For Darko, whose own wartime story inspired this one

Prologue

Korčula, 1996

She watches him as he sleeps, dark hair plastered untidily to his head, one arm flung wide over the pillow. Like his father. Every day he grows more like his father. The boy's pyjamas are decorated with faded teddy bears. He really needs a new pair. And new shoes. Things that are not easy to come by in a country that has been at war.

Her forehead creases into a frown. These have become small worries now. She had dreamed of raising a child more than anything, but not like this. All the same, the bonds of love and blood are strong. He is her sacred charge, sent by God in the hour of her greatest need. But however much she prays, He is completely silent on what she should do about the letter.

She had not recognised the handwriting on the envelope, but the postmark was clear. A woman's hand too, so she had hidden it in her bedside drawer for days before she dared to open it. And as she read those fateful words, she sank down onto her knees and wept.

Of course, she could always pretend she had never received it, then nothing need be done. They could continue as they were, and she would know the small hand in hers until he grew too big to hold it, the trust in those deep-brown eyes would be hers alone. But so many times she asks herself: what is best for the child? Best for the boy she loves more than life itself? Best for Ivan's son?

She tears herself away from his sleeping form and retreats to the solitude of her bedroom. Sleep evades her; even the half-doze she has perfected in case he wakes from a nightmare of his life before he came here. She must decide how to reply. Consider not just the now, but the years that stretch far, far into his future. Think with a clarity that is not blinded by love.

The next morning, after he has left for school, she writes her reply, first with a shaking hand and then again with a bolder one. She copies the address straight onto her envelope and sets it to one side to post. The woman's letter is trembling in her hand. There must be no trace. No trace. Her fingers fly in fury as she rips it into tiny pieces that fall like blossom around her feet.

It is a foolish gesture and means she has to sweep them up. She gathers the fragments into the pocket of her apron and sets off through the olive grove, checking the fruit as she passes. One hand on a gnarled trunk she stops, the roughness of bark sharp beneath her palm, the warmth spreading with the morning sun as it finds its way through the dappled shade. This should have been Ivan's heritage, and now it will be his son's. Her letter has made sure of that, and it is better for the boy this way. Because he will forget.

She meets no one on the short path to the rocky cove. She is alone with the buzz of the bees and the scent of wild thyme. On the deserted beach she fingers the smooth wooden beads of her rosary, while the scraps of paper spin and flow with the lacy edges of the waves until they have melted into the Dalmatian Sea. She never wants to read those words again. She has done right, right. She is sure of it.

What she does not know is that her unconfessed sin will take her from her faith, and her guilt will be etched into her soul until the day she dies. But through it all, it will be worth it, because she will know the joy of his love.

Chapter One

Sussex, 2019

"Don't mind me, I've only popped in to collect my golf clubs."

Antonia froze as the front door slammed, then hurriedly flung a corner of the duvet over her bare legs. She was still buttoning her blouse when a ruddy-faced man peered around the bedroom door.

"Oh, hi – you must be Ned's latest squeeze. Is the old bugger about?"

"N… No… He caught the early train to London. He… he's at a conference."

"Really? I thought that was just his cover story for the lady wife. Anyway, nice to meet you… er… er."

"Nice to meet you too. Geoffrey."

She sat rigid on the edge of the bed, listening to him drag his clubs from the hall cupboard, flick through the pile of post on the table next to the door, then finally, finally, leave. Oh god, the absolute humiliation. The absolute total and bloody humiliation. Ned's *latest squeeze*. Was that what she was reduced to? Geoffrey was Ned's best friend whose flat they used when he was out of town and he hadn't even known her name.

And yet she and Ned had been together for eighteen months. Eighteen months of sleeping with the boss. Which meant about seventeen months of him telling her he was going to leave his wife, he just needed to find the right moment. So around fifteen months of her actually believing him, fool that she was, and god knows how long feeling guilty because she was in love with a married man.

Shakily she wriggled into her trousers then walked across the room. In front of the mirror she shook out her thick chestnut mane and started to brush it. The rhythm was soothing, enabling her to think. But what was there to think about? She needed to get the hell out of this flat and the hell out of Ned's life. Suddenly everything felt so… so sordid. But she couldn't just up and leave, could she? She needed her job. She had a mortgage to pay, and bills, and all the responsibilities of a single mother… all right, Honey was twenty-two, but she and her girlfriend Sara were living with her while they saved for a flat of their own. She couldn't afford to be unemployed.

If she split up with Ned there was no way she could carry on working at Mediterranean Gems, seeing him every day, having to talk to him, knowing that what she wanted most dearly could never be. It was bad enough now. But at least a small slice of him was hers, and he still looked at her with what she hoped was love.

God, it was a miserable existence, loving a married man, but she'd been stupid enough to get herself into it so it was all she deserved. A sort of half-life, wound around the moments he could sneak away from his wife, knowing they would never have a proper home of their own. She looked around the bedroom, seeing it with new eyes. Not a cushion, not a throw, no personality in the pictures on the walls. It might as well be a hotel room. At least then no-one else would have had a key. Her stomach clenched with embarrassment.

She had never in a million years thought this sort of thing would happen to her, but with Honey at university she'd been so very lonely. Her attempts at internet dating had been an absolute farce... and Ned had been such a good listener that he'd moved seamlessly from boss, to friend, to... But it was wrong on every level and now it had to stop.

The trouble was, even though she knew what she should do, she was very short on the how. At the end of the day, she needed this job. Her work in Ned's travel business was far better paid than the freelance translating she used to do when Honey was growing up, and it was a regular income. Plus, she liked working with other people. And besides, there wasn't any space for her to work at home these days.

She put her hairbrush back in her overnight bag. She was making excuses, she knew she was. She was simply too empty, too exhausted by it all to be able to make a rational decision about her future. One thing was for sure; she couldn't get into her car and go home to hide under the duvet and weep, however much she wanted to. At least Ned would be in London until early afternoon so she wouldn't have to face him just yet. Was she really just his *latest squeeze*?

She felt calmer when she arrived in the office; pottering about exchanging good mornings, emptying the dishwasher, checking supplies of coffee and biscuits. After a while she felt strong enough to face her inbox and she began to work methodically through it. Close to the top was an offer of a new property to add to their virtual brochure, but the email's subject was not promising: 'New boutique hotel in Croatia – perfect for this summer's list'. For a start, Antonia didn't much like its arrogance, and for another thing, Mediterranean Gems' list had been pretty much closed weeks ago. Still, their mission statement was to make exceptions for the exceptional, so she had better take a look.

At first glance there was nothing special about Vila Maslina. In fact, it was quite an ordinary-looking farmhouse: two storeys in some places, three in others, with an irregular red tiled roof. But there was something a little different about it, and after a few moments she realised it was because the outside was painted not in the usual white, but with something akin to a paler version of Farrow & Ball's Green Ground. It softened it somehow, blending it with the olive trees surrounding it. There was no other property in sight, but enlarging the picture on her screen Antonia could see a patchwork of vineyards behind it, rising to meet dark wooded hills.

It was the content of the email that properly sparked her interest. The sender – a Damir Marić – had good English and a strong track record in the travel business. In fact, he managed Mediterranean Gems' star holiday let in Korčula's

Old Town on behalf of its owner, and Antonia knew it had absolutely rave reviews for customer service.

Not only that, Vila Maslina was offering sculpture courses, which was a pretty unusual cultural hook. Other properties had photography, writing, folklore, and art, but this would be a one-off and Antonia's skin began to tingle. The email explained there were a number of sculptors and artists living near the village of Lumbarda who would be prepared to tutor visitors and give evening talks. Her curiosity well and truly piqued, she opened the other photographs but was disappointed to find they only pictured a pony-tailed sculptor at work in his studio and a view towards the sea beyond an olive grove, which could have been anywhere.

She definitely needed more pictures before she even took this seriously, so she replied expressing cautious interest and went to make her mid-morning coffee. Back at her desk she had barely started to nibble her low-calorie biscuit when Damir's reply arrived in her inbox, suggesting a video tour. He'd obviously spoken to the owner of the house in Korčula Town about their process, and that was impressive. She sat back, wrapping her hands around her mug. Vila Maslina and its owner might just be the real deal.

She liked Damir the moment he appeared on the screen in front of her. He was not a tall man, but his almond-shaped eyes and fine features topped with close-cropped dark hair and a deep tan made him quite attractive, albeit at least ten years too young for her. But his most endearing quality was his palpable energy as his words tumbled out, explaining that his aunt had died at the end of last year, and he was converting their former home into a boutique hotel.

Antonia stopped him there. Converting or had converted? He looked confused for a moment, as though he did not quite understand the difference, then told her she could decide once he'd shown her the house.

During their conversation he had been standing outside the front door, which was freshly painted a deep olive-green, but after taking a visibly deep breath he opened it onto a building site. The wide entrance hall was all but blocked by a cement mixer and the plaster on the walls was chipped and cracked, the stairs rising in a cloud of dust sheets.

"Oh, I see."

His disembodied voice came from behind the camera. "No. You should close your eyes for this part. It makes sense to finish the entrance last, yes? Workers with dirty boots come and go."

A heavy pine door in need of some TLC swung open and Antonia found herself in an elegant living room. After the hall it was as though she had fallen down a rabbit hole into another world. The centrepiece was a massive fireplace with a mantelshelf carved from brilliant white stone; above it was an abstract painting in swirls of blue, instantly evoking the sea. The walls were the colour of the palest possible sky and swags of white muslin framed the windows. Bleached pine floors; low, squashy sofas; mismatched antique occasional tables – Antonia could almost smell the beeswax – this room was perfection.

Damir seemed to take her praise for granted as,

gesticulating wildly with his free hand, he talked her through the paintings on the walls and the sculptures dotted around the shelves.

"It is a place for relaxation and to show off the work of our local artists. The cupboard in the corner will be an honesty bar."

"It's beautiful. It feels so... calm." And this despite his bouncing around with his phone.

"Yes, calm is what I want for people who stay here. Calm to clear their heads of everyday things and to be creative."

She watched through the eye of the camera as Damir stepped back across the hall and into a dining room detailed with rich terracotta hues. He explained that most days guests would be able to eat on the terrace, so the room would be mainly used for evening lectures. Then he flung open the French windows to reveal a broad sweep of sparkling white crazy paving looking onto an expanse of olive trees, their silver-green leaves shimmering in the pale sunlight.

It was as Damir showed Antonia the finished bedrooms, one of which had the view towards the sea from the picture he had sent, that she made up her mind. She barely listened as he told her there would be three doubles and two kings, which could be split to twin beds if required; she was completely entranced by the light flooding the windows, the carefully mismatched antique furniture, and the up-to-the-minute en suites with their honey-coloured stone washbasins and tiles. If she found herself longing to be there, then with the right photography it would look fabulous in the brochure and the bookings would come streaming in.

Hauling herself back to reality, Antonia asked Damir who his interior designer was, but he just laughed, saying he couldn't possibly afford one. The fact that the sense of style and incredible eye for detail were his own absolutely clinched it.

He led her past a narrow staircase heading upwards and she asked if there were more letting rooms above.

"No. In the attic I'm making an apartment for the housekeeper. I need someone who can be here all the time, to look after the guests, to talk to them and cook for them. And make sure the cleaner does her job properly because it will be my friend's niece and she will spend too much time on her phone."

"And what will you do?"

"Run the business side of things, be the tour guide and chauffeur. And of course I have other holiday lets to manage."

"You'll be very busy."

"I hope so."

Antonia knew there was no way she could let her heart rule her head without seeing the numbers, so once the virtual tour was over she asked Damir to send her his pricing for room rates, as well as the courses and mentoring from the sculptors. For a moment he looked a little crestfallen, then explained that there was actually only one sculptor, but he was the internationally renowned Vincenzo De Luca so he didn't want any of his guests to have second best.

As soon as she finished the call, Antonia ran an internet search on the guy and found that Damir wasn't blagging. De Luca was Italian and exhibited regularly in New York, Paris, and Florence, and his work commanded astronomical prices. So why was he on a tiny island like Korčula? His website told her it was because of the local stone. While not as famous as its neighbour Brač, there were quarries on the island and De Luca eulogised about the texture, strength, and quality at some length.

Rather than eat her sandwich hunched over her desk, Antonia put on her coat and slung her handbag over her shoulder. The lane outside the barns ran down to the creek, and she scanned the bare hedgerows for any sign of life. The skies overhead were leaden, the sullen water lapping at the slipway reflecting them, and for the second time that morning she found herself longing for the dazzling blue of the Med. Perhaps she would book a break at Damir's property herself, maybe even a sneaky peak before the season started.

She had never been to Croatia, but had seen brochure pictures of crystal-clear turquoise-blue seas and jumbles of terracotta roofs. She hugged her arms around her against the cold. Apart from anything else, a holiday would get her properly away from Ned to think. Looking over the mud-grey water, her mind slid off into a fantasy where Ned would be able to come to Croatia with her and she began to picture them walking through the olive grove, sipping wine on the terrace… a whole glorious week together and not just a few snatched hours. She pulled herself up short. As if that would ever happen. Rather than daydreaming she should be thinking about how she was going to end the affair and still be able to earn enough to eat and to pay the mortgage. Apart from her languages, she didn't exactly have many marketable skills.

By the time Antonia returned to the barn, Ned's BMW was in the car park. After this morning's mortifying encounter with Geoffrey it was harder than ever to put on her professional face, but she took a deep breath and gathered her laptop from her desk, balancing it on her arm to stride up the stairs to Ned's office.

She fixed on her brightest smile. "I think I've found our latest gem. A real gem, too."

He put his phone down on his desk. "I was just texting you. I wondered where you were."

She shrugged. "Late lunch. I fancied a walk. Why? Did you need me?"

"I always need you." He smiled, his head on one side and his grey eyes sparkling. Oh, she wished he wouldn't do that, not in the office, anyway. It turned her inside out.

"Well I'm here now. And let me introduce you to Vila Maslina on Korčula."

"We already have a place on Korčula."

"This is different and brand new. The owner's just putting together some prices, and I'm having the flights checked out..."

"For this year?"

"Yes. If we don't snap it up someone else will."

"I thought we agreed no more untried..."

Antonia leant forwards. "As we say, there are always

exceptions for the exceptional. Finca el Parro only opened last season and you know how well it took off."

"It was the exception that proved the rule. I think we have more than enough—"

Oh no, he was going to be arsy because she hadn't been here when he came back. Well, she had even more reason to be arsy with him, except he probably didn't even know it. Unless his mate Geoffrey had told him he'd found her half-dressed on his bed. "You haven't even looked at the pictures."

He turned to his computer screen. "Show me the figures then I'll decide."

Antonia's voice was trembling as she swept her laptop from his desk. "No, Ned. You've always told me I have the final say on new properties and we're going with this one, whether you like it or not."

As usual, Antonia was the last to leave the office. Her argument with Ned had shaken her to the core because she couldn't remember them falling out before, but as she was drying her angry tears in the ladies' and reapplying her mascara she had started to think. She wasn't the type to stomp and scream, but there was a strange sort of empowerment in holding her own and the more she reflected on it, the more it felt like a win. A small win that might just give her the courage to go one step further, if only she could work out how to pay the bills afterwards. And how to deal with the huge hole in her heart. To be honest, she didn't know which was more frightening. How the hell had she ever let herself get into this impossible position in the first place? What was wrong with her?

She was too distracted to achieve anything at her desk. Besides, she was longing to be back in her kitchen, pottering around, creating something delicious for supper. She had always been able to lose herself in spices and sauces, and having other people to cook for was one of the best things about the girls living with her. It almost made up for queuing for the bathroom in the mornings and the tide of domestic chaos that one day soon would surely engulf them.

The tiny cottage had been home since her divorce when Honey was eight years old. It was the place they had built together, packed full of all manner of stuff they no longer needed and happy childhood memories only they shared. It was special – it was theirs – but Antonia was acutely aware that once Honey and Sara had enough for their deposit she would be left there alone. It was inevitable, and for Honey it would be a good thing, but it was hard to face it all the same.

Antonia rinsed her mug before squeezing it into the dishwasher, loading a tablet and turning it on. It hummed as she put on her coat. Outside it was dark and raining, so she stopped under the porch to fish in her handbag for her umbrella.

"Here, let me."

"Ned!" Her heart was pounding nineteen to the dozen. "What are you doing creeping up on me like that?"

"I came back, I..."

Hold your own, she told herself. *Hold your own.* "Not just to say goodnight, I take it, given you didn't bother when you stalked past my desk at four o'clock."

"Toni, please. Don't make this any harder than it is. I was wrong and I've come back to apologise. I feel like such a shit." His voice was choked with emotion and Antonia ached to reach out and touch him. However wrong it was, she loved this man. She couldn't help it.

Hauling her shattered resolve back together with some difficulty, she started to walk towards her car but he followed her.

"Do you have time for a drink?"

She stopped. *Say no, Antonia, just say no.* But instead she found herself asking, "Do you?"

"I'll make time. I want to put things right."

In the glow of the car park lights she could see the honesty in his eyes. And she was torn. More torn than ever between herself and him; between what she should want, and what right at that moment she actually wanted; between their weakness and her tiny green shoots of strength. Then he stooped to kiss her and she leant into him, her head on his shoulder as they made their way through the rain.

She knew she would regret it later, and probably descend into that all too familiar pit of self-loathing, but right at that moment this morning was forgotten and she just needed him to love her.

Chapter Two

Korčula, 2019

In a rare moment of calm, Damir leant against the door jamb, plate in one hand, mug of coffee in the other, gazing out over the olive grove. In front of him the trees were sleeping, but soon the pale sunlight would strengthen, and they would wake to begin their work. Every year, just the same. And he liked that.

His world had shifted sideways the moment he'd found his aunt, his *tetka,* dead in her bed, her body still and cold but her face as serene as if she had simply been sleeping. Tetka never slept beyond six in the morning, and when he had woken to find no sharp aroma of coffee filling the house he had known something was wrong.

The suddenness of losing Tetka had been the worst part. He knew he should be pleased she hadn't suffered, but it was like being cut off in the middle of a conversation, one he could now never complete. To be fair, he couldn't actually think of anything important he should have asked, (except, perhaps, how to handle the kitchen range) but the times he still thought, 'Oh, I must tell Tetka that', were far too many to count and made him feel just a little bit lonely.

Vila Maslina had felt so empty around him the only course of action had been to change it, fill it; give it a new life that would secure his future as well. But despite his grand plans, something was missing and he was unable to pinpoint quite what it was.

Even if he couldn't be entirely sure of the question, keeping busy was the answer. It was what Tetka would have done, he was sure. Well, she wouldn't have completely gutted the house, but she would not have sat around moping if she had been the one left alone.

His work managing holiday lets all over the island had given him plenty of opportunity to observe how the wealthy owners and visitors were able to live. He had not been brought up poor – far from it – but somehow there had never been quite enough. Not food on the table – that had been plentiful – but the little extras, or even essentials, that made life just a bit smoother. Like a car that started first time, an up-to-date iPhone, clothes that weren't designer knock-offs from the market. He wanted better, and although he would swap it all in an instant to have her back, Tetka's death had given him the opportunity to reach for it.

He perched on the edge of the terrace and checked his mobile. Still nothing from Mediterranean Gems. It had been two days now, and he was beginning to get nervous. The woman, Antonia, had sounded so positive – had something gone wrong? Of course, if push came to shove, he could put the rooms on Airbnb for the summer, but that was not his dream. For his dream he needed a high-end travel company.

Damir worked in tourism – he had a diploma in tourism, of which Tetka had been very proud; he understood its importance to the economy in all its forms. But he wanted visitors to his beautiful country to see the best of it, to learn about its culture and its history, not simply sit on the beach and drink in the bars. He wanted to share his passion. And earn a great deal of money, not to mention respect.

Perhaps he should send Antonia some more pictures. He planned to finish another bedroom that afternoon, but then he would need Petar's help to haul some more furniture down from the attic. Petar was a plumber and tended to turn up when he didn't have another job, but turn up he would. They had been friends since they were six years old and, particularly given his childhood, Damir considered Petar's loyalty remarkable.

As the sun disappeared behind a cloud, Damir stretched his legs across the grass. Tetka would sit on this terrace in summer, the scent of the jasmine that clambered up the wall of the house enveloping her, embroidering handkerchiefs and lavender bags to sell to the tourists, or passing the time of day with her friends over coffee. If he listened carefully, Damir could almost hear her voice. He took a cigarette from the pack in his shirt pocket and tapped it down. He had given up before and he would do so again. Once he heard from Antonia. Once things were settled. He checked his emails once more.

In the end it was not an email, but a call. He was waxing the last section of floorboard on the landing and was glad to unbend his back to answer it – especially when he saw the English number.

"Damir Marić, can I help you?"

"Oh, hi. It's Antonia Butler from Mediterranean Gems. When will you be ready? I mean, really ready. A definite date."

Straight to the point. He liked that. He sat back on his heels and calculated. "Three more days for the bedrooms. Then I must complete the housekeeper's apartment before the hall. So... as you say, worst case scenario, three weeks."

"So the end of February." She paused. "If you were to open in early April that does leave a little time for slippage, I suppose."

"There will not be slippage."

"So once the house is ready there will be nothing else to do?"

"Find a housekeeper. That is all." He needed somewhere to sleep himself but that was a minor detail. Even in his wildest dreams he never presumed that Vila Maslina would be at full capacity early in the season.

"And do you have anyone in mind?"

"No, because I do not want a local. I need someone who can talk to the guests in their own language, cook the food they enjoy. Not everyone likes goat meat."

"If the person you choose is on a month's notice, you don't have much time."

"But it is difficult. Without a letting contract it would not be right to employ someone." There was silence on the other end of the phone and he wondered whether his gentle push had been a step too far.

"OK. Listen, Damir, I'm sticking my neck out for you. My boss doesn't want to do this but I do and it's my call. But if you let me down and you aren't ready, I will be more than angry and there will be compensation to pay. Do you understand?"

"I understand."

"Then I'll send the contracts over."

Once Antonia rang off, Damir leapt up and punched the air, then ran into Tetka's room. Her bed had been given away, her other furniture distributed around the house, but somehow the sweet smell of lavender lingered.

"Tetka, I've done it. I hope... this is all right." His voice trembled, his words weighed down by the tears he had been unable to cry. He took a deep breath and pulled himself up to his full five foot nine inches. On Friday night he would go to the bar and get drunk with his friends.

In the meantime, he had an attic to clear to make space for the housekeeper's apartment. He wanted it to be as beautiful as the letting rooms, to attract the right sort of person, but first there were boxes to sort through and store in the boarded-off area under the eaves. There weren't very many, but each one was laden with memories: Tetka's nativity scene that came out every Christmas, the beekeeper's hood he hadn't seen her wear in years, faded sheets and duvet covers he remembered well. There were plenty of things he should probably throw out, but somehow it seemed just a little too soon.

The next box he peered into contained a pair of delicate

silver candlesticks resting on a pile of papers, and he recognised them as the ones from the shrine in the living room that Tetka had kept for a year after his father's death. He had completely forgotten about that; should he be doing the same for her? Had he somehow disrespected her memory? There used to be a photo of his father too, in a silver frame. He delved into the box, finding it beneath a couple of envelopes, one of which was almost worn away by handling, the other pristine.

Looking at the picture, Damir found himself gazing at a man he resembled a great deal. Younger than Damir was now, he guessed, and certainly more relaxed than in the only other photo of his father he'd seen, the one in his army uniform Tetka had produced every Victory Day. Here he was sitting in the courtyard behind the house, wearing a checked shirt and smiling at the camera. The picture was black and white but somehow Damir knew his eyes were the same deep brown as his own. Maybe he remembered them, but he didn't think so. There were only shadows of the time before he came here.

He began to wonder if there was a decent photo of Tetka somewhere. If so, he could have an enlargement made and put it in a frame in the hall to welcome the guests. That would be far better than setting up some sort of temporary shrine. The worn envelope contained a few pictures, but most were blurred and there were none of her alone. He guessed some were with her parents, and there was one with his father as children, Tetka looking as though she was dressed for her First Communion.

Damir turned to the other envelope. It was small, fitting

on the flat of his hand, and was addressed to Tetka. It felt wrong to read her letters but he peeped in to see it contained just one sheet of paper, folded in half, with a photo tucked inside.

It was a wedding photograph and the bridegroom was his father, but it was the smiling woman standing beside him that caught his attention. He gripped the photo harder. His mother. His beautiful mother, almost exactly as he remembered her. Except, until then he hadn't remembered, and the thought was astonishing, shocking almost. He rocked back onto his heels, wrapping his arms around him as the picture fluttered to the floor. His mother. His *mother*. He doubled over, forcing back red-hot tears. He would not cry. He would not. It was too long ago.

Why had Tetka hidden his mother's photo, and told him none existed? Why? Was it because she knew how much it would hurt? With shaking hands, Damir unfolded the note to find it was from his father. Just a few words, saying how sorry he was that the flu had kept Tetka away from his wedding, because it was the happiest day of his life. He had underlined the last part for some reason Damir didn't understand. But then, he didn't understand any of it…

All he wanted was to run through the olive grove to the dark sanctuary of the old press house at the end of the drive. It was where he had hidden as a little boy, but somehow seeing his mother's picture had transported him back to childhood, for a brief moment at least. But he was not a child anymore so he could not behave like one. Taking a deep breath, he scooped the picture from the floor and without a glance, folded it back into the envelope with the letter before shoving it to the depths of the box. Then, brushing the dust from his jeans, he jogged down the stairs and into the sunlight.

The wind whipped along the coast, forcing Damir to cut through the village to the seafront taverna, Konoba Pecaros, rather than take the coastal path. There may have been darkness around him and doors closed against the chill air, but still there was life; the whine of motorcycles on the main road, voices raised against the news blaring from a television, a cat slinking past. The cat stopped and he stopped, bending down to caress its soft fur as it wound around his legs before disappearing about its business.

The breeze carried diesel mixed with seaweed in its salty sting. As Damir emerged onto the seafront he inhaled deeply, then closed his eyes for a moment, pictures of childhood *kuna* earnt helping to unload fish flashing through his mind. Turning his back to the wind, he strode into the shelter of the bay and towards the beckoning lights of Konoba Pecaros.

In winter the bar was reclaimed by the locals, its pizza ovens only fired on Sundays when, instead of English and German, the place was filled with the chatter of Croatian families. Tonight it had hunkered down, the thick plastic protecting it from the elements snapping against the metal poles as the wind tried to find its way inside.

Mirjana, the owner's wife, was behind the bar, her auburn hair straying from beneath a broad bandana. Damir nodded to the fishermen playing cards in the corner before perching on a stool in front of her.

"Quiet tonight," he said.

She shrugged. "It's early. And so, my friend, are you."

"I'm celebrating."

"Oh yes? Then you'll be ordering a bottle of my best Pošip?"

"I may be celebrating, but that does not mean I've become a rich man overnight." He laughed. "The village white will do fine."

He watched as she poured a generous glass then set it on the counter in front of him.

"So?"

"So?"

"What are you celebrating?"

"The house has been taken on by a very high-end travel company, so come April the guests will start pouring in."

"Damir, that is excellent news. You've worked so hard this winter."

"Not without help..."

Petar's timing was perfect as he walked into the bar, accompanied by his wife Lorena, his muscular bulk shielding her from the blast of air that followed them until the door slammed shut. In three strides he was across the room, enveloping Damir in a bear hug.

"We must celebrate your news!"

Damir drained his glass and Mirjana muttered something which sounded like, 'He already is,' but she could not possibly understand what this meant to him in the same way as Petar did. The two of them had slaved together all winter and tonight was their night.

"At the end of the season when the money comes in we will drink champagne, but for now wine will have to do," Damir told them, and ordered a large carafe before they drifted towards a table in the centre of the room, well away from the flapping plastic.

"It's stormy out there," said Lorena, unbuttoning her coat before sitting down.

"I intend to be too drunk to notice," said Damir.

"You men. Why do you do that? You'll only feel like shit in the morning when you have work to do."

Petar shrugged. "It's the way to mark a special occasion. And we'll go to work tomorrow anyway. We'll just drink coffee and moan a lot." He turned to Damir. "So when do the guests arrive?"

"Not until the beginning of April, but there is still a great deal to do. We need to arrange the furniture in the last bedroom, then we can start on the attic."

"Is that where you're going to live?" Lorena asked.

"No, it's for the housekeeper."

"But I thought Ana..."

"She will make beds and clean, but I'm aiming for the international market so I need someone experienced, preferably with more than one language..."

"An older lady," Petar winked.

"But of course. I need someone reliable."

"And someone you can shag..."

"Oh, don't start that again." Damir folded his arms.

Lorena reached out to pat his shoulder. "No, it isn't kind to tease. Damir, if not the attic, where will you live?"

"Like I said, he'll cosy up to the housekeeper..."

"Petar!"

"I'm only joking... She won't be rich enough. He only goes for old women who can give him a taste of the high life."

Damir shook his head, laughing, but inside he was unsure which was worse: Petar's teasing or Lorena's sympathy. But he knew both were only doing it because they were his friends. Petar had always teased him in his gentle way, although he had never made cruel fun of him as some of the other children had. But one day, one day very soon, those children would be laughing on the other side of their faces.

Nothing was going to spoil Damir's evening and they carried on drinking until the fishermen left and they were the only people in the bar. They drank, and talked about plans and dreams, and gossiped about neighbours. They drank, and they laughed, and eventually came back to the subject of where Damir was going to live, but by that time he was past caring. They drank until Mirjana told them she wanted to go to bed.

Outside Konoba Pecaros they went their separate ways. Damir plunged his hands into his pockets as he headed along the waterfront. The incoming tide was rocking the tethered boats in an alarming manner, his head spinning in time with their dances. Maybe Lorena had been right – already he was regretting drinking quite this much.

Vila Maslina was Damir's dream. Somehow, when Tetka

was alive, working hard to manage other people's holiday villas – and, he had to admit, playing hard as well – had been enough. But once Tetka died it had hit him like a sledgehammer that if he was to keep his home, never mind improve his lifestyle, he needed more money. Much as losing Vila Maslina was inconceivable, inviting others into it was not. He loved the idea of being able to share his pride in the place where he had been brought up with people who would also appreciate it. His pride in the country his father had died fighting for.

A soldier, hammering on a door with the butt of his rifle… Shouts of "Izlazite Bosniak!" Children screaming. The acrid tang of sweat…

Damir shook his head. Too much wine. Definitely too much wine.

On autopilot he took the path along the coast. In the distance, lights flickered on the mainland, but once he passed the harbour the velvet darkness embraced him. Here there was only the wash of the waves, and the rain nudging through the trees that would shield him from its force until he rounded the headland. There was no moon, no stars, but he had walked this way too many times to need them.

He turned the corner and the storm hit him in the face, bringing with it the spray as the sea whipped the rocks. He upped his pace, past the locked gates of the holiday villas towards the inland track home. Cypresses gave way first to close-cropped vines and then to olive trees. Their olive trees. No, *his* olive trees. The trees that had sheltered and fed him since he was six years old. A debt that honour, and being a proud Croatian, meant he must now repay.

Maybe it was because of this that he was drawn to the old olive press at the bottom of the drive. The door swung open on broken hinges and as he shone the torchlight from his phone up towards the gallery there was an angry flap of wings and a dark shape disappeared through a hole in the roof. The earthen floor was damp in patches where the rain had crept in but still he found comfort in the old walls and the musty tang of bitter olives in the air.

With the flat of his hand he brushed the dust from the circular stones of the press and lowered himself onto the horizontal one. These days his feet were too big to fit in the trough that surrounded it like a moat, so he balanced them on its edge, the curve of the lip sliding neatly beneath the heels of his shoes.

Resting his back against the wooden hopper, he closed his eyes. He could still hear the sea and the rustle of the rain against the olive trees. He pictured their slender leaves swaying in the darkness. When he first came here the press had been in use; was it possible to bring it back to life? To process the olives – his olives – in the traditional way, instead of sending them to the co-operative? He was sure Tetka had only done that because, being a woman on her own, she'd had no choice. Her father, and his father before him, had pressed their own olives and Damir desperately wanted to do the same. It would be a suitable way to honour Tetka's memory and to rekindle the Marić family traditions.

Tetka had died three days after last year's harvest was complete. So like her, Damir thought, not to leave a job half-done. Even he was the finished article. When he first came here he would run in blind terror through the olive grove, darting from tree to tree, finally stumbling into the press house to hide from the sparkling blue of the sea and the dangerous skies. Hide from the flowers and trees and everything beautiful. This musty, dark barn had been the only place he had felt safe, but over the years Tetka had changed all that.

Tetka had taught him so many things, and one of those had been that after a certain age, boys did not cry. Boys were brave, especially boys whose fathers had been war heroes. That way boys grew up into men. So tears were not permitted for the woman who had raised him, but Damir was determined that through Vila Maslina and its olive grove, he would honour her memory in other ways.

Damir did not move when he heard Petar's van in the courtyard behind the house the next morning, merely winced as the door slammed, clutching his mug tighter. Petar slunk into the kitchen, dropped onto a chair next to the old scrubbed pine table and demanded coffee.

"How much did we drink?" he moaned. "Even Lorena was grouchy this morning and she never has too much."

"I wasn't counting."

"I must give you something towards the bill."

Damir waved his hand in the general direction of upstairs. "You're about to. And you already have."

They had known each other long enough to sit in silence over their coffee, and for Petar not to comment when Damir lit a cigarette. Over the years Petar had perfected the art of being patient with Damir, and for that and more Damir would be eternally grateful. Petar had first proved his worth as a friend by not telling the other boys that when an exhaust had backfired as they walked home from school, Damir had wet himself. They had been six years old.

Eventually Damir stood and stretched. "Come on, we need to achieve something today."

"I have. I've thought of the perfect place for you to live."

"You've found somewhere?"

"It's under your nose."

"Where?"

"The old press house."

"But it's practically a ruin."

"Rubbish. It will take no more work than converting the attic. I'll cost out a little bathroom..."

"No!"

Petar frowned. "Why not?"

Damir rinsed his coffee mug in the stone sink, uncertain why Petar's suggestion had given rise to such a strong reaction. "I'll think about it."

After Petar went home, Damir made his way through the olive grove, ducking into the dappled shade beneath each tree to check the progress of the buds. So much rested on them – not only this year's harvest but the next – and he was absorbed in his task when his phone buzzed in his pocket. He angled the screen away from the sun and could just make out it was an email from Antonia. The message came from her personal account, and she'd sent a CV for the housekeeping job. Damir punched the air. He had known when he mentioned it to her that she wouldn't let him down.

There was no name and no photograph but that only piqued his curiosity. The summary read:

Mature woman with excellent linguistic skills seeking new challenge.

Beneath was an impressive list of languages spoken — some fluently, others a working knowledge. No Croatian, but that wasn't important. The woman clearly had a good ear so should easily pick up enough to get by.

Actual housekeeping experience was rather thin on the ground, apart from running her own home for the past twenty odd years. And cooking for friends' dinner parties, but not professionally. It seemed she had been working in an office and claimed excellent organisational skills and experience of managing staff. It could be enough – to a mature, sensible woman, Damir knew his requirements wouldn't exactly be rocket science.

But could she engage his guests in more than idle chit-chat? The CV listed no hobbies or interests, so it was hard to tell. He would need to talk to her to find out. He fired a quick reply to Antonia:

Looks promising. Who is she? Friend of yours?'

He slipped his phone into his pocket and continued towards the old press house. It was drawing him, like a magnet, but given Petar's idea he had a practical reason to check it out. Once inside he climbed the wooden ladder to the gallery, testing each rung with his toe before putting his weight on it, but apart from one near the bottom they were all sound. Light streamed through a gap in the roof, motes of dust dancing as he moved about, but on closer inspection the holes he could see were all quite small. Some felt and a few tiles should fix them, and although the old stone walls were cold, away from the biggest opening they were perfectly dry. The gallery stretched halfway across the building and there was enough space up here for a bed, a wardrobe... a chest of drawers, even... He began to see it in his mind's eye.

Downstairs was different. The only light came from the entrance and that couldn't be left open all the time. But if it were made into a stable door, and a window put in the opposite wall, then a corner screened off for a bathroom... The plumbing would be a nightmare. Still, that was Petar's department. Damir's problem was the press; if it were moved, would it be possible to use it somewhere else? He started to feel in his pocket for his cigarettes, but instead closed his eyes to envisage how his potential new home might look.

In the very act of doing so, it was then, not now. The mustiness drew him back to the past, small chubby fingers gripping the stone while his mother's eyes faded from view. Eyes in a face he had so easily forgotten, but which were once again etched into his brain.

Suddenly his phone was ringing. It was Antonia's name on the screen, so he steadied himself against the ladder and cleared his throat to answer it.

"Antonia, how are you?"

"Yes, fine." Silence. "Look, that CV… it's mine."

Had he heard her right? There was something uncertain in her usually confident tone. "You want to leave your job at Mediterranean Gems?"

"I don't want to, but I have to."

"Do you mind if I ask why?"

There was a pause while he imagined her taking a deep breath.

"So many reasons. Personal ones. Look, if it's not right just say so, but please don't mention this to anyone at the office..."

"I'd never do that."

"Thank you."

He gazed at the circular stones, the upright in shadow and just a small segment of the horizontal dazzling in a shaft of sunlight from the door. As his eyes followed it outside he knew exactly what he would do about the press. And as far as the housekeeper was concerned, there was no decision to be made.

"The job is yours."

Another silence. "You're sure? Really sure? Because if I hand in my notice and—"

Damir wished she could have seen him smiling at her. "You took a chance on me," he said, "now I will take one on you."

Chapter Three

The bus had been flirting with the coastline all the way from Dubrovnik, but now a huge expanse of sparkling silver-blue sea stretched in front of Antonia, dotted with the deep greens of the islands, the richer colours close by becoming muted as they faded into the distance. But the sheer beauty was not enough to lift her, and she closed her eyes against the late afternoon sun. It had been a long day. A long week. A long month.

The trouble with closing her eyes was that Honey was imprinted on the inside of her lids. Honey at Gatwick, her mop of blonde hair mingling with Sara's shiny plum-dyed bob as she clung onto her, trying to smile, and both of them waving for all they were worth as passport control swallowed Antonia up. She had waved too and smiled. Then, blinded by tears, she'd blundered her way through security, forgetting to put her phone in the plastic crate and causing no end of fuss.

If Antonia had known how hard it would be leaving

Honey she would never have embarked on this crazy adventure. As she gazed out over the sea, she forced herself to try to analyse it, but it was just too painful. The absolute longing to hold her daughter made her arms ache with emptiness, and even though she hadn't shed a tear since taking off at Gatwick, her eyes still felt as though she was crying a river. And the state of her poor battered heart was somewhere it was really not a good idea to go.

Antonia had never been apart from Honey for longer than three or four weeks when her daughter had been at university, and even then it had been just a couple of hours' drive to Bristol if Honey needed her. Which she sometimes had. *What if she needs me now?* Antonia thought. Already she had been travelling for most of the day, and she wasn't even there yet. All right, her journey was longer because the catamarans linking the islands to Dubrovnik didn't run outside the tourist season, but all the same... Why, oh why, had she ever thought this was a good idea?

Of course Antonia had seen maps of the Dalmatian coast, and pictures. Since accepting the job at Vila Maslina she had studied guide books and YouTube videos, but the view from the bus window was real, and glorious, although a far cry from the calm waters promised to the tourists for the summer months. Waves broke against the rocks below the road and, across the expanse of silver-blue, matching plumes of spray beat against the islands. The sunlight may have made it all appear benign, but she was already feeling a little queasy at the thought of the ferry crossing.

Hotels and holiday villas began to appear, boarded against the elements, but then the gears of the bus started to grind as they turned uphill and inland. Vineyards were interspersed with olive groves and pastures for sheep and goats, and chickens roamed the villages between the well-kept houses with their red roofs and white-washed walls. Consulting Google Maps on her phone, Antonia realised that when they next hit the coastline she would catch her first glimpse of Korčula.

The one good thing about the agony of separation from Honey was that it put the pain she'd been feeling about Ned into perspective. It was nothing but a gnat bite. But even they could flare up and itch like buggery. And get infected if you scratched them.

It had all happened so damned quickly – just a single crazy Friday night. One moment she had been chatting to her best friend Lynn about Damir needing a housekeeper and the next they'd been poring over Antonia's laptop, trying to put her CV together. Whenever she had wavered, Lynn had told her it was high time she did something for herself, and reminded her how often she'd said how guilty she felt about the affair. Thank goodness she hadn't told her about the humiliating scene with Geoffrey or she'd have been even more insistent. But some things were just too embarrassing to share with even your closest friend.

Antonia had drawn the line at actually emailing Damir there and then. They'd both had a fair bit to drink, so she had insisted she slept on it. Besides, she'd needed to talk to Honey, because this decision would have a big impact on her too.

So once Sara had gone to work on Saturday morning, Antonia and Honey had taken a long walk on the South

Downs. In the distance, nestled on the edge of the steel-grey Solent, was the cottage where they had lived for the past fifteen years. How would it feel to be somewhere else? This was home, the place she belonged, and she'd comforted herself with the thought that even if she was away all summer, it always would be.

Antonia had not been surprised when her daughter had admitted that her relationship was under strain because she and Sara didn't have their own space, although she was at pains to point out they were grateful for the opportunity to save for a deposit on a flat. So much she had suspected, but she had been truly shocked when Honey had told her in no uncertain terms that it was high time she ditched Ned.

"He's no good for you, Mum. He'll never make you happy, and I hate seeing you put whatever you're doing on hold to run around after him whenever he can sneak away from his wife." Hearing her daughter speak in this way had made the affair seem even more sordid and she'd felt thoroughly ashamed. What sort of example was she setting her? She'd honestly believed one of the only things she was good at was being a mother, and now she was failing even at that.

As soon as they'd returned to the cottage, Honey had watched, hand on Antonia's shoulder, as she composed a careful email to Damir and, closing her eyes tight, had finally pressed send.

The last thing she'd expected had been for him to make a split-second decision, but then Antonia had been instantly faced with telling Ned. Notice first, or break up first?

Essentially, they were the same thing. At least, they had been to her.

She'd suffered thirty-six hours of pure agony, wavering this way and that. She was going to hurt Ned so much, and she loved him. But if she changed her mind and didn't go to Croatia it would mean letting down not only Damir, but Lynn, and Honey and Sara – but particularly Honey, with whom she needed to regain her reputation as a sensible and reliable parent. What she wanted for herself hadn't seemed important, because really, she had no idea what it was. In the end it had come down to putting Honey above Ned (which was in itself a no-brainer), but all the same she'd tossed and turned and cried most of the night.

Having convinced herself Ned would make her walk the moment she told him, she'd spent the Monday making sure her work was up-to-date. Much as she'd wanted to, there was no way she could put this off; it had been hard enough avoiding talking to him all day, looking at him out of the corner of her eye, wondering if she was going to hurt him as much as she was hurting herself. Every time she faltered she made herself picture Geoffrey breezing into the bedroom. Her decision had been bloody hard won and she was going to act on it.

By late afternoon her colleagues had started to drift away, although the sales team had still been busy in their corner; they were Antonia's protection against there being a scene. She spent a long time gazing into the mirror in the ladies, seeing only sunken eyes with dark circles beneath, Lynn's voice in her ear telling her she deserved better. And better – or at least different – was within her uncertain grasp.

All the same, it was remembering Honey's words that catapulted her out of the loo and back into the office to collect the envelope from her handbag and climb the stairs one at a time.

Ned glanced up from his computer, "Hang on a tic and I'll be with you."

"I could just leave this..."

He swivelled away from the screen. "What is it?"

"My notice."

There was nothing she could read in his face. Finally he said, "I've been thinking about that too. Long term, it's probably better we don't work together as well as... you know. I'm glad we're on the same page." He smiled at Antonia. "As long as you're not going to a competitor."

"I'm going to work for Vila Maslina. On Korčula." A flicker of anger started to build inside her. *Long term.* He clearly had no conscience, no feelings of guilt at all. Towards her or towards his wife.

He rocked back in his chair as though someone had shot him. "You're going where?"

"Korčula. I've signed a contract for the season." Antonia forced herself to sit down opposite Ned. This was no time to get mad. She needed to be able to think clearly, act like the reasonable person she was. "So what would you like me to do about finding my replacement?"

"Well, it's only temporary, isn't it? Although I have to say on another level... why didn't you talk to me about this,

Toni? I'd have thought it was the sort of decision we should be making together."

She leant forwards, fingers gripping the edge of his desk. She had to say this plainly – not stumble over her words, not mumble. "Ned, do you understand? I'm not just leaving Mediterranean Gems, I'm calling time on us as well."

"Holding a gun to my head, more like."

How little did he know her? After eighteen months of so-called being in love. Maybe she was just his latest squeeze after all and more than anything, that felt like the final straw. She stood up. "No. No gun. This is hurting me, probably more than it's hurting you, but it's for the best. I'll take a day off tomorrow, while you decide what you want to do about my notice period."

Although she had tried to distract herself by baking, Antonia had been on pins all the next day waiting for his call, but the last thing she'd been expecting was a knock on the door at three o'clock.

His shoulders were hunched, hands buried in the pockets of his overcoat. More telling was the puffiness around his eyes. She'd opened the door wider, and he'd stepped past her into the hall. They had gazed at each other, and in that moment Antonia had thought her heart would shatter, but somehow she'd shown him into the living room and told him she'd make some tea.

She took her time in the kitchen, deciding whatever he said she would hear him out. As far as work was concerned, she would do what he wanted, but as far as their relationship was concerned there was no going back. Both

Lynn and Honey had told her it would be impossible to find real happiness when she wasn't being true to herself and, in her heart of hearts, she knew they were right. The problem was that she wasn't even sure anymore who that self was, although one thing she did know was that she wasn't a marriage breaker.

Ned spoke before she had even put the tray on the coffee table. "I've had the worst twenty-three hours of my life. Please, just give me until Ollie's finished his GCSEs... It's only a few months. If you need space I'll still pay you. We can say you're ill or taking a sabbatical or—"

"I'm sorry, Ned. It's over. I'm going to Croatia. That should give us both enough space." Oh, God, he really was hurting and it was all her fault.

"I... I thought you loved me." He was struggling to hold back his tears and it was all Antonia could do not to cross the room to hold him. Instead, she gripped the teapot, white spots appearing on her knuckles.

"You know I loved you. And I know you loved me. But we need to face it, Ned – we just didn't love each other enough."

"And if I left Diana tomorrow?"

She put a mug of tea on the floor next to his left foot then stepped back. "You won't do it. If your future had been with me, you would have done something months ago. Just accept that I need to get away to get over you – and to let you get over me."

Until Antonia had left Honey at the airport that morning, watching Ned cry without offering a crumb of comfort was the hardest thing she had ever done.

The ferry crossing from Orebić was mercifully short, but even so Antonia spent it on the deck above the assorted vans and cars, clutching a wheeled suitcase in either hand to stop them rolling away in the swell. At the beginning of the journey the diesel fumes had made her stomach churn, but as Korčula crept closer, the sun dipping low behind the island, she became transfixed. Buildings slowly emerged from a backdrop of green, and way to her right the smudges of red, white, and grey became the old town rising above its sea walls, topped by the narrow tower of an Italianate church, pointing like a finger to the sky.

As the ferry approached the port she scanned the expanse of concrete for Damir, but the only person waiting was an elderly man in a battered pickup and Damir had told her to look out for a dark-blue people-carrier. Antonia started to feel sick again as the reality of what she was doing hit home. She knew nothing about this man, this country. She was entirely reliant on a stranger – for a roof over her head, for money, for companionship even… What would she do if he wasn't there? Was there even anywhere she could stay tonight while she worked it out? Having to turn around and head for home would be even more humiliating than the episode with Geoffrey, because at least only she knew about that.

The tannoy burst into life, and although she didn't understand a word of it she took it as her cue to make her way down the stairs to the car deck, pathetically grateful for the kindness of a truck driver who carried her cases. She told him, *'Hvala'* – one of her few words of Croatian – and he grinned at her. She fingered her phone in her pocket as the ferry lurched against the concrete apron. She had Damir's number; she could always phone him. But what if he didn't answer?

When Antonia emerged into the dusk, Damir was waiting, wearing a smart black leather jacket over his jeans. He rushed forwards and took her hand, holding it between warm palms.

"Welcome to Korčula, Antonia. Now, we must go because at home there is a problem." He grabbed her cases and strode towards the car. Oh God, Antonia thought, what sort of problem? Was the house not as finished as he'd made out? Had the plumbing given up the ghost already?

"My afternoon has been eaten up by it. All afternoon, and I had such plans for your arrival. Dinner in the old town, I had thought. But instead... is she stupid? Or selfish? Or lying hurt somewhere? I just don't know."

This really did sound like a crisis. "Who, Damir?"

He slid the car into gear and glanced across at her. "Mackalina. And what is worse, she simply turned up out of nowhere, as if I needed another problem. And now this! Today, of all days..."

Antonia tried to picture this Mackalina. Who could she be? A girlfriend? An elderly relative prone to wandering?

"Did she say anything that might give you a clue?" she ventured.

He took his hands off the steering wheel and flung them into the air. "Of course not. She's a cat. Not even my cat.

She's half wild but the old olive press has become her home as well and..."

Was he serious? "So you're telling me you have lost a semi-wild cat?" If he was going to panic at the smallest thing, this really was a huge error of judgement on her part. She looked over in time to see him arch his perfectly formed eyebrows.

"That would not be unusual. But this morning she had four kittens. In my wardrobe. Already I have been struggling to keep the smallest one alive. And they need milk, so I have been away longer than is perhaps wise." He paused to take a breath. "At least the ferry was on time."

Somewhat relieved, Antonia settled back into her seat. "Is it far?"

"My best is seven minutes."

She did not dare to open her eyes until she felt the car slow and turn onto a rough track. She had been telling herself it was better that way, so she could concentrate on praying the other drivers on the island's roads weren't in such a mad hurry as Damir.

They stopped outside a squat square building with olive trees on three sides, and Damir jumped out, grabbing a plastic bag and calling to her to follow. He hauled open a stable door and flicked a switch, flooding her path with light and making her blink furiously as she stepped inside in time to see him climb a broad-stepped ladder to a gallery.

Almost immediately a stream of what sounded like invective filled the room and Antonia fervently hoped none of the kittens had died. Then Damir's head appeared, and he was grinning.

"Mackalina's back. Oh, she is a bad cat, but now she's feeding her babies. Come and see."

Leaving her handbag next to the strange circular stone trough in the centre of the room, Antonia headed for the steps. The wood was old and smooth beneath her hands, and for the first time she noticed the rich patina of the railing that edged the gallery as it glowed in the light. When she drew level with the floorboards, the first thing she saw was a red and gold antique Turkish rug, on one side of which was a simple frame bed and a stained pine chest of drawers. Against the rough stone wall on the other, Damir was kneeling in front of a wardrobe so huge it must have been carried up there in pieces.

He beckoned to her. "They do not need my milk after all."

The mother cat was thin, her eyes wary and her tortoiseshell coat uneven. Four tiny balls of fur were suckling her; one tortoiseshell, two black, and one a patchy mixture of both. They were lying in a nest of towels on top of a stack of jumpers on the wardrobe floor.

"See," Antonia told him, "they'll be all right."

"But what if she goes away again?"

"She will. After all, she needs to eat too."

"Then I must buy cat food so she does not have to hunt. How stupid of me not to think of it." He smiled, shaking his head at his own folly, but never once taking his eyes from the cats.

After a while Antonia cleared her throat. "Perhaps we can go to the house so you can show me my room and the kitchen, then you could go back to the shop if it's still open, while I cook us some dinner?"

Finally he nodded. "You are sensible, Antonia. Usually I am sensible too, but somehow... this has touched me..." He formed a fist over his heart. "Exactly here."

Chapter Four

Lynn's message woke Antonia from the deepest of sleeps and it took her a few moments to focus before she could read it.

Did you get there? Or were you whisked away by a handsome Croat and danced until dawn in Dubrovnik?

She wriggled up the bed, rearranging the pillows to protect her shoulders from the brass bars.

I was too knackered to call, let alone dance. Long day.

So how is it?

Antonia considered. Of course it was far too soon to tell, but after a good night's sleep under the fluffy duvet and beautiful sculpted pastel-blue bedspread, she did feel more positive. Anyway, she'd made her bed so now she would have to lie in it. And be grateful it was so damn comfortable. She chose her reply carefully.

Promising

Lynn sent a thumbs-up to end the conversation, then Antonia swung her legs off the bed and padded across the polished floorboards to look outside. From her vantage point on the second floor the view was astounding, out across the olive grove they had driven through last night, towards a squarish bay with a rocky shore lapped by silvery-blue water. Closer to hand, its sloping roof and stone walls peeping above the trees, was Damir's little house, and if she craned her neck to her left she could see a few more terracotta tiles, so they weren't as isolated as she had first thought.

Her suitcases were spread open across the floor in front of the stone chimney breast. There was no fireplace but instead shelving, which looked as though it was made of highly polished olive wood. The perfect place for Honey's photo once she'd unpacked properly.

Unpacking could be left for the moment so she pulled her shampoo and conditioner from the plastic bag poking from one corner of her case and headed for the bathroom. No expense had been spared, with a state-of-the-art Grohe shower and floor-to-ceiling off-white stone tiles. She ran her finger along the smoothness of the smoked-glass shelves, savouring the fact that this was her space and hers alone. Would the girls' makeup and potions have already spread to fill the space on the windowsill left by hers? The pain surged inside her, but she could not give in. This was her new life and she needed to be strong. After gathering herself for a moment she pushed the button to turn on the shower then stepped inside the screen to surrender to bliss for as long as she liked. And she had to admit, much as she was missing Honey, that was a definite upside.

Once Antonia was dressed, she took her pad and pen downstairs to the kitchen, her need for coffee over-riding her desire to look into each of the guest rooms as she passed. Already she knew they would be as stunning as they had appeared in the videos and photos, and a flicker of outrage at Ned's reluctance to take on this place surfaced. Shaking her head, she recognised it was probably just where she was following their breakup; she'd done tears – copious amounts of them – and now it was anger. She really hoped she wouldn't move on to regret any time soon.

Above the hall table was a charcoal sketch of a woman with fabulously crinkled skin. The lines around her eyes told of laughter and sorrow, and although there was kindness in the curve of her face and she was smiling, her lips were pressed firmly together. A cross hung around her neck, just visible above the buttons of her shirt. It was a fascinating piece of art, so much feeling packed into so few strokes, and Antonia found it hard to tear herself away.

"So you have met Tetka?"

Antonia had been so absorbed she hadn't heard the kitchen door open. "It's a wonderful picture... She has a fascinating face."

Damir nodded. "Vincenzo did it for me when I couldn't

find a suitable photograph. He's the sculptor who'll be tutoring our students."

"Who is she?"

"My aunt. She brought me up. Come, I have fresh bread from the bakery and I will show you how to make coffee."

"Show me?"

"Your coffee is different, I think. In Croatia coffee is important."

So Antonia stood next to the Aga-like stove while Damir fetched two long-handled enamelled pots, the larger one chipped and green and the smaller one navy blue, together with a canister of ground coffee from the larder. At right angles to the stove was the outside wall, with its long metal-framed window above a stone sink and old-fashioned wooden draining board. In complete contrast, an enormous American-style larder fridge purred in the opposite corner.

"This is *dzezva,*" Damir explained, indicating the jugs. "Normally they match but a handle broke and we couldn't find the same colour. We use them always to make coffee. Never with a kettle." He filled the larger pot with water and set it on the hotplate to boil. "Now we wait, and to make use of the time, I'll tell you a story. In the olden days, when a man wanted to marry a woman, he would visit her family's home for coffee. This is what I mean; coffee is important. We decide business, marriages, all over coffee.

"So, the girl will make the coffee and if she likes the man, she will put in sugar, and if she does not like him she will put in salt. There may be many people in the house, so the salt tells him to... um... piss off, without anyone else knowing."

Antonia laughed. "That's so subtle. I love it."

The water was almost boiling so Damir turned his attention to the smaller pot, filling it with coffee grounds almost halfway up.

"That's going to be strong," she ventured.

"It's morning. It needs to be."

Slowly he added the boiling water, then put the smaller pot on the stove to heat again. "Now I'll stir while you fetch the cups."

There was no hint as to where the cups might be, so Antonia opened the large wooden cupboard next to the larder. One side was packed with kitchen utensils, which she'd discovered last night were covered in a fine layer of dust, but on the other was a set of plain cream-coloured mugs, bowls and plates, with the slightly lopsided look that gave them away as hand crafted.

She turned back to Damir. "These? They're beautiful."

He smiled. "I am glad you like them. They are old, but for the guests we must have new that will go in the dishwasher."

Yes, Antonia thought, perhaps this was going to work. Damir may live life at a hundred miles an hour and be a little eccentric, but he had his head screwed on as well.

Despite the warm air drifting through the open door, Damir insisted it was far too cold to breakfast in the courtyard. Instead, they sat at the vast pine kitchen table, scrubbed almost white by age, which would clearly be her main worksurface as well as a place to eat. The coffee was rich and delicious, and had a kick that Antonia knew would keep her going until lunchtime. Over thick slabs of soft white bread drenched in local honey, Damir told her the kittens had survived the night, then moved on to his plans for the day.

"As soon as we've finished breakfast, we will go to Korčula Town so I can show you the market before it closes. It's where we will buy all our fresh food. I think the guests would prefer us to support local farmers, and anyway, it is what we do here. If they like, perhaps you could take them sometimes when you shop. Of course we'll use the supermarket as well but they need not go there." He winked. "Then after the market we will walk around the old town and I will take you to lunch to celebrate your arrival."

"That's kind of you, but—"

He carried on as though she hadn't spoken. "There are big differences between your culture and mine, and you must learn as much about my culture as possible in the coming weeks. First lesson: we have lunch. More important than dinner. Of course, when the guests arrive it will be different, but until then you must remember lunch is not a sandwich. Dinner is a sandwich. Or leftovers from lunch."

Clearly food was a priority for Damir, and Antonia sensed it could be common ground between them. Likeable as he was, he was definitely talking at her, not to her, and she needed to find a foothold and make it a proper conversation before she drowned in wave after wave of words.

"We haven't discussed what you'd like me to cook for the guests, and that's really important before we start shopping. You're obviously proud of your culture; will I need to learn to make local food?"

"Definitely not. Well, perhaps one or two dishes, but not everyone likes to eat goat."

"They won't want English food either. Some sort of Mediterranean fusion perhaps?"

"Yes, that would be suitable." He picked up his mug and threw the dregs into the sink. "Come on, let's go."

"But I'm not ready, I—"

"I know, I know. You are a woman so there will be a million things you need to put in your handbag. And lipstick, of course put on lipstick. And perhaps a spray of perfume."

He rolled his eyes, but there was laughter and a sparkle in them, so it was beyond Antonia to be more than a tiny bit exasperated. She smiled at him. "No, nothing like that. As soon as you let me finish my coffee in peace, then we can go."

The Rotonda outdoor market, nestled as it was below the walls of Korčula Old Town, gave an impression of solid permanence, as though it had been in the same place for centuries. Which it probably had, Antonia thought. There were a dozen or so stalls selling fruit and vegetables beneath blue and white striped awnings, and Damir explained that in the tourist season they would be joined by many more packed with cheap clothing and souvenirs.

"Now it is for the locals only. In the summer we still

come, but very early in the morning before it gets too crowded. And there will be a better choice because the farmers will have more; tomatoes, peppers, melons... Here, traditionally, we eat with the seasons." He grinned at her. "Also we eat pizza. Real pizza I mean, not just from the supermarket."

"Pizza?"

"The Italian influence is very strong. We were Venetian until almost 1800. Marco Polo was born here."

"Really? I thought—"

Damir put his finger to his lips. "Probably. But it is our one claim to fame."

Antonia gazed around her at the golden-grey town walls, warming in the sun, and the broad stone staircase with its elegant balustrades sweeping down from the tower's rounded arch into the marketplace. A row of palm trees stretched towards the waterfront, swaying in the breeze beneath a pale blue sky and from somewhere she could smell baking.

"Why do you need fame when you have such beauty?"

"I ask myself that every day. Come, I will show you the best stalls."

Given what Damir had said about shopping at the market, it surprised Antonia when he was welcomed like a long-lost son by some of the traders, but she understood so little of the language she had no way of knowing what was being said. She had learnt a few basic phrases, but any comprehension was impossible as word followed voluble word in rapid succession. She needed to learn more – and quickly – although she suspected most people spoke at least a little English, if not Italian, in which she was fluent. It would probably be enough for her to get by, but that wasn't the point.

More important was to learn what would be in season when so she could devise some menus. All of a sudden the task seemed too daunting, and coupled with the strangeness of the language all around her, tears threatened, so she walked away from the stalls to stand beneath the palm trees, wondering what the hell she'd done. Back at home, Honey would be flying out of the house to work, no doubt having skipped breakfast, but beautifully turned out in the smart-but-scruffy look she'd perfected. And she'd have managed it all on her own; she didn't really need micro-mothering anymore. Antonia told herself she would do well to remember that, but her common-sense lecture did little to fill the gaping hole in her heart.

She had just about pulled herself together when she realised Damir was standing beside her.

"I am sorry," he said. "It was rude of me to ignore you that way, but some of these ladies are friends of Tetka's and I haven't seen them since her funeral."

"I thought you said you shopped here?"

"Not me personally, although I enjoy the romance of the idea. You understand?"

Antonia turned to face him. "Not really, no."

"I think now, for young people at least, across the world we are the same. We shop at supermarkets, we spend too long on social media, we drive the same cars, wear the same clothes. But I want visitors to understand the best of my country, how perhaps we should be living. How our parents' generation lived. The things that are uniquely Croatian."

There was an intensity in his brown eyes she had not seen before, although a hint of it had been there last night when he'd realised Mackalina was safe. His hand rested briefly on her shoulder, and for a moment he seemed as old as the hills and just as strong.

Antonia nodded. "Yes. I understand. Damir, will you teach me Croatian?"

The grin returned, but it was a slow one. "Of course. But first, let me show you the old town."

Instead of entering through the ancient arch at the top of the stone staircase, they followed the long ramp outside the walls towards a ruined tower overlooking the water.

"First we walk around, then we walk through," Damir explained. "It makes better sense that way because I can explain the geography."

"The geography?"

"Perhaps I'm using the wrong word. The town as it was planned. Of course, it started as a defensive post in ancient times, because the position is so perfect, but when the Venetians arrived it became so much more than that."

Korcula Town was perfect in more ways than one. The buildings were piled onto a promontory surrounded by sea on three sides, and the clear, calm waters of the bay to their right as they walked offered sheltered anchorage. When Antonia mentioned this Damir laughed, telling her about the winds that whipped up and down the channel between the island and the mainland; the freezing Bura from the north and the stormy Jugo from the south, the bringer of rain and, according to some local people, illness and bad temper.

"We love the sun," Damir told her, "so it is hardly surprising the wet wind is blamed for bad things."

He went on to explain the layout of the town was due to these winds. Stopping next to one of the narrow streets rising to their left, he pointed out that not just this one, but all of them, were slightly curved, and if you looked at the pattern on a map it resembled a herring bone, reducing the Bura and the Jugo to little more than soothing breezes.

"Clever," Antonia murmured.

"Oh, we Korčulans are very practical. It is probably our Venetian blood."

They strolled along a broad promenade lined with trees, the lap of the waves on the rocks below echoing their footsteps across the empty flagstones. It reminded Antonia of an English seaside town in January, with tables and chairs stacked outside the shuttered buildings, except here the air was fresh and bright – warm even, where the sunshine was finding its way through the branches.

"In summer all the best restaurants are here, because of the views over the sea. Very expensive food for the tourists, but good all the same."

"So what do people do in winter?"

"Spend their money!" Damir turned to her, looking serious. "That is for the owners, of course. For the people who work for them, life on the islands can be hard. It is not surprising some leave for the cities to find year-round jobs."

His words made Antonia wonder what would happen to her come the end of October. She would go home, but to what? The hope that Honey and Sara would have saved enough for a deposit on a flat. But then the cottage would be impossibly empty, and so would her life. The thought choked her up again. She needed to get a grip.

"You've never been tempted to go?" she asked Damir.

"Everything I need is here. And anyway, I do not like cities." For a moment he seemed to be suppressing a shudder, but when Antonia looked into his face he was smiling, so she must have misread him.

After a complete circuit, Damir took Antonia inside the old town, through the archway near the market, which had a Croatian flag fluttering on its tower. On the other side of the entrance the road widened, and to their left was a covered square with stone seats lining its walls behind low rounded arches with decorated corbels, which Antonia thought would be a deliciously cool place to chat on a hot summer's day. Damir stopped next to it, commanding Antonia to look back at the tower above the entrance, which was far more highly decorated inside than out. It was as though whoever had built the town wanted to show its strength to those beyond the gates but offer beauty and grace to those within.

Narrow alleys disappeared in three directions, ornate wrought-iron lamp fixtures and brightly coloured window boxes breaking up the grey stone walls. Antonia and Damir strolled down the main street, the paving beneath their feet worn smooth by age. On either side, carved shutters in rich mahogany hid dusky interiors from the world, but from the signs hanging above them Antonia guessed they were shops which would open when the season started. The season again. The town seemed to be waiting with bated breath, while she needed every second she had just to get her bearings.

The road opened into a square lined with impressive buildings, their facades flooded with sunshine. The pale grey stone was dazzling, but the strong light made it easy to pick out every last sculpted detail of the pillars, archways, and fine balconies suspended from the upper floors. Damir flipped his sunglasses from the top of his head onto his nose, the epitome of cool in his cashmere jumper. She added that to the ever-growing list of words to describe him. There were starting to be too many for Antonia to easily fathom him out.

The star attraction in the square was the church of Sveti Marko, with its barley-sugar twisted columns at the door and the tower that dominated the town's skyline. Damir told her you could climb it for the view and she would have dearly loved to, but all he allowed was a brief peep inside the incense-filled interior, before proclaiming it was definitely lunchtime.

They ate in a restaurant which in summer would boast a terrace overlooking the cruise ship harbour, but now they were shown to a table in the narrow interior, which was already crowded with locals. The aromas drifting from the kitchen were tantalising, the mixture of meatiness and herbs making Antonia's mouth water. Damir ordered a carafe of white wine and she pushed the thought that he would need to drive them home to the back of her mind. Perhaps after a few glasses she wouldn't feel she had to close her eyes the moment she climbed into the passenger seat.

There was no menu as such and a large man wearing an apron came to their table and rattled off what sounded like a list of food. Damir began to translate but Antonia stopped him, asking him to order for her so she could begin to understand the local cuisine.

"Very well," he said, "we shall have *makaruni*." Then, without pausing for breath, he embarked on a detailed history of the town.

The wine worked its magic and, despite Damir's lecture, Antonia was feeling quite mellow by the time their food arrived – fat worms of pasta coated in an aromatic meat sauce, not dissimilar to a bolognese. For a while they ate in silence, then Damir asked if she was enjoying it, his face splitting into his already familiar grin when she told him how delicious it was.

She put down her fork. "You are very proud of Korčula, aren't you?"

"Of course. It is my home. Are you not proud of your home?"

Antonia considered. "Of the village and the city nearby? No, not especially. But of the actual home I created for my daughter, and the adult she's becoming, yes. That's what I'm proud of." So proud, in fact, she felt close to tears again and took another gulp of wine.

"How old is your daughter?"

"Honey's twenty-two. She has a degree in textiles and works for a fashion company. She and her partner Sara both live with me, but they need their own space. I think I said... it's one of the reasons I wanted to get away."

"And the other reasons?"

"I admire what you're doing with Vila Maslina and I needed a change." Oh, that was such a pat answer. She wasn't being interviewed now… or was she? She traced her finger around the rim of her wine glass. "I'd got a bit stuck, you know, with everything..."

"I see."

But she wondered what he did see. A sad middle-aged woman on the run from herself? She certainly didn't want him to regret employing her, so, summoning every shred of confidence she could muster, Antonia looked him in the eye, smiling.

"Well that's quite enough about me; what's your story? Earlier you said that your aunt brought you up."

Damir put his head on one side, biting the corner of his lip for a moment before shaking his head.

"Some stories are perhaps too long to tell, or too long ago, anyway. Tetka may have been my father's sister, but she was my mother in every other way. And I think that is all you need to know."

Chapter Five

The darkness was so complete that opening his eyes meant nothing, yet still the ear-splitting, earth-shaking rumble and crump ricocheted around the enclosed space. Burrowing beneath the thin blanket, he raised his hands to cover his ears in a vain attempt to keep at bay the devastation hurtling from the sky.

Damir's hand touched warm fur, lurching him into wakefulness, his heart thudding so hard it made him feel sick. He fumbled for the switch and the gallery flooded with light, the kitten lying on his pillow blinking as furiously as he was. Scrabbling for the dimmer, he twisted it to its lowest level before flopping onto his back and gazing at the ceiling, trying to calm his breath.

To fight the feeling of panic, he eased himself up on his pillows, the kitten arching its body in disapproval. It was the little black boy, who he had named Marco because he was always exploring. Damir picked him up in both hands, holding him above his head for a moment before settling him into his lap. Marco curled into a tiny ball and began to purr.

Was it the kitten jumping onto the bed that had sparked the dream? He vaguely remembered suffering from nightmares as a child, but for years there had been nothing. Perhaps he should attempt to unpick it somehow. Damir tried to recall what had come before the sound of the bombs. The drone of aircraft... something else... a sickening descent through a concrete stairwell, glass shattering around them...

He could not do this; it was a struggle to remember and the tiny fragments he could recall were too damn frightening. His hand trembled as he reached into his bedside drawer for his cigarettes. There were only two left in the packet, kept for emergencies. It had been a little easier to try to give up since Antonia arrived and he wasn't so alone.

Already she was filling the house with her warmth. And she was as fascinating as she was capable. He had found himself looking at her in the quiet moments, at the way she tucked her hair behind her ear when she was thinking, or ran her finger around the rim of her wine glass. But the quiet moments had been few; in the week since she'd arrived, she had concocted menus and filled store cupboards, and every lunchtime had been a culinary delight as she experimented. In the evenings they drank wine and Damir taught her Croatian, and already she had more than a few words. Last night he'd taken her to Konoba Pecaros to meet Petar and Lorena, and when they spoke slowly she'd seemed to understand, although she lacked the confidence to say much herself, which was something he very much wanted to try to help her with.

Perhaps it was the *rakija* that had sparked the dream? He did not drink it often; the spirit was too strong for that. But Mirjana had given them a bottle to welcome Antonia, so of course... They had all drunk too much, except Lorena who was far too sensible, so he suspected Antonia would have a thumping headache this morning.

Damir moved his watch from the ashtray on the bedside table and stubbed out his cigarette. It was barely five o'clock so time to sleep again, but he dared not turn off the light in case the dream returned. And he could not lie down because if he moved he would disturb Marco. Instead he reached for his phone. Half an hour to check his emails and acknowledge any new bookings, then he would get up and walk along the beach to watch the sunrise. Perhaps, as darkness gave way to the cool light of dawn, he would come back into himself.

When Damir arrived in the kitchen, Antonia already had the coffee on and was sipping some fizzy and no doubt curative concoction from a glass.

"You look as rough as I feel," she told him.

He didn't feel rough, as she put it, at all, having dressed carefully in clean chinos and a freshly pressed shirt for his meeting with Josip Beros, the extremely wealthy and successful owner of three of the best holiday villas he managed.

"Remind me never to drink *rakija* again," Antonia continued.

"It's impossible to avoid. Almost everyone will give you a glass to welcome you." Damir wagged his finger at her. "Just remember, one glass does no damage."

In reply she rolled her eyes, then turned to take the coffee pot from the stove, half filling two mugs with the thick, dark liquid.

"Come on," she said. "I need fresh air."

With his cashmere jumper over his shoulders, Damir grudgingly agreed, although he was careful to dust both their chairs before they settled in a patch of sunlight in the sheltered courtyard which was formed by the two wings of the house and the long, low sheds opposite the kitchen. A cigarette would have been just perfect, and to distract himself from the craving he drummed his fingers on the edge of the metal table.

Antonia winced. "What's wrong?"

Should he tell her the truth or would she think less of him for it? So much of what he let people see of himself was a veneer, but it would be hard to work closely with someone and hide everything. After all, in the grand scheme of things, the odd cigarette was not so big a flaw. "I haven't long given up smoking and this helps."

"Really? I never realised."

"I actually stopped ages ago, but when Tetka died, I don't know... I sort of slipped back into it."

"That's understandable. It must have been tough."

"It was very sudden. But I have kept myself busy so there is no time to grieve."

"Grieving's important, Damir. Both my parents are still alive, but when my marriage ended I discovered I had to mourn it before I could move on. It's the same with any loss: you need to work through it. But just remember, time is a great healer."

Damir considered her words as they sipped their coffee in silence. Did time heal? The pain of losing his mother had been as overwhelming in the moment he saw her photograph as it had been at the time it happened. Which was odd, when he thought about it, because he couldn't really remember it happening. His world had begun when he arrived on Korčula. It had had to be that way. After all, he had been so very young.

He jumped to his feet. "Shall I make more coffee?"

Two more cups and a slice of bread and honey later, Antonia set off for the harbour where the fishermen would be selling their catch. It was Friday, so of course they would be eating fish, as was the tradition, but it was impossible to know what would have been found in the nets overnight. Still, it would be good practice for when Antonia wanted to cook fish for the guests.

Damir prowled around the courtyard until he guessed she would be at the end of the drive then stopped outside the shed where he and Petar had stored the pieces of the old olive press. He left the door open a crack then sank onto one of the stones, exploring the familiar pits in its surface with his fingers. All his life he had been able to find solace in the cool darkness of the press house, but in moving the press itself it seemed the comforting magic had gone.

No, this was too fanciful. He could not blame moving

the press for his nightmare. But all the same, something needed to be done about it; he couldn't leave it mouldering here in pieces when he would need it to process his olives. The only sensible course of action was to put it back together at the bottom of the drive, where it would also become a symbol of Vila Maslina and a source of personal pride. Yes, he liked that thought, and what's more, Tetka would have approved of it too. Decision made, he brushed down his trousers and set off for his meeting.

Josip Beros's villas were on the coastal path to the village, their slightly raised position giving stunning views across the sea to the mountains on the mainland. Before Vila Maslina they had been the jewels in Damir's crown: three traditional houses gutted inside to resemble loft apartments with sleek, modern furnishings and infinity pools carved into the close-cropped grass of their lawns. There was nothing Damir didn't admire about Beros, and his wildest dreams were all about achieving Beros's level of status and wealth. Over the last year or so he had watched him closely, emulating the important things about him, like his eye for detail and his refusal to compromise on quality, in the hope that it would help him obtain the same result.

He was about to unlock the gate to the largest house, which the Beros family kept for their own use, when Antonia rounded the bend from the harbour, a cool bag slung over her shoulder. She waved when she saw him, so after checking his watch he stopped.

"What have you bought?" he asked her.

Already the colour had returned to her cheeks and she laughed. "I'm not entirely sure. A couple of sea bream – I recognised those – then a bigger fish that sounded like *mali tuni*."

He leant towards her and unzipped a corner of the bag. "That's right. Tetka used to cut it into cubes and make a stew with tomatoes and aubergines."

"Then that's what we'll have for lunch. Where are you off to?"

"I am meeting a client, a businessman from Dubrovnik. I look after the three villas behind these walls. They are spectacular – when he has gone home I will show you." His hand was on the gate again.

"Can't I just peep in now?"

He hesitated, wanting to impress her, but he could not afford for Beros to see such indiscretion.

"Certainly not. It would be unprofessional. I'll see you later."

Beros greeted him from the terrace as Damir walked up the path, running a critical eye over the tightly clipped balls of the oleander trees on either side. Josip had a habit of zoning in on any small imperfections, but as Damir had expected, he was smiling.

"*Dobar dan*, Damir. How are you? You have wintered well?"

"I have been exceptionally busy. And you?"

"The same. But it is a glorious morning, so shall we take our coffee on the terrace? Lana will make it, won't you my sweet?" He waved his hand in the general direction of a skinny blonde at least twenty years younger than him, and Damir marvelled at the success with which the bald and slightly portly Josip had managed to play the field since his divorce. It must run in the family – his sister Vesna liked younger lovers too – as Damir had discovered to his advantage.

They exchanged pleasantries until the coffee arrived and Lana disappeared indoors. Then Beros sat back.

"I have inspected the villas and the only problem is a small tear in the pool cover next door. You will need to fix it before the first letting. When is it?"

"20th April. Unless, of course, there is a last-minute booking, so I will see to it straight away."

"Thank you. I did wonder if your service levels would slip now you have your own venture."

How had Beros known? Damir smiled in what he hoped was a sincere manner. "My long-term clients are always my first priority. And anyway, I have employed an English housekeeper who will run Vila Maslina so it will not be a distraction."

"You are making quite an investment."

"Quality is important to me. I have learnt so much from looking after villas such as yours. Being the best is the only way to build a business."

Beros fingered his Omega Seamaster watch, its polished steel bracelet glinting in the sunlight. "Then your instincts are good. I will watch your progress with great interest."

Damir put down his cup, delighted that Beros approved of his so-called instincts, but all the same nervous in case anything might be behind his comment. He couldn't afford to upset Beros; the prestige of working with him was immense and he made sure he told everyone about it. "If that is all, then I would like to photograph the pool cover so I can arrange the repair. Are you here for Easter?"

"No. Lana wants to see New York. Shopping. And Vesna is keen to come instead. She sends her regards, by the way."

"Then please be so kind as to return my good wishes."

They shook hands, then Damir walked around the house to the shared driveway and into the next-door garden. He knew Beros would be watching, so he completed his task briskly, all the while thinking about Vesna's impending visit. He ought to have been looking forward to seeing her again, but for some reason the thought was making him uncomfortable.

He bit his lip, then shrugged; he had almost a month to work it out, and maybe once she arrived he would feel quite differently. If she wanted to see him, he would have to agree – she was Beros's sister so he couldn't afford to upset her either.

Chapter Six

Ned's message was economical in the extreme. *I miss you x*

That was all it said, and Antonia had no idea at all how she was expected to answer. Much as she'd been wondering how he was and what he'd been doing, now she knew his silence had been a blessing. Just those three words had whipped up a welter of emotions and brought them blistering to the surface, painful and raw.

OK, OK, her and Ned's circumstances had been far from perfect, but they had loved each other, she was sure of it. Well, maybe she had loved him more than he'd loved her, but wasn't that sometimes the way? And those three seemingly innocent little words had made her remember all the things she'd been trying to forget, like the way he called her Toni when no one else did, and always bought her favourite wine, and that sweet little cough he used to clear his throat…

No. No. Think of Geoffrey barging in. That could never

be allowed to happen again. It was a good thing it was over. A very good thing. She still felt sick inside at how the affair had made her look in Honey's eyes, especially as she had been so careful with men while her daughter was growing up. Was that why Ned had been able to get so close to her? Had her loneliness been so apparent that she'd been a pushover? A fatal flaw that made her respond to a bit of attention from any man? Whatever it was, she had to use these months on Korčula to work it out and the last thing she needed was Ned texting her while she did it.

But neither could she ignore the message because that would be just plain rude. Far better to play for time.

Busy now – will email

And however much she longed to feel his lips on hers, definitely no kiss.

Busy was absolutely true. Working with Damir was like living on top of a mini-tornado. With him, everything was now, in the manner of an exuberant toddler, but with just a hint of ruthless efficiency underlying it. As well as visits to vineyards, artisans' workshops and the local beauty spots, they had made several trips to the supermarket to stock the larder, and the kitchen was feeling more like her own.

Experimenting with menus was Antonia's joy, and in Damir she had found an enthusiastic audience. For someone so slim, he loved his food, never leaving a scrap and always complimenting her on her creations, as well as having great ideas on how to improve her presentation. It made her dishes far more polished and she was beginning to feel less of an imposter in what would soon be a professional kitchen.

Over lunch each day, Damir would tell her stories about the island, its people and its culture. Or teach her so many new Croatian words and phrases her head would be spinning by the time he left her to do the washing up. But it was as important as it was entertaining, and every time they talked his encouragement made her feel increasingly confident with the language. And, to be honest, more confident full stop.

Confidence was something she had never considered herself lacking but she was coming to realise she had somehow – and for some reason – become almost too scared to make a decision. Being in a new environment had made her see it; when Damir asked her opinion about things – even things relating to her work – she had found she was completely without answers. And answers to questions like how often towels should be laundered, and how many hours the local girl, Ana, should work were a big part of what he was paying her for.

Once she'd recognised the problem she had been able to pull herself together – on a business level at least. Perhaps the trick was to appear more self-assured; after all, only she knew it was just skin deep. But there were flickers of real confidence too, like when Damir praised her food and how good her pronunciation was. And even better, on their Facetime last night, Honey had said that she looked so much more herself. Progress was definitely being made. Although perhaps not enough progress to be able to deal with Ned.

Much of this may have been down to Damir but she had to admit that although he was normally sunny, his moods could be unpredictable, and it was something of a lottery whether he would be practically silent over breakfast or fizzing with energy and fun. Maybe he didn't always sleep well, she thought, because the one time she'd ventured to ask what was wrong he had simply looked at her as though she was crazy.

That day Damir had been monosyllabic, so Antonia was rather surprised when she was on the landing unpacking parcels of bedding and she heard him running up the stairs two at a time.

"Come, I will take you to meet Vincenzo." She must have looked puzzled – or perhaps just stunned by his sudden pronouncement, because he continued, "Remember – the Italian sculptor who will teach our guests. Sunset is a good time to visit him and you can finish those later."

Congratulating herself on how good she was becoming at going with the flow, without a backward glance at the packs of pillowcases covering the floor she headed upstairs to collect a jumper.

Vincenzo's studio was not much more than a five-minute drive across the vineyards that covered the gently sloping ground to the south of the village. Here, Korčula was nothing but a narrow neck of land, and his place overlooked a cove on the opposite side of the island. While the sandy beach nearest Vila Maslina would have a bar and a windsurfing operation in summer, this one was rocky and wild, waves tumbling along the shoreline with a constant wash and drag.

Damir brought the car to a halt on a platform of scrubland just above the bay, and perched amongst the shrubs and stunted trees were two stone buildings, the plate glass frontage of the single storey one glinting in the late afternoon sun. A tall, rugged-featured man with a salt and pepper ponytail stepped from a vine-covered terrace to greet them.

"Antonia, welcome!" He grasped both her hands, the roughness of his firm against her skin. "How do you like Korčula so far?"

"I've hardly had time to think about it, there's so much to do."

Vincenzo smiled to the considerable depths of his dark-brown eyes, then Damir spoke.

"Shall we show Antonia the studio? Explain what our guests will do?"

Vincenzo laughed. "And only then can we relax with a drink, I know. But you are right because the sunset could be spectacular tonight and we will miss it if we're not on the terrace in time."

They followed Vincenzo into the workroom, which was flooded with pale afternoon light. The air carried a lingering taste of dust, and motes danced in front of the windows. Near the glass was a block of stone about a metre square with just one of the corners roughly rounded off, an electric angle-grinder resting on top. Vincenzo picked it up.

"Damir will not want the students to see me using this, but power tools are a fact of life. There is no difference to the finished piece if I use them for the heavy lifting, although of course for conservation they are not allowed."

"So what sort of work do you do?" Antonia asked.

He shrugged his broad shoulders. "Anything anyone will pay me for. Some sculptors consider themselves pure artists and create only their own pieces, but I enjoy repairing stone too, bringing it back to former glories. Or making bespoke pillars and balustrades for holiday villas. Or teaching." He grinned at Damir.

Damir turned to Antonia. "Vincenzo is very modest. His own work sells all over the world, even New York. It is why you see so little of it here."

"I would like to see some, if possible."

Vincenzo took Antonia's hand but somehow it didn't feel creepy, just confident. "Then I will show you."

At the back of the studio was a rack of shelving and on it stood the sculpted head of a man with high cheek bones and a square chin. Its very smoothness made Antonia want to reach out and touch it, but the back half of the stone, where the hair should be, had hardly been worked at all, just roughly chipped, and the contrast was stunning.

"Wow."

"Thank you. It is for a collector in Milan who wanted a portrait of her lover. Unfortunately the man is bald and that was not flattering. This way nobody knows. But come, the sun will set without us if we are not careful. Let's go to the terrace and relax." He turned to Damir. "Yes, even you, my friend."

Vincenzo disappeared inside the house while Damir and Antonia settled themselves on a high-backed wooden bench looking towards the bay. Above them was a trellis, the vine growing up it scattered with bright new leaves. Already the sun was low in the sky and an orange-pink tint crept along the horizon.

"This is just beautiful," Antonia murmured, and Damir smiled at her and nodded.

When Vincenzo returned he was carrying a tray with wine and three glasses, together with small plates of plump green olives and thin triangles of caramel-coloured cheese in oil. He pulled a corkscrew from his pocket while Damir examined the bottle.

"I am paying you too much," he said.

"You, my friend, will pay me very little until you are on your feet, and you know it. However, this is a special celebration to welcome Antonia so of course we drink Pošip." He turned to her. "It's a wine of the area, but the highest quality, sold in the best restaurants, and even our president drinks it. The best in Croatia, and made just a few miles away."

"You are all so proud of Korčula."

"Yes, even those of us who weren't born here, we love it like home. I also love Italy, of course, but it is not the same. Home isn't always where you are born, after all, but where you choose to make it." And as they sipped wine and watched the sun become a glowing ball and slide through a layer of purple clouds into the sea, he told Antonia about how he had settled on the island at the end of his studies in America, how the quality of the stone and the light had brought him here, and how he would never leave.

"But surely it's more than what you need for your work that keeps you here?" Antonia asked.

"Of course it is more than that. It is the people, the

friends you make. You have to feel… some kind of connection. It's very hard to describe, but you know when it's right. For me it's when I have had enough of the world, and Korčula is the only place I want to be."

Night fell with all the brief transience of a Mediterranean dusk, and they went inside to sit on low leather sofas around the fire to eat bread and cured meats, and more of the delicious Pag cheese. Damir explained it was a Dalmatian speciality, the saltiness coming from the sheep feeding on one particular island, where the Bura blew the taste of the sea onto the land.

What would Lynn say if she could see her now, sipping wine with a gorgeous but very different man on each side of her? What would Honey? Or Ned? But that wasn't really the point, was it? With the strange flash of clarity that sometimes comes from drinking almost too much, Antonia knew what mattered was what she herself thought, not anyone else's opinion. And right at that moment, she would say she was content. And that was better than she'd felt for a very long time.

Even though her head was beginning to spin, she found herself looking from Vincenzo to Damir and back again, and for the first time Antonia really believed she could make her home on the island, if only for a little while. As Vincenzo had said, it was all about the people, and she had the feeling she was beginning to make two very good friends.

Chapter Seven

Damir crept into the shed before dawn and sank onto the nearest stone, its chill seeping through his jeans and onto his skin. There was no comfort in the olive press anymore, just parts stacked around a dusty shed. It certainly wasn't stopping his nightmares. *A man's body, hanging from a lamppost, greenish-grey hands limp in bloodstained sleeves. And as many times as his mother had hurried him away, they came across the same lifeless body at every turn of the street.*

Had he really seen the awful things he dreamt about? He had no real memories of that time so he could not be sure. Some nights he was able to sink into the healing sleep he so badly needed and others became a terrifying carousel of slides like the ones the teachers used to use at school. Whir-click. Whir-click. Never knowing quite what the next sickening image would be.

Enough.

Action.

This mess of wood and stone was going to be reassembled into a working press if it was the last thing he did. It would never make a suitable memorial for Tetka gathering dust in here. Vincenzo would know how best to make it happen, so after breakfast he would give him a call. Damir patted the battered wooden hopper before creeping into the kitchen to make the coffee.

Once he had arranged for Vincenzo to come over later to discuss the press, Damir set off through the olive grove to search for the first buds. Perhaps it was a little early, but there was no harm in looking, as it would give him an indication of how good the harvest might be. As he neared the seaward corner of his land, he could smell salt in the air.

The wind was changing, a stormy chop on the green-grey sea as the Jugo began to make its presence felt. There would be no fish in the coming days and it would be a lesson for Antonia to be flexible. Already, menus had been written and rewritten until in the end she had thrown up her hands in horror (well, as much as any Englishwoman did) and told him she would cook with whatever she could get.

It had made him laugh so hard she had hit him with a tea towel; she'd looked so mortified he had started laughing all over again. But it had been the moment when her reserve began to crack, and he found himself fascinated by what might be behind it. She was so unlike Vesna and the other women he knew; what attracted him to them was their upfront manner and their confidence of knowing exactly what they wanted – from life, and of course in bed. Perhaps this was where Antonia was so very different. Although she was perfectly competent, she seemed to lack that easy confidence he'd seen in other women her age.

He spied Antonia on the drive, shopping basket over her arm and phone in hand.

"Did you find *lepinja* in the village bakery?" he asked. She nodded, but she was glancing at her screen.

"Is there a problem?" he enquired further.

"No, it's fine. As you said, they're like fluffy flatbreads and I'm sure they'll work with the recipe…"

"I meant the way you're looking at your phone."

She shifted the basket to her other arm, sliding her mobile into it. "Honestly, it's a personal thing so..."

"Are we not friends?"

"Yes. Yes, I hope so."

The contents of the basket seemed particularly interesting and Antonia couldn't meet his gaze.

"Look, when I told you why I wanted to come here I didn't tell you the whole truth."

Oh no, what was coming? She wasn't going to leave, was she? Not only was she good at her job, but he was coming to rely on her. This could be an absolute calamity before the season had even started – Vila Maslina couldn't function without a competent housekeeper – and he felt sweat pool in his armpits. Even so he did his best to smile encouragingly. "Then perhaps you feel you can tell me now? If something is making you unhappy..."

"You're right, I should. But I hope you won't be too shocked, or think badly of me. You see, I was having an affair with a married man."

Was that all? Damir shrugged as he leant against a tree. "It happens."

"And that married man was my boss, Ned, the owner of Mediterranean Gems."

"OK…" This was potentially more serious.

"I knew I had to finish it. It was just so wrong on every level, but, well, I was in love with him. And the opportunity to come here made it possible to leave him and still have a job."

"But all the same you are sad here?"

"No. No, I'm not. I miss Honey dreadfully, and of course I miss Ned too, but most of the time it's fine. Absolutely fine. But then, out of the blue, Ned will text me and I feel like shit again, because he'll say something that reminds me how much I still care."

"Then you should tell him to stop."

Antonia wound her fingers more tightly around the handle of the basket. "I've told him it's not helpful but he won't listen. I don't want to be too forceful, because of Vila Maslina."

"You think he could make problems for us?"

"I don't know. Legally you're protected, but he could still influence the sales team. I don't think he's a spiteful man, but hell hath no fury and all that."

"Hell hath no fury?" Damir repeated the words slowly.

"It's a saying from an old English play. It means there is no one more dangerous than someone rejected in love. Generally applied to women but I don't see why it couldn't cut both ways."

"So what will you do?"

"Ask him to give me the space and time I need. As much as anything because it's the truth."

Again, Damir found himself casting around for the right thing to say. "You said time heals. And perhaps space too, so it is just as well you are here."

Finally Antonia smiled.

As they walked back to the house together, Damir found the words 'hell hath no fury' rolling uncomfortably around his head, accompanied by a mental image of Vesna. Her visit was little more than a couple of weeks away, and despite Josip's message, he still did not know whether she would want to see him.

Towards the end of her holiday last October there had been an unfortunate incident when she'd accused him of flirting with one of her friends. Obviously it had been rubbish – he'd only been, perhaps, a little over polite – but Vesna had barely contacted him over the winter. Of course she had written an eloquent letter of condolence when Tetka died, but there had been no reply to his text thanking her. Until Josip had sent him her regards it was almost as if he had been completely forgotten.

Not that it had been anything like a love affair, but he had enjoyed her company and, of course, the sex. He had felt proud to lunch with her in the island's best restaurants, but if she found another young man to replace him this time when she visited, then he would feel like a total fool. It would be just what he deserved, but people laughing at him was the one thing he could not bear.

No, that had to be avoided at all costs. If necessary, he would woo her again, and just accept that he would probably be erased from her consciousness the moment the catamaran disappeared in the direction of Dubrovnik at the end of her stay. It would be a small price to pay to continue to be linked to the Beros name in the eyes of those on the island who had dismissed him as nothing.

Chapter Eight

Damir stood at the kitchen door, twisting the keys to the people-carrier between his fingers. It was the only thing about his appearance that gave away his nerves.

"Well, this is it."

"Yes." Antonia smiled at him. "A big moment. Good luck."

"I hope I will not need it."

She took his hand. "It's just a phrase... something to say. You've worked so hard for all this; the guests are just going to love it."

She watched as he strode across the courtyard and reversed the vehicle out of its space. For once he had left plenty of time for the short journey to the catamaran quay in the old town and she figured she had almost an hour to herself.

The house was silent around her as she checked the bedrooms one more time, straightening a perfectly placed towel here, plumping an applique cushion there. She was just taking a moment to gaze at the view from an upstairs window when her phone buzzed in her pocket. She smiled; it was probably Damir with a last-minute instruction, but instead Ned's name flashed on the screen. Not again. Not now. How could she ever get over him properly if he kept doing this? It was hard enough when for eighteen months all she had dreamt about, all she had wanted, was for them to be together, but if she was going to survive she had to put the past behind her. Even though her heart still thudded against her ribs when she saw his name.

Without reading the message she went downstairs. In the kitchen she checked the fridge where the antipasti stood ready in its terracotta bowls and the room was filled with the spicy aroma of lamb tagine. It was the first meal she had cooked professionally and there were butterflies in her stomach. Hopefully she was good enough; she would hate to let Damir down.

She started to rinse the couscous, but Ned's message was burning a hole in the pocket of her skirt so she set the colander on the draining board and opened it.

I can't stand this anymore. I'm leaving Diana.

Antonia felt as though the air was being sucked from her lungs. He mustn't do this, not for her...

And yet...

For a moment a world flashed in front of her: a brick and flint house in the South Downs with a large garden, Honey and Sara being able to stay in Antonia's cottage, Ned coming home to her every night... God, how every fibre of her being longed for it. Home, security, the man she loved. But it was a dream, wasn't it? And Honey would never respect her again. Unless, of course, Ned was a single man.

You mustn't do it for me. You must do it for yourself.

She watched Vincenzo cross the courtyard from the shed, where he had been working on the olive press.

"I'll be on my way before they arrive."

He spoke in Italian as he had taken to doing when they were alone, sanding down each plank of the hopper then applying layer after layer of marine-grade varnish, ready for the blacksmith to put it all together again.

She nodded. "See you tomorrow."

"Smells amazing, by the way."

"Thank you."

He kissed Antonia on both cheeks, and she watched as he slid his motorbike from its stand and swung his leg over it. The brief contact with another human being had made her feel so much more able to push Ned to one side and focus on the task in hand.

Vincenzo must have all but passed Damir on the drive. The moment she heard the people-carrier, Antonia rushed through the hall to fling open the front door and put on her best smile to welcome the very first visitors to Vila Maslina.

Antonia showed the guests to their rooms while Damir organised their cases. They had practised this routine so many times, but now it was real it seemed easier, smoother. All the same, she wished it was Damir hearing the arrivals exclaim over the comfort of the beds, the carefully chosen pictures, the hand-painted water carafes and glasses, because it was all his doing. Once everyone was settled, she stood for a moment on the landing, revelling in the hum of people around her and laughter from the twin room. Then there was another sound, deep in her pocket.

Read the message or not? She bolted to the privacy of her own little staircase up to the attic and perched on a step.

Why else would I do it, if not for you? Come home, Toni. I love you. We can make our dreams real.

Antonia was trembling inside. Two months ago it would have been everything she ever wanted and part of her still wanted it now. To go home to Ned, to love and security – the thought was turning her inside out... Or home to another empty promise. And more stolen hours in bloody Geoffrey's bed as Ned's *latest squeeze*, the woman so unimportant she didn't even warrant a name. That would most likely be the truth of it.

A trail of cigarette smoke led her to where Damir was standing on the opposite side of the courtyard.

"Everything all right?" she asked.

He gave her a brief nod.

"The guests love it."

"I know."

OK, it was stressful, but right at this moment she was having enough trouble dealing with her own emotions. Antonia shrugged and returned to the kitchen.

Over dinner, Damir was the perfect host. Wine flowed and the tagine dish was scraped clean, the evening only marred by Antonia's phone ringing as she served the syllabub for dessert. Putting the last dish down, she apologised and hurriedly turned it off.

Thankfully, nobody wanted a late night so Antonia was able to creep into the kitchen to check her messages. Ned. She'd known it would be. His voice ran through her, begging, pleading for her to come home. He loved her, he would make it right. They could weather the storm of his divorce together and it would be fine. There were tears in Antonia's eyes as she clicked to end the voicemail and gazed out into the darkened courtyard. How could he continue to taunt her with dreams she knew would never come true? It was selfish of him… and just plain cruel.

"Can't you leave your phone alone? You're worse than Ana."

She spun around. Right now she could really do without one of Damir's bad moods. "And what if it was something important?"

"It rang at the table. It should have been on silent. I was so embarrassed..."

"So was I, and I apologised to everyone, so that should be the end of it." She swept back to the dining room to collect the glasses.

Damir was behind her, hands on hips. "And was it important?"

The words were out before Antonia even had chance to think. "As it happens, yes. Ned's leaving his wife and he wants me to go home."

"So he does this, tonight of all nights. And still you are thinking of going? Are you?"

There was a tap on the dining room door. "I am so sorry to bother you, but my toilet seems to be blocked."

Damir's angry face morphed into the brightest of smiles. "Do not worry – we are here to look after you. Let me see if I can fix it."

Antonia finished collecting the glasses and took them to the kitchen. Putting them on the draining board, she fired off a text to Ned.

Don't do this to me.

Straight away flashed back:

So you do care!

She closed her eyes and took a deep breath. God, this hurt. But Damir had been right when he'd said *tonight of all nights*. Ned must have known it was the opening day of their season. Probably even the time the guests would arrive. No, she was not being manipulated in this way. She was stronger now. Just a little bit anyway. She could survive this.

Not anymore. Do what you want, but don't involve me.

Tears streaked Antonia's cheeks as she blocked his number then switched on the dishwasher before running the water into the sink to wash the glasses. There, it was done. And once again, she'd been the one who'd had to do it. If she hadn't acted in the first place, he'd have just carried on using her – probably until his wife found out – and then she would have been out of a job and a relationship so fast her feet wouldn't have touched the ground. Why the hell hadn't she realised before?

But now she had a bridge to build. She'd wanted to lash out at somebody and in doing so had almost deliberately misled Damir, despite knowing how stressed he was. Well maybe there had been fault on both sides, but perhaps it was best to just say sorry because there was no way she could deal with any more upset tonight.

The kitchen door opened and she caught Damir's reflection in the window in front of her.

She cleared her throat. "All sorted?" she asked as cheerfully as she could manage.

"No. It is not all sorted," he snapped. "Petar must come tomorrow. Also, it seems, as you did not answer my question, that I need a new housekeeper." He gesticulated towards the kitchen table, where there was a bottle of *rakija* and two glasses. "I had planned for us to celebrate, but this is no success. It's a disaster, a disaster. And you, Antonia, have let me down worse than anyone in my life. You should be ashamed, really ashamed." In two strides he was across the kitchen. "We will talk of this tomorrow."

Antonia had been about to speak, but the door slammed behind him. She was so shocked by his outburst she could do nothing but slump at the table, put her head in her hands and sob. Could she do nothing right? And what if… what if Damir made her go home? What would she tell Honey? And how would she face Ned if she saw him?

She let herself cry as the emotion drained out of her.

Reaching for the *rakija* bottle she poured herself a small glass in the hope it would stop the trembling inside. Come on, Antonia, calm down. She knew she had done the right thing over Ned, and Damir really should not have spoken to her like that. It wasn't acceptable. But on the other hand, they were both tired and stressed. Things would surely feel better in the morning, and even if they didn't, there were seven guests who had paid a lot of money for their holiday and needed looking after. That should be their priority, their common cause. Surely they could be adult enough to work together to make sure it happened?

"*Jako mi je zao.*" Damir stood at the kitchen door, his eyes dark holes above his strong cheekbones. "Your 'I'm sorry' does not say it enough. You were hurting and all I did was make things worse."

Antonia felt her shoulders sag with relief; she'd been awake most of the night worrying that their working relationship was in tatters.

"Your apology is accepted, as long as you accept mine too."

"You did nothing wrong. I was just so impossibly stressed over our first night, and then I was frightened you would leave. I woke at two in the morning and I understood what I had done. How I was last night would be enough on its own to make you go. Have you decided?"

"I am not going back to Ned."

"So you will stay?"

"Yes."

He nodded. "Good. A cigarette and some coffee, then I will help you with breakfast."

Antonia watched him retreat to the courtyard. Mercurial was not the word for Damir, but she would need to learn to live with it. His apology had been sincere enough and he had clearly been just as worried as her about the consequences of their misunderstanding, but all the same it unsettled her. She preferred her life to be calm and ordered, and she was coming to recognise that working with Damir this was unlikely to be the case.

Shortly after ten, Vincenzo arrived to talk to the guests, then he and Damir took them to Korčula Town for a guided walk to show them the beautiful carvings incorporated into the stonework of many of the buildings. Antonia would have loved to have gone with them, but someone needed to wait for Petar to arrive to repair the toilet. And anyway, she wanted to talk to Lynn, who was a counsellor, about last night and how she might deal with Damir when inevitably something similar happened again.

Petar arrived before she had a chance to make the call, and although he fixed the toilet within half an hour, seemed in no hurry to leave. In his halting English he told Antonia it had done him a favour, because he was missing Sunday lunch with Lorena's grandmother who always cooked some sort of tasteless stew and complained endlessly about everybody under forty.

It seemed churlish not to offer him a meal, but the best Antonia could come up with using unspoken for ingredients was an omelette. She put Petar to sit in the courtyard with a glass of wine while she beat eggs and grated cheese, wanting to make the tastiest, fluffiest concoction imaginable. Luckily there was leftover syllabub for dessert.

Putting his plate in front of him, she thanked him again for coming out on a Sunday.

"It's my job. But I was not pleased about the way Damir told me last night."

"That could have been partly my fault. Our first night was stressful enough, and then my phone went off at the dinner table and... anyway, it put him in a very bad mood." She thought for a moment. Petar clearly knew Damir well. "Do you mind me asking, is he often like that?"

"Almost never. He is a very positive person. Even when he is stressed he is not angry; normally he runs around like this." Petar did a fair impression of a rabbit bobbing up and down to avoid imaginary gunshots and Antonia laughed.

"Yes, I've seen that too. Last night though, he was determined to have a fight."

"Damir never fights. Not even at school. At first when he came here, it could have been a problem. But I was big and my brother even bigger so we made sure it was not."

The opportunity was too good to miss. "So Damir wasn't born on the island?"

"No. He arrived at about the time we started school. His father had died in the war and it made him a little... strange? No, perhaps that is the wrong word, but I do not have another one. My mother said because of it I must be his friend."

"Strange?"

Petar looked thoughtful. "Things as a child I did not understand. Like, if my mother gave us cake he would hide some away, but I knew with Tetka he could not be hungry. And at first he did not want to play outside either, and then only in the olive grove. But we had good games in the olive grove." He smiled.

"What about Damir's mother?"

"I do not know. Dead too I think, because he always lived with his *tetka*. Things were not easy for him for a while. Other children teased... sometimes very cruel. But then we all grew up and it was fine." He took the last piece of bread from the basket and wiped his plate. "Antonia. You are a very good cook. Thank you."

"And you are a very good plumber. So good that there is dessert."

He grinned at her. "I'll tell you when we're going to Nona's house for lunch again, then you can ask the guests to block another toilet."

Chapter Nine

How one week had become two, and two had become three, and Easter weekend had come and gone, Antonia could not imagine. To be fair, she was a little short on imagination this morning anyway, because last night after supper they'd had a wine tasting from a local grower and it had turned into something of a party. She was doubly glad of her coffee, although a little surprised Damir hadn't turned up to share it.

Instead she received a text, just as she was restocking the breakfast buffet with homemade croissants. There was yet another issue at the Beros villas he needed to attend to urgently, so would she mind driving the guests to Vincenzo's?

Apart from the mildest of hangovers she had no particular reason to feel as miffed as she did, because it would take her all of half an hour, but she needed the time to talk to Honey. Her daughter had messaged at some point during last night's wine tasting to say she'd had a massive row with Sara and would call once Sara had gone to work. Which would be precisely the time Antonia was loading the guests into the people-carrier. Damir was really asking too much of her this time.

She pulled herself up short. Of course he wasn't. He had a real reason to ask her, not just one of his increasingly frequent morning moods. He knew nothing of the drama being played out back in Sussex and helping Damir to look after the guests was central to her job. It was just that the timing was bloody awful and for the first time ever she would need to put her daughter second on her list of priorities.

She'd been here the best part of two months and right now the pain of missing Honey didn't seem to have faded at all. The desire to hug her daughter, to smell her hair in her face, was almost physical and it ripped her in two. Especially when Honey was hurting and she couldn't even give her a cuddle to make it better. Oh, how she longed to be back at home. At least Lynn had been talking about coming out for a week in the not-too-distant future and that was something. Of course it would have been better to have been able to see Honey, but she couldn't afford the airfare and neither could the girls.

What she needed to do right now was to message Honey to let her know it would be a little later before they could talk, which they could do as soon as she left the guests at Vincenzo's. She remembered his words about home being the place you needed when things were tough and right now that place felt further away than ever. How could she be the best possible mother if she wasn't even there?

The morning clouds were lifting as she drove up the slope to the studio, the sunshine creeping down the hill, over the rocks, and into the crystal-clear silver-blue of the bay. In a couple of months' time it would be a beautiful place to swim, and Antonia knew that on a day like today she should focus on these small positives. She jumped out of the car to release the guests and Vincenzo appeared, kissing her on both cheeks.

"Good morning, Antonia. Have you come to see how our students are progressing?"

She shook her head. "I'm afraid I—"

"Oh, please. I'm so excited." This from a gentle-voiced American who was especially nice, so it was impossible for Antonia to refuse. But at least she summoned up the resolution to tell her she had an important call to make first.

Vincenzo put his hand on her shoulder. "Feel free to go into the house."

Antonia thanked him but instead chose to perch on the bench on the terrace, gazing out over the bay as the watery sunshine licked the tops of the waves and the tendrils of the old vine fluttered above her head.

While Honey's phone was ringing she barely noticed the view, picturing instead her kitchen at home, the table strewn with the debris of more than one meal, her daughter standing at the window, gazing out at the pots of tulips in the tiny courtyard garden. Over and over again Antonia told herself she needed to put her own unhappiness to one side and be strong for Honey. After all, a large part of coming here had been to prove to her that she was.

"Why aren't we Facetiming?"

This was not a good start. "Only because I don't have a great signal, my darling, and I didn't want to leave it a moment longer to talk to you. How are things this morning?"

"Better, I suppose. Sara doesn't like sleeping on an argument."

"Well that's good."

"Not really. We didn't actually, you know, resolve anything."

Antonia sat back on the seat, arching her shoulders against the wooden boards. "So it was a biggy, then? What was it about?"

Honey sighed as dramatically as only she could. "Money. Again. She's always on about money."

"In what way?"

"Like, we have to save every penny. Like, there's never any left over to have any fun. Or for new clothes."

Now they could be getting somewhere. Honey had always loved clothes. "So what did you buy?"

"Nothing expensive – it was from the seconds shop at work. It was just the cutest print T-shirt, new for this season, and it's not as though I didn't buy one for her as well."

"Oh, Honey. You know you're meant to be sticking to your budget."

"She didn't have to throw it back at me. Literally. I mean, really literally." Her voice started to break. "Oh, Mum, if you'd been here she'd have never dared to be so… so cruel."

Oh God, this was hard but she had to say it. As gently

and firmly as she could. "But I'm not there, Honey. And part of the reason I'm not is so you can learn to live together on your own."

Silence. If Antonia had been sitting next to Honey she could have wrapped her arm around her shoulder, let her have a little weep about the unfairness of it all, then gradually talked her round. The miles between them meant that almost half her armoury was missing.

But suddenly there was a comforting hand on her shoulder, as Vincenzo leant over and put a steaming mug of cappuccino in front of her before padding away as silently as he had arrived. Gratitude for his simple kindness flooded through her, and telling herself to buck up her ideas, Antonia took a deep breath.

"No, Sara didn't have to throw the T-shirt at you, but then perhaps you should have discussed buying the tops first."

"But they were only forty quid. It was nothing."

"Forty pounds isn't nothing, Honey. Not when you have bills to pay and you're trying to save."

"The bills would be smaller if you were still here."

Antonia closed her eyes. "Honey, we talked it all through before I even applied for the job, and you wanted me to go."

"I didn't know I'd miss you this much."

It was agony picturing her hunched at the table, tears streaming down her face. "I miss you too, my darling. But as I said, the whole point was to give you and Sara the proper space to live together. To find out if you could live together."

There was a very long silence. Were their differences something they could reconcile? What if they couldn't? If that was the case, Antonia knew she would have to go home, and then she'd be letting Damir and goodness knows how many holidaymakers down. And besides, it was much too soon to risk bumping into Ned. She had to – *had to* – help Honey find a way through this. Then inspiration struck.

"You're very like your dad with money. We used to have rows like you and Sara are having, especially when I was on maternity leave. But we talked about it and worked it out. If you and Sara love each other, you need to do the same."

"How did you and Dad sort it?"

Antonia fiddled with the handle of her mug. "You probably won't like my answer, because we agreed I would take control of our finances. Only for a year, until I went back to work and things eased. Once you and Sara have enough for your deposit, things will ease for you as well."

"But she won't let me have any treats at all!"

"Then negotiate your treat budget up front. Agree that if you can save a bit elsewhere, you can spend at least some of it on non-essentials. Relationships are about compromise, after all."

"But she won't shift..."

"I bet she will if you explain it right. And if she doesn't, well... you've learnt something."

Silence. Antonia was tempted to fill it. If she'd been there she would have been holding her daughter's hand while she worked it out.

Eventually Honey said, "I do love her, Mum."

"Then isn't it worth trying? If you want help with the budget we could always Facetime when I'm back at the villa on the Wi-Fi."

"Then where are you?"

"Sitting on a bench overlooking the most beautiful bay. I had to drop the guests here. I'll send you a picture when we've finished."

"Send me a selfie. I want to see your face."

"Only if you send one to me."

"I'm a bit blotchy..."

Antonia's heart twisted in her chest. "But do you feel better?"

"Of course, Mum. I always feel better when I've spoken to you."

"Selfie time then?"

There was a pause, then a gasp. "Shit, Mum, I've only just realised the time and it will take me an age to repair my face for work. Love you – talk later."

And she was gone. Oh, how easily the young mended, Antonia thought as she gathered her coffee cup, while she would feel shaken and upset for most of the morning.

When Antonia arrived back at Vila Maslina with the shopping, the top half of the stable door of the old press house was open, so she pulled over under the olives. The trees were almost in full flower, covered with sprigs of the tiny cream balls that Damir told her would, at the end of the season, give fruit. By that time Antonia would be on her way home, which made it seem even more of an age before she would see Honey again and she badly needed a bit of company to distract her.

Damir was at his desk in front of the window and jumped up when she knocked on the door.

"Everything all right at the Beros villas now?" she asked. "You seem to be over there all the time at the moment."

"It is one problem after another, all so small it makes me wonder if perhaps they're making them up, but it is Beros's sister so of course I have to go."

"So the guests are higher maintenance than the house?" He frowned and she explained the English phrase.

He smiled. "Yes, that is good. Very good. I will remember it."

"Right. I'll leave you to your paperwork. I can cook you a bit of lunch later, if you like."

"Sorry. I have to meet someone."

"Then see you this evening."

Antonia was about to leave when her phone rang. She pulled it from her bag to see a call from Lynn on the screen.

"Hello?"

"I've found some cheap flights for next week. Andy's working from home so he can feed the kids, so shall I book? I'd get into Dubrovnik on Wednesday morning."

"Hang on, hang on, let me ask Damir." He had gone back to his desk and was scooping one of the black kittens from his keyboard. "Damir, my friend Lynn – I told you she was looking for flights – she could come next Wednesday for a week. Is that OK?"

"We certainly have a room until Saturday." He held the

kitten to his cheek. "And after that too, although if it is booked in the meantime..." Suddenly he grinned. "...I would be able to find a place in the village. Tell her to come."

"Do it, Lynn. Book that flight and email me the details. Oh God, I can't wait to see you."

Lynn hung up and Antonia turned back to Damir. "Thank you so much. I'll pay for her food, of course..."

"No. Just looking at your face I can see this is making you happy. And that makes me very happy too."

His simple pleasure at her excitement was deeply touching and made her feel so much better. "Thank you," she said. "You are so very kind to me."

He grinned at her. "No worries. We're a team."

Chapter Ten

Damir was full of advice as he drove Antonia to the catamaran on Wednesday morning. Already he had gone above and beyond, suggesting she take some time off and arranging a guest house in Dubrovnik where she and Lynn could stay the night. Antonia had instructions about where to eat, when to avoid the old town, and the best place for coffee. When pressed, he'd reluctantly revealed he never visited himself but had a friend who lived there who kept him up to date.

Both the ferry port and the main bus station were in Dubrovnik's new harbour, a sheltered inlet edged with modern functional buildings. A bewildering number of people eddied to and fro on the concrete expanse of waterfront, and for a moment Antonia wondered how she and Lynn, who had taken a bus from the airport, would ever find each other. Gripping her rucksack, she looked left and right, then her phone pinged a message; Lynn was waiting under the canopy, next to stand number three for the shuttle bus to the old town.

There was barely time to hug before they had to board, but Antonia was so happy to see her she never wanted to let her go. They slid into a seat, surrounded by a sea of backpackers and locals pouring from the ferries, gabbling at each other like a couple of loons. It was hectic and hot, the air filled with sweat and diesel fumes, but they clung together as the bus swerved around corners, laughing at the craziness of it all.

Clutching Damir's hand-drawn map, Antonia led Lynn away from the crowds at the old town's Pile Gate, through a dusty park then down some shaded steps with the honeyed walls of Italianate villas on either side, their white shutters closed against the heat of the day. At the bottom was a concrete plaza, edging a bay which was dominated by the town walls that soared high to their left, and on the right an imposing castle that seemed to grow out of the rock it was built on and into the sky.

The enticing aromas of grilled meat surrounded them as they passed the restaurants lining the waterfront, but it was the crystal-clear sea that captured Antonia. Every stone, every fish, rippled just below the surface and a kayak-hire operation was doing brisk business from a long, narrow jetty.

They dropped their bags at the guest house, which overlooked another cove a little further on. Here, the red-roofed properties were cheek by jowl, but compared to the area just outside the old town it was a peaceful backwater with pots of herbs lining the steps and bougainvillea climbing the walls. The owner, who seemed to have some sort of connection to Damir's friend, welcomed them then pointed them in the direction of the nearby taverna.

"This is amazing," Lynn said as they sat down at a table right on the edge of the small quay. "I didn't expect it to be like this at all. The sea, the castle... all these pretty houses."

"I don't know what I did expect," Antonia told her. "I bought a guide book but I haven't had time to open it."

"So the job's keeping you busy?"

"Yes. But first, tell me how Honey really is. She said you dropped by on Saturday."

The waiter brought the carafe of white wine they had ordered then proceeded to take an impossibly long time going through the menu. One of the specials was a squid risotto so Antonia opted for that, and Lynn chose swordfish, saying she'd never eaten it before. Eventually he left and they returned to their conversation.

"I'd say she's all right."

"But?"

Lynn laughed. "There is always, always a *but* with you."

"It's the way you said it."

"I said it because… Look, I hope you don't mind me mentioning this, but Honey's a very young twenty-two, don't you think? I mean, in general and compared to Sara."

"I hadn't really thought about it." Antonia took a gulp of wine. She wanted to hear how Honey was, not suffer one of Lynn's lectures, especially if it involved her parenting skills. It was all right for her – she hadn't had to raise her kids alone.

"Well I think she is, and maybe it's because you still treat her like a bit of a child. You know, slipping her money to make her feel better, and if you were still at home I reckon you'd still be picking up her clothes too."

"Don't be silly. I haven't done that for years."

"Well, figuratively speaking."

Antonia folded her arms. "So it's just as well I'm not there then."

"Maybe. Are you cross with me for saying it?"

"No, of course not."

Lynn held up one eyebrow with her little finger, in a joke they'd shared for years and Antonia had to laugh. "Anyway," she asked her, "how did Honey and Sara seem together?"

Lynn screwed up her nose. "They're OK, but not exactly love's young dream anymore. I could be being unfair though. It's hard to be especially lovey-dovey when you're pole-axed by period pains, which Sara was."

"Did you sense there was anything wrong between them?"

"Not at all. Perhaps they're just settling down to the long haul of their relationship. It's been a while, hasn't it?"

"Coming up to two and a half years." Antonia ran her finger around the rim of her glass. "Am I wrong to be worrying so much, Lynn? I mean, part of the reason I left was to give them space to find out what it was really like living together."

Lynn covered Antonia's hand with hers. "Honey's your child. You are going to worry. But you can't fight her battles for her. Remember, you came out here for yourself as well."

Having drunk too much wine, they retired to the guest

house for a siesta. Lynn had had an early start, but Antonia was far from tired so she took a shower to freshen up then sat in the shaded courtyard under a bougainvillea, working her way through a large bottle of water. The guide book was in her hand, but all the same she was pre-occupied by what Lynn had said. Was she really in part responsible for Honey's troubles now, because she'd sorted everything out for her in the past? But even if she was, she couldn't just turn around and tell Honey it was all down to her now – it wouldn't be fair. One thing was clear: she shouldn't go running home at the first hint of trouble at the cottage. Learning to resolve their own problems was all part of giving the girls space.

She knew Lynn was right to remind her she had come here for herself as well. How many times had Damir said, whether choosing ingredients for new dishes or dealing with difficult guests, or any time she was prevaricating really, 'It's what you think that matters'? And every time he did, she felt just a little bit more confident that he was right. He really was proving to be a wonderful friend, supporting her as he did – not to mention giving her this time off and finding them such a gorgeous place to stay. It was such a pity he suffered from those difficult moods and she wished she understood the reason for them because she wanted to help him too.

Lynn appeared at half past five and they made their way towards the walls of the old town. The immense structure towered above them, grey stone forbidding even in the bright sunlight. Circling the town completely, the walls were far higher and sturdier than Korčula's, making

Antonia think that in bygone days the populace must have felt so very safe living inside.

They approached the Pile Gate across a bridge with an elaborate stone balustrade. Despite the number of tourists there was a lazy magic to the late afternoon, perfectly suited to wandering around and exploring. The sea sparkled at the end of the old moat below, and Lynn stopped to take a photo on her phone.

They strolled under the tower, Antonia momentarily plunged into darkness as her sunglasses adjusted to the light. A tour group blocked the steps in front of them so instead they took a wide stone ramp, which sloped first left and then right. Halfway down was a map of the city and they paused to get their bearings, but it was the slightly rusting sign next to it which grabbed Antonia's attention.

"Lynn, look at this." It was a map of the old town, covered with black dots and red blotches. "It says it shows the damage caused by the aggression of the Yugoslav army, the Serbs and Montenegrins in 91 and 92. I never realised..." But of course, Damir's father had been a soldier. The Balkan war. "I remember hearing about Bosnia on the news, but not here."

"We were probably a bit too young to take much notice," Lynn said. "But I do remember my gran being sad because they'd come here on a cruise just a few years before and she said it was beautiful."

Stepping through another arch they found themselves in a bright square dominated by an enormous covered water fountain. Its creamy stone glowed in the sunlight, its carving almost too perfect, which made Antonia wonder if perhaps it had been rebuilt after the war. Ahead of them was the long, broad main street, Stradun, a church tower rising at its end, dwarfed by the mountains behind. How much of this, too, was new? There had been an awful lot of black dots on the map at the gate. Was this the place where Damir's parents had been killed? Had he himself lived through that awful bombardment? Despite the heat, goosebumps appeared on Antonia's arms. He said he never came here – perhaps that was the reason.

As they strolled down Stradun, Antonia tried to shake the thought. It was hard enough to think of war blighting this beautiful place, let alone someone she was becoming fond of having experienced it. The stones beneath their feet were glossy with wear, and on either side shop awnings and restaurant tables encroached on their dazzling smoothness. Even this late in the day the street was still crowded, a convivial buzz of holiday-makers eating, drinking, and shopping around them.

At the far end, Stradun opened out into an elegant square, the slender grey bell tower of the church piercing the deep blue of the sky. Beneath the portico of a medieval-looking building, under a colonnade of yet more delicate arches, was a group of folk singers, their voices soaring above the people who had gathered to listen.

"This is amazing," Lynn breathed. "I must get a video. Let's see if we can squeeze around the side for a better view."

As they were making their way through the ragged edges of the crowd, a gap appeared when a handful of people left the building through a door half hidden behind the performers. Lynn ducked into the space and Antonia started to follow, but was distracted by an enticing glimpse across the stone threshold. Inside was a two-storey atrium with one row of beautifully rounded arches above another. Next to a small door to her left was a sign which read 'The Memorial Room of Dubrovnik Defenders'. She returned outside and gave Lynn a nudge.

"There's a memorial room in here. I'm going to take a quick look."

And it really was just a room. Boards lined the walls, covered with black and white photos of men. Mainly men so young Antonia thought her heart would break. There was a single cabinet in the centre, and a television silently played a documentary in the corner, accompanied by the haunting voices of the singers on the colonnade outside. Above the pictures hung flags, and a terrifying montage of the city in flames. Alone in the room, Antonia moved methodically around the photographs, barely admitting to herself she was looking for the surname Marić, which thankfully wasn't there.

Lynn had appeared without Antonia noticing and was standing in front of the television. The singers had fallen silent and Antonia's sandals echoed on the parquet floor. In the cabinet were documents and black and white pictures of civilians in the ruins of the city and one in particular seemed to draw her in: a young woman in a headscarf holding a child of three or four, who in turn was clutching a struggling cat in his arms.

It seemed to Antonia that their eyes met across the years. There was a common thread between them – the bond of motherhood – but when Honey had been the boy's age her biggest drama had been falling off the plastic slide at nursery school and breaking her wrist. Even now Antonia remembered sitting in the hospital corridor, waiting for the doctor to come. But what if there had been no hospital? No doctor? No plaster and no Calpol? No shop to take her to, to buy the latest Bratz doll to cheer her up. No shops to buy food, even. Oh my God, how had this mother coped? Not in some faraway land decades ago. But here. In Europe. And very much in living memory.

That young woman would have had dreams for her child too, when she held him in her arms as a tiny baby and saw a wonderful future spread out in front of him like a glittering trail. Perhaps she dreamt of him becoming a teacher, or a lawyer. Or even a hotel owner in the growing tourist industry. She would not have imagined war, or hunger, or bombs hurtling from the sky to blow their world apart. Overcome by the pain that woman would have gone through, Antonia wanted to weep. And yet the eyes in the photograph showed only tenderness and love.

Lynn moved away from the television and stood behind her. "It's awful. I don't think I can watch any more."

Antonia dragged herself back into the room. "Damir's father was killed in the war. His mother too, I think."

"You think?"

She lifted her sunglasses to rub a tear from the corner of her eye. "He's never mentioned it. His best friend told me about his father and he wasn't sure. They were very young when Damir came to the island."

Lynn shuddered. "Poor kid. Probably blocked it out. Just as well."

Suddenly Antonia was interested. Could Damir's past have anything to do with his moodiness now? "And does the counsellor in you think that's the right thing?"

"Children can be strangely resilient, you know. Come to think of it, there was actually some long-term research done on young people who lived through the Bosnian part of the conflict and very few of them had any major issues when they grew up."

They climbed the city walls to watch the sunset then bought a takeaway pizza and some wine to drink in the small garden behind the guest house, but even though they talked about home, Antonia found she was haunted by the black and white faces of the woman and her child. In the smallest of hours, when it was hardest to sleep, they came back to her. During those few short months when their lives had been turned upside down in the most unspeakable way, she would have been starting her lower sixth year and lusting after Ryan Symonds who worked in the HMV shop, more worried about whether ripped jeans made her bum look big than some remote conflict. Why, oh why, hadn't she paid more attention? Why hadn't she cared about it more? But of course she could never had guessed she would be living and working in this country, so why would it have mattered?

Apart from fellow human feeling, why did it matter now? It could only be because of Damir… But maybe Lynn was right. He didn't seem badly adjusted at all and lots of people were a bit iffy in the mornings. She was probably reading too much into it, and worrying too much. As usual.

It was a glorious late afternoon when they arrived on Korčula, the sunlight giving the stone walls of the old town a magical golden glow that had Lynn snapping photos from the catamaran window. To Antonia's surprise, it was not Damir waiting for them on the quay, but Vincenzo, leaning against his truck and watching the life of the harbour with his artist's eyes.

As they reached the end of the ramp he approached, and after kissing Antonia on both cheeks did the same to Lynn, then took her bags.

"Where's Damir?" Antonia asked.

"There is an emergency at one of the apartments."

"He's had a poor run of luck so far this year."

Vincenzo shrugged and started to walk towards his vehicle.

Arriving at Vila Maslina, Antonia flew into a panic when she realised that not only had Damir failed to meet them, but he'd forgotten to put the *pastitsio* she'd prepared for dinner in the slow oven. Vincenzo rested a steadying hand on her arm and told her not to worry, before making for the larder to prepare dishes of olives and cheese in oil. Within minutes he had them on a tray and was heading for the lounge.

"I will keep the guests talking," he promised. "They won't even notice dinner is late."

It was past nine o'clock when Antonia heard someone in the hall, and through the crack in the kitchen door glimpsed Damir slipping into the room to listen to the end of Vincenzo's talk. She and Lynn were sitting at the table, an almost empty wine bottle between them as the dishwasher hummed.

"So I will get to meet Damir tonight," Lynn said.

"Looks like it. He's had a bloody awful start to the season with his other rental properties – it's been one thing after another."

"Sounds as though he'd never have coped without you."

"Luckily he doesn't have to."

She topped up her glass. "You're fond of him, aren't you?"

"Yes. He's a bit of an oddball, and sometimes I don't know what to make of him at all. One minute he's the polished businessman, the next leaping around the place like an exuberant puppy, or morphing into a monosyllabic teen."

Lynn laughed. "You realise you have just described almost every man I know. Most of them can revert to childhood at the drop of a hat. I mean, look at my Andy..."

"I guess so. Maybe not Vincenzo..."

"He does kind of exude masculinity." Lynn growled.

"Stop it. You're happily married."

"Yes, but you're not. Don't tell me you've never looked at him that way."

Antonia thought about it. "Not especially, although now you come to mention it, he is quite hunky. But honestly,

Lynn, it's too soon after Ned. My head's not in the right place for a relationship – you know that."

"There's more than one sort of relationship. How about a bit of good old no-strings sex? It might do you no end of good. It's clear Vincenzo fancies you – he can't keep his hands off you. I bet he'd be up for it."

Lynn's musings were making Antonia feel increasingly uncomfortable. "That's just the way he is. He was like it with you as well."

"Not so. He kind of lingers around you a bit more."

"Rubbish."

Lynn leant forward. "Seriously. Think about it."

At that moment, the subject of their conversation retreated to the kitchen, together with Damir, leaving the guests to enjoy the honesty bar.

Antonia jumped up. "Hello, Damir. Are you hungry? I can make you an omelette or something."

He smiled, shaking his head. "No, I am not hungry. And this must be Lynn." He held out his hand. "Welcome to beautiful Korčula. I hope you enjoy your stay on my island home."

"I intend to," Lynn said. "And the house – it is absolutely gorgeous. You have done a fantastic job."

"Thank you," he replied. "But if I made the house, it is Antonia who makes it a home."

Vincenzo headed for the door. "I must be going. I need to call the gallery in New York before I turn in."

Damir shook his hand. "Thank you, my friend, for all you have done this evening."

Vincenzo laughed. "On the one hand it was a pleasure,"

he nodded in Lynn and Antonia's direction, "but on the other, you definitely owe me. Big time."

Damir turned to them. "I will leave you too, ladies. It has been a long day." He followed Vincenzo outside.

"I think I'll hit the hay after this glass," said Antonia. "I had a shit night's sleep last night."

"Me too. I'll just WhatsApp Andy and tell him I'll call tomorrow."

"Good idea. I need to message Honey."

They tapped away in companionable silence as the men's voices rose and fell in the courtyard, Damir's intensity against Vincenzo's rumbling bass. Lynn raised an eyebrow and asked if they were arguing, but Antonia shook her head, explaining how harsh Croatian sounded until you became used to it.

Chapter Eleven

Antonia and Lynn had known each other so long that after just a day her friend fitted into her new life like a comfortable old gardening glove, although when Antonia told her so she threw a tea towel at her, knocking the basil off the windowsill and leaving them both giggling like schoolgirls.

Damir seemed to be leaving them to their own devices, which Antonia appreciated because time with Lynn was precious and the week was flying by far too fast. But on Monday evening he invited them to join him, Petar, and Lorena at Konoba Pecaros for a drink.

When they arrived, Petar and Lorena were already in the taverna, a bottle of *rakija* on the table, although Lorena was drinking Coke. The old men were playing cards in the corner, and the plastic sheeting had been rolled down against the evening chill, but even in early May there were plenty of tourists and the aroma of rich tomato sauce and baking olives wafted from the pizza ovens.

Petar poured the *rakija* into four small tumblers and raised one. "To your welcome, Lynn. I am sorry it is delayed but it was difficult for Damir to find a time."

Lynn grinned at him. "It is very kind of you," she replied slowly. "I did wonder if perhaps Damir was hiding from me."

Damir laughed but did not look her in the eye. "Of course not. And you are here to see Antonia, not me. It has been a difficult few weeks with the lettings, that's all." He drained his glass and poured another. "In fact, there is more to come and I have a favour to beg from Antonia."

"Oh yes?"

"A favour, and perhaps an opportunity for Lynn to see more of the island before she leaves."

Lynn sipped her *rakija,* screwing up her nose. Antonia leant towards her and whispered, "Drink it, then we'll order some wine. You can't be rude." Lynn gulped down what was left in her glass, which only prompted Petar to refill it.

"You like it?"

"It's... it's different." Antonia felt the ball of Lynn's foot grind onto her toe.

"So, Damir," she asked. "What is this favour?"

"The Dobsons want to visit the famous cave of Vela Spila tomorrow and I said I would take them, but now the pool at Beros's own villa is turning green again. Beros's sister is not happy so I have to meet the engineer…"

Petar smirked. "She's a very demanding woman, isn't she?"

Damir shot him what to Antonia looked like a warning

glance. "She can be... temperamental. If I don't do this she could make trouble with her brother."

"But it's my last day tomorrow," Lynn interrupted, "I was going to take Antonia to lunch at one of the fancy fish restaurants in the old town."

"There are good restaurants in Vela Luka. It's very near the cave, so after your visit you can go on there. If you like I can book a table at a place I know on the harbour. Very good fish, and local dishes too if you'd like to try." He pulled out his phone. "I'll speak to them now."

Seeing Lynn was about to argue, Antonia gave her a gentle kick. This was part of her job, after all, and Damir was doing everything he could to make it right.

Once they finished the *rakija* they moved onto the wine, but while Antonia simply sipped her glass, knowing she needed to be up to cook breakfast, Lynn knocked hers back with enthusiasm, while trying to coax a few words of English from Lorena. The result was a blinding hangover, which Lynn promised to sleep off while Antonia went to Vela Spila, and when she told the Dobsons a little white lie that she needed to be back early in the afternoon to prepare dinner, they did not bat an eyelid.

When Antonia returned, Lynn was lying on a sunbed on the terrace reading her book. In the olive grove, a small flock of bee-eaters flashed yellow and gold as they flew in and out of the patches of sun between the trees.

"Feeling better?" Antonia asked.

"Physically, yes. Otherwise spitting feathers."

She dropped onto the lounger next to her. "Why? What's happened?"

Lynn sat up and swung her legs towards Antonia. "Damir. That's what's happened." There was a dangerous flash of anger in her eyes, one Antonia recognised as usually reserved for Ned. Or even further back, for Honey's father, Simon, when they'd been going through their divorce. Her palms felt sticky so she wiped them on her skirt.

"I felt OK by about twelve so I went to the beach. And there, bold as brass, was Damir, rubbing suntan oil very slowly and sensually into a woman easily old enough to be his mother."

"What?" Antonia stared at her in disbelief.

"You heard me. He totally bollocksed our last day together to spend time with some old tart. Old being the operative word. He's not running a gigolo service on the side, is he?"

Antonia balled her hands into fists, anger driving her close to tears. "He lied. He sodding lied to me."

"Probably more than once. All those other times there was an emergency... Like Thursday night..."

"The little shit." How could he be so deceitful? And there had been no reason to lie in the first place. That made it worse. She'd thought they were friends. She'd trusted him and now she felt like a total fool.

Her shoulders slumped. "I've done it again, haven't I?"

"Done what?"

"Let myself be taken in by some guy who talks a good talk."

Lynn put her hand over her mouth. "Oh my God! You're not… you and Damir…?"

"Of course not. Nothing like that at all. It's just I thought... there was friendship, understanding. But obviously I was wrong. I'm just a bloody liability, Lynn. Every time – *every* time – I let myself be taken for a ride."

"Oh come on, don't beat yourself up. It happens to everyone at some point and this is nowhere near as big a mistake as Ned."

"But it is! I'm stuck out here, miles away from home, with a boss I can't trust any further than I can throw him. I'm going to be so bloody lonely when you go home." A thought struck her. "Unless of course I come back with you."

"And would that be the right thing to do?"

Antonia folded her arms and glared at her. "You've got your counselling voice on again. Are you talking about Honey? That it's better I leave her be?"

"No, actually, I'm talking about you."

"Me?"

"Don't sound so surprised. You matter and you need to believe it. Already you have some of your old spark back so maybe you should stick this out. Prove to yourself you can rise above it and not be taken for a ride again. And you needn't be lonely; there's always Vincenzo."

"Don't start."

"I'm not starting. I meant as an ally, a friend. Damir's lied to him as well, remember."

Of course Lynn was right. This wasn't personal and it wasn't her fault. Damir was to blame for this mess and it shouldn't send her running home with her tail between her legs. And besides, without a housekeeper Vila Maslina would fall apart – at least until Damir found someone else – and then Ned would be proved right about not taking it on, and that she couldn't bear.

"All I can say is, I hope Damir doesn't show his face in the kitchen tonight."

Lynn's lips were pressed firmly together. "I doubt he will. I made very sure he saw me."

It was bleak on the harbour in the early light, and Antonia hugged Lynn for all she was worth, not least to hide her tears. "You're going to keep standing up to him, aren't you?" Lynn asked. "Not get all mealy-mouthed just because I'm not here."

"Of course. I'm still angry."

"That's my girl."

She waved to Lynn until her face in the catamaran window became too obscured by spray for her to make out. The cruise boats, which had been lining the harbour three deep when they'd arrived, were slipping away one at a time. Antonia remembered on her first day on Korčula Damir had told her how they moored up in turn, in just the right order to leave in the morning. She could hear the laugh in his voice, see the mad waving of his hands. Had all the fun and friendship been an act? Somehow the thought was particularly hurtful. He'd said they were a team, but now it seemed he'd been using her all along.

The same as Ned really, only in a different way. He'd sold her the idea they were meant to be together and it was just a case of him finding the right moment to tell Diana, but that had been a load of bullshit too. Even so, she'd fallen for it. It was all very well Lynn saying everyone did, but things felt very different this morning now she was on her own. She should have just cut her losses and left. She didn't even know how she was going to face Damir, let alone work with him for the next five months when she couldn't trust him at all.

Tempted as she was to go online and book her ticket home, she knew she needed time and space to think before she did anything, and the quiet beach below Vincenzo's studio was calling her. She might even pluck up the courage to go to talk to him once her head was a bit straighter, because it was only fair he knew he was being lied to as well.

On her way back to the car she slipped up a side street next to the Marco Polo museum, the scent of citrus and caramelised sugar drawing her to her favourite bakery. After gazing at the trays of sweet and savoury goodies stacked behind the counter in the tiny shop, she decided on a takeout coffee and a bag of *kroštule* – delicious lemony pastry knots a bit like churros – and jumped into the car to head across the island.

No sooner had she settled on a rock than her phone flashed a WhatsApp call. Honey. What a wonderful surprise. She must have known Lynn had just left and that Antonia would be feeling a bit down.

"Oh, it's lovely to hear your voice," she told her. "How are things, my darling?"

There was a pause. "So-so."

"That sounds a bit ominous."

"I don't know, Mum, most of the time it's OK but then all of a sudden I can't do a thing right."

Antonia dug her toes into the coarse sand. She supposed she could have guessed there was a reason for a call at this time of the morning. "In what way?"

"Little things. Like stacking the dishwasher. Or giving Maxi too many treats. She even said... she even said... 'She's my dog, not yours.'"

"That's not very nice."

"I know, but when I told her so she went off on one about who feeds her, who walks her, and all that sort of thing."

Antonia eased the lid from her coffee and gazed across the bay. There was a lone swimmer ploughing from left to right. "And do you feed and walk Maxi?" Antonia was pretty sure she already knew the answer.

"Sara walks her at work. I don't get the chance."

"And at weekends?"

"Whose side are you on?"

Such a childish thing to say. Maybe Lynn had been right. Perhaps Lynn was right about a lot of things… but just at this moment Honey needed her.

"I was only trying to make you think. Listen, Honey, the way I see it, the most important thing is whether you're communicating properly. It's no good telling me how you feel if you can't tell Sara. And if you can't tell Sara, you need to ask yourself why."

There was a silence, then Honey said, "This relationship stuff is tough, isn't it?"

"Which is why it's only ever worth it if you really, really love someone."

"And I do. Love Sara, I mean."

"Well tell her so, then explain how you're feeling – in that order, mind – and see what she says. Look, I'll put some money in your joint account so you can go out for a night, have a bit of fun. Would you like that?"

"Mum, you are just the best."

Honey sounded cheerful when she rang off, but in order to make her happy she'd just done exactly what Lynn had told her she shouldn't. But talk was easy, wasn't it? The doing was so much harder. Lynn had said she should stay, but all Antonia really wanted was to be at home. She longed to see Honey, talk to her face to face, give her a hug. Be a proper mother. But was she even doing that right? Yes, the offer of money had made Honey happy, but for how long? It hadn't really solved anything. Maybe she was better off keeping out of it and letting her and Sara find their own way. It was their life, after all, and she wasn't exactly making a good fist of hers, stuck on this bloody island with a lying boss and nowhere to go.

The swimmer had emerged from the water and was making his way up the beach, towel slung around his neck. As he got closer, Antonia recognised the long salt-and-pepper hair. She was wondering whether Vincenzo had seen her when he raised his hand and called, "Ciao, Antonia. If you'd come sooner we could have swum together."

She needed to pull herself together, try to act as though everything was fine, then pluck up the courage to tell him about Damir. "It's probably still a bit early in the year for me," she laughed.

"Nonsense. You should try, but maybe later in the day when there is more sun. Perhaps another Wednesday when I have no students. I could cook you lunch."

It was impossible to look him in the eye so instead she found herself gazing at his muscled chest with its covering of silvered hair. "That would be lovely. But I do need to talk to you before then."

"Ah, so you're not here just to check out my rippling pecs." Oh God, was that what he thought? Antonia was trying so hard not to blush, and he laughed, gesticulating at her cardboard cup. "Stop drinking that filth and come up to the house for a proper coffee. It won't take me five minutes to shower and dress."

Trying to recover some of her equilibrium Antonia rattled the paper bag in his direction. "And I have *kroštule*."

While Vincenzo was upstairs she turned on his Gaggia coffee machine and filled it with water, but could get no further with the beast so retreated to a sunny spot on the terrace. Already the day was becoming warmer and she glanced at her watch. Ten o'clock. By rights she should be getting back, but what for? Yes, there were jobs to catch up on and Ana to supervise, but that could wait. Let Damir wonder where she was for a change.

Antonia heard Vincenzo in the kitchen and shortly afterwards he appeared with the pastries on a plate as the Gaggia snorted into life. She started to speak, but he raised his finger.

"One moment. Coffee first."

The moment stretched to almost five minutes and the wait seemed endless while she framed and reframed her words, but finally he sat down next to her and handed her a cappuccino.

"So, what do you need to talk about?"

"Damir has been lying to us. Lynn saw him on the beach yesterday with a woman, after he'd ruined her last day by dreaming up an appointment with a pool technician so I had to take some guests to the other end of the island."

Vincenzo leant back. "He has been lying to you, but not to us. I am so sorry, Antonia, but if I had realised last Thursday was more than a one-off, I would have told you."

"So you know about her?" Why did she feel so let down?

"You have to understand that Vesna is demanding; she causes difficulties for Damir if he is not sufficiently attentive."

"Lynn said he was being pretty damn attentive. And that she's old enough to be his mother."

"And you mind?"

"Of course I don't mind. I only mind that he's lied to me constantly over the last few weeks and he spoiled Lynn's last day just to get his end away."

"Don't worry, Vesna is going back to Dubrovnik on Friday. She was the one who arranged the guest house for you – it belongs to her gardener's cousin."

"Her gardener?"

"She is Josip Beros's sister. Very rich." He rubbed his fingers together.

"Oh, so money's the attraction for Damir, is it? Lynn wondered if he was getting paid."

"No!" Vincenzo was clearly shocked. "It is not like that at all. It is simply his taste: older women who come on holiday, wanting a fling. He says he finds them interesting, and that he can concentrate more on his business without a steady girlfriend. But with Vesna, she comes to the island a lot so perhaps he has bitten off more than he can chew."

"And I'm meant to feel sorry for him?"

"No. He has been lying to you and that is very wrong. He must apologise and be honest in future."

"Do you think he's embarrassed, you know, to admit to me he has a much older girlfriend? Or just guilty because it means I have to do so much more work?"

"Embarrassed? I would be surprised. He has never hidden these things before, not even from Tetka." Vincenzo shrugged. "I do not really understand the attraction for him, but we are all different. Of course, I like mature women," he raised his coffee cup in her direction, "but then, I am a mature man, not a boy of thirty."

He reached across to pick up a *kroštule,* his fingers brushing hers and lingering for a long, quiet moment. Perhaps Lynn had been right after all. He did seem to be flirting with her just a little, but attractive as Vincenzo was and despite the butterflies fluttering around her stomach, Antonia told herself she had quite enough to worry about already without having to try to remember how to flirt back.

Chapter Twelve

The morning after a sleepless night plagued by nightmares was not a good time to be juggling, Damir thought. More yoghurt, more coffee, more fruit – he had only one pair of hands. Then some woman wanted tea. She was not sick, so why did she want tea? The English were very strange.

But of course he smiled and laughed with them as usual. It would do no good to take his irritability out on the guests. Or on Antonia, when she eventually returned. But it was difficult when things did not run smoothly, especially when he was so damned tired. He had to remind himself he was not an angry person – the exact opposite, in fact. Was it Vesna making him this way? Or the nightmares? Or Antonia? Or all of them, even?

He leant against the sink, the smooth stone of its edge cold against his hands. The catamaran would have left some time ago and it was clear Antonia was in no hurry to get back. Lynn must have told her. She must have. Yesterday on the beach he had thought she was going to walk right up to him and Vesna, but she had veered off at the last minute. But she had seen them. And she had looked very, very angry. To be fair, he understood that. Why the hell had he not told Antonia about Vesna in the first place?

Of course, if he was being honest with himself he knew the answer to that particular question, although he struggled to put it into words. Last year, having Vesna on his arm had made him feel important, more of a man, but now everything seemed different. She was still beautiful, of course she was. And still interesting. But he was so much at her beck and call, so scared of upsetting her and therefore her brother… and now someone else was coming down the stairs like an elephant, just when he was trying to think.

Damir fixed a smile on his face and carried the pots of tea and coffee through to the terrace, where the guests were making plans for their free day. He was doing his best to listen to them attentively when Vesna texted.

He excused himself and returned to the kitchen. Vesna wanted to know what time he would be at her villa, and she would not like his answer at all. And if she continued not to like his answers she might find someone else and then he would become a laughing stock; she may even turn her brother against him, and he would have upset Antonia for nothing. He felt in his pocket but he had smoked his last cigarette in the small hours of the morning.

Damir swore out loud when Vesna texted again. Then replied that he was serving breakfast.

Where's Antonia?

At the market. She took her friend to the early cat.

Then by now she should be back.

Perhaps the wisest thing would be to turn off his phone.

Damir took some of the guests to Korčula Old Town for a morning of sight-seeing, but although he had a quick look around the market he could not see Antonia. Returning to Vila Maslina, he parked by the old olive press. Antonia or Vesna? Vesna or Antonia? He wasn't sure he could face either of them. He just wanted to sleep. God, he was such a coward. Why could he not be even half the man his father had been? His war hero father. But now the war was haunting him, and he was finding *he* wasn't very brave at all.

Sranje! He couldn't talk to Antonia right now. He wasn't in the mood for a grovelling apology, which was certainly what was needed. Not if he had to face Vesna and grovel to her as well.

When he arrived at the Beros villa, Vesna was lying by the pool, reading her book. He gazed at the curve of her buttocks and thighs, trying to conjure up at least some hint of excitement. It was probably useless, but he had to try; had to be the Damir she wanted, and certainly not the strange, messed-up, sleep-deprived Damir he felt inside. He didn't want anyone to see that.

He crept up and whispered in her ear. "Oh, such a beautiful woman."

"And that sounds like my beautiful man." She twisted

her head towards him, then rolled over, shading her eyes. "Sit down next to me."

Damir perched on the edge of the lounger, and Vesna propped herself up on her elbow. "You look tired, my sweet," she said. "Is Antonia making you do all the work?"

He shrugged. "Well, as you know her friend has been staying, and Antonia is a long way from home so it is good for her to see her."

"Yes, I suppose so, but I assume Antonia came here of her own free will."

"Of course. But she has a daughter who she misses very much and that has not been easy."

"As a mother myself, that I do understand. I miss my son, but it takes only an hour to fly to Zagreb and I am free to visit whenever I like. Poor Antonia, perhaps she is not the one being difficult after all."

Damir knew Vesna well enough to know any answer could put him in a lose-lose situation, but she was looking up at him, her head on one side.

"It simply means we are both busy," he told her. "But I am never too busy for you."

"Except this morning..." She reached up and removed his sunglasses. "And now you arrive with those unflattering bags beneath your eyes..."

"I am never too tired for you either."

"But do you tire of me?"

"No. No, of course I don't..."

"I am only wondering."

"Because I could not come earlier?"

"Because of a hundred small things that can give a man

away. But if you tell me everything is fine, for the moment I will believe you."

Although her tone was light and relaxed, to Damir her words carried more than a hint of threat, but he only had to carry on with this play acting until she went home on Friday. Just a few more days and then she would forget all about him, and as long as she didn't complain to her brother, nothing would be lost. He leant down and kissed her. "Of course everything is fine. Now what can I do to convince you?"

Daylight followed the rain across the sky, creeping in through the window as the birds began to sing, and Damir resigned himself to the fact he would not sleep again. He had to talk to Antonia to apologise but there were no easy words to explain his behaviour, so what could he say? Perhaps this morning he'd just say sorry, and tell her they could talk properly after Vesna had left and he was no longer in this difficult position. Maybe after that her English reserve would mean she would remain silent on the matter.

And if it didn't? What if she said she was going to leave? Certainly Vila Maslina couldn't function without her; she had become its beating heart. Of course, he had created the house, but it was Antonia who had turned it into a home from home by filling it with not only wonderful food, but also the warmth of her personality. All the guests said how marvellous she was, how her thoughtfulness had made their holiday in a thousand small ways. And there was no doubt in Damir's mind that she had made his life better too.

He slid off the bed, surrounding Marco with a nest of blanket before pulling on his jeans and a sweatshirt and heading for the beach. There was a freshness to the air that would vanish all too soon when the sun appeared over the grey banks of mountains. He kicked off his flip-flops and dug his toes into the cool sand as he gazed eastwards. The hills he could see were on the Pelješac peninsula, but beyond them was the mainland proper, and further, Bosnia & Herzegovina. Thirty-two years ago today he had been born there, to a woman he had thought little about for most of his life but who was now increasingly haunting his dreams. He shivered. Without Tetka to remember it, his birthday would be impossibly grim.

Once he had showered and dressed he made his way through the olive grove, the warm air filled with the sweet liquorice scent of the blossom. At this rate the harvest would be early, coinciding with the end of the tourist season. Within a few weeks they would be fully booked until September, perhaps even October. He needed Antonia more than ever. He needed to apologise for practical reasons as well as personal ones. Already it was impossible to imagine Vila Maslina without her calm and comforting presence, and his foolishness had put something very precious at risk. He stopped in the shadows beneath a tree as a bitter memory drifted half in then out of his brain. He was left with the impression it was not the first time something lacking in himself had led to a terrible loss, but he could not remember why.

He spied Antonia through the kitchen window, pushing a strand of hair behind her ear as she sliced a melon. Girding himself to seize the moment, he opened the door.

She glanced up. "Good morning, Damir." She was not smiling.

"Look, Antonia. We need to—"

"Not now. There are guests waiting for their breakfast." She wiped her hands on a cloth and poured water from the kettle into the teapot. "I must take this through. If you want coffee, perhaps you could drink it in the courtyard?"

"Antonia, I just want to—" But he was speaking to her back as she disappeared down the hall.

Given how busy Antonia claimed to be, she was spending the longest possible time on the terrace. Damir took the *dzezva* from the stove and poured coffee into a mug, knowing full well it was his own fault he had been dismissed from his kitchen. He told himself it was not the end of the world; he wanted a cigarette, and needed to deal with his emails and update Vila Maslina's Instagram feed with the pictures he'd taken in the olive grove. This was a battle he couldn't afford to lose so maybe it would be best to pick a moment when they were both less busy.

Less busy did not come. Vesna was taking him to lunch for his birthday at one of the smart tourist restaurants in the old town, where she presented him with a beautifully soft leather Alexander McQueen bag, but he had to limit himself to one glass of champagne as he was driving. All the same, he did his best to sparkle, but on returning to her villa he was dismissed from there as well when she said she needed to pack.

Damir lay on his bed, listening to the birdsong and distant shouts from the beach. *The mattress narrowed, the ghosts of model aeroplanes swung in the breeze from the window, the murmur of his parents' voices floated in from the next room. He was straining to hear what they were saying, but the words were lost in time, and the not knowing filled him dread .*

Damir may have been clutching a fine white linen sheet, not a duvet decorated with brightly coloured cars, and there was daylight outside, not darkness, but that feeling of dread still lay heavy on his heart. But dread of what? What didn't he know? Or was it the dread of what might happen with Antonia that had transferred itself to the dream? He rubbed the unshed tears from his eyes. Even in sleep there could be no rest.

The next morning Damir found himself on the catamaran quay, surrounded by matching Chanel luggage, most of which he had carried from the car.

Vesna turned to him, her hand on his arm. "So, Damir."

"So, Vesna."

"You are a beautiful, young man, but I sense you are not the carefree boy I met last summer." He shrugged and she carried on. "Perhaps it is the weight of business on your shoulders, but perhaps you tire of me."

"No! I already told—"

She placed a warm finger on his lips. "I am not saying you know it if you do. I am saying you have changed."

"I'm sorry."

"Don't be. Everyone does, sooner or later." She said something else, but it was impossible to hear over the engines of the catamaran, which had burst into life.

Damir kissed her on the lips. "It is time for you to go."

"So we should say goodbye."

"For now."

"For now, and perhaps for rather longer. Be good to yourself, Damir, and remember, wherever life takes us, I will always be your friend."

They kissed again and Damir wheeled her cases to the bottom of the ramp where Vesna smiled at a couple of backpackers who gallantly took over. Hands in pockets, Damir watched as she disappeared inside without a backward glance.

He told himself he should be feeling relieved it was over but it wasn't that way at all. Not wanting company, instead of going to his favourite café he bought a takeout espresso from the stall at the harbourside and stood in the shade of the town walls to watch the catamaran leave. Inevitably he would see Vesna again, but it would be different. He had to accept that. It had become too exhausting keeping up appearances, and yet appearances were much what the relationship had been about. For both of them, he guessed. And that was a pretty damn shallow reason to be together. In fact, the whole thing had been shallow. Maybe he was shallow too – not like other people. Perhaps he would always be that strange, different boy everyone had laughed at. Always looking at Vesna and Josip Beros's world from the outside, never really gaining admission. Being tolerated, maybe, but never accepted. It was becoming the story of his life.

Miserable as he was, the business of the day would not wait. He had two apartments in the town to check before guests arrived later, then he needed to drive out to the blacksmith to fetch the hopper from the old olive press, and make sure he returned to Vila Maslina in good time to talk to Antonia before collecting the guests from Vincenzo's studio. Tomorrow they were moving the press so this afternoon would be his only chance to put things right. He couldn't afford to lose Antonia as well.

But there was a problem at one of the apartments, and the blacksmith was desperately slow making out the bill, so by the time Damir had returned to Vila Maslina and unloaded the hopper outside the press house, he was left with precisely twenty minutes before he had to leave again. Certainly no time to say what he needed to Antonia. After yesterday morning he knew apologising would not be enough; he would have to explain himself fully, and possibly – probably – beg her to stay. And he would have to do it, because without her his dreams for Vila Maslina would be crushed like an olive beneath his feet.

Damir dropped onto his haunches next to the hopper, the scent of grass mingling with the wild mint that straggled along the boundary wall. Even though the metal bands had been enamelled black they looked impossibly shiny and new. He ran the flat of his hand over the wood. The same wood as it had always been, the ends of the planks smoothed by use and age. Vesna had said everyone changes; every*thing* too.

She said he had changed and Damir had to accept that she was right. The moment he'd found Tetka dead in her bed he had no longer been able to be the carefree boy Vesna spoke of. The responsibility for Vila Maslina had become his alone. The responsibility to earn enough money to live and to maintain his home, without Tetka's help and pension. Right now, he felt adrift from the life he had always known, with no one to turn to and no way of even gaining a foothold.

But that wasn't quite true. The warmth from the hopper spread through his hand and up his arm. The press and all it represented was what mattered now. It wouldn't bring Tetka back but it would honour her memory, honour their family. He owed it to the woman who had given him so much. After all, the dead would never let you down.

Chapter Thirteen

Laden with vegetables, Damir nudged open the larder door. Antonia was at the kitchen table, the aroma of chocolate drifting from the oven while she kneaded a ball of sticky dough. The remains of a lemon and an orange next to the bowl made Damir wonder if she was attempting to make *kroštule*.

Putting his purchases down he called to her that he had everything on her list.

"Thank you, Damir. Saturdays are much too busy for me to go into town, especially when you are already there."

"It was my pleasure." He smiled at her, but all she did was nod and tuck a stray hair under the chignon she wore when she was cooking.

The hoover bumped upstairs, telling Damir that Ana was suitably occupied, and he knew Petar wouldn't be here for at least half an hour.

"Antonia, we need to talk."

She paused her pounding and swept the table with her hand. "I've only this minute told you how busy I am."

"I know, but I have to apologise to you. I don't want to put it off any longer."

"An apology is meaningless if you intend to do it again."

The tiny flicker of hope Damir had managed to drum up as he fought his exhaustion to battle around the crowded market was extinguished. He started to bite the corner of his lip, then turned his back on her. He was well aware this was of his doing, but there was no need for her to be deliberately difficult. She knew how much he had to do today and she hadn't even meant it when she'd thanked him for doing one of *her* jobs.

A vehicle rumbled to a stop outside. Not Petar's van, but Vincenzo's truck. As Damir turned back to Antonia he saw that for the first time she was smiling.

"It's Vincenzo," she said, as though it was not already obvious.

He jumped from his vehicle and strode across the courtyard. "When you said you were moving the press I thought I'd come to help. Easier on my truck than in Petar's van."

"I thought you said you don't have enough time for your own work as it is."

"I always have time to help a friend."

Vincenzo was in the kitchen and on the other side of the table before Damir could reply, kissing Antonia on both cheeks in greeting. It was what he always did, but for a moment his hand rested on her neck, just below her ear, and she smiled up at him.

"That's kind of you, Vincenzo," she said. "Damir, put the water on the stove and once I've finished kneading I will make you both coffee." There was the sound of another vehicle. "Petar too."

Outside, Damir lit a cigarette, unable to look Vincenzo in the eye. Why was he really here? Had Antonia told him they had fallen out, so now he was trying to worm his way into her affections? No, Vincenzo was his friend. But what if Antonia had poisoned him against him? But if that was the case, why was he here to help? Or was he? This train of thought was confusing his befuddled brain even more, so he ground his butt into the paving with his heel and opened the shed door.

"Where's the hopper?" Vincenzo asked.

"Already down by the gate. I collected it yesterday and there didn't seem much point hauling it all the way up here just to take it back again."

Vincenzo shrugged. "I only asked, my friend."

"I do have the sense I was born with, you know," Damir snapped.

Vincenzo and Petar exchanged glances. "Are you hungover or something?" Petar asked.

"I have a lot to think about, that's all."

"Ah, the beautiful Vesna has gone home." Petar teased.

"This is nothing to do with Vesna. The press is far more important. It is critical – *critical* – that it can be made to work again."

Vincenzo leant against the door frame. "I hope you are not serious, my friend. Naturally we will try, but…"

"Of course I am serious." He eyed Vincenzo suspiciously. Had he come to make mischief after all? Had Antonia put him up to it?

"But what about the trough?" Petar asked. "It's in the middle of your living room."

"It will be a simple thing to form a new one from concrete once the press is in place. I can do that at any time before the harvest."

"But Damir..."

Vincenzo was interrupted by Antonia's arrival with coffee and brownies warm from the oven. He took the tray from her as Petar and Damir turned their attention to discussing how best to lift the parts of the press onto Vincenzo's truck.

"At least the spars will be easy," Petar said.

"Yes, but we need to wrap them in something first," Vincenzo replied. "After all the work Antonia put into them we wouldn't want them scratched. Damir, do you have any old sheets, by any chance?"

Oh, yes, of course. They mustn't damage anything *Antonia* had done. He was just trying to think when she spoke. "There's a box of linen in the eaves off my room. Anything suitable in there?"

"Could be."

"I'll fetch it."

Damir watched Vincenzo watching her cross the courtyard, the sculptor's eyes locked onto the sway of Antonia's hips.

How the hell did Antonia know what was in his attic? His most personal, most painful memories were locked away there. It was a place that even he did not dare to go and if she had been snooping… The trust he had felt in her was slipping, oozing away like blood from a wound. Forcing the image from his mind, he started to follow, calling over his shoulder,

"I need to help her. She won't know what to bring."

Damir's ears pounded in time with his feet as he raced across the courtyard and through the kitchen. Ana was struggling down the stairs with the hoover, phone in hand as usual, and she jumped when she saw him but he had no time to tear her off a strip now. She stepped to one side as he grabbed the banister and squeezed past, upwards, ever upwards, to where Antonia had no business to pry.

All Damir could see was her bottom as she tugged something backwards from the eaves.

"Get out of there!"

She stopped, reversed, and finally unbent. "But you told me to..."

"I did no such thing. There are private things in there, private. How did you know the sheets were there in the first place?"

She spoke slowly, as though he was an idiot. "Because, if you remember, Damir, when I first arrived you told me to put my suitcases under the eaves..."

"I did not—"

"Do you have to lie to me over even the simplest thing?" she yelled.

"I am not lying, I—"

"So you're saying I'm the liar? Is that it? Making out I

don't know what's right and what's wrong to put you in the clear?"

"You must not go into the attic!" Damir was screaming now.

"Then fetch the bloody box yourself." She turned her back on him, folding her arms. Thankfully the linen was just inside, next to her suitcases, and he could reach it easily, slamming the door behind him.

Antonia's shoulders were heaving. Oh God, what had he done? He had never, ever made a woman cry before, never mind one so precious. What the hell was wrong with him? He shifted the box from arm to arm. "Antonia..."

"No." Her voice was breaking. "No. Just go away, Damir. Go away and leave me alone."

The men wrapped the spars in Tetka's old bed linen, so carefully acquired over the years and now faded from constant use. Pastel colours, swirls of flowers, everything she believed to be beautiful, and seeing them again made Damir want to weep. Tetka would be so ashamed of him, the way he'd yelled at Antonia. Just like when he was eight and one of the girls in school had mocked him so badly he had pulled her hair. He was the one who'd had to apologise, of course – Tetka had made him – and although the memory still smarted, he knew in his heart of hearts she'd been right.

At the end of the drive, Vincenzo took charge of re-assembling the press and, lacking the mental energy to argue, Damir let him. He was spent, absolutely, but all the same he and Petar worked at Vincenzo's beck and call, flattening the earth to make a base, then setting the first stone in place. They stood on it to slide the upright spar into the hole, but it wobbled alarmingly when they let go. Vincenzo jumped from the stone and stood back.

"You are sure you want it to work again?" he asked.

"Of course I do. How many times have I said as much this morning?"

"I know, I know. It's just it would be safer if we could use concrete to secure it."

Damir folded his arms. "Definitely not."

"All right. We will try to wedge it with wood."

They were securing the second stone when Antonia emerged from the olive grove with some beers and freshly baked bread rolls stuffed full of cheese and tomatoes. She did not need to do this; perhaps it was her way of showing him she was prepared to let him make amends. Damir scanned her face for clues, thankful there was no sign of redness in her eyes, but before she turned deliberately away from him, he noticed she was wearing subtle makeup.

He started to move towards her but Vincenzo was in front of him and took the basket, his arm brushing hers. As Damir watched, she leant into him just a fraction, but it was enough. If Damir had been lying to her, then they were both lying to him. Keeping secrets from him. For the second time that day the blood started to pound in his ears but he knew he could not let this strange anger win so he grabbed a beer and retreated towards the press house. When he turned to tell them he needed to check his emails, three pairs of eyes were locked onto him. He was almost sure he could hear them laughing at him as he closed the door, but that could not be right, because Petar had never done that, not even when the other children… No, Petar would not be laughing. He knew that in his heart and he clung to the thought like a drowning man. Whatever had made him believe that he would?

Damir rested his head against the wooden planks on the inside of the door. How the hell could a bunch of nightmares push him to doubt everyone around him? Everything about himself, even? And he was scared – no, terrified – that if he didn't get a grip soon he would lose the friends he cared so much about.

With darkness surrounding him, Damir did not know if the whimpering was then or now, nor the stone pressed against his cheek. Lost halfway into sleep, he did not know anything, except he knew everything. Everything that had happened and was about to happen again, screened like a movie in front of his eyes.

They were playing in the shelter when Kemal told them he'd heard there was going to be a food drop. Damir did not question how he knew, or how the Red Cross knew they were hungry, because Kemal was nine and so much older. The only reason he played with Damir was because he had toy cars. Dragan was there too; probably for the same reason, because he was eight.

They crouched together on the concrete floor, Kemal whispering. He was saying they would make a good search party for food parcels because he was clever, Dragan was strong, and Damir was small and nimble so could be lifted into trees if the packages caught in the branches as they rained down, or he could crawl through small holes to get into abandoned buildings if they fell through the space where the roof should be.

They were not allowed to leave the shelter. That much had been made clear by their mothers, but Kemal had done it before and it was easy. He reminded them their fathers were fighting, so finding food for their families was the least they could do. They edged their game closer and closer to the iron doors and they waited in the shadows cast by the gas lamps until there was no one around, finally finding their moment to slip through.

The cold bit into Damir's face and hands, but the chance of a hot meal made the wind less bitter. The planes were still overhead, but straight away they could see Kemal was right and they were not dropping bombs. Damir ran ahead of the others, arms outstretched, mimicking their banking motion in the clear grey sky, the joy of breathing outside air making him forget his fear.

Kemal called Damir back, reminding him this was a serious business, and of course he was right. Once the planes left there would be many more people hunting for the parcels. There were thirty of them in their shelter so they needed to collect as many as they could.

According to Kemal the park was a good place to start because the pilots liked to aim for an open space away from snipers. The trees were winter naked, the grass and earth churned into mud. In spring Damir's mother had taken him there to play, but now the swings were no more than twisted stumps of metal in the concrete. But he did not mind because he was too grown up for such things now. If school started again in September he would be old enough to go.

But there were no parcels waiting. They scoured the craters and gazed up into fractured branches, but there was nothing to find. Kemal stopped where the gate used to be and looked up and down the empty street.

"Right," he said, "we should head towards the river."

"But it is so far…"

"It is less than half a mile," said Dragan. "And if you are going to be a baby we will not bring you again."

As usual Kemal was right, and they found the first parcel outside an empty-eyed tenement in a side street. Further on there were two more, and then another. Each one was wrapped in brown plastic with a number on it and words in a foreign language Damir could not read. But he could recognise the numbers and liked 8 best because the biscuits had chocolate on so he could take his half to a quiet corner to lick off and pretend he had a whole bar.

They walked through what used to be the building's entrance hall into the yard behind, and soon Dragan's rucksack was so full he was bending over like an old man. At the end of the street, in front of a patch of wasteland that used to be a supermarket car park, they stopped, and Kemal told Dragan to take their booty home while he and Damir searched on. Already the sky was beginning to darken, and Damir was envious as he watched Dragan go.

Kemal told him they should separate to cover more ground, and Damir was rewarded almost instantly by finding a parcel in an old planter. He raised it into the air in triumph, calling to Kemal, but as he turned there was a crack and Kemal somersaulted into the air, time slowing as his back arched and he fell with a scream like no other Damir had ever heard.

Damir threw himself behind the solid concrete drum of the planter. He had no idea where the shot had come from, but here he had at least a chance of being safe. He made himself as small as possible, curling his body over the parcel, the hard edges of the plastic sticking into his palms and chin. Was Kemal dead? But no, he cried out again, splitting the eerie silence. Damir knew he should go for help, but if he moved he might be shot too and his mother would weep like she had when their neighbour's husband was killed.

When Damir dared to raise his head, the light was fading behind the distant mountains. Once it was dark he could move because the sniper would not see him. Go to Kemal or go for help? Perhaps Dragan would come to look for them. He could not bear to hear Kemal moan. He wanted to call to him, tell him he would get help soon, but his voice had left him.

It was almost dark when Kemal yelled for his mother, made a strange gurgling noise and then was silent. Blood stuck to Damir's hands from the sharp edges of the parcel and the concrete froze against his back. He curled himself tighter. He knew Kemal was dead but he would not leave him.

When they found them, Damir could not move, could not speak. Dragan's grandfather lifted him in his arms and he tasted salt tears. He heard a woman keen; an eery, unearthly sound...

The keening Damir heard now was his own. The concrete planter was the solid stone of the old olive press and the night air was warm around him. To the east there was a glow over the distant hills and on the other side, Kemal was dead.

Chapter Fourteen

Antonia paused in front of the mirror, lipstick in hand. Was the deep red too dark? Yes, these days her skin was tanned, but all the same… although her favourite peachy-coral tone would never go with this top. It was the third top she'd tried and she was certain it looked the best, with just enough cleavage showing – just a little bit, not too much. She didn't want Vincenzo to get the wrong impression.

She dropped down onto the bed. She didn't even know if this was a date or not. Over the last couple of weeks she had become acutely aware of Vincenzo's physical presence, but maybe that was because Lynn had put her in mind of it. Maybe he had always touched her neck when he kissed her hello or goodbye. Maybe his eyes had always lingered on her hips.

And what if it did all mean something? She was so not ready for sex with another man. But why not, if it was just a fling? But she didn't do flings – she never had. The idea was so alien she found herself crossing her legs, only to uncross them again for fear of creasing her skirt. For goodness' sake, what was she so scared of?

She knew the answer to that all too well. She was scared of being taken for a ride. Again. Of being promised a dream that could never be delivered. Whether that dream was of love, or friendship, it didn't matter. She had been let down so badly by two men she cared about and she wasn't going to let it happen a third time.

She had no intention of risking her friendship with Vincenzo. He'd been an absolute rock since her falling out with Damir and she would have been very lonely without him. Every night after finishing his lecture he would wait for her in the kitchen with a glass of wine, and once she had settled the guests in the lounge or on the terrace with their drinks they would talk. Not about anything serious, just chat really, about their days. And then last night he had asked if she would like to come to dinner. Perhaps simply because it was Wednesday so she didn't have to cook, but perhaps there was more to it. She'd certainly been left with the impression there was.

The words he used to greet her only re-enforced the feeling. "I am so pleased you could come, Antonia. I needed to get you alone, away from the prying ears of Vila Maslina."

Her hand felt clammy in his as he took it and led her to the table, where a bottle of her favourite Gavi wine was waiting.

"So I'm not just here for supper." She forced a laugh.

He sat down next to her, grinning. "That as well, of course. Can you not smell the cannelloni in the oven?"

The rich aroma of tomatoes and herbs was drifting onto the terrace, and Antonia nodded. "Of course I can. And I can see the sun preparing to sink into the sea, which is just as you promised too." She smiled at him. "So what is it?"

"Damir."

Antonia shifted along the bench away from him, cross with herself for feeling just a little disappointed. OK, she wasn't ready for him to make a move on her, but it would have been nice to have been asked there for herself. "So what dirty work has he asked you to do this time?"

"Nothing. He has asked for nothing. But you have brought him down and I cannot bear to see him like that."

"All I've done is stand up for myself. I'm fed up with men who take advantage."

Vincenzo picked up his glass. "Do you want to tell me what has happened between you?"

"You know very well what's happened. He lied to me over Vesna and he's not taking me for granted again."

"No, it is more than that."

They watched as the orange-purple glow filled the horizon, just like it had on the night Damir first brought her here when she had been so full of hope for the season. She rolled an olive around her mouth, savouring the sharp saltiness. Antonia didn't blame Vincenzo for his concern over his friend. Even from the distance she'd been keeping, it had been impossible not to see how Damir had faded, like a rose in a vase that someone had forgotten to water. But if she didn't stick to her guns she would end up losing every shred of her hard-won self-respect. "Perhaps it isn't me. Perhaps he is missing Vesna."

Vincenzo shook his head. "If anything he was relieved to see her go. No... I think... last Saturday – did you have an argument?"

"Yes, but it wasn't my fault." Antonia was afraid she might have sounded a bit petulant so she continued, "Look, I know there are always two sides, but this blew up from nowhere. I suppose... well I did... you know, lose it a bit with him."

"Ah, so there is passion beneath that quiet demeanour," Vincenzo murmured, but she chose to ignore him. She may be out of practice, but it still felt wrong to flirt in the middle of a serious conversation.

"It was the straw that broke the camel's back, that's all. He'd barely apologised for lying to me while Lynn was here, and then he accused me of being the liar. It's no wonder I flipped."

Vincenzo passed her the plate of stuffed vine leaves. "So you told him you would be leaving."

"Where did you get that idea from?"

"I just assumed. It had to be something pretty major to affect him like this."

"Then perhaps it isn't me after all."

"Well, maybe not you alone but I am sure he would be better if you could be friends again."

"I think he's just sulking."

Once again Vincenzo shook his head, more vigorously this time. "Damir does not sulk. I have never known it. But I have never known him withdrawn like this either. It's as though someone has flicked a switch and the lights have gone out."

"He is... I don't know... going through the motions with the guests. From what little I've seen."

"Will you talk to him?"

Antonia sat up straight and swivelled to face him. "Will you?"

"I cannot resolve any part of his problems, but I think you can."

"Why?"

He shrugged. "Because I am not the person he is afraid of losing."

She picked up her glass and sipped as the sun became a glowing orb singeing the distant surface of the sea. Vincenzo sat in silence next to her, and for that she was grateful. Yes, she was angry with Damir for the things he had done – and said – but now Vincenzo was asking, and if he really was suffering so much, it was all but impossible to stand by and do nothing. In any case, to keep Vila Maslina running smoothly they had to at least communicate. It wouldn't work otherwise and she needed it to succeed for so many reasons: to show Ned he'd been wrong in not wanting to take it on, for one, but increasingly because she loved the cooking and making the guests smile. Adding the personal touches that made Vila Maslina a home from home for them was something she could be really proud of and it had gone an awfully long way towards restoring her self-worth.

And it wasn't just about her, was it? The black and white image of the woman in war-torn Dubrovnik clinging to her child reared up from nowhere. The little dark-haired boy holding the cat. Damir loved cats. She ran her index finger slowly around the top of her glass.

Eventually she asked, "How good would you say Damir is at dealing with his emotions?"

"Perhaps better at burying them than dealing with them."

"Petar says... when he's stressed he normally zooms around at a million miles an hour. Taking charge of a situation, or an avoidance tactic, do you think?"

Vincenzo removed an olive stone from his mouth. "Bit of both. He is practical. Tetka taught him to be practical."

"And how did he grieve for her?"

"By working on her house night and day." There was another silence before he continued, "What are you thinking?"

"I'm not thinking anything, just gathering information."

"But will you do something?" The fire from the setting sun reflected in his eyes.

"OK. You offer to bring the guests back to the villa tomorrow and I will find the time."

His touch was light on her arm. "Thank you. You are a good woman, Antonia. Good as well as beautiful."

Just when she thought she understood Vincenzo's intentions, now she wasn't so sure.

Antonia had expected Lynn to be cross when she told her Vincenzo had persuaded her to offer Damir the proverbial olive branch, but she didn't know whether to be infuriated or relieved that her friend was more interested in how her supper with the sculptor had gone. Lynn hadn't taken the Damir issue seriously at all when Antonia had WhatsApped her after she got home, but when she was alone in the kitchen the next morning she finally received a proper reply.

Until recently, at this hour Damir would have been leaning against the sink, coffee in hand, chatting through menus and gossiping about the guests, and Antonia had to admit she was missing the easy warmth between them. It had made her feel less far from home to have someone to share the minutiae of the day with, to laugh with about the silly things, and although Vincenzo had tried hard to fill the gap, she still did not entirely trust his motives. Not that she could trust Damir's anymore either, but she'd promised she'd try to put this right and if nothing else, she was a woman of her word.

LYNN: You're sure he's not just sulking?

ANTONIA:That's what I thought but Vincenzo says not. He hasn't been near me since our row but even from a distance I can tell he's not himself.

LYNN: In what way?

ANTONIA: Like I said, going through the motions. No spark.

There were footsteps on the stairs and Antonia broke off

to follow the first guest onto the terrace to ask if they would like tea or coffee before escaping back to the kitchen..

LYNN: So what are you going to do?

ANTONIA: I have to talk to him but I need some counselling tips. He might be depressed or something and I might make it worse.

LYNN: You expect to learn counselling via WhatsApp?

ANTONIA: And in about five minutes – the guests are starting to come down.

LYNN: OK. Just three lessons you need to know.

The kettle boiled and Antonia poured the water slowly over the coffee grounds before setting the plunger on top and carrying it through to the terrace. Already there was warmth in the sun, teasing the delicate scent from the jasmine flowering under the bedroom windows.

Back in the kitchen, Antonia read Lynn's next message.

LYNN: Unconditional positive regard.

ANTONIA: Is that one lesson or all three?

She couldn't resist the quip, even though she was fairly sure she knew what Lynn meant.

A gif arrived, showing a slapped wrist.

LYNN: Lesson two: if you suspect he is clinically depressed or anything like, get him to see a doctor. It's way above your pay grade.

ANTONIA: All this is above my pay grade.

LYNN: And yet you're going to do it?

A bedroom door opened and closed, accompanied by voices.

ANTONIA: More guests on the way down.

LYNN: And I must head for the shower so lesson three: never counsel a friend.

Thanks a bunch, Lynn, Antonia thought. *Thanks a bloody bunch.*

An internet search confirmed her understanding that 'unconditional positive regard' meant accepting someone exactly as they were without judging them, and then supporting them. To Antonia the phrase summed up motherhood and it was exactly what she had tried to give Honey all her life. But the article also said not to try to resolve the other person's problems for them either. Just like she was learning to do with Honey. But what could you do when you felt someone had wronged you and should apologise?

But surely there was something bigger than both her and Damir at stake here? They both needed Vila Maslina to work. For Damir it was a means of keeping his home; for her it was the reason for her growing self-respect. And it *was* growing, little by little. She'd read the guest reviews; she knew how well she was doing, and when Honey had seen them too and congratulated her, she'd felt as though she would burst with pride. And once again she could look the world in the eye.

All the same, the risk of trying to put things right and failing, of making things worse, was pretty high. She only had one chance at this, or everything they had built so far could come crashing down around their heads. She knew she couldn't counsel anyone; she didn't have the skills to unwrap Damir's myriad problems, couldn't help him to deal with bottled-up grief or whatever was really behind this. But what she could do was offer to be Damir's friend. It wasn't about letting him walk all over her; she would need to make him see that wasn't going to happen, and making the first move would certainly put her in the driving seat. She could show herself to be the bigger person. She could say, 'I forgive you.' Depending on his response, she might even mean it.

As the afternoon wore on, finding Damir became Antonia's most pressing concern. The first time she walked through the olive grove, the people-carrier wasn't outside the press house, and later when it was, the stable door was shut and there was no answer. After checking the outbuildings around the courtyard Antonia resorted to subterfuge and texted him.

I need you at the villa – there's a problem.

And she waited, frying aubergines and courgettes, mint and caramelisation filling the air as she turned them again and again. After a while her phone bleeped.

On my way.

She set the pan to one side and put the large green *dzezva* on the stove to boil, while spooning coffee into its smaller navy companion. Remembering the tale Damir had told her, about a girl accepting a man if she put sugar in his coffee and refusing him with salt, she wondered if that was a way to start the conversation, so she fetched the packet from the larder. When she returned, Damir was at the kitchen door.

"I'm making you coffee. Sugar, not salt." She managed the words in halting Croatian.

His eyes opened unnaturally wide and he sagged against the door frame.

"What's wrong? Are you ill?" Panic began to rise inside her.

"No. Just thankful, so very thankful." He straightened up a little. "Well, maybe a bit light in the head because I have not been hungry."

"You mean you haven't been eating? Oh, you stupid boy." After just a few seconds she had found herself judging him, but it didn't matter. She wasn't Lynn – she wasn't a counsellor. She was doing this her way. With compassion – and with food. She took his arm and dragged him onto a chair next to the table. "I'll make you an omelette, and then we can talk."

"I am not a child." There was a flash of the animation that had been missing when she'd overheard him talking to the guests, and Antonia found her relief was more powerful than her desire to bite back.

"OK, but you sure are hangry."

"Hangry?"

"A mixture of hungry and angry."

He looked up at her. "Yes, yes, I see."

Antonia finished making the coffee at the stove, spooning in the sugar.

"There is no need to do that. You have made the point."

"And you need the energy."

"You're still treating me like a child. I do not need a mother." As he said it there was something unbelievably dark in his eyes.

Antonia sat down next to him. "Then do you need a friend?"

He squeezed his lids tightly shut, as though fighting back tears, but he took a deep breath and picked up his mug. "Is it possible, after I lied to you?"

"Of course it is possible. I think... I will need to understand why you did it. And why you are so angry all the time, when I don't think it's like you. But not today. Today we are just going to be nice to each other and I am going to make you eat an omelette. Nothing more."

He half smiled. "No bread with the omelette? No cake for afterwards?"

Close to tears herself, Antonia punched his arm. "As much bread and cake as you can eat."

Over the next few days they took small steps, but Antonia thought that most of them were in the right direction. They somehow found time to sit on the old olive press to watch as Damir left the stable door open for Marco to take his first steps into the outside world, making them laugh when he rushed straight back inside on encountering a large bee. Then on Saturday he helped her to battle through the crowded market before rather shyly asking if he could buy her lunch on Wednesday, so they could talk.

Antonia had assumed Damir would take her somewhere in Korčula Town, but instead they turned inland, the road twisting upwards through the small agricultural village of Žrnovo, its grey stone cottages lining the hillside between walled pastures and dark bands of cypress. They continued to climb, through the cool darkness of the Aleppo pines onto a series of S-bends threading their way up an escarpment, which even Damir took relatively slowly, much to Antonia's relief. Beyond a town with the enchanting name of Cara, the road was straddled by a mixture of woods, pastures, and vineyards, and it was outside one of these they drew to a halt.

"The food here is excellent, and so are the wines. I put their advertising in the properties I manage so they'll give us their best table," Damir explained.

They were shown through a cool dining room with terracotta tiles on the floor, and onto a terrace. At the far end, on a slightly higher level than the rest, was a vine-shaded arbour with a view across the valley and a tantalising glimpse of the sea in the distance. It was both beautiful and quite private, and within moments a plate of olives and two glasses of crisp white wine appeared in front of them, so chilled Antonia was able to write her initials in the beads of condensation on the glass.

"This is breath-taking," she told him. "Thank you."

"I wanted a suitable apology. I should not have lied to you about Vesna and I am sorry. But it is over between us and I will not hide things from you again."

"So is that part of the reason you've been so upset?" Although Antonia knew Vincenzo's opinion, she wanted to hear Damir's own answer.

He shook his head, but it was impossible to read his expression behind his sunglasses. "Vesna... it was meant to be fun, and last year it was. She is clever, beautiful. But she is also demanding. And I became scared... if I did not do as she asked she would complain to her brother that I was bad at my job. So it was not fun anymore."

"So you ended it."

He squeezed an olive between his forefinger and thumb. "I wish I had been that brave. But I am not brave, Antonia. And that is hard for a man to admit."

"It is brave for a man to admit."

"You twist clever words but that is not how it feels."

She took a sip of her wine. "So how does it feel?"

"I thought you might ask this question and I cannot say. The words don't come... not in the Croatian in my head or the English I speak."

"Your English is pretty damned perfect."

He shrugged. This must be so hard for him, Antonia

thought, and yet he was making a really good fist of it. He had never spoken directly of his feelings before and she was touched he felt he could. But all the same the speed with which they had moved from silence to confidences was a little unnerving, and perhaps it was time to lighten the conversation.

"Have you ever been to England?" she asked.

"Never. I have not travelled. There wasn't the money when I was growing up and I hardly left the island. Just a few times to Dubrovnik or Split but I was not comfortable in a city. I do not trust cities."

"Trust?"

"This time I am sure I have the right word. I want you to understand... where I came from, why I am here." He took a gulp of wine.

The waiter brought an oval dish of tuna carpaccio and two small plates, then lingered to top up their drinks from the ice bucket he'd placed at the far side of the table, just beyond their reach. Damir watched him leave, then selected two choice morsels of fish loaded with fresh capers, and put them on Antonia's plate, before looking studiously at his own while he spoke.

"I was not born on Korčula. I am not even Croatian by birth, although my father was from the island. I am from Bosnia & Herzegovina, a city called Mostar. It was not a good place to be born, because very soon the war came there. My father was a soldier, so he had to go to fight. My mother... she disappeared."

The food on Antonia's plate seemed to swim in front of her. "Disappeared?"

"I suppose it was a kind way of telling a child she was dead – I cannot really remember. My mother was Bosniak, a Muslim, and someone told me it happened everywhere because Croats and Bosniaks could not live together."

"Your parents clearly could..."

"Yes, but if I was half Bosniak, half Croat, where could I live?" He gazed out over the countryside for a long time, but Antonia was too close to tears to interrupt his thoughts. She could see that little boy so clearly in him still – lost, confused, alone – and the compunction to mother him was strong. But he had said he did not need a mother and she must respect that.

He was speaking again. "Of course, the answer was to become Croatian, like Tetka told me to. So that is what I did."

"And you are very proud of your country. Rightly so."

"I am proud of its beauty, its culture... those things. But politics I avoid. Tetka did too. She said life was easier when we were Yugoslavia because there were no choices to be made and there were no arguments. No wars either."

"Do you remember much about the war?" Antonia asked.

"I try not to. But sometimes... sometimes it remembers me. Things come back. After we argued... that night..." He was pushing a piece of tuna around his plate.

"Can you tell me?"

"No." He looked at her, but his smile was shaky. "And anyway, it is time to eat, to enjoy the view." He drained his glass. "And for you to finish the wine because I will have to drive us home."

Antonia put her hand over his. "Thank you for trusting me, Damir. Your honesty means a lot."

It meant a lot, but it changed a lot too. Perhaps he had only told her his story to explain his behaviour, but it would have been no easier for him to tell than it had been to hear. She didn't believe for one moment all that pain had been erased by the years, not after the way he'd said 'the war remembers me'. Perhaps that was where his moodiness stemmed from? Perhaps that was the answer?

But it remained to be seen whether his confidences would draw them closer together or tear them apart. The latter must be avoided at all costs, for the sake of Vila Maslina and for their own sakes too. For very different reasons they were both lonely people and they both needed a friend.

Chapter Fifteen

The cool tingle of seawater on Antonia's skin melted into a delicious freshness, contrasting with the warmth of the sunlight flooding the deserted bay. Vincenzo had been right about how wonderful it was, and she ploughed through the gentle wash of the crystal waves to tell him.

"Now you have tried you must come every day. Make the most of it."

"I certainly couldn't do this at home at the beginning of June. Even though I live near the sea I rarely ever go in. It's too bloody cold."

Vincenzo flipped onto his back to float. "I swim summer and winter. Every day. When I have to travel I miss it; a hotel pool is not the same."

Antonia joined him, gazing up into the pale blue sky. "Do you travel very often?"

"Only when I have to visit galleries if there is a show of my work, or to meet important buyers. This winter it will be

Amsterdam and Tokyo. I've never been to Japan before – it should be cool."

"I'd love to travel more."

"Then do it. When you finish here in October, see the world."

She laughed, then started to swim towards the shallow sloping rocks that lined the bay. "Not possible."

"Everything is possible."

"Only if you can afford it. And anyway, I miss Honey too much." Below her the water was so clear she could make out every frond of seaweed, and every tiny fish that darted between them.

Already Vincenzo had caught up with her, and they floated again. "You have missed out on travelling; I have missed out on children. We only have one life, and very few people can have it all."

"We must just make the best of what we have."

His arm touched Antonia's as a wave rolled in beneath them. "And what we have right now is today." The promise in his words fizzed through her, and this time she was sure there was promise. Or perhaps she was just ready to hear them in the way they were meant. With Damir on an even keel and no more tearful calls from Honey, maybe it was time to do something for herself. All the same, it was a frightening prospect with plenty of opportunity for humiliation and hurt. She still hadn't quite managed to erase the ghost of Geoffrey from her mind and being naked in front of another man was going to be more than difficult, however kind and understanding Vincenzo was.

Sitting on the terrace with a glass of wine in front of her, Antonia messaged Lynn.

ANTONIA: I've been swimming with Vincenzo and I'm having impure thoughts while he's in the shower. It's all your bloody fault.

LYNN: I'll take the credit, if that's what you mean.

ANTONIA: Ya-di-ya. What the hell do I do?

LYNN: Go and hold his towel for him.

ANTONIA: Nice fantasy, but no way. Even if I was that brave I'm still not sure I'm properly over Ned.

LYNN: Why does there always, always, have to be a but with you? You don't have to be over Ned to have sex with Vincenzo. He's a nice single man and so obviously into you. Get up to that bathroom right now.

Much as Antonia was tempted, she didn't want to feel a fool.

She was thankful that when Vincenzo returned he busied himself with cutlery and plates, then asked how Damir was. This was safe, normal conversational ground and Antonia told him he was much better, although on Monday morning he'd been pale and had struggled to light his cigarette with his shaking hands.

"Did he say why?"

"He said the war remembered him again. I guess he meant he had a nightmare or something. Did you know he was in the thick of the fighting in Bosnia before he came here?"

"No. I knew from Petar he was orphaned but I never really considered the details. Poor bloke. If it's still screwing him up maybe he should get some help."

"I'm sure you're right, but he finds it pretty impossible to talk about. It must be awful to be haunted by it like that. And yet... when I first came to the island he seemed fine."

"Perhaps it comes and goes. Maybe next time you should ask him."

"Have you any idea how hard it is to have a conversation in between making coffee and toast for the guests? And being nice to them, and replenishing the buffet plates when they fall on them like gannets."

Vincenzo rolled his eyes. "That part I do know – I make them lunch."

"If it's lunch like this it's a wonder they eat supper." Antonia surveyed the plates covering the table; tomato and mozzarella with fresh basil, plump olives dressed with lemon and herbs, *boquerones,* courgette and aubergine *agrodolce.*

"No. This is a special lunch because it is for you."

Not knowing where to look, Antonia helped herself to some more bread.

"You are even more beautiful when you blush."

"I'm not beautiful..."

"Of course you are. Look at me." She turned to him, and he took her chin gently between his forefinger and thumb. "Your cheekbones; strong, high. Your nose, yes, a little uneven but a certain lack of symmetry is good – it makes a face interesting. Eyes – more round than almond-shaped, and so expressive. And your lips. Well, it does me no good to think of your lips." He released her chin to run his little finger along them, his touch making them tingle.

She pulled away, laughing. "Is this how you seduce all your women?"

The playfulness left his face. "I seduce very few women, Antonia, and if I am to continue to seduce you a serious conversation must happen first."

"Go on."

"It is simple, and yet it is complicated. At the end of October you will go home and I will stay here." He smiled. "Perhaps we could travel to Tokyo together, but that would just delay the inevitable."

Antonia turned her wine glass under her hand. "We lead very different lives."

"We do. And those lives have brought us together only for a brief time. We have become friends, we are attracted to each other, but love... love is out of the question. I do not want us to hurt each other. Anything we decide – today, next week, next month – it must be good for us both."

So a summer fling, going in with eyes wide open. Antonia wondered if she was even capable of it. But his touch still lingered on her lips and she laughed, nervously. "What is it the kids call it? Friends with benefits?"

"I do not like the expression, but yes, I suppose so. Friends first. Friends always." He threw up his hands. "I don't know why I am even suggesting this – it is madness – but whenever we touch it's like fire through my body and I cannot resist the flames."

"It is the same for me, but this is so strange. I need time to think."

"Of course you do. Of course. This is craziness on my part. If you will excuse me, I will make the coffee."

He swept up the empty plates and disappeared, leaving Antonia gazing at the sea. With Ned, love had crept up unannounced and unwanted, and she was frightened it could happen again. But what she had also learnt was that the pain didn't last forever; already she knew she was moving on. Time did heal, and space too. At some point she would have to dip her toe in the ocean again, and perhaps this was as good an opportunity as any. After all, it was underpinned by friendship, and friendship meant honesty and trust. But all the same, casual sex just didn't feel like her.

Antonia stopped, Lynn's voice in her head. There was always a but. Always a reason to hold back or not to put herself first. After a moment she drained her glass and with her heart vibrating scarily through her ribs, followed Vincenzo into the coolness of the kitchen.

Antonia had told no one except Lynn about Vincenzo, and even then she'd spared her the details. They had spent a glorious afternoon in the coolness of his bedroom, the soft breeze from the sea finding its way through the blinds and onto their skin, a gentle counterpoint to the warmth of their hands on each other.

They had made love, laughed, talked. And it had been very good. Afterwards they'd eaten pasta with capers and anchovies on the terrace as the sun set over the sea and Antonia had driven home through the darkness, creeping up to her room and hugging the memory to her; the salt perfume of his hair filling her nose, the rough pads of his sculptor's fingertips tingling across her body all over again.

But a few days later, as she stood in the courtyard watching the swallows feeding their young, it occurred to her that in not telling Damir she was being as bad as he'd been over Vesna. But on the other hand, what was there to tell? It didn't feel right to say Vincenzo was her boyfriend, because that implied a degree of permanence. That he was her lover sounded far too pretentious, and anyway, it had only happened once.

All the same, she didn't want secrets between them and already she wondered if it was a cause of underlying tension. Damir had been in a black mood this morning and when he'd rounded on her for dropping an egg on the floor she had felt so jumpy she'd almost bitten back. She hadn't, but only because he'd laughed and muttered something about 'plenty more chickens in the sea', and they had cleared up the mess together. But it had been a close call.

Since Damir had told her he had lived in Mostar, Antonia had wanted to learn more about the Bosnian war, and she hoped today she would finally find the time to do so. If she knew what had happened around him when he was a child, perhaps she would be better armed to help him if he mentioned it again.

Instead of taking her lunch into the courtyard, Antonia carried it upstairs to her room and turned on her laptop, homemade lemonade fizzing on her tongue as she waited for it to warm up. Typing the words 'war in Mostar' into the search engine, inevitably Wikipedia was the first site to show up, but it was the bank of images appearing on the search that riveted her; the empty shell of a red brick apartment block, a soldier in khaki pointing a gun across a river at a tumble of buildings on a hillside, and a whole load of pictures of an elegant arched bridge – perfect in some, a blackened wreck in others. She simply could not imagine being in such a place; what happened to the families who lived in those apartments? Where had they gone? Had they ever been able to go back to their homes?

She clicked away from the sickening pictures and headed for Wikipedia. Here she learnt there had been two phases of fighting in Mostar: three months from April 1992 when, like in Dubrovnik, the Serbs were the aggressors, and then a year later when the Croats and Bosniaks had started to fight each other. She checked back; in the initial siege, they had been fighting together.

And how old would Damir have been when all this was going on? Antonia checked his age on his Facebook profile; in 1992 he would have been five years old. Little more than a toddler, living in a city under perpetual shelling from the 17,000 enemy forces surrounding it. 90,000 people had left, so why hadn't his parents? Maybe because his father was a soldier. Maybe they'd had to stay.

The article began to mention East Mostar and West Mostar as if they were separate entities, and from its tone Antonia gathered that the Bosniaks lived in the East and the Croats in the West. People in the wrong place were beaten then expelled, some ending up in concentration camps. That phase of the war was definitely in and amongst the general population, and the thought of children being caught up in it brought red hot tears to her eyes.

But on which side had Damir lived? Impossible to tell, given his heritage. No wonder he'd said something about not knowing who he really was — it could have quite literally been a matter of life and death. And he had been just a tiny, tiny child. Antonia remembered how small Honey's hand had felt in hers when she was five, on her first day at school. She would have fought battles single-handedly to protect her, and she'd shed copious tears in secret once she'd settled her into her classroom and left her in the company of strangers.

Antonia could read no more. She had never expected her emotions to be churned up like this, and as she put her laptop on the floor beside her, she thought how often she had watched reports from war-torn corners of the world which had washed over her. People just seemed numbed to it. Perhaps they had numbed themselves, because if you really thought about the true horror of living through a conflict, right-minded folk would be taking to the streets in their millions to make sure it never, ever happened again.

Before turning off her laptop she bent down and

bookmarked a BBC documentary filmed in Mostar in 1993. She had no stomach for it now; in fact she felt tearful and slightly sick. Instead, she texted Honey to tell her how much she loved her then headed for the shower to wash the second-hand horrors away.

Chapter Sixteen

Just as Damir put his hand on the door handle of the old press house to slip outside, the sound of an engine split the early morning birdsong and he froze. He recognised the car; he had driven it himself for years, and there was only one place Antonia could be coming back from at five in the morning. But he had known, really he had known, although the confirmation of his fears added yet another layer of gloom to his already jaded mood. He had seen women come and go in Vincenzo's life and if he hurt Antonia in any way, he didn't know how he would ever be able to forgive him.

But it was more than that, much more. Although not because he wanted Antonia for himself – not in the way Vincenzo clearly did, anyway. He didn't want flirtation and mystique, he wanted… He struggled to find the words in his head. He needed… her calm good sense, her warmth, her trust. But how much could he trust her with his secrets when she was sleeping with his friend? Perhaps he had already opened up to her too much?

Maybe trusting Antonia had been a bad decision. Much as taking Marco to the beach was turning out to be. The other kittens had been found homes and he'd looked a little forlorn left alone in the press house but he was certainly less than happy now, squirming and yowling in Damir's pocket. Stopping as he turned out of the drive, he hauled Marco into the early morning light by the scruff of his neck.

His father pulling a kitten from the pocket of his khaki uniform jacket; a mewing, squirming bundle of tabby and white fur. Damir had been jumping up and down on the red circular rug in the middle of their living room, but his father made him sit on the sofa before he set her gently on his lap. He crouched in front of him.

"So, Damir, would you like to look after her?" Too full of excitement to speak, he had nodded. "What are you going to call her?"

His mother appeared, wiping her hands on a tea towel. "She is such a little sweetheart – just look at her tiny pink nose."

Damir had looked at the kitten, then at his parents. "Then I will call her sweetheart." He stroked between the kitten's ears with his finger. "Do you like that, Dusa?" She purred.

But the fur between Damir's fingers now was black. The grey dawn was around him, and he was standing at the side of the track to the beach. Not asleep in his bed. Surely, surely, the flashes of the past were not going to invade his daylight hours as well? But even so, the memory was a good one. Which was as astonishing as it was unsettling. Everything good came from his life on Korčula.

As Damir continued towards the beach he wondered how much was buried in the depths of his mind. In this memory, his father had been wearing a different uniform to the one in Tetka's picture, yet Damir had known it straight away. And he had not seen a photograph of his mother until just before Antonia arrived. But in the memory his mother's hair had been longer, and she'd been wearing a blouse with embroidery on the collar, and he'd seemed to recognise that as well.

It was almost as hard to shake the memory as it was the nightmares, but shake it he must. Damir walked towards the sea, close enough to let the water wash over his feet and Marco shifted. He held him more tightly against his chest, suddenly terrified of dropping him in the waves and losing him. What had happened to Dusa? Damir tried to remember, but he couldn't.

He remembered other things though, like pictures from an album: being in the country somewhere, with grass higher than his knees; finding a caterpillar and dropping it onto his mother's hand, making her scream. And his father laughing. And his mother's voice singing – not that time, but somewhere else. And her hand guiding his finger along the words in a book as he said them out loud.

It was as though Damir was standing outside himself, watching the man in shorts on the edge of the sea as he observed someone else's life. The chill from the water spread to his ankles, bringing him back down. If he hadn't been holding Marco, he could have dived in and purged those thoughts. Swum and swum and swum until he was too exhausted to care.

After the last guest had gone to bed, Damir and Vincenzo joined Antonia in the kitchen. She was holding a tea towel in one hand and a saucepan in the other, staring into space.

"What is wrong, *mia cara*?" Vincenzo asked.

"I think... I should go home." The look of horror on Damir's face must have been apparent as he tried to absorb the full impact of what she'd said, because she carried on, "For a while, at least."

"Why, what's happened?" He somehow managed to squeeze the words out.

"It's Honey and Sara... they might be on the verge of breaking up." She looked close to tears.

Vincenzo took the pan from her and guided her to a seat at the table, while Damir plunged his hands into his pockets. He watched as they sat down and Vincenzo pulled his chair next to hers so he could hold her.

"I'll get us a nightcap," he said.

Even though the *rakija* was close to hand, Damir lingered in the larder, trying to order his jumbled thoughts. If Antonia went home, she might never come back, and then what would he do? Without her everything would fall apart… No meals on the table, no pile of freshly laundered beach towels in the hall, guests complaining about everything (and rightly so), an impossible workload for himself at a time he could barely cope with what he already had. Without Antonia, he might just as well give up.

No, he shouldn't be thinking like this – he should be thinking about what was right for her. Tetka's favourite jug was on the shelf, and he ran his fingers over the stippled surface before grasping the handle to draw strength from the place she had held so many times. He owed Antonia so much, not just for all the hard work she put into Vila Maslina, but for actually seeming to like him when he felt so damn unlikeable himself. Maybe if he could make this one thing possible he would go some way towards repaying her. And making sure she came back.

Returning to the kitchen, Damir set three glasses on the table and drew up a chair on the other side of Antonia, putting his hand over hers.

"Tell us what's happened," he said.

"You guys... you are just the best. You really are..." Antonia sniffed.

Vincenzo uncorked the *rakija* bottle with his teeth and with his free hand sloshed drink into their glasses. *Trust him to be so bloody macho*. Damir focused his attention back on Antonia.

"Go on," he encouraged her.

"Oh, I don't know. Honey is so unhappy, but it's hard to pin down what's really wrong. One minute it's fine, then the next... But she loves Sara, and I've spoken to Sara and she says she feels the same, but Honey isn't taking saving for their flat seriously at all. But perhaps Sara is taking it too seriously – Honey says there's no fun in her anymore. She said if I was there I could get to the bottom of it and maybe help them to sort it out. I feel so useless..." Her voice was cracking and Damir squeezed her hand while Vincenzo hugged her tighter.

"Then you must go," Damir told her, hoping he

sounded more confident than he felt. "I can manage. Well, for a week or so anyway. I am sure Ana can do some extra hours."

"And I can cook Italian a couple of nights," Vincenzo chimed in. "We can find another artist to give the talks while I'm on kitchen duty." Vincenzo may think he was superman, but cooking was not his job, and Damir was about to remind him of this when Antonia spoke.

"You guys..." A fresh tear streaked Antonia's cheek.

"Come on," Vincenzo said, "this is meant to make you happy."

"It is... it is... but there's something else." She took a sip of her *rakija*. "This is a bit awkward, but the flights are really expensive this time of year. I couldn't... I'll need to... ask you for an advance against my wages. You see I'm still paying my mortgage back home, and..."

Damir tried to think how much money was in the bank, but Vincenzo looked over Antonia's head and gave a slight nod. Damir knew he was right; if he delayed payment to him he could do this, and after all Vincenzo was a wealthy man. He could probably buy Antonia the moon to fly home on if he wanted to.

"That is no problem at all," Damir told her. Except now they were both beholden to Vincenzo. But he must not be bitter. He knew Vincenzo was doing his best to help. If only he could find the same generosity in his own heart then his life would be so much easier. Like it used to be, before the past had re-emerged to tie him up in knots.

"Oh, thank you. Thank you so much. I know it's a busy time and I'm letting you down."

Damir shook his head. "Of course you're not. I know how much Honey means to you."

"And I will ask my travel agent to sort out your flights," said Vincenzo. "Leave it all to me." Vincenzo seemed to puff up his chest as he pulled her to him, away from Damir. He must have seen the look on Damir's face because hastily he qualified. "To us. Of course, leave it to both of us."

Good to his promise, it was just a few days later when Vincenzo called after Damir as the guests were settling into his studio. He stopped halfway back to the people-carrier, keys in hand, while Vincenzo caught up.

"I've had an idea. How about, instead of Antonia going home, we bring those girls out here? What do you think?"

The relief that flooded through Damir was tempered with caution. "I think it is genius, my friend. But how will we do it?"

Vincenzo grinned. "I've already messaged Honey through Facebook – I noticed she was following my page, and she says she will talk to Sara and see about getting some time off. She sounded very excited." So he had acted first, and then asked him. But Damir could not allow his irritation to show. Vincenzo was the best sculptor on the island, the only one he wanted to tutor his guests, so it would not do to upset him. And anyway, Antonia staying on the island was good for them both. And, of course, for Vila Maslina.

Even so, there were practical considerations he clearly hadn't thought through.

"But if Antonia doesn't have the money for one flight then..."

Vincenzo waved his hand. "My travel agent is used to working with budgets."

"And accommodation? We're fully booked until the end of September."

"Perhaps they could have Antonia's room at the villa and she could stay with me. No hardship."

But Damir did not want Antonia moving in with Vincenzo. For so many reasons, although as the more logical ones ran through his head he was well aware there were others swirling beneath, ones that might not show him in a good light were he to examine them too closely.

He played with the car keys in his hand. "Well let me know when you hear from Honey and I will try to find somewhere in the village for them to stay."

Vincenzo grinned at him. "Good idea. We work so well as a team, you and I, even to help our lovely Antonia."

But Antonia was not theirs, she was her own woman. Maybe that was it, that was what had been irking him about Vincenzo's attitude. It was so… proprietorial, not to mention old fashioned. That's what was making him angry with his friend. All right, Antonia was half a generation older than him, so maybe she didn't mind, but all the same he couldn't imagine Vesna ever standing for being referred to as a man's possession. Vincenzo had a powerful personality… certainly strong enough to crush Antonia's fragile shoots of self-confidence if she let him.

Perhaps, now Vincenzo had solved the problem of Honey and Sara single-handed, what Damir should concentrate on was protecting Antonia from Vincenzo. But how? She was a grown woman. Why should she listen to him, especially when he couldn't even hold down a second-rate love affair like he'd had with Vesna. He was the last person in the world who should be giving relationship advice. Or advice about anything. The strange boy, the outsider.

Resisting the temptation to rage and scream at Vincenzo for reminding him of who he really was, Damir managed a tight smile before leaping into the people-carrier and slamming it into gear then bumping down the track. In his rear-view mirror he could just make out the sculptor watching him through the cloud of dust.

One thing Damir knew he could contribute to Honey and Sara's visit was to find them a place to stay. The obvious candidate was Petar's mother Sanja, although Damir felt more than awkward that he hadn't visited her for some time and was only going now because he needed a favour. As soon as he handed over the lavish flowers he'd bought her, Sanja asked what he wanted, reminding him painfully of just how shallow he was, but then she enveloped him in a hug that reminded him of Tetka's and said she knew because she understood him as well as her own sons.

Sitting on her terrace with its lush vine covered with tiny grapes and its view towards the wooded mountains behind the village took Damir back to his childhood. In the summer holidays he would play here all day, and Sanja would make him and Petar sit in the shade for lunch, which was always traditional food like *makaruni* or lamb *peka,* however hot it was. Life had been so simple then, and drinking coffee and eating Sanja's homemade *fritule,* the round balls of fluffy dough drenched in sugar and rich with vanilla, a tiny part of that feeling of ease drifted back. They talked about friends in the village, and when he asked after her grandchildren she positively glowed.

Damir felt his shoulders relax and he closed his eyes, drinking in the pungent scent of the geraniums in their mismatched pots, listening to Sanja gossip and imagining himself in happier times. But his life could not be like this anymore, so reluctantly he hauled himself to his feet.

"I am so sorry, but I have work to do."

"Always busy, Damir, just like your *tetka.* Even when we were children she could never sit still." She kissed him on the cheek. "Come to visit me again, my son. Never forget you are part of my family too."

Her words echoed around Damir's head during the short drive back down the hill to Vila Maslina. He parked outside the old press house and wandered into the shade of the olive grove. Sanja may have meant well, but she was wrong. He had no family. Antonia had Honey, and even Vincenzo had sisters back in Florence, but he had no one. The sense of isolation was so strong he had to steady himself on a tree, the gnarled bark digging deep into his hand.

But it was metal cutting his skin… and something hard,

circular, the pattern of a tiny tyre on the soft flesh of his thumb. He was curled into a ball around it, adults talking just outside the flickering arc of yellowish light, words he did not strain to hear because he did not want to. 'Sam na svijetu.' Over and over again.

If the phrase 'all alone in the world' had continued to haunt Damir as he went about the business of the day, it came into sharp relief that evening as he watched Antonia fling her arms around Vincenzo in delight.

"You wonderful, wonderful, man. However did you even think of bringing the girls out here, let alone make it happen?"

"It wasn't just me, it was Damir as well."

Damir shrugged. "Just a small part." He knew even that was far from the truth as he had done precisely nothing, except beg a room from Sanja, which she had been delighted to give.

But for now, Vincenzo's arm was draped around Antonia's shoulder as he told her how hard his travel agent had worked to find seats on just the right flights. Apparently the girls didn't need to worry about anything now; like some improbable, long-haired, superannuated Disney wizard, Vincenzo had waved a magic wand and covered them all in stardust. By the look on Antonia's face it had worked a treat and he was winding her further into his web, pulling her away from Damir and once again he was on the outside. Outside looking in.

Damir drained his coffee. "Right. I must be getting on. Back to the paperwork. Leave you two lovebirds to gaze adoringly at each other." Out of the corner of his eye he saw them exchange a glance. Of course he had said the wrong thing. He had worked so hard to make this place his home. Everything about his identity was tied up with this village, this island… this country. He had been nothing before and without it he would be nothing again. He was falling, falling, back to the moment he had arrived on Korčula, blinking in the light like a mole. He remembered that light, the searing sun that had hurt his eyes. But there was a disconnect; one moment he'd been emerging from the shelter in Mostar and the next he'd been in Lumbarda. He stopped and shook his head. It could not have happened like that.

Damir made his way through the olive grove, but tonight it was full of ghosts as the leaves whispered around him, and one part of him battled to remember the first time he'd seen it and the other tried to forget. That, together with the sultry heat, made him feel a little dizzy, so instead of going inside he sat on the cool stone of the olive press. Vincenzo's motorbike had not passed. He and Antonia were probably still talking about him.

He closed his eyes but the darkness was different, the yellowish gloom of the shelter. *He was playing with his toy cars, the colours indistinct as he pushed them along the concrete floor. And he was alone, not with Dragan. He did not play with Damir anymore. Perhaps because Kemal was dead, and they were watched like hawks to make sure they did not go outside. But Damir did not want to go outside at all.*

It was his mother who went out. In the early morning, when he was only half awake. She kissed his forehead but he barely responded. Every day she went, sometimes alone, sometimes with the other women. But that day she did not come back.

Damir opened his eyes, fumbled for a cigarette and lit it between trembling fingers. He didn't have to remember this. It was gone. Over. The sweat on his back made his shirt stick, damp and cold against the stone as he smoked. He ran his free hand over its roughness. Its solidity. His mother may have died in a far-off city, but here in his olive grove he had always felt safe. Now there was nothing but emptiness and doubt, eating him up inside.

Chapter Seventeen

On the day Honey and Sara arrived, Antonia was on the dockside a full twenty minutes before the catamaran was due, so she distracted herself by watching the dances of the cruise ships as they moored up one against the other, the noise of their engines carrying across the water as they moved back and forth to line up their doors so the passengers could walk across. Groups of visitors clustered around their flag-waving guides beneath the palm trees on the harbourfront under the bluest of skies. It was July, so the town was at its busiest, but Antonia loved the joyous vibrancy of it all.

Even with the distractions it still seemed an age before the catamaran appeared, the flume of white behind the only hint of its speed. She twisted the car keys in her hand. Would the girls be on speaking terms when they arrived? Would their problems have changed Honey? Pulled her down? Had she really done the right thing leaving them? But this was no time to be besieged by doubts because finally the cat was slowing down to begin its interminable arc towards the harbour, the crew on the prow throwing ropes to their colleagues on shore to secure it, their shouts drowned out by the thrum of the engines. Antonia searched every window for Honey's face, but then the door opened, and she and Sara tumbled down the gangplank, dragging their cases behind them as they raced towards her.

Honey's hair filled Antonia's nose and four arms embraced her. She held them both close, elation overtaking her sudden urge to cry. But there were tears streaming down Honey's cheeks.

"Oh God, Mum, I've missed you so much."

"And I've missed you. Both of you." Antonia added.

Sara grinned at her. "Oh, come on, Mum-two, you've missed Honey more, but that's as it should be. And she's been a right bloody mare without you at times."

Honey punched Sara on the arm, but there was a softness in her eyes. "Don't start, you. Not tonight. We promised."

"No, not tonight," Sara agreed. "We want to see this island first."

Antonia steered them through the crowd towards the car, basking in the glow of having her daughter beside her. "You're not going to see the whole island in one night. Maybe not even in a week. It's bigger than you think. But for now I'm going to take you to your room and introduce you to Sanja. Damir's given me the evening off so once you've freshened up we can go to the restaurant on the beach for a pizza."

"Pizza? That doesn't sound very Croatian," Honey said.

"Oh, but it is. There's huge Italian influence here."

"Like Vincenzo." She nudged her.

"Yes, like Vincenzo."

"Is he your boyfriend?"

"No, he's a friend..." Oh God, was there a way of putting this without sounding like a teenager? "With benefits," Antonia finished.

"Mum!"

Sara laughed. "Go for it, Mum-two. We've checked him out online and he's much more exciting than dreary old Ned."

So that was Antonia told. Maybe Ned had been dreary. Maybe she had become dreary too. But all the same she wasn't quite comfortable with this no-strings sex business, especially admitting it to her daughter. But nothing, nothing, was going to spoil this evening and with Honey bouncing up and down in the front seat next to Antonia, life was as good as it could possibly be.

Antonia left Honey and Sara to shower and unpack, and she took the car home so she could have a drink with dinner. Damir rushed out when he saw her, concerned some disaster had struck and the girls had not arrived, but when she told him her plan he agreed it was a good idea.

"Keep off the *rakija,* though," he grinned. "You don't want them to be hungover for the first day of their holiday. And I don't want to have to cook breakfast."

Antonia was impatient to get back to the girls, but they weren't ready so she spent a pleasant half hour sipping coffee on the terrace and chatting to Sanja in her stilted Croatian. She thanked Sanja again for putting them up, but she told her Damir was like her third son, and nothing was too much trouble for him. It occurred to Antonia to ask her about how he had arrived on the island, but she wasn't sure her language would be up to understanding Sanja's answer, and anyway the girls appeared, Honey in a cute miniskirt and halter-neck top Antonia hadn't seen before, and Sara in her habitual combats, although she too had a new skinny T-shirt in a bright scarlet that matched the current dye in her hair.

They strolled through the quiet streets, the white tower of the church on the rise above them gleaming in the evening sun. At the end of the road they turned towards the sea, and Sara let out a sigh.

"This is glorious. Just an ordinary little village with such a beautiful bay. It feels very... I don't know... real."

"It is. There are just a couple of small restaurants in this part, although if you walk on around the shoreline to the left it's more of a town, really, with a big harbour for yachts, a couple of hotels and all sorts of cafés and bars. And then if you walk the other way, there's a little quay for the fishing boats and around the headland a second bay – that's the closest beach to Vila Maslina so you'll see it tomorrow."

"And meet Damir and Vincenzo?" Honey asked.

"Damir most likely, but it depends what he needs to do. He normally manages to make it home at some point though. Vincenzo will be teaching so you probably won't meet him until Saturday."

"I kind of forget you're working, and not on some sort of perpetual holiday."

"Sometimes I forget myself."

They arrived at Konoba Pecaros to find Damir had paid for a large carafe of wine for them. As Mirjana told the girls about the specials, Antonia texted to thank him, then ordered a seafood pizza for herself.

"You've learnt a lot of Croatian, Mum," Honey said. "We heard you yabbering away to Sanja."

"It's really only enough to get by and I don't get as much practice as I should. Sometimes Damir makes me speak it so I learn new words, but we're too busy to mess around most of the time."

"So is he a good boss?" Sara asked.

"Yes. Given how young he is, he has a sound business head and he's not afraid to make decisions. And he can be such great company too."

"Can be?" Honey pounced on her words and Antonia cursed her slip of the tongue.

She shrugged. "No one is one hundred percent sweetness and light. Especially not when you're with them pretty much 24/7. We've had our moments, like everyone does, but nothing we haven't been able to sort out."

Sara laughed. "Of course, Honey's perfect."

"No I'm not." There was a tiny edge to her voice when she said it, but then she smiled and carried on, "Well, only some of the time."

"I'm glad to hear it," Antonia told her. "You'd be unbearable to live with if you were perfect – or, heaven forbid, always right."

"Are you lecturing us in an oh-so-gentle way?" asked Sara.

"Not at all. Unless you need a good talking to, then I'm happy to oblige."

Honey ran her finger around the rim of her glass in exactly the same way as Antonia always did. "The thing is, Mum, we've agreed a few ground rules for this holiday: two days to chill, two days to talk, and then the last two to call in the cavalry if we need to."

"To be honest, Mum-two, we really need the break..."

"Sara especially," Honey added.

"Why's that?"

"We're a nurse down at the vet's and they aren't exactly hurrying to replace her so Kathy and I are doing no end of overtime and extra shifts. I felt so bad coming away, but at least it means they have to do something, and they've found someone from an agency."

"The upshot is, Sara is tired most of the time," Honey gave her hand a squeeze. "And just a teeny, weeny bit grumpy with it."

"And that," said Sara, "is the last word on the matter until Sunday."

After supper, Antonia walked them back through the soft, velvety night to the end of Sanja's road before heading past the church and down the hill in the opposite direction. Perhaps they didn't need her to sort out their differences after all; maybe they could do it themselves and she sincerely hoped so. But she would never forget Vincenzo and Damir's kindness in giving them the space and time they needed.

As she rounded the last bend in the road, Antonia heard Vincenzo's motorbike heading away from the villa. She was sorry to have missed him; she wanted to hold him and thank him again for bringing the girls here, and now that would have to wait. As she walked through the olive grove she heard voices on the terrace where Damir was drinking a beer with some of the guests, talking about the island's history. From the darkness under the trees she listened to the cadence of his voice, his enthusiasm shining through.

Then, then... someone asked about the war in the 1990s. Antonia stiffened, but nothing changed in Damir's demeanour as he answered, "We were lucky, the conflict did not touch us here." And he carried smoothly on to tell them about a folklore performance in Korčula Town the next day, and that they could delay the farewell party a little if they would like to see it.

The consummate professional. But Antonia knew he must have been asked the same question so many times. She smiled to herself as she skirted the house to the courtyard. She probably worried about Damir far too much – as it seemed she had been worrying about the girls. She climbed the stairs as if she was floating on air, right at this moment the happiest she'd been since arriving on the island.

All the same, Antonia was a little concerned when Damir didn't appear while she was preparing breakfast – indeed, he rushed in just ten minutes before the guests were due to leave for Vincenzo's, and grabbed a coffee from the stove while she was clearing dishes from the terrace. They passed each other in the hall and he told her his alarm hadn't gone off.

"Is there anything I can do?"

"No. You have your cooking and Honey and Sara. I want to meet them but I haven't checked my emails yet so my day could be anywhere."

Antonia touched his arm, "Then let me take the guests to Vincenzo's and go on to the market from there."

"You are too kind to me." He shook her gently away and disappeared to drink his coffee outside the front door by the people-carrier, leaving Antonia feeling rather puzzled.

Once Antonia had finished the shopping she stopped by Sanja's to collect the girls. It would have been insulting to give their hostess pastries, so instead she'd bought her flowers, and Sanja exclaimed over them as though she had never been given any before. Honey and Sara were surrounded by the debris of their breakfast, but Sanja refused all offers of help to clear away, so they grabbed their bags and followed Antonia to the car.

She could not help but feel proud as she drove through Vila Maslina's gates. In her own small way she had helped Damir make this place magical and for a moment she was almost overwhelmed by the achievement. Who would have believed it, just a few short months before? With growing excitement, she pointed out the old press house where Damir lived and Marco, who was sitting on the press itself opposite, cleaning his paws.

"What happened to the other kittens?" Sara asked.

"Two went to a vineyard not far from here and the other is still in the village. It bothers me Mackalina hasn't been spayed but Damir doesn't seem to be getting around to it."

"You worry too much, Mum," Honey told her. "Maybe he liked having kittens in his wardrobe. Maybe they were company for him."

The girls helped Antonia carry the shopping into the coolness of the kitchen where she put it away. The hum of the hoover told her Ana was working upstairs, so she showed Honey and Sara the living room, then led them through the dining area and onto the terrace.

"It's as perfect as you said it was," Honey breathed. "Amazing."

"Damir certainly has a good eye," Antonia agreed.

Sara wandered back into the hall and stood in front of Tetka. "Who's this lady?"

"That's Tetka, Damir's aunt. It was her house and she brought him up. Vincenzo did the sketch."

"It's brilliant – what a face! Every wrinkle tells a story."

"Yes, but what story? I can never work out what she was like from the picture."

Sara put her head on one side. "I'd say she was strong. Loving – there's definitely some softness in her smile. It's welcoming, but all the same I reckon she was a woman who knew her own mind."

"How can you tell?" Honey asked.

"I watch a lot of faces. When it comes to their pets, people's emotions are stripped bare and you learn a lot about them."

Antonia packed a cool bag with lemonade, pastries, and fruit, and together they walked to the beach. The square bay lacked the lazy charm of Antonia's favourite swimming spot below Vincenzo's studio and the narrow strip of coarse sand was already dotted with tourists. The girls staked their place in the shade of the old stone wall that stopped the vineyards behind from tumbling into the sea, and before Antonia had even left Sara was stripping off and heading for the water.

"You can join her," she told Honey. "Your stuff should be perfectly safe."

Honey pulled her Kindle from her bag. "For the moment I just want to feel the sand between my toes and chill." She tilted her face for a kiss. "Love you, Mum. I really do hope you can join us later."

"I'll do my best."

Antonia's best wasn't until about half past two when she figured she could snatch an hour or so. The stable door of the press house was open when she passed and she peered in to see Damir hunched over his computer.

"How's your day panning out?" she asked.

He stretched, and swivelled around to look at her. "Better than I expected. There were three new bookings overnight: one for October and two for next year. And no problems with the rental properties when I did my Friday checks."

"So not a bad morning to oversleep?"

He turned back to his screen. "You're going to the beach?"

"Yes. I don't suppose you have time to come with me? The girls are dying to meet you."

"Oh no... what have you told them?"

"That you're charming, funny, kind, handsome..."

He threw up his hands. "Lies, all lies!" But all the same he looked pleased as he glanced at her over his shoulder. "You go on – I need to turn off my computer and change into shorts. And somehow become this superman you have promised."

Damir was, indeed, all charm when he arrived at the beach. He was the Damir he presented to the guests, and Antonia was a little disappointed he did not share anything of himself with the girls. He looked every inch the young, successful businessman with his designer shades and Ted Baker beach shorts, and she certainly could not accuse him of any lack of sparkle, because he had them laughing within minutes of sitting down. Antonia told herself she was being silly – Damir was being the best he possibly could be. But as she watched them race into the sea together, a slow realisation dawned. Did he genuinely believe the real Damir wasn't good enough? And if that veneer cracked, what then? There was a moment of dread when she wondered how firm Vila Maslina's foundations really were, then Honey called her so she pulled her sundress over her head and followed them into the gentle waves.

Chapter Eighteen

At the Friday night party, Vincenzo suggested Honey and Sara should spend the next day on his side of the island. Knowing Saturday was especially busy for Antonia, he offered to show them the cove and make them lunch. It was so thoughtful of him, but although she knew it would be hard to snatch any time with the girls, she still wanted them close. They seemed fine though, so good together… but what if they were just ignoring their problems rather than solving them? Then she reminded herself of their timetable. A day with Vincenzo would be a wonderful way for them to chill. And a night with him would be good for her too.

The velvet darkness was warm and still, the wash of the waves drifting up to Vincenzo's terrace. He held her in his arms and kissed her, then suggested a walk on the beach. But there he undressed her, and took her by the hand to swim naked under the stars. The beauty of the moment was so intense that Antonia wanted to weep so she was thankful it was too dark for him to see her face. Back on the beach the soft silkiness of the water against her skin was replaced by the familiar touch of his hands as they made love on their pile of abandoned clothes.

It was rather less romantic waking up with her bedsheets full of sand, but still, Antonia lay in her attic room in the calm of the dawn replaying the moment. Was this living without buts? Six months ago she would never have even considered doing such a thing. She had come such a long way from the confidence-starved woman who'd arrived on Korčula; there was a freedom in being with Vincenzo that she could have never achieved with Ned. Perhaps because with him, she had cared too much. Maybe this time she didn't care enough, and perhaps that was the reason this affair didn't sit too easily with her.

Last night had felt so very adventurous, but it wasn't the first time she'd made love on a beach. When they were students, she and Honey's father, Simon, had skinny-dipped while backpacking around Greece, chasing phosphorescence with the thud of music from the tavernas behind them. She knew in her heart that carefree girl had long gone, so was it the right thing to try to bring her back? Or should she be moving forwards?

Antonia stood on the front steps to wave off the guests then returned to the kitchen to pour herself another mug of coffee, carrying it upstairs to sort out the fresh laundry ready for Ana to make the beds. She would miss coffee made in the *dzezva* when she went home; she would have to buy herself a set to remind her of this glorious summer. And as she gazed out over the olive grove from the window of one of the guest rooms, it occurred to her, would she come back next year? And if she decided she wanted to, was anything stopping her?

But she had already done enough navel-gazing for one morning. Once the linen was sorted she grabbed her bags and jumped into the car to head for the market. There was a trail of sand on the driving seat too and as Antonia flicked it out of the door she smiled to herself. Lynn would be so proud.

Vincenzo brought back the girls mid-afternoon, staying only long enough to steal a brownie from the cooling rack, explaining he was just starting a special piece he wanted to get ahead with.

"Did he show you the studio, or did you spend all day on the beach?" Antonia asked as Honey settled herself at the table and Sara filled the kettle to make a pot of tea.

It was Sara who answered. "Yes, he's pretty amazing, isn't he? I mean, we know from his Facebook page he sells all over the world, but it's only when you can actually see and touch the sculptures first hand you realise why. For stone, they're gloriously tactile."

"Like Barbara Hepworth's. Do you remember the sculpture garden in St Ives, Honey? I suppose you were quite small when we went, but the whole idea was to be able to touch things. It does bring a new dimension."

Honey frowned. "I'm not sure I like the idea of some creepy bloke touching the one you're modelling for."

"I'm not modelling for anything. If Vincenzo is working on a female form then it doesn't mean it's me, just because we're... sleeping together."

"But it is, Mum. I can tell from the sketches."

Antonia bent to take the lemon polenta cake from the oven, glad Honey couldn't see her face. Surely he wouldn't have… he had never asked to sketch her, although she'd been aware of him drinking her in with his eyes while they made love. No, it wasn't possible. She tried to make her voice light. "He showed you some sketches?"

"He didn't have to," Sara said, "they're all over the wall next to his workspace."

Antonia gripped the tin more tightly and stood, resting it on the stove top while her heart beat at a million miles an hour. They couldn't possibly be right, could they?

"They could be sketches of anyone. Or no one in particular."

"Well I can't be sure about all of them," Honey continued, "but the woman in one is definitely wearing that skirt of yours with the poppy fabric... and not much else. To be honest, Mum, it was a bit embarrassing. I wish you'd told us." The betrayal of trust was so unexpected, so huge, Antonia was struggling to digest it. She swallowed hard, the image of Geoffrey bursting into the bedroom while she desperately tried to cover herself coming unbidden to her mind. But this was worse, far worse. This was deliberate, not some mortifying blunder. Vincenzo had sketched her without her knowledge – and put the images in his studio for anyone to see.

All the same, a part of her found it hard to believe this

kind and thoughtful man would really do something so awful. Antonia wanted to see the sketches herself before saying anything, but making it happen wasn't as easy as it sounded. Sundays had a strict routine which saw Vincenzo come to Vila Maslina to talk with the guests, then he and Damir took them to Korčula Town. This time Honey and Sara would be going as well, and that left Antonia free, but not at a time Vincenzo would be at the studio. Her only chance was to hope he returned home for lunch so there would be a window of opportunity before Damir brought the guests for their practical induction at half past two.

But it wasn't to be. When Antonia drove up to the studio at half past one, Vincenzo's motorbike wasn't there and she guessed he was lunching in town. Shielding her eyes from the light and pressing her nose against the glass, she tried to peer through the windows, but although she could make out some sketches pinned at his work area they were too far away to see properly. She would just have to hope they weren't recognisable to anyone other than her daughter.

Why was it down to her to hope? She wasn't the one in the wrong; Vincenzo should not have done this. It was an abuse of trust to a massive degree. Turning away from the window, Antonia found she was shaking; it was her body, and even if they were sleeping together he had no right to use her. No right at all. There was no way she would give him the opportunity to do it again and just as soon as she could get him alone she'd tell him so, in no uncertain terms.

Wednesday was Honey and Sara's last day, and Sara still wanted to see something of the island, so straight after breakfast Antonia loaded a picnic and some beach towels into her car and set off down the drive. She had had no time at all to get up to Vincenzo's studio, and she was still upset with him. Over the last few days, the fact that without him the girls wouldn't be here had taken the edge off her anger, and she clung to the thought that perhaps there had been some mistake, or he had at least taken the sketches down before the guests arrived in his studio. Yet it was gnawing away at her and she wanted to find time to address the matter before they all met for a farewell dinner that night.

Damir had suggested they visit one of the small sandy beaches on the southern side of the island. It was tucked at the end of a long inlet, so protected by the shrubs and trees on either side it almost appeared to be a lake. The water was as clear as a mountain stream, the dark shapes of the rocks that edged it in stark contrast to the pure white sand beneath. The waves rippled so gently they couldn't resist stripping off and running straight in, the cove ringing with their laughter as they splashed each other under the cloudless sky.

Afterwards they sat in the shade of an old holm oak, cicadas chirping around them and the warm breeze drying the salt onto their skin as they ate their picnic. Honey's tan was almost as golden as Antonia's own, but Sara, much fairer, complained she was little more than off-white.

Honey reached over the rug and hugged her. "I love you just as you are."

Antonia seized the moment. "So," she asked, "how did

the strategy of two days chill, two days talk go? Am I right in thinking you didn't need to call in the cavalry?"

"You are so right, Mum. It turns out what we needed was time together. We hadn't really realised there wasn't any. You see, when you were around you did so much for us we had all the time in the world."

"I spoiled you, you mean."

Sara squeezed Antonia's hand. "Yes, you did. But you also knew when it was time to give us space to see how we would cope on our own."

"I think fate intervened there. If Damir hadn't been looking for a housekeeper... but it's all worked out for the best."

"And when you come back we're going to take turns with everything," said Sara.

"But it won't be for long," Honey chimed in. "We have a proper financial plan so we should be able to start looking for a house in the New Year. And Sara's seen a few better paid jobs advertised and I'll get a rise in January so that will help. It's all worked out." She looked so proud of herself, as though it had all been her idea, and when Antonia caught Sara's eye it was all they could do not to burst into fits of giggles.

All the same, Honey was growing up, moving on. The fact the girls had resolved their own problems underlined that, and although Antonia was delighted for them there was no doubting the tiny hole in her heart. Lying on the sand, in the dappled sunlight beneath the oak, it occurred to Antonia that instead of running neatly parallel, from now on her and Honey's lives would diverge and converge, like train tracks from a junction. Her daughter was certainly ready for it – but was she?

They lounged on the beach far longer than they intended, then had to rush back to Lumbarda where Antonia left the girls to get ready and pack for the morning, before heading to Vincenzo's studio. Her palms were sweating as she parked in front of the plate-glass windows and Vincenzo emerged, brushing a thin film of white dust from his arms.

"*Mia cara,* what a lovely surprise. What brings you here?" He moved to kiss her on the lips but Antonia stepped away.

"Honey says you have some sketches of me in the studio and I'd like to see them."

He shook his head. "Of course. But I am so stupid. It was meant to be a surprise. I should have taken them down but was absorbed working on the piece and I didn't think... Come, anyway."

He put his arm around her shoulder and guided her to his workspace. The urge to pull away was strong and she had to keep reminding herself it was best to deal with this in a calm and adult manner. However she felt – and whatever he had done – they had to work together in future, because if they couldn't it would make life incredibly difficult for Damir.

The lump of stone was barely formed, but behind it were half a dozen sketches of a naked woman. Antonia recognised herself immediately from the faded Caesarian scar on one of them. And of course the skirt. The skirt anyone would know was hers. And the gold chain she wore around her neck, the fall of her hair... Even without a hint of a face... This was far worse than she had ever imagined and she was choked with anger, although she was determined not to show it.

She moved away from Vincenzo. "Please take them down before anyone else sees them. It's bad enough Honey recognised me..."

"I am sorry for that, but it was only because she knows you so well. No one else..."

"Take them down. Please." Her fingernails were digging into her palms.

He shoved his hands into his pockets but he nodded. "And how do you feel about the finished piece? Are you allowing me to continue?"

Allowing him? If it was a question of allowing then he'd have asked in the first place.

"My work... it's pretty figurative, you know," he continued. "No one would ever be able to tell who the model was, but all the same I can't understand why you are so ashamed of your beautiful body."

This was just too much. Making it sound as though she was making a fuss about nothing. She had spent days worrying about this when she should have been enjoying herself with the girls. Something inside Antonia snapped.

"I am not ashamed of it, not one bit. But it is *my* body, and you should have asked."

She turned on her heel and stalked across the room, determined to leave on that parting shot. But tonight was the girls' leaving party and she didn't want to spoil it...

And she would have to see Vincenzo again tomorrow, and the next day… and there was Damir to consider as well…

She hesitated, and in that moment Vincenzo was behind her, wrapping his arms around her and nuzzling the back of her neck.

"I am so, so sorry. Believe me, Antonia. I will remove all the sketches and lock them away. It was meant to be a surprise for you, that was all."

He was trying to make it right, although she knew inside the damage had been done.

She twisted around to face him, taking a deep breath. "Thank you. I don't want this to come between us. I want us still to be friends."

He stroked her cheek. "Friends in the way we are?"

No, Antonia wanted to scream, *a thousand times no,* but she kept her voice calm. "I think, perhaps, this is not the best moment to discuss it," she told him. "I need to go and get ready. I'll see you at Pecaros later."

There was no time to deal with her emotions – barely time to shower and change – but once she had done so, Antonia found Damir in the courtyard with a mug of coffee and a cigarette. Realising how badly she needed to share his moment of calm she sat down, moving her chair away from the drifting smoke, and asked him how his day had been.

Immediately he stubbed out the cigarette. "Sorry, I am sorry."

"It's OK."

"It's not. I need to give up, but the more I smoke the harder it gets."

"You could give your cigarettes to me to look after so it's not so easy to just light up."

He shook his head. "You wouldn't like me searching your bedroom at three in the morning."

"Really? You smoke in the middle of the night?"

He waved his hand. "I'm joking, I'm joking. We should go now or we will be late."

They followed the path around the shore, every valley and tree on the hills on the mainland opposite brought into sharp relief by the evening sun. Music drifted from the villas, and they stopped to watch two fishing boats slip out of the harbour.

"I will meet Ivica with his catch in the morning," Damir said. "You'll be taking the girls to the catamaran."

"I know. It's gone too quickly."

"You will miss them."

"That doesn't even begin to cover it, but I've done it before and I'll live. At first it will feel as though a limb has been ripped off, but it will settle down after a while. Life goes on."

He put his hand on her arm. "Yes, because it has to, it does."

After that he was quiet, but once they were settled in the restaurant the polished, charming Damir reappeared, pouring wine, telling stories, making everyone laugh. At one point he went outside to smoke and Sanja had a few sharp words to say to him, most of which Antonia did not understand but could guess. She rolled her eyes in Antonia's direction and tutted, muttering, '*glup dječak*', which Antonia translated to herself as 'stupid boy'.

They were late leaving Pecaros as Antonia found herself clinging to every last moment with Honey and Sara, but eventually common sense prevailed and after hugs all around, and saying goodbye to Vincenzo before he jumped onto his motorbike, they walked together through the village.

In front of the church they went their separate ways, and when Damir kissed Honey and Sara on both cheeks Antonia was a little sad they hadn't seen the real man she was coming to know. All right, so that man wasn't as perfect as the front he put on, but he was warm, and kind, and despite the vulnerability which came from his troubled past, in so many small ways had become her rock. And she his, she hoped.

As they began their silent walk down the hill to Vila Maslina he put an arm around her shoulder and Antonia realised just how privileged she was that he had let her behind his mask.

"Thanks, buddy," she whispered.

He gave her a squeeze. "I am here for you. We are friends."

Chapter Nineteen

It was all Damir could do not to yawn as, for the guests' sake, he pretended to inspect the trail of ants snaking across the courtyard of the converted barn on the outskirts of Zrnovo. This was the countryside, and he was not God, but all the same these idiots expected him to control the insect life. He told them he would buy some spray from the mini-market on the main road.

After a run of stifling days and nights it was a little cooler so he decided to walk through the winding streets. He was hardly walking anywhere these days. And eating far too many bad foods with Antonia's rich cooking. It occurred to him this could be contributing to his lack of sleep so he resolved to buy some salad as well as the ant powder.

The produce was not as good as he would find at the market in Korčula but he had no time to go there as well. He picked up tomatoes, peppers, then reached for the last lettuce at almost exactly the same time as an elderly lady.

Naturally he stepped back and let her have it, and she thanked him. But he was not in Zrnovo, and it was not a lettuce. It was not even his hand: *he was watching his mother reach out to an almost empty shelf for the last cabbage before somebody snatched it away.*

She turned to him, dark eyes troubled. "Do not worry, Damir, that lady must have needed it more than we do. We have plenty of food at home."

Despite the air conditioning in the store, the sweat trickled down his back. For a moment Damir thought he was going to throw up, but he took an enormous breath, put a head of chicory into his basket and made his way to the till, reaching almost the front of the queue before realising he had forgotten the ant poison. His skull was pounding, but he made it around the store again, managed to pay without a fumble, then stepped into the sun.

There was a low wall outside and he dropped onto it. That had been more than a memory of his mother; it had been as though it was happening there and then. As though she'd been standing behind him. The soap she'd used, with its delicate perfume, still lingered in his nostrils. It was bad enough the past was plaguing his nights without it invading his days as well.

After dealing with the ants, Damir parked in a lay-by outside the village, taking a long drink from his water bottle before resting his head on the steering wheel. The tall conical shapes of the cypress trees rose in front of him, their shadows stretching towards the distant sea. Beyond them the land dropped away to the coastal plain, and although Korčula Town was hidden from view, he could just make out the red roofs of Lumbarda. Home. But no longer his sanctuary.

He had fought hard to make this his home too. It had not been easy, when the other children had teased him. The Croatian football shirt Tetka had bought him for his ninth birthday and which he had worn so proudly had made no difference; they had still called him *Bosanac*. But over the years he had shown them; he knew far more than they did about their country's traditions and customs, of the real Croatian life that lingered beneath this modern facade. He was bringing tourists to Korčula to appreciate it; they were waiting tables.

The bubble of pride gathering inside him burst like a pricked balloon. What did it matter anyway? He had done all this – and more – but now the past, hidden for so long behind the smoke-distant mountains on the mainland, was seeking him out even here. How long before it defeated him completely? Engulfed everything he had battled for, and washed him clean into the sea. That was by far his biggest fear; that he would cease to be able to cope, to function. Even to exist.

The urge to be at Vila Maslina was strong, although of course it wasn't Tetka in the kitchen, it was Antonia who was making meatballs. The aromas of cinnamon and frying onion, so comforting, so familiar, drew Damir towards the stove. Antonia smiled and levered one of the cooked *polpetta* onto a plate and handed it to him.

"What do you think?"

He blew on it, then took a bite, the warm spiciness all but bringing tears to his eyes so he closed them, as if considering. "Perhaps a little more oregano, but otherwise perfect."

"As good as Tetka's?"

Still, tears stung behind his lids. "Almost."

Antonia's hand was warm on his arm. "Damir, what's wrong?"

He pulled away and rubbed ferociously at his eyes. "It's nothing. I think some ant powder may have blown into them and they itch, that's all."

She picked up her wooden spoon and began to stir. "It wasn't because I mentioned Tetka, was it? I thought perhaps I'd struck a raw nerve. You don't really seem yourself at the moment."

So she'd noticed. She cared. But even if he could find the right words he couldn't trust her anymore. Not while she was so close to Vincenzo. But all the same… to lie and say that everything was fine seemed wrong. He needed to put her off the scent.

"It's guilt. I should take flowers to Tetka's grave, but somehow I do not go." At least a credible reason had popped into his head.

"Would it help if I came with you?"

He shrugged. "It would mean I had no excuse."

"Where is she buried? The church doesn't seem to have a graveyard."

"No. The cemetery is the other side of Korčula Town."

"We can go on Wednesday; buy some flowers on the market first. How does that sound?"

"You don't want to spend your free time with Vincenzo?"

Antonia walked over to the windowsill and picked some leaves from the oregano plant. "No, not really."

"And is there a reason?" Damir asked, as casually as he could.

"This is so difficult. I know Vincenzo's your friend…"

Hope. A tiny grain of hope. "But you are my friend too. A very dear friend. You can trust me. Tell me what's wrong."

"I know I can trust you, but I don't want to make things awkward with Vincenzo because we both have to work with him. I was so stupid – I should never have let this start. I should have learnt my lesson about not mixing business with pl— Well, you know…" A blush rose up her neck.

"If you want to finish with Vincenzo then you must do it. I will not have him making you unhappy."

"I know I must. But I'm still worried it might make things awkward."

Damir pulled himself up to his full height. "I will not permit that to happen. If he makes problems then I will talk to him."

Antonia was smiling. Right to her eyes, and right at him. He just hoped that if push came to shove he could be good to his word. Much as he did not want their affair to continue for personal reasons, in business terms there might well be fallout he would find it hard to manage right now. But Antonia was speaking again.

"I'd like to think it will not come to that, but thank you for understanding. And it will be an honour to visit Tetka's grave with you on Wednesday. It's the very least I can do to thank you for making this so easy for me."

The last time Damir had driven up this dusty road was for Tetka's funeral, but then it hadn't been dusty, because it had been deep in the winter. In the days since he had committed to visiting her grave he had begun to wonder if somehow it would help, and although he was nervous, in a strange way he was almost looking forward to it.

It was only as he reached into the back seat for the extravagant bouquet of deep-purple velvety roses with toning alstroemeria he had bought from the florist, that he realised he had nothing to put them in. Already he had failed Tetka; he had got this one thing he could still do for her wrong. but he turned to see Antonia pull a vase and a bottle of water from the boot, explaining she had grown up taking flowers to her grandfather's grave so knew exactly what they would need.

Tetka's resting place was marked by a plain wooden cross with a small metal plate for her name. He knew straight away it was not good enough, and Damir told Antonia that at the end of the season he planned to organise a proper monument. A big one. An impressive one. One suitable for a Marić. Tetka had been so precious to him that he was determined she would have the best he could afford, cut from beautiful local stone that everyone would admire.

Antonia set the plain glass vase she'd found in the back of

the larder onto a level patch of earth and filled it with water, while Damir stripped the excess leaves from the stems. Most of the other graves had chrysanthemums growing in pots so perhaps cut flowers weren't right; but he knew stripping the leaves was; he remembered Tetka teaching him when he was so small he'd had to stand on a stool to reach the kitchen table. She had always grown ranunculus and marguerites to grace their home. She'd said it was good to have beautiful things to look at, and that nothing was more perfect than nature. The memory made Damir smile and he shared it with Antonia.

"Perhaps you don't need to visit the grave so often when you put fresh flowers in front of her picture every week."

He crouched to arrange the roses in the vase. "No. Because she isn't here. If she's anywhere, she's there, looking after Vila Maslina."

"Keeping an eye on you." There was a laugh in Antonia's voice and he looked up, smiling.

"She always did." In just the same way Antonia always had the knack of saying the right thing to make him feel better.

Suddenly he had an idea about how to thank her. "Come, if we drive a little further there is something that will interest you. You ask always about cooking *peka* and my friend has a restaurant nearby and it is the right time of day."

As they parked next to row after neat row of vines tumbling down the hill towards the sea, woodsmoke drifted towards them from a covered terrace. On seeing Damir, the chef, Jakov, stepped forwards and embraced him, telling him it had been far too long, and he would be delighted to show Antonia how to make *peka*.

They stood by a long metal table stationed next to the outdoor oven. Damir watched the look of fascination on Antonia's face as Jakov placed cuts of lamb in the round metal dishes, then chopped potatoes, peppers, and carrots before throwing them on top with a juggling flourish that made them all laugh. He kept up a constant stream of commentary, which he could tell by the questions she was asking Antonia understood perfectly, and Damir glowed with pride at how much she had learned.

She expressed surprise when the dishes went under their bell-shaped lids in the oven without any liquid and Jakov explained that the wine was added later. And talking of wine… he led them to a spot beneath the jumbled stone wall that supported the terrace where two sofas had been placed under an olive tree, and brought them a glass each, his own he told them proudly, before disappearing back to work.

Antonia looked at her watch. "It's only eleven in the morning."

Damir winked at her. "It's only one glass."

She raised hers to chink against his. "To friendship! *Zivjeli*!"

It was a rare moment of peace.

Chapter Twenty

It was unusual for a guest to book in for two weeks, and even more novel for them to arrive by car. Damir and Antonia had been playing guessing games about Declan Walsh, but his email address had given nothing away. Their ideas ranged from a retired gentleman on a grand tour of Europe to a hippy art student, and they reckoned the latter was more likely, given he was taking the sculpture course in his second week.

Walsh was, in fact, neither young nor old. Damir didn't see him arrive so met him after Antonia had settled him on the terrace with a beer in hand, and a plate of olives and her homemade cheese melts next to him. He was leaning back, long jean-clad legs stretched outwards, resting the glass on his stomach. His eyelids were closed so Damir hesitated, but he must have heard him because he turned his head and looked at him with eyes so green he had to be wearing contact lenses.

"Welcome to Vila Maslina. I'm Damir."

Walsh stood to shake his hand, half a head taller. "And I'm Declan. It's a beautiful place you have here." There was a hint of Irish lilt in his accent.

"Thank you. You like your room?"

"It's perfect. So peaceful. Although I guess if there's a late party on the terrace it won't be."

With his black rock band T-shirt and unruly sandy hair Declan looked as though he would be in the thick of any party, but all the same Damir said, "You'll find some earplugs in the drawer of the bedside table."

Declan grinned at him. "No need. I never travel without my own."

Antonia appeared through the French doors. "Great, you guys have met. Damir, can I get you some lemonade? A coffee?"

"Coffee would be good."

"Another beer, Declan?"

"No, I'm fine thanks. Now I know where the honesty bar is I can look after myself."

They sat in silence until Antonia came and went with Damir's coffee and a slice of fruitcake. It didn't escape his notice that the Irishman gazed after her.

Declan popped a cheese melt into his mouth. "You've found yourself one hell of a cook."

The way Declan had looked at her had absolutely nothing to do with her skills in the kitchen, but Damir still trotted out his usual line."Antonia's my housekeeper. We say I made the house, but she makes it a home."

"Very neat. She sounds English so how come she's working on Korčula?"

It was more than neat. It was the absolute truth and Damir felt as though he would burst with pride when he said, "She came here to work for me."

Declan took another sip of beer and picked up an olive. "Your own?" he asked, gesturing towards the trees.

"Sadly no. Last year our crop went for oil, but I hope this year will be different and we will press the olives here. It depends on the harvest, but I would certainly like to see a Vila Maslina label on some of our own products."

"What sort of things?"

"Soap, polish. My aunt used to make them to use herself, but naturally I'd take them up a scale. And if the fruit is good enough, then jars of olives too." He just hoped he could find the energy to do it all, because shortly after the harvest Antonia would be going home. How on earth would he manage it all without her?

"Sounds cool. I'd certainly appreciate a jar of these olives as a souvenir. They're awesome."

There was something infectious about his easy manner and overcoming the wave of exhaustion that swept over him, Damir asked Declan what sort of holiday he was hoping for.

"Peace and relaxation. My job can be bloody stressful so I thought, you know, chill for a week then once my mind has slowed down enough to take it in, try something new."

"You've never sculpted?"

"Nope."

"You draw, sketch?"

"Not an artistic bone in my body. But I like a challenge."

Teaching someone from absolute scratch would be a

new experience for Vincenzo, and this guy didn't seem the type to hang on his every word. Damir grinned, then went on to ask Declan how he planned to spend his first week.

"Initially, sleeping."

Damir laughed, but Declan carried on.

"No, I mean it. You know when you're so shattered you can't think straight and everything crowds in on you? This holiday hasn't come a moment too soon, I can tell you. But after a few days I want to get out and about, explore the island. Hike a bit in the hills. I guess you know some good trails?"

Damir knew exactly what he meant about feeling shattered, but there was no way he would ever admit it. Instead he smiled at him. "It would be a pleasure to help you to discover the secret places of my beautiful island." And it wasn't just his normal tourist-speak; there was something eminently likeable about Declan that made him mean it.

As he strolled through the dining room on his way to collect the other guests from the catamaran, Damir began to realise that part of the reason he felt so comfortable with Declan was his openness about his failings. And if that was a good thing in someone else, why was he so scared to admit his own? Declan had probably never been laughed at, and that made all the difference. In front of Tetka's picture he paused to deadhead a flower. Strength was what she had taught him and strong was what he needed to be.

Damir had been ready to tease Antonia about the way Declan had looked at her but she wasn't in the kitchen, and when he spied a hatchback with Bosnian plates as he walked towards the people-carrier he jumped in, slammed it into gear and sped down the drive.

The tiny flag on the numberplate was not even the same one he remembered as a child; that had been red and this one was yellow and blue with a slash of white stars, so there was no reason for it to stir him up. It was not even the flag they had been taught to recognise at school. Or rather, the flag Damir had refused to recognise.

Damir had not wanted to learn about Bosnia & Herzegovina or its war. How could it be history when his own father had died in the fighting? So he had shut his ears and instead made drawings of animals and flowers. When he'd been small it had been tolerated by the teachers, although it had been another reason for some of the children to make fun of him.

And he saw, just for a moment, in a corner of his mind, a tattered old red flag wrapped around the body of a soldier, with his boots sticking out at impossible angles. The colour of the flag did little to disguise the blood seeping onto the paving stones... Damir's hands slid on the steering wheel and nausea burst through him. He pulled onto the verge next to a vineyard just in time.

Had they wrapped his father in a flag when he died? Damir saw his boots on the doormat of their apartment. Black, shiny, but worn down at the heel and the laces frayed. When he opened his eyes it was no different; he could not make them go away. So many dead soldiers, and for what?

He knew he must not think about this now. Nor let dead soldiers' boots haunt him, although Damir feared they would return in his dreams. He needed to be on the quay when the catamaran came in, a welcoming host. The man you would want to meet when you arrived in a foreign land. A strong, capable man. Somehow he had to find him in the last few minutes of his drive.

Declan was true to his word; it almost seemed as though he did sleep for a couple of days. He missed breakfast, and Antonia gave him tea and toast when he emerged late in the morning, then found him dozing on the sofa with a book over his nose.

Much as Damir liked the man, he was eaten away with envy. Damir's nights were more than broken, and he'd had to buy some tablets to make sure he didn't fall asleep at the wheel. He woke at two in the morning, wondering what had happened to Dusa, his cat. He needed to know with a strange urgency, but he could not remember. After smoking a cigarette to help him to sleep he curled under his sheet, but all he could see were the labyrinthine corridors of the shelter. *Paint peeling from the walls and sticking to his clothes, the stench of sweat and worse around him as he searched and searched until, not even knowing what he was looking for, his fingers closed around a dead mouse with the longest tail he had ever seen, its putrid flesh oozing between his fingers.*

At first light, Damir went for a swim but rather than invigorating him it sapped his last reserves of energy so he resorted to setting his alarm for eight thirty and snatching a few hours, which was barely enough. He told Antonia he was fine, but there was disbelief in her eyes and he felt guilty about lying to her. Much as he wanted to tell her the truth, Vincenzo had said something that had made him think she hadn't finished with him yet. And anyway, when he returned she was serving Declan a late breakfast on the terrace.

Damir could have followed Antonia into the kitchen, but Declan asked him about hiking on the island. Damir told him it was perhaps too hot, but he said now that he was refreshed he would set off early. So Damir suggested he took the first bus from the village to Korčula Town then walked across the island through the vineyards to Rasohatica, with its peaceful, sheltered beach. Even if he stopped in the old town for breakfast before he left he should be there not long after nine o'clock, and after Declan had enjoyed a swim either he or Antonia would drive over to collect him. It wasn't a long walk back to Lumbarda, but there was little shade in the vineyards and scrub, and Damir was afraid Declan's fair skin would burn.

Because Declan chose to go on Wednesday, Damir decided to drive to Rasohatica himself. He loved the quiet beaches on the seaward side of Korčula, away from the glowering hills on the mainland. He had fond memories of Petar's father bundling them into his car to leave them there all day on summer Saturdays to swim, and play, and jump off rocks. Right now, when his nights were filled with a past he would rather forget, even those innocent, carefree memories made Damir feel tired and old.

When he arrived he couldn't see Declan on the strip of sand so decided to swim. The beach was at the end of an inlet so Damir ploughed towards the open sea and back, the salty freshness of the water coursing through him, and by the time he'd finished Declan was standing on the shoreline, damp shorts clinging to his legs.

"Good morning, Damir," he called. "I thought it was you zooming around out there like some sort of fish."

Damir shook the droplets of water from his eyes. "Sorry. I didn't see you."

"Aw, I'm not much of a swimmer so I stuck to the edge. Where I grew up there were only about three days a year you'd want to venture anywhere near the sea, although I still miss seeing it."

They walked up the beach together. "So where are you from?" Damir asked.

"Ireland. Place called Donegal. It's the arse end of nowhere, but it's very beautiful all the same."

"I think perhaps your home is always beautiful."

"And you and I are very lucky to have homes."

Declan said it with such conviction Damir asked him what he meant.

He shook his head, laughing. "It's my personal crusade. I've worked with refugees all my life. But for God's sake don't ask me how it started, because I couldn't tell you."

They sat in the shade of a tree at the back of the beach to dry, sipping water from their bottles. It seemed polite to ask Declan more about his work.

"At the moment I'm seconded to a housing project in Sarajevo. Very rewarding, but oh so political. That's what's been stressing me out. I just want to get the job done but every decision takes almost forever. It's practically impossible to make any meaningful progress and there are so many displaced people. Not just those arriving from Syria as we speak, but folks who have been without a proper home since the war in the 90s. Imagine! Twenty-five years... that's half a lifetime."

Damir murmured how sad it was, but he did not want this conversation about Bosnia & Herzegovina and its war. *Shattered walls and blank windows pressed into his eyelids and the distant crump of guns filled his head. Only the shelter was safe. He must get to the shelter...* But Declan was saying his name and as he came back into focus Damir found himself removing his hands from his ears.

There was a short silence, then Declan asked Damir how old he was.

Sranje. How had he known? Had he said something out loud to give himself away? His heart was pumping at the base of his throat, words he did not want to say spewing from his mouth. "Almost five when the war started. Six when I came here to live with my aunt." He managed to recover himself and shrugged. "For me it was over quickly."

"But it isn't over, is it?"

Shut up. Shut up, you stupid Irish bastard. "How the hell do you know?"

Damir hadn't meant it as a question, but Declan replied. "I see it sometimes. Not often, but I do. In all sorts of people. When there's a trigger..."

Damir stood up and pulled his polo shirt over his head. "It's time we were heading back. I have work to do."

Declan nodded. "Sure. Just remember, you're not alone."

Of course he was alone. What a ridiculous thing to say. The man pretended, but he knew nothing. Nothing at all. And worse, they would be stuck in a car together for the best part of half an hour. Sweat pooled on Damir's back. What if Declan mentioned it again? He couldn't exactly put him out on the side of the road, much as he wanted to. And then… inspiration. Without even waiting for Declan to do up his seatbelt, Damir punched Petar's number into his phone and talked volubly and determinedly all the way back to Lumbarda.

Chapter Twenty-One

It was becoming increasingly difficult for Antonia to convince herself she wasn't avoiding Vincenzo. It had been ten days since their awkward discussion in the studio and nothing further had been said, but she wasn't entirely sure he'd got the message. And being fair to him, the message hadn't exactly been clear. A couple of nights ago his fingers had brushed the length of her arm as he'd asked if she was coming over, but then Damir had appeared, complaining they were running out of beer because Declan was drinking too much.

His moaning had been completely unfounded as far as Antonia could see, but it had become patently obvious Damir did not like the man. He had never taken against a guest this way before and his thinly veiled animosity was unprofessional and verged on the embarrassing. As a result, Antonia found herself compensating for his behaviour; in fact, she was putting the strong teabags Declan favoured into a pot when Damir arrived at the kitchen door.

"I am sorry. I need something... from the attic in your room. I can find it?"

Antonia thanked her lucky stars she was not like Honey, leaving her dirty underwear strewn across the floor. "Of course," she told him. He nodded his thanks then disappeared.

She discovered what he'd fetched when she crossed the hall to the dining room to put slices of melon on the buffet. Next to the flowers beneath Tetka's picture a black and white photograph of a man in army uniform had appeared. Balancing the plate across her arm, Antonia picked it up; it had to be Damir's father – he had the same straight nose and wide cheekbones, although his lips were thinner. He was young too, and it suddenly struck her that he was probably only around Damir's age when he died.

Antonia shuddered. She had long recognised that young men cut down was one of the tragedies of war, but somehow standing in front of this picture it was frighteningly real. She set the photograph carefully back next to the flowers, wondering why Damir had brought it out today but when she found him in the courtyard he simply shrugged, telling her it was Victory Day and Tetka had always done it, then returned to tapping on his phone. She wanted to ask him more but shortly afterwards he disappeared back to the press house until it was time to take the guests to Vincenzo's.

When Antonia returned to her room to collect her bag to go shopping, the door to the attic was slightly ajar. She was about to close it when she remembered the argument she and Damir had had about her going in there. She couldn't resist a peep inside and sure enough there was a box she hadn't seen before next to her suitcases. But tempted as she was, what was in there was nobody's business but Damir's so she shut the door and ran back downstairs.

She was not the only one who was curious about the picture in the hall. In the lull between dinner and Vincenzo beginning his talk, Antonia was in the kitchen when she overheard a lady guest asking Damir about the photograph. She didn't catch his reply, but the woman was effusive about how like his father he was, then asked if he lived on the island too. Antonia gripped the handle of the frying pan she had just lifted from the draining board, but then Declan's voice filled the silence, teasing that she was thinking he'd be about her age, and asking if she was after a holiday romance. It was only when their voices faded down the hall that she released her fingers to put the pan in the cupboard.

When she turned around, Damir was behind her.

"Are you OK?"

"Do you know how many times you ask me that?"

"Do you know how many times you don't answer?"

He nodded. "I should have expected questions. Perhaps next year I will not do it, but all the same it would have been Tetka's wish."

"Did she talk about him?"

"She said he was a hero. I guess she had more memories than I do."

"I expect as a soldier he was away a lot, even before the war."

He frowned. "Sometimes. Maybe. I don't really know.

Anyway, I am meeting Petar for a drink. You do not need me here?"

Antonia smiled at him. It was rare he took an evening off and some downtime would do him good. "I think I can manage. Have fun."

As she watched Damir cross the courtyard and disappear into the dusk, it occurred to her that his slow gait and hunched shoulders were anything but those of a young man heading for a night out. He had been far from himself in recent days – one moment irritable, the next withdrawn – but perhaps it was down to Victory Day and the memories it must be stirring. If it was upsetting him so very much, she hoped the photo of his father wouldn't have to stay on display for very long.

Antonia finished in the kitchen then went to check the honesty bar, surprised but rather pleased to find Declan sprawled across one of the sofas, browsing a book on the flora and fauna of Dalmatia.

"You're not listening to Vincenzo's talk?" she asked.

"It's probably incredibly rude of me, but I am really not interested in art history. And I figure as I'm on holiday I can cut myself some slack."

"That's what a holiday's all about." Antonia opened the fridge to see what she needed to load into it for the evening's drinking.

"Tell me, was Damir all right earlier?" For a moment she didn't know what to say, but he carried on, "About his dad's picture?"

"You deflected the questioning very well." Antonia

stood and turned to face him. "How did you know it was necessary?"

Declan swung his long legs onto the floor. "Perhaps I shouldn't say, but from the way you phrased your question I guess you know something about his issues. The fact is, Damir and I had a bit of a chat when he met me from my walk. Well, I say chat, but it was rather one-sided."

"What happened?"

"I was talking about my work and something I said triggered him, but although he admitted he'd been a small child in the war in Bosnia that was as far as it went."

She sat down next to him, conscious of how close she was when she caught a hint of his distinctive sandalwood aftershave. "How do you mean, triggered?"

"I've seen it before. I have a colleague whose brother's body was found in a mass grave in Tomašica. Not just her brother, but his wife and baby daughter as well. And she is fine, most of the time, but there are moments she just isn't in the here and now. When that happened with Damir, given his age, I guessed."

So Antonia had been on the right track about what was wrong, but of course there was nothing she could say to someone they barely knew, despite the fact Declan seemed to understand. "Your lips are sealed," he said, "and that's fine. So are mine. But I did tell him he's not alone, and if he needs help..."

"Thank you." Antonia was staring at the floor between her clasped hands, a knot in the polished boards half hidden by the cream tassels of the rug. It was hard not to be mesmerised by those stunning green eyes, but this was important and she didn't want to be distracted while they talked. "So, is that what you do in Bosnia? Help war victims?"

"In a way. I'm seconded to a housing programme in Sarajevo for a couple of years and although it's so very worthwhile, the politics is a killer. No wonder I'm perpetually stressed." He laughed, running his fingers through his hair. "But all the same, thanks to EU funding and banging a few heads together we have actually managed to deliver 1,400 new homes. Imagine, some of those families haven't had a place to call their own for twenty-five years."

"That's amazing."

He grinned. "More like a bloody miracle. Even I might have said a few Hail Marys when they were finished."

"So you're not the praying type?"

"Growing up so close to the Northern Irish border I learnt it was better not to be religious. And since then, from what I've seen, even if religion doesn't actually cause conflict, it can be a damn good excuse for it."

Antonia settled back onto the sofa. "You must have led a really interesting life."

"Well, it's suited me, but it wouldn't have been for everyone. In the main I've worked with refugees – all over the world. And I loved being at the sharp end; setting up feeding stations, doling out blankets. When you're there on the ground you really feel as though you're doing something to help."

"It sounds to me as though you're helping now."

He sipped his beer. "Yes, but it's different. I spend a bit

too much time behind my desk and on the phone for my liking, but at least Sarajevo is better than being stuck in Brussels sitting on a ton of EU money nobody quite knows how to spend."

"So why did you stop actually working in the camps?"

"Partly it's to do with age and experience. Like any job, you get promoted away from the coalface. And for me it had to happen because I had a nasty dose of malaria in Somalia a few years ago so they won't risk sending me back. You don't want to become a liability when you're the one meant to be helping."

"I guess not."

He stretched his arm along the sofa behind her head. "Well I've jabbered on about me for long enough, what's your story?"

How could anything she had to say be half as interesting as him? But when she glanced at Declan he looked attentive enough. "Nowhere near as exciting, I'm afraid. Or as worthwhile. Married young, had a baby, divorced when she was eight. Did some freelance translating then worked for a travel company to keep the wolf from the door. Then this. My daughter's twenty-two now, finding her own life."

"How can you say you've done nothing worthwhile when you've raised a child?"

Antonia frowned. "I meant in the bigger sense. From a personal point of view there's nothing more important to me."

"You do realise that if every child had the chance to be raised in a proper home like your daughter, the world would have far fewer problems?"

"My daughter didn't have to live through a war."

"Are we speaking generally, or are we back to Damir?"

Antonia was saved from answering by voices in the hall as Vincenzo's talk broke up. "I need to get some more beers and another bottle of wine. It's been really interesting having the chance to talk to you properly."

"You too." Declan stretched. "But if you're busy I may as well go out onto the terrace and be sociable for a while."

They were standing next to each other when the door swung open and Vincenzo's head appeared around it. "Oh, there you are Antonia. Are you coming over later?"

To ask in front of a guest… To imply… Was he deliberately trying to embarrass her, to call her out? It was time she dealt with this once and for all, but now was definitely not the moment. Instead she smiled and shook her head. "Damir's gone out."

"Fine. Then I will see you tomorrow. You too, Declan. I hope you had a relaxing evening, ready to start again." There was an edge to Vincenzo's voice but once he'd gone Declan started to chuckle.

"What is it?" Antonia asked.

"He doesn't think I'm trying hard enough, but I am bloody useless." Declan grinned. "I won't let it beat me though. I'm a tenacious bugger, if nothing else."

Damir's father's eyes seemed to follow Antonia every time she crossed the hall the next morning, which was hardly surprising, because his son was nowhere to be seen and she was becoming increasingly anxious. At eight thirty she phoned Damir, and again five minutes later, but there was no answer. So after making sure everyone's teas and coffees were topped up she ran down the path to the old press house. It wasn't like him not to answer his phone by the second ring and the possible scenarios for it flashed through her head, each more awful than the last. Had he met with an accident? Or worse…? Oh, God, please let him be all right.

The door was closed so she hammered on it, her heart echoing the thud of her fist. There was no reply so she tried calling Damir's name, two, three times, shattering the backdrop of birdsong and cicadas.

His voice came from behind her. "I am here."

Antonia spun around to see Damir sitting on the ground next to the old olive press, wearing a frayed T-shirt and beach shorts. He was pale and his eyes were red rimmed. In two strides she was across the drive and crouching next to him.

"It's OK, I've been swimming," he said. "I do it when I wake early."

"It's coming up to nine o'clock."

"Time... time is doing strange things. Or perhaps I dropped off. I'm just so tired, Antonia, so tired of all this."

Oh God, he was right on the edge. Why hadn't she tried harder to find more time for him, to talk to him? She'd been so preoccupied with bloody Vincenzo… But that was just an excuse; it was Damir who was important. Without him, Vila Maslina would struggle to function, and it would be the end of everything he'd worked for. She could not allow that to happen. She had to do something. Make a difference. She took a deep breath and as calmly as she could she told him, "I think you should see a doctor."

There was a long silence; a stillness in the olive grove when even the birds seemed to stop singing."No, I am not ill," Damir answered finally. "What can a doctor do about nightmares and memories? There is no medicine."

His voice was wrung through with the hollow flatness of despair. It was as though something was shattering inside him, sweeping away the last vestiges of the front he hid behind so well. If the front was all that was holding him together… She tried again.

"But this isn't just nightmares and memories, is it? This is some sort of delayed post-traumatic stress and you need help."

Damir hauled himself to his feet, staggering against the press. "Can you take the guests to Vincenzo's? I need a shower."

"Of course I will, but I think what you need is to go back to bed and rest."

"Perhaps later. Perhaps I should not have drunk so much wine last night." He started to make his slow way across the drive. He was shutting her out, making excuses, hiding again. Tears burnt red behind her eyes; tears for Damir, for his dreams – for his sanity even.

"Damir, please, let me help you. I'll do anything."

He turned at the door. "Antonia, there is something. Put my father's picture back in the box. As soon as you can. Victory Day is over."

Antonia gazed at the photo as she carried it upstairs.

What had happened to this man? And to his wife? Did Damir know? Or was it not knowing that was causing him so much anguish? Antonia stopped, just inside her bedroom door. Had she just had an epiphany, or was it a crazy idea? Could you find out what had happened to someone in a war? She needed to understand more about it and she wondered if perhaps Declan might know.

But that would have to wait. She tucked the picture back inside the lid of the box, grabbed her purse and ran back down the stairs to bring the people-carrier to the front door. Today she needed to do the work of two people. And finally make the status of their relationship clear to Vincenzo. Because if Damir was about to crumble then she needed to pull every available resource together to make sure he didn't take Vila Maslina down with him.

Antonia had been relieved when Vincenzo had agreed to see her that night; after blurting out about them in front of Declan, she had wondered if he was going to start playing games. Much as Damir needed Vincenzo's friendship right now, and much as she was determined to help Damir, she knew sleeping with him to keep the peace was not a price she was prepared to pay. She was worth more than that. And she was going to tell him so.

Vincenzo was waiting for her on the terrace, and had poured her a glass of the Italian Gavi wine she loved before she had even sat down. He leant over to kiss her on the lips, but she pulled away.

"I am sorry, Vincenzo. I haven't come here for… that. I've come here to talk."

"Is that as ominous as it sounds?"

"I… I don't know." It had been so easy when she had rehearsed the words but here under the midnight stars her courage was failing her. For Damir, there was so much at stake.

Vincenzo edged closer along the bench. "Are you sure you want to spoil such a beautiful night? Can't we just sit for a while to enjoy it?"

No – she had to be clear. About what *she* wanted. "Of course we can, but as friends. For me the other side of our relationship is over."

Vincenzo picked up his glass and cradled it in his hands. "For any particular reason?"

As if he didn't know. But this was no time for recriminations and she chose her words carefully. "We said at the beginning it had to be good for both of us and it isn't what I want anymore, that's all. I mean, don't get me wrong, it's been great, but…"

"It's time for us to move on."

"Yes."

He put down his wine and took her hand in his. "Then thank you, *mia cara,* for our wonderful nights together."

"Thank you, too."

He loosened his grip and picked up her glass, wrapping her fingers around it. "Then we shall drink to friendship. *Salute*!"

In the end, it had been easy. She remembered how hard she'd had to try not to stutter or mumble when she had finished with Ned, but looking back, those had been the very first and palest green shoots of assertiveness. She hadn't recognised them at the time and she had almost trampled them underfoot, but somehow they had grown until she had been able to do this. To put what she wanted first, but in such a way that she and Vincenzo were able to remain friends.

Finally, Antonia felt able to relax, and she leaned back against the bench and tipped her head upwards. Through the gaps in the vine the stars were twinkling and the waves were washing the rocks in the cove below. "I don't think I'll ever forget this place," she said.

They sipped their wine, lost in their own thoughts, Antonia's turning to Damir. She'd found time to speak to Lynn about what had happened that morning, and she'd said Antonia's gut reaction of getting him to seek proper help was the right one, but all the same she shouldn't push too hard and close down the channel of communication between them. They'd both had a sense that perhaps Antonia was the only person Damir had even hinted to about his troubles and it felt like one hell of a responsibility, and a lonely one at that.

She turned and looked at Vincenzo; even though Damir was his friend she wouldn't feel comfortable confiding in him. But somehow she knew that if push came to shove, Vincenzo would pitch in and help with whatever needed doing at Vila Maslina. Petar too. She wasn't alone after all. These men who loved Damir had become her friends too. They were loyal and reliable, and together they would do whatever it took.

Antonia couldn't help but remember the first time Damir had brought her to Vincenzo's. It had been the moment she'd begun to feel at home on Korčula. So much had happened since and that feeling was stronger now; she was so much more comfortable in herself and a good part of that came from Damir, from the myriad small ways he had made her feel confident during her first weeks on the island, the difficult days when she had needed it the most. And now it was her turn to repay that debt and do everything in her power to help him.

Chapter Twenty-Two

He was half sleeping, half waking, when his father came to him. He had been listening to his voice for a while, a murmur in the background as he talked to his mother in the other room. Unusually, their conversation had risen to a sharp crescendo, but Damir could not make out the words. He could never make out the words.

He came to him in the darkness, yet Damir knew it should be in the early morning light. He was wearing his uniform and his boots would be next to the front door of the apartment. He could barely see the expression on his face as he told him he was going away, perhaps for a long time. He asked if Damir understood his job was to fight to protect them all and he nodded, but it was only a child's understanding. He was seeing it all from a child's point of view. And as his father leant over to kiss him, he made him promise to look after his mother. He promised him then and he promised again now, but the skin had fallen from his father's face just inches away; a sneering skull, the sweet smell of death.

The snap of a sheet sucking the air from his chest.

Wooden steps. A rug beneath his bare feet sliding on the tiled floor. Night air on his face, then the familiar shape of the cold stone of the olive press was beneath his arms and chest. And, for the first time he could really remember, he sobbed.

For a moment the hand on Damir's shoulder was his mother's, but then he realised it was Antonia saying his name again and again. He felt himself crumble beneath her touch and she sank onto the ground, wrapping her warmth around him as he shivered and wept.

It was when she started to stroke his hair that he began to come back into himself. Tetka had done this too, so many times, so many times when he'd been a frightened child. But now he was a frightened man, because his father had been at his bedside, reminding him of the promise he had broken so many years before. No… no… he couldn't have been there. It was just a dream… It must have been a dream, but the terror of it held him in its grip. He knew it could not have happened, yet he could not rid himself of the feeling it had. Antonia's jumper was soft and warm against his face as he clung to her but he did not dare not look up. Had his mind completely gone this time?

Eventually Antonia disentangled herself enough to drag him up then bundle him into the car. The headlights picked out the yellow hue of the leaves scattered on the cracked earth beneath the olives. Damir closed his eyes. What if he saw his father in the shadows between the trees?

The house slept around them. Antonia made Damir sit at the kitchen table while she fetched him one of her fleeces. He struggled into it, enveloping his chin in her perfume, while she warmed milk on the stove. He ran his hand along the grain of the table, feeling the almond-shaped knot under his palm in the way he had done since childhood, searching for comfort, anything to cling to. But there was nothing. He was adrift in the torrent of his emotions with no foothold to be had.

It seemed an age before Antonia put a mug in front of him and sat down.

"Damir, you have to tell me what happened."

He couldn't. He couldn't say those words. But how could he not say them? He needed to do something, anything, to rid himself of these ghosts.

"I do not know... I do not know... if it was a vivid dream or if my father was haunting me. But he was there, sitting on my bed... and the skin on his face fell away because I had broken my promise." The words rushed out one after the other, but Antonia's response was calm.

"And what promise was that?"

"To look after my mother." He swallowed a sob. Already there had been too many tears. But he had said it, said it out loud.

Antonia held his hand, while Damir searched for more words that might help make sense of the chaos in his mind.

"I do have very real dreams," he ventured. "Especially about the past. The memories... they come to life in the darkness. I used to think the darkness was safe, but not anymore."

"So when did this start happening?"

"It feels as though it has been going on forever, but I know that isn't the case. Perhaps weeks, perhaps months ago... I started to remember the time before I came here. A time better forgotten."

"But it's inside you all the same."

"Fragments only. Sometimes..." But no, he could not tell her about Kemal. He had said too much already. *Retreat. Or try to.* "Sometimes good, and sometimes bad."

"Tell me about the good ones."

"It is too hard."

"Because I am asking the question in English?"

"That I barely noticed."

They sat in silence as Damir sipped the hot milk he did not want. Antonia had made herself a mug of tea and he wanted tea even less. He wanted to be anywhere but here and he certainly did not want to talk about his memories. But the words were pushing up inside him like molten lava – his silence was choking him, burning him – so haltingly he told her about his parents taking him to play in the park.

"Before the war?"

"Yes. In the war the park was..." And he saw the devastation, the shattered branches of the trees, that he had witnessed the day Kemal—

He shook his head. "They are not whole memories."

"Tell me what else you remember that was good."

"When a food parcel contained chocolate. We would share, so only a small piece each, but I can still almost feel its smoothness in my mouth. And in the shelters, we would race toy cars. That was fun. In the shelters... it was where we were safe."

There were tears in Antonia's eyes. "Your good memories are in a shelter?"

"Yes, because outside bad things happened."

"Oh, Damir..."

Damir gripped Antonia's hand as the images crowded in on him and she squeezed his back. Eventually she asked, "And tonight's memory. Was that in the shelter too?"

"No, in my bedroom. Before. My father – you know he was a soldier – he came to say goodbye..." Damir couldn't go on. Tears were streaming down his cheeks but how could they be, because he did not cry. Men did not cry. But he had no way of stopping himself. Perhaps it didn't matter. Perhaps nothing mattered anymore, except the solid wood of the table and Antonia's hand in his.

"Tell me, Damir, you must tell me. Get this awful thing out. Tell me about the promise."

"I broke it. I broke it. Because of me my mother had to go outside and she never came back." He buried his face in the fleece that covered his arms. "Now will you please leave me alone?"

Antonia let Damir cry, and then she took him upstairs to her bedroom, his feet dragging after her with exhaustion. The grey dawn was creeping through the window, and the chirping of the fledgling swallows rose from the courtyard below. She led him to her bed and opened the quilt for him to climb under, before telling him she was going to shower then make breakfast for the guests. Damir said he would help, but she shook her head and he was relieved, uncertain how he would have found the strength. Instead, he curled himself into the tiniest ball and listened for the pulse of the water. But he was asleep before it came.

When he woke, the first thing he did was grope for his

phone, panic filling him when he couldn't find it. Was it back in the olive press, or had he dropped it last night? It was the lifeline of his business and he leapt out of bed, throwing on the trousers and sandals that had appeared next to it, then took the stairs two at a time, the silence of the villa echoing around him.

Antonia was sitting at the kitchen table, the fragrant aroma of *mali tuni* – tomatoes and aubergine – filling the room, just as if Tetka had been cooking. And next to her was Damir's mobile. He sank onto the nearest chair in relief.

"Ah, so this is where I left it."

"No, you didn't leave it. I fetched it from the press house along with your clothes. And you needn't worry because Petar is looking after the maintenance issues and I have replied to the email queries on your behalf. Vincenzo is driving the guests, so it looks as though we have everything covered."

So they all knew. They knew how weak he'd been. The protection he'd so carefully built around himself over the years… all gone in an instant. Damir put his head in his hands. No one would ever respect him again. "And what have you told them?"

"That you are sick. An upset stomach you need to sleep off. Oh, and I fed Marco while I was in the press house, although I have to admit he did seem rather lonely."

Only now did Damir dare to look at her. His secrets were safe. "You are an incredible woman."

She covered his hand with hers. "I am your friend."

He was close to tears again. He had no defences left, but the urge to rebuild them was strong. He needed time. He needed space. He needed the courage to think all this through. He levered himself to his feet, patting his empty pocket for cigarettes. "I must get on."

"There is nothing for you to do. Let me make you some coffee. And maybe something to eat? After all, you did miss breakfast. And lunch."

"Then what ti—"

She stood too. "But did you sleep well? Did you rest? I looked in a couple of times and you were dead to the world."

Damir rolled his eyes. "Thankfully the dead stayed away."

"I was wondering how much of last night you would remember."

"How about every impossibly embarrassing moment?"

"There's no need for you to be embarrassed. You were a small child in a war zone. There are going to be scars."

He sat back down. Maybe, maybe to work this through with someone who had proved themself worthy of his trust? "But why are they coming back now?"

"Perhaps it was the same when you were younger, but you blocked those memories too."

Damir considered. "It's possible. I do remember some things... when I first came here I was nervous around loud noises. And I couldn't get used to the sunshine and sky. I used to hide in the... somewhere dark."

"Oh God, Damir, and you've carried this all your life?"

No, he could not do this. Could not tell her the worst of it. "It has not been all my life. Tetka made me better very soon so I forgot about it all. And I'm OK now. Really, I am

OK. Much better after sleeping, so thank you. Now, just a quick coffee and I need to get on."

Antonia opened her mouth to say something else, but he turned his back on her and strolled into the courtyard, hoping she could not see his nails digging into his palms. She was his friend – he shouldn't lie to her. But some truths were unforgiveable and never to be shared.

The most surprising thing for Damir was that Antonia's demeanour towards him did not change. He had expected her to be wary of him, or worse, pitying; or to treat him like a sick child, but she did none of those things. He marvelled at the fact she knew how weak he was and yet it seemed to make no difference.

In fact, he had the distinct impression it had somehow drawn them closer. She materialised in the press house the next lunchtime bringing octopus salad, and they had a picnic under the olive trees, laughing as they fended off Marco's attempts to steal a succulent morsel. And once again in the evening they sat together in the courtyard while fireflies danced around the lamps, making vague plans to restore Tetka's *peka* oven, which was currently hidden behind the washing machine in one of the sheds. And she had confided in him how hard she'd found it at first, to finish her relationship with Vincenzo, but she had finally done it. And they talked about the freedom that could be found in saying the hardest of words out loud.

As he was walking back through the olive grove Damir

thought about those most difficult of words; about talking about the nightmares when they happened. And talking about the memories. But how could he when they continued to float from corners of his mind at unexpected moments? If he shared each and every one of them with Antonia, they would talk of nothing else.

It was as though the wall he and Tetka had built to hide his past had cracked so it was seeping through. More than seeping. The other night it had been a raging torrent he'd been powerless to stop, and if it hadn't been for Antonia every last part of him would have been washed away. He needed her more than ever, and yet in a few months she would be gone. Then what would happen to his life? To his dreams?

Somehow he had to find a way to move on while she was still here to help him.

Chapter Twenty-Three

Declan's invitation to go for a hike with him came so naturally from their conversation over breakfast that Antonia found she had agreed before she'd even thought it through. It was his last day and he had given up on his sculpture, saying he would rather enjoy his holiday. And despite the fact she would have to race through her morning's work, and he would be leaving tomorrow, Antonia wanted to enjoy some time with him too.

Damir had been less than enthusiastic, telling her rather sharply that it was taking guest relations too far, but rather than start an argument she had simply shrugged and reassured him dinner would be on time. Given Declan knew about Damir's wartime past she could understand his antipathy, but it would be a good opportunity for her to find out what Declan knew about the war in Bosnia and its terrible aftermath, and what records from that time might still exist.

Antonia decided to take Declan into the hills around

Cara, where it might be cooler, and they could go to the spectacular vineyard restaurant she'd visited with Damir for a drink. She wanted the last afternoon of his holiday to be memorable, and if she was honest with herself, she wanted him to remember her too. But this wasn't a date – of course it wasn't – and even though she showered after a morning running around preparing buffet food, her perfume and lipstick remained untouched on the bathroom shelf.

After half an hour on the track through the vineyards, Antonia wondered why she had bothered to shower at all, but the views across the plain towards the sea were spectacular. They paused in the shade of a solitary Aleppo pine to drink from their water bottles and cool off before their route took them back towards the village with its ornate white church tower, then into the blissful shadows of the woods that rose above the red roofs of the houses like a dark green amphitheatre.

Declan was easy company. He told Antonia about growing up in Donegal, his widowed father in his bungalow next to the pub, his sister and her family who had taken over their former home. And memories of fishing trips and kicking a football around, and all the normal childhood things. Antonia talked about Honey, and Sara, and the labour of love that was the reality of living in an old cottage; the birdlife on the nearby shore, and the yachts that crowded the harbour but were never sailed.

Before they knew it they were outside the vineyard. The shaded terrace felt sleepy in the afternoon sun, although they could hear the clatter of cutlery from a kitchen somewhere below. Antonia ordered a glass of white wine, while Declan opted for a beer, the look on the waiter's face when he did so making them dissolve into laughter behind his retreating back.

"Probably not the done thing in a vineyard," Declan said.

"You could even call it a little tactless."

"Yes, but I'm thirsty and anyway, I have to drive back to Lumbarda."

While they waited for their drinks they admired the view towards the sea, a distant sliver of blue just a shade deeper than the sky.

"This is pretty neat," Declan sighed. "I could get very used to it."

Antonia nodded. "I'm lucky."

"You are that. Both to live here and have someone like Damir to show you all the best places. He's so very knowledgeable about the island and a bright young man."

Antonia drew a circle on the tablecloth with her forefinger. This was the moment, but should she say anything? Instinctively she trusted Declan, yet she could never betray Damir's confidences. On the other hand, he might be in a position to help. And if he wasn't, well, he was leaving tomorrow and they would never see him again. The trick would be to tell him just enough and no more. She looked up.

"And a troubled one."

"Yes."

"You said... your colleague... I mean, does anything

help? Has she had any... professional intervention you know of?"

"She's a good talker. She said that after the war she was fine for a long while; everyone she knew had the same experiences so it didn't feel strange, and for her, having lived through conflict and having been displaced herself is a motivator to help others. She's Bosniak but bears no malice to any ethnic group, although she said when her brother's body was exhumed she discovered a lot of anger inside her she didn't know she had. So she took up kick boxing.

"The thing is, Antonia, everyone is different. If you think about it, in Sarajevo I am surrounded by people who lived through that terrible conflict and in the main they are fine and lead completely normal lives. I kind of struggled to fathom it when I first arrived, but I talked to a mate who works in Cambodia and he said it's the same there. Because they all experienced the terror it's become part of the normal background noise."

"So for your colleague it was finding her brother's body that opened the wound. Perhaps for Damir it was Tetka dying."

"I'm no psychologist."

"Me neither. That's the problem." The waiter arrived with their drinks and a dish of olives. Declan thanked him, then looked at Antonia, waiting for her to carry on. "It struck me the other night, although I could be barking up completely the wrong tree, does Damir know what happened to his parents? And if not, would it be a good thing to find out? Would it give him some sort of closure?"

"Or would it push him over the edge?"

Antonia had been in the process of picking up her wine glass, but she put it down again. "I hadn't thought of that." Was it really a good idea to mess with something she understood so little about?

"You are a kind, kind, person, Antonia, but he would have to make that decision himself. Remember, it was a brutal conflict and some terrible things happened."

"It could be that he does know and just doesn't talk about it."

"Then perhaps it's better to let it lie."

Antonia looked sideways at Declan. "But if he did decide he wanted to know, is it possible to find out after all this time?"

"And I thought I was a tenacious old bugger," he laughed.

She grinned back. "That famous Irish charm. Such flattery…"

"Well, if it's flattery you want, then you're a tenacious youngish bugger with just about the most amazing smile I've ever seen. Happy now?"

And despite the fact he hadn't answered her question, and he was leaving the next day, Antonia found that she was. There may be practical reasons they couldn't get together, but at least Declan had shown her that kind, interesting, attractive, single men did still exist.

"I don't know, Damir, perhaps it would do you good to go to Vesna's party. Have some fun."

He helped himself to coffee from the stove, then leant against the sink. "Are you serious? It is August."

"Yes, and her birthday is on Wednesday, so I can cover for you. Even with a lie-in the next morning you'd be back from Dubrovnik by mid-afternoon. I'll look after things here and I'm sure Petar will deal with any urgent maintenance. We've done it before."

"Then it is not right to ask you to do it again."

"You are not asking. I am offering."

He waved his hand. "Pfft! Words. Your twisty English words."

Antonia repeated the phrase in Croatian, leaving Damir momentarily open-mouthed.

"You learn too fast," he said.

"And the party?"

"I will think about it."

He took his cigarettes from his pocket and headed into the courtyard, while Antonia carried on with her Saturday baking. When she glanced through the window he was tapping on his phone and she wondered if he was replying to Vesna. She hoped he would say yes. Perhaps a change really was as good as a rest, and as there was nothing she could do to persuade him to take some downtime, maybe a break from the island and a damn good party would be just the thing.

Her own phone trilled and she smiled to herself. The alert from the Scrabble app told her Declan must have made his next move. She wished she knew more about what his life was like. She'd seen some gorgeous pictures of Sarajevo online but of course he'd lived there a while now and wouldn't be spending his free time wandering around like a tourist. She could picture him in his flat though; she'd had a glimpse of it when they had played a proper game of Scrabble via Facetime on Wednesday night, and before he'd angled his phone over the board she'd caught sight of a couple of well-stocked bookshelves and a collage of photographs on the wall.

The Scrabble games had been his idea and she had been delighted he'd found a way to stay in touch. When he'd hugged her goodbye on the day he left she'd felt genuine affection as he wrapped his arms around her, and she'd found herself hoping he would kiss her. But of course there would have been no point. Sarajevo was six hours' drive away in a different country, and she was going home in less than three months.

But with no expectation came no pressure. Looking back, even though her relationship with Ned had been driven by her loneliness, the moment it started tipping into more than friendship there had been an edginess to it; first from fear of discovery, then from the increasing discomfort of knowing they were doing wrong, and from the small ways he had tried to control her. She hadn't really seen it at the time, but she could now. And as for Vincenzo, well, she'd let Lynn talk her into it in the first place, and although it had been fun, she had never been totally comfortable with that either.

Even so, Vincenzo had proved a good friend and there was no animosity in him. They had simply flipped back to how they'd been before he'd run his fingers over her lips just a few months ago. She felt like a different person now;

one who was beginning to discover what it was she really wanted.

She still missed Honey, of course she did, but it was easier as things had settled down between her and Sara. Her daughter was carving her own life, and so was she. But there was still a huge question mark over what would happen after the end of October. Going home to Honey would be wonderful, but to what else? She would have to start all over again; find a new job, a new life even, once the girls had a home of their own. For so long, home had meant Honey, and she had to face the fact that very soon that would no longer be the case.

The other consideration was how hard it would be to walk away from Damir the way things were. He had helped her so much on her journey, with the encouragement and support he gave so naturally, and now she wanted to be there for him. As she looked out of the window he got to his feet and started to walk across the courtyard waving his phone.

"It seems I have no choice about the party," he told her. "Josip has emailed saying he's delighted I'm going as he has a business proposition we can talk about over lunch when I arrive."

Antonia grinned at him. "Then it is doubly worth the trip. Enjoy it, Damir – you could do with some fun."

In the cool silence of Vila Maslina, Antonia took a glass of lemonade up to her room, stopping on her way to check the beds and bathrooms. Ana had missed one bin so she put it on the landing for later, and a couple of cushions were out of place so she plumped them and set them on their pillows.

Antonia checked her watch. Damir would be more than halfway to Dubrovnik by now, but he had been withdrawn when she'd taken him to the catamaran, she was really worried about him. She hoped he wasn't just going to meet Josip then cry off the party, or worse, sit in a corner feeling miserable all night. Despite Antonia's misgivings about Vesna as a positive influence in Damir's life she knew he looked up to her brother and a good meeting with him should buoy his confidence and hopefully, *hopefully*, he would be in the right frame of mind to have a good time and forget about his troubles for a while.

But even if it was the best party in the world, Antonia knew in her heart of hearts it wouldn't solve anything, and she suspected he did too. But what could he do? What could she do to help him? There must be something. The closed door to the attic under the eaves was just in her field of vision as she sat in her armchair and flicked through a copy of *Good Housekeeping* that a guest had left behind. Only the tiniest of breezes trickled through the open window, carrying with it the familiar background of cicadas and birdsong. For once, Antonia's time was her own, but all she could do was worry about Damir.

If Antonia was wondering how this would ever stop, what must it be like for him? She closed her eyes, but there was no way she could even come close to imagining. Did the box in the attic hold any clues? He hadn't wanted her near it; or at least there was something tucked under the eaves he didn't want her to see. Would knowing what was in there help? Antonia was biting her lip so hard she could taste blood. She could not do it. It would be a massive breach of trust.

Then she remembered the documentary about the war in Mostar she hadn't been able to watch all those months ago. It might at least give her some idea about what it had been like for him. She searched the bookmarks on her iPad with some trepidation, but the time had come for her to know. And this programme had been made during the conflict in 1993, so there would be no air-brushing, no bias of history. This should show her how it had really been.

Within just the first few frames, the level of destruction was terrifying. As the presenter's voice intoned that Mostar had been the most vicious theatre of the war, images flashed across the screen of apartment blocks blown to their concrete shells, burning rooftops and swirling clouds of smoke. It was truly the stuff of nightmares. Damir's nightmares. Women ran along the street carrying shopping baskets as the sound of mortar fire ricocheted around them. How did they find food? What of the very basics of life?

The horror continued, but she forced herself to watch. A man was taken to what passed for a hospital, but he died, leaving his widow weeping and wailing. They looked dishevelled and poor, but before the war she had been an accountant. Everyone was reduced to ragged ghosts, so it made Antonia smile to see one young woman at least had managed to find some lipstick for the cameras. A small, defiant step of normality in a war zone.

The programme was made from a Bosniak point of view

at a stage of the war when they held the east of Mostar against the Croats holding the west. How old would Damir have been then? Five or six? And which side was he living on, with a Croatian father and Bosniak mother? What if they had been on the wrong side? But how could Antonia know which was right and which was wrong?

People had certainly been displaced from their homes. She was reduced to tears at the sight of two elderly women being helped across the divide by their neighbours, having left their every last possession behind in a hail of bullets. Their whole lives abandoned in a moment, only to be looted by strangers. Bad enough to have no roof over your head, no food… but what of those irreplaceable treasures that make up a home? Gifts from their children, photographs of their husbands. Nothing left from their pasts and the most uncertain of futures ahead of them. How could they have even borne it?

But there was more to come. Towards the end of the programme was some murky footage of refugees crossing a no-man's land outside the city after dark, carrying only their children and telling of the slaughter left behind. This was the reality of ethnic cleansing on the ground. Antonia tried to imagine soldiers appearing at her cottage and ordering her and Honey to leave, never to return, but it was an act so evil she could barely comprehend it.

The reporter interviewed some of the women. One was shown only in profile, her face darkened against further intrusion. She had been raped by Croatian soldiers and had expected to be killed. Struggling to breathe and trying not to cry she told the interviewer that sometimes her brain stopped working and she could not think; that she was fighting this battle on her own. What had become of her afterwards? What was her life like now? Antonia could bear to watch no more.

In the silence of the house she walked slowly downstairs, tears streaking her cheeks. She stood in front of Tetka's picture.

"What did you know?" she whispered. "What did you shield him from?"

But as ever, Tetka kept her own counsel.

Chapter Twenty-Four

Damir was lucky enough to find a window seat on the catamaran, but all the same it proved impossible to catch up on his sleep. The thrum of the engines reverberated through his back and into his skull, and the sparkling spray made his eyes ache when he opened them. He was relieved when the wooded slopes of the mainland near Dubrovnik appeared in the distance, and he splashed water from his bottle onto his face then used the rest to wash down two painkillers in an attempt to ease the throbbing in his head.

The quay was rammed with people but Damir spied Josip waiting for him, craning his head and waving from the front seat of his Mercedes convertible. The boot slid open as Damir approached, and he put his overnight bag into it. It closed silently at just the merest touch of his finger.

"Good trip?" Josip asked.

"Honestly? No. Far too crowded, although of course we need the tourists."

"The constant dilemma. I assume none of them have trashed my villas yet?"

"Of course not. Yours are a very select clientele."

"Wealth and good manners do not always go hand in hand." Josip started the engine. "We need to be on our way; we are highly honoured because Vesna has offered to cook us lunch – on her birthday as well. Then we can use her study to talk in private."

Damir had been hoping for a little longer before seeing Vesna, not least because he had no idea why he had been invited, having heard nothing from her since she left the island in May. In her text all she had said was that she needed a presentable partner for her birthday party. And when he'd accepted she'd told him not to book a hotel because he would be staying in her guest room.

It was a short journey from the new port to the smart suburb of Lozica. As soon as they crossed the elegant Franjo Tuđman Suspension Bridge they were on the road behind the villas clinging to the coastline, half-hidden from their view by the luxurious vegetation planted to screen them.

Inevitably, Vesna's house was the most impressive of all. The wrought-iron gates slid open and Josip drew into a courtyard landscaped with cypress and palm trees, in front of what appeared to be a bungalow. But Damir had seen this area from the catamaran and he knew the building would cascade through many levels down to the sea.

Vesna greeted them at the door, resting her arms lightly on Damir's shoulders and leaning in to kiss him on both cheeks.

"I am so pleased you could come, Damir. Your bedroom

is on this floor, so you can drop your bag and freshen up before lunch. Josip will come down with me to make the cocktails."

"Happy birthday, dearest Vesna," Damir said, returning her kisses. "You look radiant as ever."

"And I have not even been to the hairdresser yet. Still, you always did flatter me." She opened the door to a room with tall windows looking out onto its own balcony and an enormous double bed covered with cushions and throws in various shades of green, an oasis in a desert of travertine tiles. Damir made suitably appreciative noises and with the instruction to be no more than ten minutes, Vesna followed her brother downstairs.

Damir had little to unpack. Given there was a white dinner jacket hanging from the wardrobe he guessed he wouldn't be needing his own clothes for the party. He pulled Vesna's birthday present from his bag; a perfectly wrapped bottle of her favourite scented oil, but so far there was no hint whether or not she would expect it delivered right to her skin and the uncertainty was adding to his unease.

Instead of heading to the bathroom, Damir stepped onto the balcony and lit a cigarette. The breeze was coming off the sea, so the smoke should at least drift upwards. He perched on the marble wall and watched two cruise ships cross in front of the long, low island of Daksa. Vesna's was a beautiful villa in a beautiful place, and for the moment at least he was expected to be one of the beautiful people. He'd just have to make sure he could pull it off.

They lunched on the terrace next to a swimming pool

lined with burgundy tiles to stunning effect. Damir exclaimed over it; in fact, he felt as though he had been exclaiming over the whole house – the broad circular staircase that wound through its levels, the glass-walled open-plan living area stretching its whole width, the eclectic mix of modern and antique furniture.

Josip said the same architect had designed his home and he would like to work with her again, but Damir thought nothing of it until they were settled comfortably in the mezzanine study with their coffee, and Vesna had set off for the beauty parlour. Josip came straight to the point.

"I am impressed with you, Damir, now more than ever. You have built a whole new business without your existing one suffering a jot. And I have been keeping an eye on your bookings for Vila Maslina. They are very good."

"Yes, we have been lucky..."

"No, it is because you have read the market exactly right and I wonder, are you interested in expanding further?" Damir remained silent, waiting for him to carry on. Josip swept his arm across the mahogany desk, indicating the villa. "You like this place, don't you? But do you aspire to it yourself? How hungry are you to be this successful?"

At the moment, success seemed like a long-forgotten and far-away dream, but all the same there was only one answer he could possibly give. "Very."

"Then listen to what I propose."

Josip told Damir that having watched the progress of Vila Maslina he had found a suitable property in Korčula Old Town he would like to buy, and wanted to do something similar. But not in competition with Damir; he had no intention of stealing his idea, but with him as his partner. Josip's capital and Damir's expertise. A new company with both of them as directors. Boutique hotels specialising in culture and the arts. If they worked together well, all over Dalmatia. Perhaps, all over Croatia and even beyond.

It was hard for Damir to grasp the scale of the opportunity. It would mean many, many changes to his life. Last year he would have jumped at it, but was he strong enough to handle it now? Would he regret it forever if he turned it down? He absolutely knew he would, but if he took it on and failed? That didn't bear thinking about because not only would it mean public humiliation, but he would also have to accept that he wasn't man enough to make his dreams come true. The way things were at the moment, that was a very real possibility.

His mind whirling, Damir told Josip he was interested but needed time to think. Perhaps to look at the property. A little time to consider branding. All credible business speak, to which Josip nodded and said of course. But was there disappointment in his eyes that Damir hadn't grabbed the riches he was offering, like a kid with a piece of candy?

Once Josip left, Damir went for a swim; not in the pool but diving from the rocks below the villa into the sea. The coolness of the water as he cut through it helped him to focus on the here and now and stemmed his rising panic. He needed to put Josip's proposal to one side for the moment. The most important thing was to find enough resolve to push away the lurking shadows so he could at least try to be the Damir Vesna wanted and Josip clearly expected him to be for the rest of the day. It was going to be a tough ask.

He climbed the ladder to the lower terrace, shaking the droplets from his body like a dog. Vesna was sitting under an umbrella, wearing a brightly patterned sundress, and she raised her tortoiseshell Oakleys to look at him.

"Ah, Damir. Beautiful as ever. I forget when I do not see you for a while."

"So that is why you have not called or messaged me." He pretended to pout.

"No, I have not called because that side of our relationship is over. Although looking at you now I have to say I am just a little tempted to resume it."

"Then I'm in the guest room for a reason, not for propriety." That, at least, was a huge relief.

"Yes. I have a new lover, but he would not feel comfortable in my social circle. You, however, know how to behave."

"Damir Marić, escort services." He gave an over-dramatic bow.

"Damir Marić, my friend – I hope."

"But of course."

She threw him a towel from a pile on the seat beside her. "You will want to shower after your swim. Try on the suit I hired for you as well." She frowned. "I know your size, but I fear you have lost some weight. No matter, we can somehow pin the waistband and it will be hidden by the cummerbund. But it bothers me, because there are lines around your eyes too, that do not come from laughter."

"Perhaps you can recommend some of the creams you use."

"Ha! How can you suggest my beauty is not natural?" It was her turn to pout. "But seriously, my friend, are you sure you're not ill?"

"Of course not. Perhaps a little tired, and perhaps I have tried too hard to lose the extra kilos from Antonia's rich cooking."

"If it is so irresistible you must invite me to lunch at Vila Maslina when I come to Korčula in October. Now go – you are dripping on my terrace."

It was quarter to seven when Vesna nudged open his bedroom door, a glass of champagne in each hand. She set Damir's on the dressing table while he finished tying his bow tie, something he'd been attempting to master with the help of YouTube for the last fifteen minutes. But he must have got it right, because after looking him up and down, all Vesna did was straighten his cummerbund.

She was wearing a shimmering gold sheath dress, which most women of her age would have failed to pull off. Damir took her hand, raising it high above their heads as she twirled.

"Stunning. As ever," he told her. "Clever touch that my accessories match your dress."

"I want everyone to know I have a partner for the night. A young, attractive partner."

"Your boyfriend doesn't mind missing out on the fun?"

"I told you, he would not fit in. And I am taking him to Zagreb for the weekend to make up for it."

"Should he not be taking you?"

She smiled at him. "It will seem that way, but I will be paying. Of course he has offered, but I would not like the sort of hotel he could afford."

"You should be careful..."

"And you sound like Josip. But thank you for caring." She put her hand on his arm. "He is a good man, Damir. He may lack your polish, but he makes me happy."

"Well that is all that matters." Damir raised his glass. "Once again, happy birthday, dearest Vesna."

Vesna had decided to receive her guests at the bottom of the curved staircase. The caterers had transformed the main living area and terrace into an elegant party space, with small tables covered in bronze and gold cloths set around the edges for people to put down their glasses. There was little seating inside apart from the two long sofas so it was clear the idea was to mingle – and perhaps, later, to dance. The lights were low and garlands of twinkling stars festooned the terrace, turning it into a subtle wonderland.

Damir was not only the youngest guest, but he would have wagered he was the only one in a hired suit. Not that it mattered to anyone who he was, and Vesna introduced him as her 'very dear friend' with a suggestive flutter of her eyelashes, and he overheard Josip telling a man tailored in head to foot Savile Row that Damir was someone he hoped to be doing a great deal of business with.

Standing alone in a corner for a moment, Damir looked around. His life could be like this. It was a strange idea but

Josip was prepared to put things he had hardly dared to dream of within his grasp, if only he could find the courage. He could be someone on a larger stage than Korčula and the idea was seductive, but so far outside his comfort zone it was hard to contemplate. For so long the island had been his sanctuary, his refuge. Was he too much of a coward to leave it?

He had always known that part of his desire for material success was to show the children who had laughed at him at school, who had called him *Bosanac*, and thought he was strange, to show them he was the better man. And until recently he had always believed he could do it. But now, just when he was plagued by doubts, he was being offered vastly more and he was surprised how much he found he wanted it. Maybe it was the wine affecting his thoughts, but if Josip believed he could do it, then perhaps he could gather together enough shreds of his tattered confidence to at least act as though he believed it too.

He could not think with all the noise inside and outside his head, so he escaped to the terrace where the chatter of the party was muted, and Josip followed. Damir turned to face him.

"You have given me a great deal to think about, but I am very excited by the opportunity."

"I did not see you as overly cautious, Damir, and I do not think there can be a downside to my proposal."

"Far from it. But let me see the property you have in mind before I give you my final answer. It is important to me we share the same vision, because otherwise it will not work."

"The vision will be yours alone. I am just a simple businessman." Josip rubbed his thumb and finger together. "All I bring to the table is money. And I want to spend it soon."

Was he becoming so insistent because he had drunk too much champagne? Or was he already impatient with Damir's prevarication? Common sense told Damir he had no reason to be, but all the same he felt wrong-footed. Did Beros want less of Damir's vision and more someone he could mould to suit his purpose? Perhaps Damir's weakness was only too obvious to him, and that was why he had been asked.

Vesna appeared beside them. "Josip! It's not fair to corner Damir in this way when he is meant to be enjoying himself. Leave the poor boy alone." She held out her hand to Damir. "Come, we will dance for a while before the grand finale."

"The grand finale? What do you have planned?"

She put her finger to her lips. "A secret."

Damir thought no more about the secret until Vesna shepherded her guests onto the terrace just before eleven o'clock. Perhaps it would be a spectacular cake, because Josip led them all in singing *'Danas nam je Divan Dan'*, but then there was a sound like mortars and Damir dropped to the floor.

He had been standing next to Vesna so everyone would have seen him. Damir cracked his glass on the tiles so it would appear he was crouching to pick it up, but a waiter appeared from nowhere to wipe away the rivulets of blood-red wine so he had to stand, although he was almost shaking too much to do so. He whispered his apology as coloured rockets and stars filled the sky over the bay. Focussing on the darkness beyond them he battled his urge to run away. He could not embarrass Vesna any further. He could not. For her sake he had to endure this.

Vesna must have felt his trembling, because very casually she wrapped her arm around his shoulder and pulled him to her. As the display reached a crescendo she cupped her hand to her mouth close to his ear and told him he could slip away if he wanted. The guests would be leaving soon, and she would tell them he had cut his hand on the broken glass. Damir shook his head. He would not let her down.

And somehow he didn't. Damir stood by her side near the front door of the villa, passing her bags of party favours to give to her guests as they left. Luckily, by the time Josip gripped his hand the trembling had stopped. He and Lana were amongst the last to go, and Damir could already hear the caterers packing up two storeys below.

Vesna closed the front door and leant against it with a sigh. "What a wonderful, wonderful, evening."

Damir could barely look at her. "I am sorry, so sorry I spoiled it."

"Spoiled it? How did you spoil it?"

"You know… with the fireworks."

"You did nothing wrong." She stepped forwards and took his hand. "Do you want to tell me what happened?"

He shook his head. "No. But maybe… maybe in the morning…"

"Yes, that is a good idea. Now I think we are both very

tired. I'll just go down to see to the caterers then I'll be turning in."

"Goodnight, Vesna."

She turned at the top of the stairs. "Goodnight, Damir, and thank you for coming. I was very proud to have you as my partner."

Chapter Twenty-Five

Damir sat on the balcony watching the light creep across the rippled surface of the sea, the first rays of sun bringing the trees on the island of Daksa into sharp relief as the night clouds drifted away. He looked at the clock on his phone – if he was going to leave, now was the time. He would walk to the harbour and catch the seven o'clock catamaran.

He had spent the last hour composing a note to Vesna in his mind, but now it was time to commit it to one of the sheets of thick cream writing paper she had provided for her guests. A simple thank you for the party, yes, of course, but what else should he say? He certainly couldn't stay to explain what had happened last night. She would tell Josip and he would withdraw his offer, and although Damir was far from decided about taking it up he couldn't quite bear to have it ripped away.

He had come to the conclusion it was better not to lie, so he simply said he needed to catch the early cat. Hopefully she would assume some emergency had arisen, and that would be the end of it. He folded the paper in half, wrote her name on it and left it on the hall table where she would see it when she got up. Then as quietly as he possibly could he slipped out of the front door.

Already the day was warm and the walk would take him the best part of an hour. He would have loved to have made a coffee first, but he hadn't dared risk waking Vesna, so he trudged along, oblivious to the birdsong and the sweet fragrance of the orange blossom draping the high garden walls. The past was crippling him and it seemed there was nothing he could do to stop it.

It was so much worse because Beros's offer had rekindled his dreams, and the party had given him a taste of what life could be. Until, of course, he'd messed it up. Thank goodness Vesna had been kind. She'd probably felt sorry for him, and that in itself was bad enough.

When he reached the port he bought a coffee from the internet café next to the cruise harbour, then made his way past the ships, the aroma of breakfast drifting from their galleys. They would all be leaving today, carrying eager tourists around the islands in the never-ending cycle that was their summer. This morning it all felt rather depressing.

Damir was asleep before the catamaran passed Vesna's villa, but even so he woke far from refreshed and stumbled onto the quay at Korčula, blinking in the light. And he was back, a child again, emerging from the shelter… He rubbed his eyes. Coffee, more coffee, then something to eat. He had time. Antonia wasn't expecting him until much later.

He didn't feel like sitting in a café so he headed for the

bakery and bought a coffee and a thick slice of *bucnica*, its layers oozing with cheese and grated pumpkin. Already there were tourists on the narrow beach at the inland end of the harbour, so he sat on the stone steps nearby and watched them. More than ever he needed the flashbacks and nightmares to stop, but it seemed nothing he tried was ever going to work.

He took the lid from his coffee and began to sip, almost spilling it when he heard Antonia call his name. He turned to see her crossing the road, her shopping basket over her arm.

She sat down next to him. "What's wrong?"

"Why do you ask if something is wrong?"

"Because you're not due back until later. What happened? Did you actually go to the party, or did you cry off?"

"I went, but I wished I had not."

"Why?"

Antonia at least he could tell, and the relief of recognising it flooded through him. "There were fireworks. I panicked."

She put her hand on his arm and he set his coffee down to cover it with his. "So what form did this panic take?" she asked.

"I… I just dropped to the floor. I was standing next to Vesna so everyone would have seen. I broke my glass to try to cover it, but I had to stand up and then I just shook like a frightened puppy." He said the last words with some disgust.

"And Vesna? Was she cross?"

He shook his head. "Far from it. She gave me a get-out – said I could go and she'd tell everyone I'd cut myself – but I couldn't let her down again."

"That was brave."

"Of course it wasn't." He pulled his hand away so fast it made her recoil, so he muttered an apology.

They sat in silence for a while, watching a young mother make sand pies with her toddler while the last of the morning's cruise ships slipped away. Damir's phone burst into life and he pulled it from his pocket to see a text from Vesna.

He turned to Antonia. "I'm in trouble now."

"Why?"

"I sneaked away this morning when I said I'd explain to her why I was such a coward last night."

"Ah."

Bracing himself, Damir read the text, but Vesna was simply asking if he was OK. He showed it to Antonia, who nodded.

"You'd better tell her."

"The truth?" He raised his eyebrows.

Antonia's gaze was steady. "Yes. Why not?"

"Because I do not know how to."

Antonia took the phone from him and typed. Exhaustion washed over him. What did any of it matter anyway? He couldn't possibly take up Beros's opportunity given the state he was in. He lifted his *bucnica* to his lips, but somehow he wasn't hungry anymore, so he broke off a corner and dropped it in front of a passing pigeon.

Antonia showed him her text. "You'll have to correct my

Croatian spelling and put in the word for flashback," she said. But it was practically perfect and he shook his head, reading the words to himself.

I'm OK. I am sorry not to stay and explain last night. I sometimes have flashbacks relating to the war, but I do not like talking about it.

Why could he not have typed that – said it to Vesna even?

"It reads… as though it is nothing," he said.

"One day it will be."

"But how? If anything it is getting worse."

"Send the text."

He did as he was told. The young woman had now made three sand pies, and her child was taking great delight in bashing them with a plastic spade. Within moments Vesna had replied.

Then even more so I stand by what I said last night. I am proud to have had such a brave man by my side. Believe in yourself, Damir.

He showed Antonia the message. "She is very kind."

"And she is right."

"How so?"

"Because however frightened you were, you stood by her. You overcame your fear because you did not want to let her down. And now you've done it once, you can do it again."

"Your twisty English words..."

Antonia spoke slowly and deliberately in Croatian. "Look at me Damir. You can do this and I will help you."

"No, it's impossible."

She wrapped her arm around his shoulder. "It feels that way because you're tired, hungry, and it's raw. Promise me you'll have a rest when we get home, then think about it. You can't go on like this forever – you owe it to yourself."

Over the following days, Damir thought of little else. The idea he could maybe beat this drifted tantalisingly around the edges of his consciousness as he went about his daily life. It even stopped him from calling Beros to tell him he would not be able to take up his offer. What if, with Antonia's help, he could do this? He would never be able to look himself in the eye if he didn't at least try.

But to move beyond his fears would require more than good intentions. Exactly what, he did not know. He mulled it over as he took the guests to the catamaran on Saturday, then viewed the property Josip had his eye on. It had the potential to be charming but there was something about it that sounded a note of caution. Whether it was the dilapidated state of the town house or his own mood he could not be certain, and that made him more than uneasy.

He knew exactly where he would find Antonia. The kitchen was filled with the aromas of citrus and spice, a tray of her special shortbread cooling on a rack as she pummelled dough to make delicious bite-sized *krofne*. Damir stole a piece of shortbread and leant against the sink.

"I need your help."

"Then stop eating the cakes before I've finished even making them."

"One slice. I've taken one slice, that is all."

She looked over her shoulder. "All right. One slice. No more."

At that precise moment she sounded a great deal like Tetka and Damir hesitated. But he trusted her, and, after all, she had witnessed the depths of his hell without batting an eyelid.

"I have decided. You are absolutely right. I cannot let the past take over my life. I have to face up to it."

Antonia spun around, hands covered in flour. "Damir, that's amazing, just amazing. What are you going to do?"

"That is the problem. I do not know."

"Oh." Disappointment was written all over her face but he could not help that. He was determined that once he had conquered this she would be proud of him. And he would be proud of himself.

"It is one thing to say I will confront the past, but I do not know what I am confronting. Or how to confront it. But you said you would help so I thought maybe together…"

"Perhaps confront is the key. Perhaps you need to find out what happened, to stop blocking it out. Let the memories come."

"Sometimes I have tried, but they are only fragments and dreams. And there is no one now I can ask – no one who was there, anyway."

Antonia looked thoughtful. "Apart from the photo of your father, do you know what's in the box in the attic?"

The box. Of course. "I looked... once, when I was clearing the room before you came. It was Tetka's family things. Old pictures, a letter from my father... That letter, it had my parents' wedding photograph in it. It upset me so much I couldn't carry on."

"Would it help if we went through it together?"

"It would. Very much."

They decided to wait until after their busy weekend to explore the contents of the box, but first thing on Monday Damir needed to return to Korčula Town to look again at the property Josip had his eye on. This time he'd arranged to meet a builder there to assess the amount of work required, but he was still plagued by doubts. It was almost a week since Beros had made his proposition and Damir knew he had to give him an answer. But it was hard to see the future with his head so much in the past.

He was early for his meeting, even after he'd collected the key from the agent. She was a girl he'd known at school; one of those who used to laugh at him, and she expressed surprise Damir was working for someone else when he had his own hotel.

"I am not working for Josip Beros – I am working with him. If we buy this property we will do so as partners." Damir scooped the keys from her desk, called 'ciao' over his shoulder and left feeling about two inches taller.

Fighting his way through the tourists, Damir walked the narrow streets around the townhouse. Its front door was on one of the alleyways leading up from the promenade of restaurants on the harbour so the approach was steep and, in places, stepped. But the neighbouring properties were well kept, with pots of geraniums outside and bougainvillea growing up the walls. Once the solid wood front door was stripped down, varnished and repaired it would make a characterful entrance to the cool courtyard behind, but still something was bothering him.

It took him until he was on the street that ran parallel to realise what it was. And then it was not so much a realisation as a question of finding it staring him in the face. Korčula's liveliest bar, silent now but with a sign outside that boasted dancing from dusk to dawn, backed onto the property. There would be no peace for the guests in this house as the music reverberated through its floors and walls. Damir was furious with himself; he knew this town, he knew this bar. And the fact he had not thought of it straight away made him wonder how much he could trust his judgement.

The builder was waiting on the front step and Damir apologised for wasting his time. He'd come from Račišcé, a village further along the coast, and Damir knew him only by sight, but he didn't seem remotely phased by Damir's announcement. Damir took him for coffee to compensate him for his trouble, and he asked what Damir was looking for.

When he explained about the boutique hotel for students of art the man looked thoughtful and asked if Damir would consider buying land and building from scratch. The idea had not occurred to him, but the builder explained that his neighbour was selling a plot on the headland above his village, with impressive views over the sea towards the island of Hvar. Although a bubble of excitement stirred inside Damir, he told him he would need to discuss it with his business partner first. The builder was the second person Damir had used that phrase with in just over an hour and it seemed he had somehow made his decision.

But acting on it – and telling Antonia about it – would have to wait. After a quick lunch of Antonia's homemade *burek,* the meat and pastry fragrant with herbs, Damir followed her upstairs, their footsteps the only sound to break the murmur of the cicadas outside. She had already placed the box on the rug in front of the chimney breast and he sat on the floor next to it while she took the chair.

"Ready?" she asked.

"Yes." He hoped he sounded more certain than he felt.

The picture of Damir's father in his uniform was caught in the folds of the lid and he set it on the floor without a second glance. There were no secrets here or in the silver candlesticks Tetka had used to make her little shrine. Beneath them was the framed photograph that went with them, the one of his father in the courtyard, wearing a checked shirt. He handed it to Antonia.

"You are very like him," she said, after studying it for a few moments.

He frowned. "I think, perhaps, he was taller. But I cannot be sure because I remember him from a child's perspective."

"And what do you remember?"

"I remember him telling me to look after my mother.

That is the strongest memory, and the most bitter, because in that I failed him."

"You've never really explained why."

"No, and if I start now we will never get to the end of the box."

"Perhaps it is the one thing you need to tell."

"But not now." He looked up at her. "Antonia, the last time I saw my mother's wedding photo it broke me. I cannot be broken *before* I see it again. I need all my strength."

"OK. Do you know where it is?"

As Damir pointed to the envelope his finger trembled. "See?" He tried to laugh. "Already it terrifies me."

Antonia knelt on the floor next to him, so close her warmth and the herbal scent of her shampoo wrapped around him like a soft blanket. "Shall I open it?"

"Please."

Antonia studied the letter and picture for so long that in the end Damir leant into her to look at it too. Between her fingers it seemed to lack the power to wound, or perhaps it was because this time he was ready for it. He took the photograph from her and cradled it in his hand. It showed his mother from the waist up, her white dress unadorned, its long sleeves a stark contrast to the khaki of his father's uniform where their arms looped together. Curls of dark hair escaped from her lace veil, but it was still drawn tightly enough around her head to give extra definition to her beautiful heart-shaped face with its wide smile, delicately drawn eyebrows, and deep-brown eyes.

And the memories flooded in. Lullabies, games, trips

to the park, walking in the country with his father. Flashes and fragments of laughter and love. Playing with his toy cars in the hall of their apartment. Scolding Dusa for climbing onto the kitchen table. The smell of a perfume Damir did not know but was oh so familiar. But he'd lost her, he'd lost all this. And despite his promises to himself he was howling like a child in Antonia's arms.

She did not move until the storm passed, did not utter a word. When his chest finally stopped heaving they untangled themselves and looked at each other.

"God, you're a snotty mess," she said. "Go and wash your face."

Damir gazed at himself in the bathroom mirror. Yes, he was like his father, but his mother's eyes held his in a steady gaze. And he was beginning to realise that he knew who he was. He felt his roots grow into the floor of Vila Maslina, down through its wooden joists and solid stone into the same soil that gave life to the olive grove, nourishing its trees and filling its fruit. He belonged here; he was in all of these things. But he was his mother's son too, part of a life that had nothing to do with this island. And perhaps that meant that one day he could follow his dreams beyond it too.

When he returned to her bedroom, Antonia was back in the chair, studying the letter. "I'm trying to translate it," she said.

"There is no need. I read it before. It's just sending Tetka a photo because she had flu and couldn't get to the wedding."

"But the underlined part – '*najsretniji*' – what does that mean?"

"Most happy."

"That's confusing – it's not like the word for happy at all. And how strange to underline it. It is as if he is trying to make a point." She frowned. "I wonder... did Tetka not approve of your mother for some reason?"

Damir took the letter from her and read it again, right to the end. The end that said,

I will bring Narcisa to Lumbarda soon, so you can learn to love her as much as I do.

He translated it for Antonia.

"You could be right. I remember... I was writing an essay once in high school, about the war. And I hated learning about the war. But I asked Tetka why she thought it happened and she told me it was because it wasn't normal for Muslims and Christians to live together. Then she said that was in most circumstances and of course there were exceptions to every rule. I assumed she meant my parents but perhaps she was just trying to spare my feelings."

"Or maybe your father did bring your mother here and she changed her mind?"

"Yes. Yes. That is probably it." He hoped it was, but he felt far from certain. With Tetka gone, was there a way of finding out?

He bypassed the envelope of photos of his father's family and Tetka in her youth, but Antonia flicked through them, exclaiming how the house had changed over the years. She paused at the First Communion one and asked if Tetka was religious. Damir shrugged. "A little. When I was small we went to church every week, but then something happened and there was no confession anymore and mass was just for the most holy days and we sat at the back. She still made me say my prayers every night, though. Until we argued over my First Communion, that is."

"What happened?"

"She wanted me to do it, but none of my friends were. I asked her why it was so important if we did not go to church anymore, and she let the whole religion thing drop."

Next there was a folder of Damir's old reports from high school, some birthday cards, a pressed carnation which he must have given Tetka for Women's Day one year, and a couple of childish drawings of animals and flowers. He showed them to Antonia, all but overcome by the fact his practical Tetka had kept these sentimental things for all these years.

"Perhaps," he told Antonia, "I should be grateful to have had two mothers."

She nodded. "And that is a wonderful gift. But sadly you are having to mourn them both."

"My real mother I mourned a long time ago."

"Did you? Did you really?"

But what did it mean to mourn? The thought was uncomfortable, certainly. It meant opening yourself up to your emotions, perhaps even losing control. But if it was lost, anyway? If the past had a way of finding you and stripping you bare? But even so, how could you mourn someone you could hardly remember? He struggled to make sense of it all as they sifted through a folder of papers to do with the house and another of family documents. There was no death certificate for either of Damir's parents and no birth certificate for him. When Antonia questioned it, he shrugged.

"I guess it was the confusion of war. I remember it was a problem when they issued my identity card, but only a small one. I think they took the information from my medical records instead."

After a while they came across an official letter to Tetka from the Croatian army, confirming the date and place of Ivan Marić's death as a hero of the nation. But Damir did not want to read it. He felt as though his heart had been scratched raw by the emotion of the afternoon already.

Three heavy items had sunk through the paper to the bottom of the box. They looked incongruous lying next to each other: a set of rosary beads made from olive wood and two small toy cars, their paint chipped from frequent use. *They were racing on the central corridor of the shelter under the flickering gaslight. He was lying on the floor with Dragan and Kemal as the cars bounced and spun from the walls against the rough concrete floor. He could hear them argue about who won, hear them laugh.*

But Kemal was dead.

Damir picked up one car in each hand, and turned to Antonia, despair burning a black hole in his chest. "For now, I have no more tears."

In a train of thought that had started when he was reading the letter his father sent with the wedding photo, Damir was left with a burning desire to know more about his parents. Not old photographs and half-memories, but to discover who they really were, if that was still possible. Somehow facts seemed safer than surrendering to his emotions and it was surprising he had never thought of it before.

In a village like Lumbarda there would still be people who had known his father. Although men sometimes moved away in search of work, there were many who stayed. Or who returned. Women too. Had he lived, Damir's father would have only been in his early sixties; some of the children he grew up with must still be here. Sanja had been Tetka's closest friend so she must have known him, and what was more, Damir thought she would understand.

The next morning, Damir called into the market to buy some flowers before visiting her. Sanja kissed him on the cheek, laughing as she took them from him.

"What is it you want this time, Damir? Are the girls coming back?"

"No, Sanja. It is time I knew more about my parents."

"So, is that what's been troubling you all these months?" Her question left him open-mouthed, but she continued, "I am not a fool, Damir. You have become nervy, thin. You smoke too much. Petar tells me it is not a woman and your business is going well, so I put it down to grief. I did not really grieve for Željko until many months after he died so I thought it was the same for you."

"Perhaps... many months afterwards for Tetka. Many years for my parents. The problem is I have so few memories, just fragments really. I need to know who they really were and you must have grown up with my father."

"Come, we will have coffee in the kitchen."

Damir followed her inside. Compared to Vila Maslina, hers was a modest house, but even though she lived there alone it was filled with warmth. Sanja removed her old tabby from one of the seats at the table and set the *dzezva* on the stove. When Damir sat down, he lifted the cat onto his knee.

"That is exactly what your father would have done. When I think of Ivan, I think of animals. He was a kind boy, compassionate. But also strong in his beliefs." She frowned. "That makes him sound like he was not fun, but he was. He was four years younger than me so in many ways he was just your *tetka's* little brother. The boys in the village used to play together and we thought we were far too grown up to join in. You need to ask Ivica the fisherman if you want to know about that part of his life – but there is one story I can tell you that I think sums up your father as I remember him."

She reached into a cupboard and pulled out a tin, loading slices of lemon cake onto a plate and setting it between them. "It was the donkey," she told him. "It was what happened with the donkey that comes first to mind when I think of Ivan." And left Damir pondering this while she finished making the coffee.

"He would have been perhaps fourteen, maybe a little older. But not much because his mother was still alive. In those days the olive press was turned by a donkey. For some reason, this particular year there was only one in the village and of course it was in great demand during the harvest, so your grandfather hired a man with a donkey from the hills instead.

"Well, when this donkey arrived it was in a terrible state – lame and with sores on its back where the harness had chafed. But to the men it was just a donkey. There was a hardness back then that grew out of poverty. We had not the money from tourists, even though the country was beginning to open up. The olives had to be pressed and that was that. But somehow Ivan persuaded his father to keep the donkey overnight and he discovered the lameness was down to a stone in its hoof, which he removed, and he put salve his mother had made on its wounds.

"The owner was indifferent. Ivan offered him the salve but he would not take it. And when he led the animal away, Ivan saw him beat it when it stopped on the path to eat. That must have been the final straw because as soon as the harvest was over, he stole the donkey."

"He did what?"

"It tells you a lot about Ivan that he waited until after the harvest. He thought things through; he knew it would be a problem for the olive farmers if there was no donkey, but all the same he did not want the beast to suffer more than it had to. So once the last olive was pressed, the donkey mysteriously disappeared.

"Naturally, all fingers pointed at Ivan. When his father asked, he told him straight what he had done, but even after a beating he would not say where the donkey was hidden and I don't think anyone ever found out. In the end, the owner of one of the vineyards stepped in and offered to buy the beast. Ivan knew he was a good man so it magically reappeared and cash changed hands. Everyone was happy, but I think your grandfather was always a little ashamed his son had resorted to theft."

Damir gazed at the dregs of coffee in the bottom of his cup. Sanja's story had painted such a vivid picture and he was desperate to relate it to the father he could remember. "He bought me a kitten when I was tiny. He must have wanted me to love animals too."

"And to learn to be kind. But you are kind, Damir, you always have been. It was your father's nature in you and besides, Nada brought you up to be as much like him as possible, although she was relieved you never wanted to leave the island as he did."

Damir shrugged. "Why would I have left? My whole life is here."

"And, I think, you eventually learnt that here you were safe. You know, when you arrived it took you a couple of years to adjust, to be anything like the other children, but that was not surprising."

That was certainly not the route Damir wanted this conversation to take. He did not need to remember the child he once had been, especially when he felt he was close to slipping back there again. He stared at his coffee cup so hard Sanja removed it from his gaze and took it to the stove to refill it.

"But what of my mother?" he asked. "What do you remember of her?"

She did not turn around. "Nothing, Damir. He never brought her to the island."

"But I found a letter... After their wedding, he was going to..."

Sanja sighed. "Nada did not want it. You have to understand, Damir, your parents met at about the time your grandfather died. Your *tetka* had expected your father to come out of the army and return to Vila Maslina, but of course he did not. Instead he married and stayed in Mostar. She never visited them either, not even when you were born. The first time she even saw you was when you arrived here, just a couple of weeks after your father died."

"I thought... I wondered if perhaps it was because my mother was Bosniak."

"When they married, I do not know. But later of course your father was killed by Bosniak forces..."

"And my mother was killed by Croatians."

Sanja returned to the table, sat down, and put her hand over his. "That, Damir, was the true tragedy of our war."

Back at Vila Maslina, Antonia was desperate to hear about his visit to Sanja's, and when Damir told her about the donkey she laughed.

"Yes, I can see you doing that as well. I remember the state you were in when I arrived, all because Mackalina had disappeared. I honestly thought she was a person, the way you were talking about it."

"But she had left her kittens—"

"I know, I know."

"You're patronising me."

"I'm sorry, I didn't mean to." She stopped chopping onions. "What did Sanja say about your mother?"

Damir wanted to pretend it did not matter, but with Antonia he couldn't. "She never met her. Tetka did not want my mother here."

"I did wonder when I saw that letter."

"So now I will never know."

Antonia frowned. "Why not? She might have had relatives who are still alive. Can you remember anyone? Uncles? Aunts?"

"I remember being taken to a village in the country before the war, but not much about it. There were goats... The grass seemed very high... But I can only see myself there with my parents so maybe it was just a holiday or somewhere we went for a day out."

"I wonder, how much do you know about your mother, Damir? I mean, in factual terms."

"Like?"

"Her full name, her birthday... that sort of thing."

"Not much." He hunched his shoulders and looked at the clock above the stove. "It is time I went to collect the guests."

Antonia pushed the pad she used for shopping lists across the table. "You have at least ten minutes. Write it down and I will ask Declan if it's enough to find anything out."

"Declan?"

"You remember Declan, the Irish guy. He works for an

aid organisation in Bosnia – he might just know his way around this stuff."

"Of course I remember Declan but I did not know you were still in touch." How could that awful, interfering man help him? But at the same time he realised he was being unfair; his dislike of Declan had stemmed from the man having seen him at his most vulnerable – and having recognised his anguish for what it really was.

Antonia returned to her chopping. "We chat sometimes, play internet Scrabble. Now stop changing the subject."

He shoved the pad back at her. "I need to think. I will do it later. After supper, while Vincenzo is giving his talk."

What Damir really needed time for was to get used to the idea he might have another family in Bosnia & Herzegovina, a family he had given no thought to in twenty-five years. His need to fit in, to be Croatian, had been so great he had refused to recognise the other part of who he was, especially when it had led to such cruel teasing. But perhaps, although he had gained from that strategy as a child, maybe as an adult there was more he had lost. Could it even be a good thing to be different from other people?

Tentatively he posed the question to Antonia as they sat in the courtyard after supper, sipping wine while the dishwasher hummed and moths flickered around the outside lights.

She wrapped her hands around her glass. "I think, as children, as teenagers even, we all want to fit in and the best way to do that is to be like everyone else. And Tetka made that easier for you; she encouraged you to be the proudest of Croatians, maybe because she knew your mixed ethnicity might be dangerous if war broke out again. But if you can embrace the part of you that is Bosnian, you may even discover it's an advantage."

"In what way?"

"Well, coming from somewhere else, learning to fit in, it's a good life lesson. Being a stranger in a new place doesn't necessarily make you less; it can make you more."

"I'm not sure I understand."

"I know it's not at all the same, but for me, coming here has expanded my horizons. I've learnt to adapt, to fit in, and I've gained in confidence because of it. I will always be English, of course I will, but at the same time, there will be a tiny corner of Croatian somewhere in my heart." She laughed. "I'll probably always make coffee using *dzezva*."

"Good thing too." He grinned at her. "Then I am not wrong to be curious about my Bosnian roots? It's not disrespectful of Tetka?"

"No. I think you need to do it. And we will start by writing down all you know about your mother." Once again, she handed Damir the pad and pen.

At the top he wrote 'Narcisa Marić', then shook his head. "That is probably everything and it will not be enough."

"Don't give up before you have even started. We can get the approximate date of her marriage from the letter in the box. If you will allow me, I can look at it later."

"Of course I will allow you."

"And perhaps her records can be traced from your birth

certificate, if it can be found. What's your full name and date of birth?"

"Damir Ivan Marić, 9th May 1987."

"And your father was Ivan. Any middle name?"

"Not that I know of."

"OK. Can you by any chance remember your mother's birthday?"

He took a sip of wine. "I was thinking about this. I cannot be sure, but I believe it was near Christmas, because I half remember my father teasing her it was not worth buying two presents. But I could be wrong. Sometimes, for the good parts, it's hard to distinguish memories from dreams."

Antonia stretched her hand across the table, her eyes soft in the glow of the outside light. "Then this is going to be harder. Any idea at all when she died? You came here when you were six, so 1993? But do you know when?"

But somehow it wasn't so difficult to answer. "A while before September at least, because when Petar and I started school I already knew him. I'm sorry... in the shelters... they were underground. You did not know the time of day, let alone the time of year."

"You were living in the shelters all the time?"

"Yes, the children... we were not allowed outside. Not after..."

The silence stretched around them into the darkness, out through the olive grove and across the sea. Eventually Antonia asked, "After what?"

And he knew if he was ever going to say the words, now was the moment and Antonia was the right person to hear them. But all the same they felt choked inside him. He reached for his cigarette packet then put it down again. It was all right; Antonia was loyal, constant – he may hate himself for what had happened, but she wouldn't hate him.

"We were stupid children, and Kemal died because of it."

"What happened?" Her voice was soft.

Something in the way she said it made him wonder if perhaps she understood it was one of the most important events in his life. And for the first time he did too, and with it came the realisation that if he could bear to tell her, the memory just might be robbed of some of its power. It might. And that was a risk worth taking. So he told Antonia about the food parcels being dropped from the planes, and about the strange fractured world they had found themselves in when they went outside, and their pride at collecting so many packages. And then he told her about the deserted supermarket car park, and the sniper, and Kemal's screams as he had died alone just feet away from him.

Antonia's face was ashen. Even in the dim light he could see it.

"I know we did wrong," he said, "but since the memory has come back, that in itself is my biggest punishment."

"You were tiny children. You were only trying to help. It was the man who fired that gun who was to blame. To kill a little boy..." Her voice was shaking. "No wonder the adults didn't let you out after that."

"But still, I should have tried to find my mother when she didn't come back. I promised my father..." The memory lay black and heavy over him, but there were no tears. He had expected tears, but this time the pain stayed inside.

"Why did she go out?"

"She went for food. The women had to queue at the community organisation for whatever there was. She left before I was awake and I never saw her again."

"So what did you do then?"

"The neighbours, the other families in the shelter... they looked after me. But then I think someone from the Red Cross came to tell me my father had died and brought me here."

"Damir, I think that is just about the saddest story I have ever heard."

"Yes, but it is my story and every day I have to live with it."

Suddenly anger at the injustice of having been born in the wrong place and time – not just him, but Kemal, and Dragan, and all the other children – filled him and he stood, pushing his chair away so hard it hit the ground with a crash. *A crash of splintering wood, of falling masonry, bombs howling above and a hand in his, dragging him along…* But no. He was in the courtyard of Vila Maslina with Antonia. He was safe. *He* had caused the dangerous energy behind the sound, not some nightmare or echo of the past. It had been his anger, driving the last of his shame from his soul. He hadn't killed Kemal. Or his mother. It was war that had taken them both.

Recovering himself, he picked up the chair and tucked it under the table. "I am sorry. But I needed to do that."

Antonia nodded slowly. "I think perhaps you did."

Chapter Twenty-Six

Antonia crossed the olive grove in the grey dawn. It was almost September and already the fruit was filling up the branches. She reached through the shimmering leaves to touch the tough green ovals that Damir had told her would be impossibly bitter for weeks to come. But there were a great many of them, and bar unseasonal storms it should be a good harvest. Earlier in the year, Damir had been talking about pressing their own fruit, but recently he had fallen silent on the matter – which was hardly surprising, given everything else going on.

The press house was silent too; silent and closed to the world. Antonia wondered if Damir was still asleep, or whether he had gone swimming. She knew how much emotional energy the night before must have cost him, energy he barely had. But telling the worst of his story seemed to have released some anger at least, so maybe he had been able to rest. They had come so far since her early days on Korčula when she had struggled to know what to make of him. First he had helped her to regain her confidence and now, in the depths of his adversity, he had opened his soul to her. Their friendship went far beyond their initial need to fill the lonely spaces in their lives and their mutual interest in making Vila Maslina a success; it had become one of the most rewarding relationships of her life. Because it was different, and unexpected – undefinable even – but she knew that each of them held a special and unique place in the other's heart. She would certainly miss him more than she could say when she went home.

The sea was calm but there was no one swimming, nothing to break the gunmetal sheen on the water as the night clouds lifted from the hills on the mainland. Although the sun had not yet struggled through, the air was warm and there was a peacefulness to the morning, broken only as a jogger passed her, the tinny thud from her earphones fading in her wake.

Over those hills was Bosnia & Herzegovina, with Mostar just a four-hour drive away. In a couple of hours more she could be in Sarajevo and there were times when she longed to be. Little by little her affection for Declan was growing, and she was letting it. It was early days, and if it turned out to be the right thing then they would find a way, and in the meantime it was fun getting to know each other better. Late last night she'd sent him an important email, although he probably hadn't read it yet as few people got up as crazy early as she had to when there was fish on the menu.

It was as she'd tried to fill in the gaps about Damir's mother that it had occurred to her, but initially Antonia had pushed the thought away. Digging back through the box she'd found the letter from the army about Ivan's death and it gave the date as 23rd April 1993. So that meant Narcisa must have been killed before that, but the question was, how long before? Just placing the likely date as 1993 tied it in with the Bosniak expulsions from West Mostar, and when pushed, Damir had told Antonia they had lived in army housing so it must have been on the Croat side of town.

The thought that had started to plague Antonia was the possibility that his mother had been forced to leave rather than been killed. In the small hours of the morning, she had replayed the last section of the BBC documentary, her heart in her mouth. Those refugees struggling across, could one of them even have been Narcisa? The chance was such a small one, but all the same she had emailed Declan to ask if there was any way of finding out. But then her hopes plummeted when she realised that if by any chance Narcisa had survived the war, she would have certainly looked for her son – and estranged or not, Tetka would have been her first port of call.

Already, Antonia was rounding the corner to the harbour and the boats were in, their red and blue hulls brightening the dawn. Ivica waved when he saw her, beckoning her over. Half a dozen choice squid lay in a plastic crate and she told him she would take them all. He named his price and wrote the amount in his battered notebook as she asked after his wife. He grinned, telling her she was well, and he asked after Antonia's daughter, before continuing to unload the crates from his boat. There was no sense anymore of her being an outsider, and realised again how much she would miss Lumbarda when she was back in England on a dank November day.

Every time an email pinged onto her phone she leapt to answer it, her tiny flame of hope for Narcisa keeping thoughts of her own future at bay. But after reading Declan's reply she found herself holding back sobs as she hung the towels to dry in the yard. The chances of Damir's mother having survived were just too small. The refugees in the documentary were the lucky ones – most displaced Bosniaks had been taken to concentration camps which few survived. It was hardly any comfort at all that Declan had offered to see if he could track down any other relatives, but if it was the best he could do, then she supposed she was grateful.

It was late morning when Damir appeared at the kitchen door, rolling the keys to the people-carrier between his fingers.

"Antonia, do you have an hour for me? Maybe longer if you have time for lunch?"

There were sheets to be washed later, and of course dinner to be prepared, but the pastry for the goat cheese tartlets was already chilling and squid was quick to cook.

"Yes, everything's under control here." She looked at the car keys. "I take it we're going somewhere?" He nodded. "OK, give me five minutes to throw on a clean top."

They skirted Korčula Town then drove along the coast road beyond it, somewhere Antonia had not yet been. The sea to their right was busy with pleasure boats and the diminutive cruise ships that plied Dalmatia. Damir had told her it wasn't a long journey, but all the same they passed through a couple of hamlets with scant strips of beach dotted with sunshades, then headed inland through a mixture of scrub and neat fields behind dry stone walls. Suddenly the sea was in front of them again, a far deeper blue this time, and the road began to curve downwards to a tongue-shaped bay lined with red roofed houses, which he told her was Račišcé.

They passed a couple of restaurants, and beyond a long, narrow jetty turned up a stony track which climbed steeply through a band of trees, then onto more scrub. To Antonia's surprise, this was where Damir stopped.

"What are we doing here?" she asked.

"We are looking at this land. It is for sale." He stepped from the car and she followed. The earth was rock hard and dry, covered with straggling thyme and small boulders.

"You can't grow olives here, can you?"

"I could, but in this case I am planning to grow another hotel."

Damir took Antonia by the shoulders and wheeled her around so she was facing the sea. They'd climbed to the headland beyond the village and in one direction the views were towards the mainland, but they were at the point where the Pelješac peninsula ended, and as Damir swung her to their left she could see past it, across an expanse of shimmering blue, to a distant island which he told her was Hvar.

"What do you think?"

"It's an amazing spot, but Damir, how would you do it? You'd just be piling stress upon stress, what with everything else going on. I can see it's a great opportunity but your timing is lousy."

"Because it is not my timing. And I have not committed, although I expect I will regret it all my life if I do not."

"Then you'd better explain. Is this something to do with what Josip Beros wanted to talk to you about before Vesna's party?" She had meant to ask him at the time and now felt guilty she had completely forgotten when events had overtaken them.

"I'll tell you over lunch."

Antonia put her hands on her hips. "No. Now. I want to at least know enough to decide whether or not I'm going to lunch with a madman." His face crumpled and she regretted her choice of words. "I'm sorry..."

"So you do think I'm crazy?"

"No... but you would be if you decided to heap more stress on yourself. What has he asked you to do?"

"He hasn't asked me to do anything. He wants us to be partners."

Antonia was about to tell him how wonderful that was, but stopped herself just in time. She didn't want to start pressuring him, even inadvertently.

Instead, she said, "It's a big vote of confidence in you that he asked."

"I know." Damir turned away from her, looking out to sea. "I think it is mostly that confidence which is giving me the courage to face my nightmares. You are right I have doubts... perhaps I am good enough, but probably I am not.

And he wants an answer. I bought time because the property he was considering was not right, but I know in my heart this land is."

"So what is he proposing? Another hotel like Vila Maslina?"

"A little larger. This time for artists instead of sculptors. And this would just be the beginning, Antonia. He sees hotels for culture all over Dalmatia, and maybe beyond. He is a wealthy man and he can make me wealthy too."

"At what cost?"

"My biggest fear is beginning then failing. That he will discover my weakness..."

"What weakness?"

Damir shrugged, then walked away towards a lone olive tree in the middle of the plot. Damn the man for offering this to him now, Antonia thought. Damn him. In just a few months everything could look different for Damir; he could have answers. He could rest at the end of the season. If this kicked off he would have no rest and Antonia wouldn't be there to help him.

She followed him across the scrub. "Tell him you need time."

"I cannot. He is becoming impatient."

"And can you work with someone like that, who is always pushing you?"

"Vesna tells me he will be better once I say yes, once things are settled."

"Can't Vesna persuade him?"

"No. This is up to me. I cannot... I don't know if you say it... hide behind her skirt, if I want him to respect me."

"Yes, I get that."

They stood in silence, gazing out over the incredible view. The gentlest of breezes whispered through the olive tree, its leaves shimmering in the midday heat. She could see from this distance its trunk was sturdy, solid, gnarled with age, and somehow seeing it standing alone made her feel connected to this land in a way that surprised her.

Eventually Antonia spoke. "You must keep the tree."

"You think I should do it?"

"I think we must work something out so that you can."

"In what way?"

"Now it is time to discuss things over lunch."

They walked back down the track to a harbourside restaurant serving simple food, Antonia's mind racing. The nuts and bolts of making this happen were one thing, but by far the biggest issue was Damir's mental state, although she had to admit there'd been a few flickers of the old Damir since Vesna's party, and he was right when he said it was probably Josip's belief in him which had done that.

Once they had ordered their lunch, Antonia pulled her pen and notepad from her handbag.

"OK, what needs to happen for this to work? In a practical sense."

"What other sense is there?"

"You know very well what I mean. Damir Marić can do this standing on his head. A sleep-deprived, grief-stricken Damir has no chance."

He looked out across the harbour. "That is my biggest fear."

"We need to find you some answers about your Bosnian

family. There must be someone who can tell you about your mother, and it occurred to me that Declan's in a good position to help. Although… I don't know… I have the impression you don't really like him."

Still Damir did not look at her. "That is not his fault. He saw me… He guessed… about my weakness. He has no reason to help."

"Vesna is helping you."

"Vesna is my friend."

"So would Declan be if you let him. And anyway, what choice do we have? He is in Sarajevo, and he knows his way around this sort of stuff."

Damir shook his head. "It could take him years or not happen at all. The answer must be in my own mind. I know it, but it is tough to deal with alone."

Antonia put her hand over his. "You are not alone."

"In two months I will be."

Myriad small thoughts and feelings were coming together in Antonia's mind, chasing each other like the fish darting through the crystal water of the bay just feet below them. Was it possible? And if it was, did she want it? She felt herself smiling – of course she did.

"Are you asking me to stay?"

Damir looked shocked. "I could not. You want to see Honey. You have your life in England..."

She tried again. This was important and she didn't want to let it go. "So you're saying you don't want me to?"

"You are twisting my words again."

Antonia took a deep breath. "Yes, I want to see Honey and at the end of October I will go home for a while. But then, if you want, I can come back. I mean... I'd like to come back. In fact, I'd love to. If we can see a role for me in your new venture, that is."

"But of course there's a role. I will need you to manage Vila Maslina completely, and perhaps in the winter help with the website and starting a proper office for the new business. Maybe there will even be time for our olive products..."

So he had wanted her around, after all. "You've got this all worked out, haven't you?"

He nodded. "I have dreamt but did not dare ask. Antonia, are you sure? It will make all the difference. It will mean... everything."

"Then the answer is yes."

Had she just done the craziest thing? But no, this had been building for a long while now, even if she had taken her time to acknowledge it. On Korčula she had made a life that was hers. Antonia's. Not Antonia the mother, not Antonia the mistress – hers. The confidence inside her was real; it must have simply been buried under the surface all along. And what was more, no one had made this most momentous of decisions for her. She had done it all herself.

Chapter Twenty-Seven

Antonia was preparing an early breakfast for the guests before their journey home when there was a tap on the kitchen door and Declan's untidy mop of sandy hair appeared around it. She grinned at him.

"I didn't expect you so early. Did Sanja not give you any breakfast?

Declan laughed, and to her delight wrapped Antonia in a bear hug which seemed to go on forever. Finally he released her and said, "Sanja gave me the most enormous breakfast, which was one of the reasons I decided to take a walk. And it seemed rude to go straight past, even though I know you'll be run off your feet until the guests leave. Besides which, I am gagging for a cup of tea if it's not too much trouble."

"Of course not. It's amazing of you to come all this way just for the weekend."

"It's hardly a chore. I found myself rather looking

forward to seeing you again." There was a delicious sparkle in his green eyes and Antonia grinned at him.

"Any news for Damir?"

"Not really, so you could say I'm here under false pretences, but there's just the small matter of building his trust, which is much easier done face to face. Good start though – did he tell you he's taking me to lunch today?"

Instead of continuing with his walk, Declan helped Antonia load the dishwasher then accompanied her to the market. Saturday was always a big shop and she was glad of an extra pair of arms to carry the baskets. And he chatted all the time – sometimes to the stallholders about their produce, then to Antonia about what she was going to cook and how she put her menus together. When they had finished, he invited her for coffee, but she reluctantly refused.

"It's such a shame – your days off are our busiest. You've come all this way and we'll hardly see you."

"Well I did wonder if you could spare a few hours tomorrow lunchtime. You know, go back to that lovely little restaurant in the hills? Then once Damir is shot of the guests to start their week of hell with Vincenzo, we can sit down together and go through the stuff related to his mum."

Antonia looked up at him. "You won't say anything about me thinking she might be alive?"

"No. Because the chances of that are way too small."

"But not impossible?"

He put his hands on the top of her arms, his eyes full of concern. "Antonia. No. Don't even dream it for him. I couldn't bear to have you hurt by this as well."

Even though Antonia didn't see Declan again, for the rest of the day WhatsApp messages flew between them.

After his lunch with Damir:

DECLAN: He seems brighter. Not so black under the eyes.

ANTONIA: Makes me worry about what you might find.

DECLAN: Stop it. He's asked for closure. It's up to him.

Then half an hour later:

DECLAN: I didn't mean to upset you by saying that – he couldn't want for a better friend.

ANTONIA: Radio silence was because I was up to my elbows in pastry. Not offended. Takes more than that. I'm a tough bugger as well as tenacious.

ANTONIA: Where are you eating this evening?

DECLAN: Taking my hostess to Pecaros as she won't accept any money.

ANTONIA: She considers Damir her third son.

DECLAN: Interesting.

Then finally:

DECLAN: Stuffed with pizza and absolutely knackered. Sweet dreams, Antonia.

ANTONIA: Sleep well. Looking forward to lunch tomorrow.

DECLAN: Me too.

In early September the island's resorts were still busy, but inland it felt as though the restaurant near Cara had been reclaimed by the locals. Antonia and Declan were the only foreigners there as tables were put together to accommodate large groups, with children flying between them. Declan fielded one toddler who tripped on a step near their table and carried her back to her mother.

"Handled like a dad," Antonia told him.

"Sadly not. I missed out on all that, but I guess it was my choice. You can't have it all."

"Was it just a case of your work coming first, or did you never meet the right person?"

"I never looked. It wouldn't have been fair. I mean, I've dated other aid workers. You kind of know what the score is, but I can't say it was especially satisfying – you know you'll both move on and most likely in different directions. Mind you, it was a tough decision once, but she made it for me."

"Love can be like that, can't it? It can creep up, tap you on the shoulder, then bugger up your life for a while."

He rested his chin on his hand and looked at her. "Are you saying that from experience?"

"Yes. I was so careful after my divorce. A bit like you putting your work first, really, only for me it was total dedication to being a mum. My friend Lynn kept telling me I was too fussy, but you know, that was fine – except then I fell for my married boss. Of all the stupid things to happen. It's why I'm here, really. I had to get away."

"And did it work? Are you over him?"

Antonia laughed. "It took a while but yes, yes I am."

"And you and Vincenzo?"

"How did you know?"

"He made it very clear to me in all sorts of not particularly subtle ways."

"There wasn't much in it anyway, kind of... friends with benefits..." Antonia blushed. "Like your hook-ups with other aid workers, I'd guess. And equally hollow."

"Yeah. Some of my uni friends who've been married since their twenties envy me for being single, and when you're young it's kind of OK, but not anymore."

Antonia smiled at him. "Likewise. I even let myself be talked into Vincenzo by Lynn, because she thought it would be good for me."

"You mustn't let anyone make those decisions for you, Antonia."

"I do know that. Well, at least I do now."

"Sorry... I didn't mean to sound condescending. You're an intelligent woman and you don't need me to tell you what to do either."

It took a while for their food to arrive. They had both been tempted by the incredible aroma drifting from the kitchen and had ordered beef *peka,* and Antonia told him how Damir had taken her to watch it being made. As they waited, they sipped their wine and people-watched. It was apparently one of Declan's favourite pastimes, but his comments, although amusing, were never acerbic, always kind.

After a while he told Antonia he'd had an interesting conversation with Sanja about how Damir was when he first arrived on the island.

"You're brave. I've never dared to ask her. And besides, my Croatian probably isn't up to understanding her answers."

"I'm not sure mine is either, but with a bit of repetition and explanation we got there in the end."

"What did she say?"

"That he was a shadow of a boy. Understandable really. He didn't speak for weeks, and hated going outside – he must have thought it was dangerous. Even years later he would hide in dark, enclosed spaces when he was upset."

"Mm."

"Are you saying he still does that now?"

"No. He told me about one of them, that was all. Oddly enough, it's the place he's living now – the old press house."

"Perhaps not so odd."

"It was his only practical option with me in the attic. What else did Sanja say?"

"His aunt was at her wits' end. She could barely leave the house, so Sanja would shop for her and come to talk.

This went on for months, apparently; Damir had arrived in early May and she had gone beyond hoping he'd be able to start school in the September. Then one day Sanja took Petar with her and he and Damir began to play. It was the start of him turning the corner. She said they are firm friends even now."

"Having another child around must have helped everything to feel more normal for Damir."

"And play is a great distraction. Anyway, he did make enough progress to be able to start school, but he was still a bit nervy and terrified of loud noises, so the other children used to pick on him quite a bit. But in a while he rose above that too and within a couple of years became properly settled. His aunt lived for him and he was devoted to her. As far as Sanja knew, little was said of his real mother because Nada hardly knew her."

"She didn't know her at all. They never met, and reading between the lines of a letter we found, she didn't approve of the marriage – or mixed-ethnicity relationships in general."

Declan sighed. "It wasn't an unusual view in Croatia then, although in Bosnia & Herzegovina before the war things were far more fluid. They're becoming a little that way again, with a new generation, but the brutality on all sides is hard for many older people to forget."

"It seems such a shame. I mean, you wouldn't forget, would you, but the fact it all kicked off in the first place was a tragedy."

"It also shook many people when the news of the atrocities came out after the war ended at the end of 1995.

Sanja said for a while Nada became very protective of Damir, would hardly let him out of her sight. She made sure he told people he was Croatian – even bought him a replica football shirt to wear; Sanja thought she was afraid of reprisals. Terrified, in fact. One day she dropped around to see her and she came downstairs looking as though she'd been crying, and that really wasn't like Nada at all.

"Sanja remembers the whole time as being very awkward, because Damir was nine and wanted to be out and about playing with the other children and it set him apart again. It took some months for Sanja to persuade his aunt it was all right, and that no harm would come to him in the village."

Antonia put down her fork. "It's not surprising Damir's having some issues now. The miracle is he's turned out so well at all."

"No, not really. As I think I said before, many people have, but then a great deal of that is through shared experience. Damir had no one in his life who knew anything about what he'd been through. That's the problem with displacement. It happens when refugee children get adopted as well. It's one of the reasons it's so important to keep communities together." He looked despondent.

"It's a very special thing you do, Declan Walsh."

"Yes, but do you know what the supreme irony is? I've travelled around so much helping other people that I've never had a home of my own. This job sure buggers up any chance you have of a decent personal life."

Antonia ran her finger around the rim of her wine glass. "Does it have to?"

He sat back in his seat, frowning. "I wish I could be sure why you're asking."

"Well I think you can probably guess, but my motivation shouldn't make any difference to your answer. This is about you." She faltered, choosing her words carefully. "I think you and I are the same, Declan, we're natural givers. If there's one thing the last six months have taught me it's that there are times when you have to put yourself first."

"You wise, wise, lady." His hand crept across the table towards hers, then stopped. "It's a big change in mindset though."

Antonia rolled her eyes. "Tell me about it. Come on, it's time we were getting back. Damir will be waiting."

As it happened they were settled in the courtyard with a jug of lemonade when the people-carrier parked up next to Declan's car. Damir breezed across the yard to sit down, but Antonia could tell he was nervous by the way he fingered his cigarette packet in his trouser pocket.

"I'm almost at the point of saying, for goodness' sake light one," she told him.

"That is not helpful. Especially when I am almost asking you if I can."

"There's nothing to stress about, Damir. Like I said yesterday, this is just the nuts and bolts of what I can do," Declan told him.

"What I want to know is how long it will take," Damir said.

"Hmmm. Like everything, that depends. I think now I have enough information to go on. Just enough. There was a big fanfare a week or so ago when the Bosnian government announced a new missing persons' database, but of course it isn't working properly yet. As soon as it is I should be able to type in your mother's name to see if there is a match. Then it's one of three scenarios." He paused for a sip of lemonade.

"Go on." Damir was sitting forward, his fingers pressed against the edge of the table.

"First one: there is a single match for her name and we have an answer. That is reasonably likely because over the years the authorities, together with NGOs from around the world, have managed to trace where most people were buried. So as soon as the database is up and running we could well know all there is to know.

"Second one: there is more than one match for her name. At that point I would need to work backwards from the information we have to try to find out which Narcisa Marić she is, and we may or may not have enough to be sure. But in time I can probably trace her marriage certificate, and that will give us her date and place of birth. I warn you though, administration in Bosnia can grind awfully slowly."

"So what's the third option?" Antonia asked.

"That her name isn't on the list at all."

Antonia's heart thudded in her chest as Damir leant even further forwards. "What would that mean?" he asked.

"Simply that no one reported her missing. And if you think about it, if you are right and there were no other close relatives, with your father dead too that is possible."

"So we would be at the end of the path?"

"No. There are many remains that have yet to be identified. You would need to give a DNA sample to see if there was a match."

The bald finality of the statement made Antonia feel slightly sick. Damir sat back in his seat and reached into his pocket. "OK." Antonia noticed he trembled a little as he lit his cigarette, but he flashed Declan a confident smile. "I cannot thank you enough, my friend. You have given me hope."

Together they watched Declan's car disappear through the olive trees. Antonia put her arm around Damir's shoulder.

"How do you feel?"

"Sometimes, I do not understand why I need to know so much. Declan says closure, but what is closure? I understand the actual word, but... anyway, if I wasn't a coward I would not need it."

"I wish you'd stop saying that about yourself."

He looked at her, half smiling. "I wish I would stop believing it. But sometimes I think I have some courage, and perhaps for now that is enough."

"Would you like a coffee?"

He shook his head. "I was planning to sulk in the press house, but I think it would be more helpful to visit Tetka's grave."

She gave him another squeeze. "Good idea."

Once Damir left, Antonia carried on preparing supper.

After her lunch with Declan, everything felt flat and she was a little worried she'd gone too far with her comment about him doing something for himself. But it had to be that way. Fond of him as she was becoming, they would have no chance at all if he went into any relationship believing it doomed to failure because of his job, but she knew he had to work it out for himself. On the one hand it was agonising, because they seemed to fit together so well, but on the other it was too important to push it. She didn't want to make another mistake; next time she was going to get it right and if that meant waiting, well so be it.

In the meantime, she needed to get her act together and tell Honey her plans for the winter. She'd been putting it off, ostensibly because she'd wanted Josip to agree to the idea first, but that excuse had been blown out of the water some forty-eight hours before. Antonia needed to pull on her big-girl pants and make that call. After the moussaka was in the oven. And the peppers and tomatoes marinating in herb oil. Then she would do it. Really.

Chapter Twenty-Eight

It was late on Monday evening by the time Antonia got around to Facetiming Honey, and Sara had gone to bed early, so there wasn't even her quiet common sense to calm Honey down. Antonia suffered a good five minutes of 'How could you do this to me?' and sobbing, which stripped her heart into tiny pieces, but she knew she had to hold her ground and after a while Honey settled down enough to talk about it rationally.

Once Antonia told her she would be home for a couple of weeks in November, and then again for Christmas, she seemed much happier. Antonia pointed out that she had no job to come back to in England, so the offer of an all-year-round one on Korčula was too good to refuse.

"You're not back with Vincenzo, are you? He's not bullied you into this?"

"Of course not. I am doing this because it's what I want. Why would you think anyone was bullying me?"

"Well, not bullying... but, you know, persuading you to keep on doing something you don't really like."

This was beginning to sound a bit like a broken record, but it only reinforced to Antonia how much she had changed. She sighed. "Are we back to Ned again?"

Honey nodded.

"Honey, from this distance Ned feels like even more of a mistake than it did at the time. And not one I intend to repeat. If I find anyone else it will be a man who's free to love me, someone with their own life who doesn't feel I have to step into it, or who wants to jump all over mine. I think it was what I was looking for all those years after I split up with your father. And whatever your Auntie Lynn says, I'm back to being picky."

Finally Honey smiled. "Good for you. And I really am happy you're able to do what you want. I'm sorry for the outburst. It was just such a shock, and I'm tired because Sara was up and down most of last night. I was so looking forward to you coming home."

"Well, as I said, I will be. But I'll take your old room. You can stay in the house longer now if you like, save up a bit more to get somewhere better. Anyway, you'll need to talk to Sara about that."

"I'm saving too, Mum. Sara's set up all these little pots in our joint account and it's quite fun. Especially working out how to spend the treat one. And there's so much more in it now that I take my own latte to work every day."

"Then that's my first treat in November – we'll go for a proper coffee-shop breakfast."

"That would be awesome, Mum."

On Wednesday, Antonia dropped Damir at the early catamaran for Dubrovnik where he was meeting Josip and his lawyer to draw up the contract. There was little sign of his nerves this time and as she turned the car around, in the rear-view mirror she caught a couple of blonde backpackers in cut-off denims eyeing him up and down. He did look a million dollars in his sharply pressed chinos and linen shirt, and Antonia couldn't help but feel just a little proud of him.

Back at Vila Maslina all was quiet. Ana had cleared the breakfast things and was busy upstairs, so Antonia collected a basket of clean bed linen from the utility area and set up the ironing board in a shaded part of the courtyard. The swallows had long gone, but a couple of blackbirds were squabbling over the breakfast scraps and she watched them for a while before setting to work.

It wasn't long before a message flashed up on her phone from Declan, asking if she was free to talk. She typed that he could interrupt the ironing any time and within seconds her mobile was ringing.

"So how's my tenacious little bugger this morning?"

"Good thanks, and I'll even forgive you the use of the personal pronoun."

"Slip of the tongue, slip of the tongue." She could hear the laugh in his voice. "Anyway, that missing persons' database is finally up and running."

"And?"

"And… a conundrum. I want to talk it through with you before approaching Damir."

She unplugged the iron from the extension lead and perched on the edge of the table. "Go on."

"I searched it for Narcisa Marić, and there was nothing. That in itself is only a little unusual, but it was disappointing all the same. So before I started to trawl through the hundreds of Narcisas of about the right age, I thought I would try Marić as a surname. And I found a Damir."

Antonia's tongue felt as though it was stuck to the roof of her mouth. "Our Damir?"

"Quite possibly, but not all the details fit, which was why I thought I would talk to you first."

It couldn't be right. It had to be someone else. "But he isn't missing. He never was. He's been here on Korčula all the time..."

Declan's voice was soft. "I know. It's hard to fathom right now. But the father's name is listed as Ivan, and Damir's last known location is recorded as Mostar in March 1993. What isn't right is his birthday – it's listed as 27th June, not 9th May, although the year is 1987. And the place of birth is Jablanica, which is a small town less than an hour north of Mostar. I wanted to ask – is it possible there are any other papers hidden away?"

"I don't think so. Damir must have pulled the house apart when he converted it, and there really isn't much in the attic. Just that one box, and we've been through it a few times now, but I'll have a word with him when he gets back."

There was a short silence. "Can you ask him without

letting him know what I've found? I don't want to freak him out too much – or to build up his hopes."

"His hopes?" So far Antonia had viewed this development as totally negative, like some sort of sick joke.

"If it is him on that list, someone must have put his name there. Now, it could have been a friend, and that would account for the date of birth being wrong. But more likely it was a family member, which means someone survived the war at least, although it's possible they have died since."

"And if they reported Damir, why not report his mother? Unless they already knew what had happened to her."

"Exactly."

Now Antonia was excited. "Is it possible to work backwards, to find out?"

"I honestly don't know. It depends when it was reported and we could end up being bounced between the Bosnian authorities and the NGOs. But I'm hopeful because the source is tagged as the Red Cross. We'll have to see."

After he rang off, Antonia stood in the courtyard for a long while, watching the blackbirds and trying to grapple with what Declan had found out. But something didn't fit. It didn't fit at all. Eventually she wandered into the coolness of the hall and stood in front of the picture of Tetka. Her face remained inscrutable.

"What did you know?" Antonia found herself whispering. "What did you know?" But whatever it was, it was a secret she had taken to the grave.

A feeling of restlessness settled over Antonia but there

was nothing she could do except wait for Declan to find out more. But what would happen when he did? Would it be good news or bad? Give Damir the closure he so desperately needed or open his wounds wider? She was glad he wasn't there so she didn't have to hide what Declan had found from him. She made a coffee, then finished the ironing, before helping Ana move the large sofas in the living room so she could hoover under them. She pondered starting on the terrine for tomorrow's supper, then tried to read her book. But nothing was enough to distract her.

Instead she was drawn to the olive grove, the hum of the cicadas accompanying her through the dappled shade. The fruit was swelling; young, fresh and so very nearly ripe, but the trees were twisted and gnarled, the bases of their trunks solid into the ground, as though they had been there forever. Damir's father would have known most of them, and his father too. The elder statesmen were interspersed with more slender trunks, but even those were twisted at the bottom, giving them a firm foundation in the soil.

There was a saying locally that an olive tree was like a mother – however long you went away for, she would be waiting for you patiently, still generous with her fruit and her love. Did Damir have a mother waiting for him somewhere?

No, it wasn't possible. Don't even think it.

But he loved these trees; they had given him shelter during his first days on the island and they sheltered him still. She would just have to make sure that whatever happened in Bosnia, he could draw on that strength and come through it.

She was coming to love these olive trees too, but in a different way. For her, home was as Vincenzo had said all those months before: it was about the people. Home would always be where Honey was, but that didn't mean it couldn't be elsewhere too. But for Damir, torn from everyone he knew at such a young age, and now having lost Tetka as well, perhaps the physical place was more important. He had learnt too early that people you loved could disappear from your life and Antonia could understand that for him, and thousands like him, home was not so simple.

Already she found herself next to the old olive press. The harvest was drawing closer. Would he be able to use it this year? More than once he'd mentioned the need to rebuild the concrete trough to catch the oil but so far nothing had been done. Perhaps this autumn it would be best to send the fruit away and not add extra pressure where it wasn't needed. There was always next year. She reached out and ran her hand over the warm wood of the hopper. Next year, she would be here for the olive harvest too.

Chapter Twenty-Nine

"Come, my friend, there is only one place to celebrate our partnership." Josip slapped Damir on the back and led him away from the lawyer's air-conditioned office and through the tourists thronging the narrow street between the Dominican monastery and Dubrovnik's city walls. It had been a long morning studying legal documents and, blinking in the sunlight where it slanted between the tightly packed buildings, Damir felt heady with the strangeness of it all. But Josip had made sure every aspect of the agreement had been explained to him in painstaking detail so he understood it perfectly.

It didn't surprise Damir that Josip had reserved a table at Restaurant 360, the only restaurant in Dubrovnik to have a Michelin star. The design of the place alone took Damir's breath away, the cubed rattan furniture in turquoise and grey in the lower courtyard contrasting in both colour and style with the honeyed stone of the old fort into which it was built. As the maître d' led them up the rough stone staircase, Damir resolved that as soon as he had made any money at all he would bring Antonia here.

They were shown to one of the best tables, standing alone in the apex of the fort, looking down over the boats swaying gently on their moorings in the old harbour.

A bottle of Krug was already chilling in a bucket under a stiff white napkin and having adjusted the sunshade over them, the waiter poured two glasses before leaving the menus and disappearing.

Josip raised his champagne flute. "And so, we begin."

Ice-cold bubbles hit the back of Damir's throat. "We do. I will try to be worth my princely share of the business."

"Already you have proved yourself, in stopping me from making an expensive mistake on the property in Korčula Town. I will send the architect and a surveyor to the island, and if a build is feasible, we can start the purchase of the land."

"But you have not seen it." Damir couldn't decide if the trust Josip was putting in him was gratifying or down right terrifying.

"You have sent me pictures and I have your recommendation. We must have trust in each other, Damir, or we will fail."

It was a huge responsibility and Damir looked away to study the menu. For the price of a starter he could have bought a whole meal in Pecaros, and it both unsettled and excited him how much his world could change. For now, at least, he would be on familiar territory on Korčula but the next steps would surely be away from the island... But not all of his past was there, not all of himself. He remembered looking in Antonia's mirror and seeing his mother's eyes gazing back at him. There was a Damir who had nothing to do with Korčula, if only he could find him. A Damir who knew what it was to belong in another place… a difficult place… No, he would not worry about that. Not today. He was going to enjoy himself. He would order octopus with lime ravioli, then turbot, as though he had been born to riches, not to war.

It did not surprise Damir that exactly forty-eight hours after lunching at a Michelin starred restaurant, he was lying on a damp floor with his arm down a drain, trying to clear a blockage that was stopping a washing machine from emptying. Such was his life, and he was grateful he was in a better frame of mind to enjoy the irony.

Damir had slept well for two whole nights and strength was feeding on strength inside. Of course, he was aware it could crumble around him at any moment, but also that it was growing, and he could perhaps manage to be at least half the man Josip believed him to be.

He fumbled around in the cold, soapy water, stretching to reach the bend in the pipe. Yes, there was something there. Something small, soft, and slimy and he grasped it and gave it a tug. Water sucked then flowed like a rocket from the pipe at the back of the machine, splashing him up to his armpit. In his hand was a shredded child's sock.

Damir left the machine to complete its cycle, and mopped the kitchen floor before removing his polo shirt and having a good wash in the sink. If he sat in the sun while the laundry finished, his sleeve would dry; it was a glorious day, although he knew that at this time of year the wind could change and the Jugo could sweep in from the south bringing its storms. It would do no good for either tourists or his olive crop.

He stepped onto the terrace, and shielding his screen from the sun, opened his phone to text the guests to tell them the washing machine was fixed and he would hang their laundry on the line in the courtyard. A few emails had come in, and a WhatsApp, which he opened to see was from Declan. He smiled. How foolish he had been to take against him, but already the man who had done that was beginning to feel like a stranger. In just a few weeks, as well. Of course the past still crept up on him at inconvenient times, but somehow since the night he'd told Antonia about Kemal, it had lost much of its sting.

How are you, my friend? We may have progress. From your father's details and with a bit of good fortune, I've traced your parents' marriage certificate. But there is something I need to explain, so best to call me when you can.

He could hear the machine had not yet reached its spin cycle so Damir perched on the edge of a sunlounger and pressed the phone icon. When Declan picked up he asked him if it was a good time.

"It is for me, but how about you? Where are you?"

"In the courtyard of a guest villa, waiting for a washing machine to do its stuff."

"And you're alone?"

"Why is that important?" This did not sound good. Suddenly Damir was not sure he wanted any news which might disturb his newfound equilibrium.

"Because what I have to say will surprise you – shock you, even."

Damir took a deep breath. "Then you had better tell me."

"The missing persons register is finally online, but when I searched it I did not find your mother. Instead, I found someone I am pretty sure is you."

The washing machine churned. Music pumped from the beach bar a couple of hundred yards down the street. Damir's sleeve clung damply to the top of his arm.

"You're pretty sure is me?" He said it slowly, as if repeating the words would help him to understand them.

"Yes. Everything fits, apart from your date of birth. I needed more evidence before saying anything and the place on your parents' marriage certificate is the same as your place of birth on the register."

"Mostar? It's a big city..."

"No, Jablanica. A small town about forty minutes' drive away. That changes the odds."

"How else does this change the odds?" The strange phrase rolled around Damir's tongue, but he understood what Declan meant.

"If you are on the register, someone must have reported you missing. Someone who survived the war."

"My mother?" It was a tiny hope.

Declan's voice was firm. "No. Not necessarily. She

would certainly not have got your birthday wrong. But a more distant relative, or a family friend could have... Damir, they may not still be alive, but with your permission I will ask the Red Cross if they have a record of who it was."

"Of course you have my permission. You have my permission to ask anyone, try anything. I understand... it is a small chance. But I am very grateful to you, all the same."

It could not have been his mother. How stupid of him to have thought it even for a moment. But in that moment, the pain of losing her resurfaced, bubbling up through his flimsy happiness and leaving him feeling exhausted and bereft.

But somehow, over the next few weeks that seed of hope would not go away. Sometimes it grew to such proportions he would dream he saw his mother walking towards him through the olive grove. One time she seemed so real that he woke with tears streaming down his cheeks, and even the salt of the ocean as he ploughed across the bay refused to wash them away.

It was not a good day to be brimming with emotion because the architect and surveyor were coming to look at the site, so he wanted to be at his best. Mia was a clever and beautiful young woman, with hair so glossy it made Damir want to reach out and stroke it. The Jugo was making its presence felt, but still she perched on a rock and sketched, the wind blowing her Jil Sander trench coat around her shapely legs. Damir watched her from the corner of his eye as he walked next to the surveyor across the field and back again, the man talking into an old-fashioned Dictaphone.

Mia continued to draw over lunch, explaining her initial ideas with sweeping strokes of her pencil. It was soothing to watch her, and the image of Damir's mother faded. Mia's ideas were traditional and radical at the same time, and he found himself nodding like some crazy donkey, which made him think of his father and once again his spirits flagged. Damir didn't want this graceful and talented young woman to consider him the village fool.

Antonia told him all this was normal, but Damir was uncomfortable about the way her interest pricked up when he spoke of Mia. He could not even think of Mia now, bar checking her Facebook profile to see if she was single. He was on the brink of everything and nothing, and the waiting seemed interminable. Declan may have forbidden him to hope, but how could he extinguish that flame? But all the same he knew he should be ready for disappointment, for the harsh reality of life to kick back in.

Damir's mother's name was not on the missing list, yet by the beginning of October Declan had failed to trace a death certificate. That could simply mean nobody had reported her, but who had reported Damir? While he waited for an answer from the Red Cross, Declan arranged for Damir to be sent a DNA testing kit, so on the morning Vesna arrived on Korčula he found himself swabbing the inside of his cheek in a state of some despondency. He'd read an article online about unclaimed bodies, and now Damir's nights were filled with rows of skeletons on table after table, bullet holes in precisely the centre of their skulls.

It was a good thing he had little time to dwell on what might have happened to his mother. Vila Maslina would be full of guests for the next fortnight, right up until they closed for the winter. The purchase of the land had begun, although to be fair Josip was handling that. And as Damir walked through the olive grove he could tell the fruit was almost ripe, and he had done nothing about building the trough he needed to complete the press, or sourcing packaging for their own products.

Had he become so wrapped up in finding his Bosnian family that he had all but forgotten the woman who raised him? Bringing the press back to life, making as much as he could of the olive harvest, was going to be his tribute to her, but somehow it had fallen by the wayside. He could not let that happen. He owed Tetka so much. He would harvest the olives and he would press them in the traditional way. He would not let her down.

Some of Damir's neighbours were picking their olives already, or laying nets beneath the trees, and although that would be easier he wanted to harvest by hand. The crates were languishing in the shed off the courtyard and he would need to inspect and clean them before they could be used. Damir was sure Antonia would help him before she went home. This year he couldn't ask his neighbours, because he was not in a position to help them in return. This dampened his mood even further, making him feel that something more had been lost. Was he growing too far and too fast from everything he knew?

He found himself mesmerised by the thought that there were wheels in motion, dragging him along like a stick caught under the bumper. Josip and his new hotel, Declan's search for his relatives; in both cases he felt entirely powerless, and although Antonia reminded him it was his life and he always had a choice, he couldn't quite persuade himself to believe it.

Vesna lost no time in reminding him about wanting to try Antonia's food. Antonia took little persuasion to invite her to lunch, despite Damir's protests that it would mean cooking two meals in one day, but she shook her head, telling him it would be the same meal twice, therefore very little extra effort. So Damir told her rather too sharply it had better be something he liked, before heading to the builder's merchant on the Račišće road to buy the cement he needed to make the trough around the old olive press.

Antonia cooked a traditional dish of bream, potatoes, garlic, and chard, after a starter of wild mushroom terrine, with *zabaglione* and shortbread to follow. They would eat together in the dining room, overlooking the terrace and the olive grove. As Damir set out the olives and cheese in oil to accompany their aperitif, it dawned on him that this meal was far from being about the food. Vesna, an ex-lover who had become a friend, was going to meet Antonia, who was the most important woman in his life. Not because he was in love with her – it had never been about that – and not because she had that comforting yet irritating habit of mothering him. No, it was because she saw him for who he was, and some days the honesty between them was the only thing keeping his world from spinning entirely out of control.

Vesna was sparkling, full of praise for everything and

gliding from room to room in her kitten heels and fine cashmere dress. Antonia's cheeks were flushed from the kitchen, but Damir knew she was a different kind of diamond, in jeans and a plain terracotta shirt, mistress of her own domain. And although their conversation was a little limited by Antonia's Croatian, the women appeared to understand each other very well.

By the time Antonia brought the fish to the table, Vesna had relaxed into her less formal self. A watery sunshine filtered through the window as they talked of recipes, and Croatian customs, and the women exchanged stories about their grown-up children. This surprised Damir, as Vesna hardly ever mentioned her son, a lawyer in an international firm in Zagreb who apparently took too much after his father. Damir looked from one of them to the other, and found it was not only the sun bathing him in its warmth.

Antonia's phone rang just as they were finishing dessert. She looked at the screen, then jumped up, excusing herself as she rushed from the room. Vesna raised her eyebrows.

"It must be important," Damir said. "I hope it is not a problem with her daughter."

Vesna rolled her eyes. "Children are always a problem. But she is a good woman, Damir. You have chosen well for your business. Josip will be pleased when I tell him."

"So you came here to spy for your brother?" He laughed.

Vesna was about to respond, but Antonia returned, her face a little pale. "Declan has some news and he would like you to call him when you're free."

"Who is Declan?" asked Vesna.

"He is the aid worker who is trying to trace my Bosnian relatives. I told you, he was waiting for the Red Cross..." Damir turned to Antonia. "He has heard from them?" She nodded. "Then I had best phone him now."

He pulled his phone from his pocket and began to dial. "On the terrace, perhaps?" Antonia said it so gently he knew it would not be good news.

"OK."

Damir sat for a long while, smoking a cigarette and gazing at the birds fluttering between the olive trees, before picking up his phone again. He would always remember that moment; the softness of the cushion behind him, the breeze carrying the scent of the sea, Antonia and Vesna's muted conversation. It was the moment before he spoke to Declan and everything changed. The moment Declan said:

"Damir, it was your mother who reported you missing, and I have found her."

Scrambling to harness his fractured thoughts, Damir cleared his throat to ask where she was living.

"Mostar."

Four hours away. Just across those mountains he had been staring at all his life.

"OK."

There was a silence before Declan asked, "What would you like me to do?"

"Do?" The news was almost impossible to process, let alone consider any action.

"I can hand the matter back to the Red Cross and wheels would grind slowly to reunite you. Or I could break just about every rule in the book and go to see her on your behalf."

"Or you could just give me her address." Then it would be in his own hands, and he would have time to think.

"I could, but I won't. Just imagine the shock it would give her; she might not even believe you were her son without some official involvement."

Damir gazed into the shadows beneath the olives. "Yes, I see that. How could she know me after all this time?"

"I probably shouldn't even have suggested I go, but I know how long these things can take officially – months, if not years."

"But why?"

"Shortage of case workers, mainly. Then once they have allocated someone they will need to 'design the project', as the jargon goes, which sounds like a load of institutional baloney to me. Plus there is no real protocol for it, because mostly it is only bodies that are found. My contact says it will take them a while to even work out what happens next."

"But you would break the rules?"

"I could... misunderstand the rules. Dragging out the whole process seems unnecessarily cruel in my book, but it depends what you want me to do."

Damir leant back against the cushions and stared at the sky. "I want you to do nothing."

Declan didn't argue, even though Damir half expected him to, so he thanked him for his trouble and rang off. What next? What now? His only option seemed to be to continue as normal, at least until the crazy jumble of thoughts spinning in his head settled down. He stood, stretched, and went back inside. Two pairs of eyes, one hazel and the other pale blue, locked onto him.

"My mother is living in Mostar," he told them. "Now, shall I make the coffee?"

Chapter Thirty

It was as though the women had made a pact not to mention what had happened, but all the same Damir made his excuses and left as quickly as he possibly could. Nothing in his life so far had given him any idea of how to deal with this thing, this enormous thing, that he could not even begin to understand.

He decided that hard physical work was the best way to stem the questions flooding his mind. After all, he was pretty sure it was what Tetka would have done. In the press house he measured the trough on the floor then sat back on his heels. The flat base would be simple; all he had to do was dig a circular hole in the ground to the exact dimensions, make up the concrete and pour. The sides would be more complicated as he needed to figure out how to mould them. Vincenzo would know, but then he would offer to help, and for some reason Damir didn't understand, he needed to do this on his own.

He had an hour or so before collecting the guests from

the studio so he marked out the shape of the trough in the earth and began to dig. After the long, hot summer the earth was hard and the sweat ran off his forehead and into his eyes. Marco sat under an olive tree to watch until the dust began to coat his fur and he stalked off in disgust.

If his mother was alive, why had she not looked for him? Yes, she had put his name on a register, but surely she would have asked former neighbours and the authorities, and if not them, then his father's only living relative. And if she had not looked for him, had she left him deliberately in the first place? Had she walked away one morning because it was his fault Kemal was dead, and she could not bear the shame?

No, he must not think of this. He must dig. He had removed the layer of scrubby grass but now he must go deeper. He checked his measurements one more time, and then his watch. In twenty minutes he needed to be at Vincenzo's, so, cursing to himself, he took the quickest of showers and managed to arrive not very late at all.

As soon as supper was over he excused himself and hurried back through the olive grove to continue his task. Clouds scampered across the face of the moon so he worked by the light flooding from the door of the press house, its beam casting his shadow long amongst the trees. But the night was cool, the salt breeze from the south making it easier for him to dig.

Damir was on his hands and knees, smoothing the edges of the hole so it would be ready to take the concrete when he heard Vincenzo's motorbike on the drive. There was no time for him to melt away between the olives, so inevitably Vincenzo stopped.

"What are you doing, my friend?"

"Building the trough for the press. The harvest will be here before we know it."

"Still, to work in the dark..."

Damir stood and folded his arms. "It has to be done."

Vincenzo switched off his engine. "There is no guarantee the press will work. I told you..."

"It will."

"OK, OK... How are you planning to mould the lip?"

Damir flung his arms in the air. "Why do you always have to put up obstacles? Because no one is as perfect as you?"

"Perfect?" Vincenzo laughed. "No, far from it. But in my workshop I have a rounded wooden brace that might do the trick. It's probably about the right size."

"It needs to be exactly the right size."

"Now it is you who is putting up obstacles. Is there something else eating you, my friend? You seem in a very bad mood."

Damir stepped back, away from the light. "What has Antonia told you?"

"Nothing. Should she have?"

"No. Not at all. Goodnight Vincenzo, I will see you tomorrow."

Damir woke to the sound of rain on the roof. So much for the earth drying ready to pour the concrete later. But at least the digging had achieved one purpose; he had slept, when he had not expected to. His shoulders ached badly though, and even ten minutes under the shower did nothing to relieve them. He thought about asking Vesna if he could use the Jacuzzi in Beros's villa, but she would have too many questions, questions he knew he could not answer. Already she had sent three texts asking if he was all right.

Antonia was the one who had been silent. But then she knew – she knew about Kemal. She must have guessed the real reason his mother had abandoned him so it was obvious she would do the same. There would be an excuse... something... She would go and she would not come back. Suddenly he understood that everybody left him sooner or later because of some flaw that made him let them down so badly he was impossible to love.

The hole around the press was half full of water and the very sight of it made Damir want to weep. He hadn't even had the sense to cover it. The direction of the breeze last night should have told him rain was on the way. He messaged Antonia, asking her to take the guests to Vincenzo's, and set about emptying the hole with his coffee mug and mopping it with his spare towel. The wind was still fresh, so with any luck the earth would dry quickly.

He hid in the press house when he heard the people-carrier through the trees, preparing to stay there until it passed again on its way back. But it didn't pass; the engine stopped. Antonia knocked on the door, then called his name, and Damir ducked into the bathroom in case she came in when he did not answer. But after the longest silence ever he heard the vehicle continue towards the house. Had she wanted to tell him already that she was going to leave?

Under the door was a scrap of paper torn from her notebook. With shaking hands he picked it up.

'You know where I am if you need me. We all are. We're your friends and we love you. You are not alone. But if you want to be for a while then I understand. xx

How could she possibly mean it? Even his own mother hadn't wanted to know him. She'd probably just put his name on that register because someone told her she should. After all, she'd got his birthday wrong. Probably deliberately so there wouldn't be a match.

With that devastating thought, the final piece of the jigsaw fell into place; the last shred of hope that maybe he was wrong and his mother had loved him and wanted to find him disappeared. He stood at the door and looked across at the old olive press. What was the point? What was the point of anything? Except... the olives would still ripen, and they would need to be harvested. Like they did every year. An olive tree would never let you down. Tetka had never let him down. And he would repay that faithfulness.

The sun flitted in and out of the clouds as Damir carried on mopping and reshaping the hole where the water had washed the edges in. After a while it was perfect once more. He checked the forecast on his phone; if he mixed and poured a thin layer of concrete straight away it had every chance of setting before it started to rain again.

It was lunchtime by the time he finished and he was almost weak with hunger. Antonia's note was on his desk and he turned it under his index finger. She'd said she understood if he wanted to be alone, and he did. He needed to come to terms with his mother's rejection. To find her and lose her all in the same moment... it was just too much. And there was nothing more he could do with the press until the concrete dried. He texted Antonia, asking if she could make him a sandwich and leave it in the courtyard for him to collect in half an hour. If she really understood, that would be exactly what she would do.

When he arrived in the courtyard, Antonia was nowhere to be seen, but on the table was a plate covered in foil, which had a note tucked under it in Croatian saying 'Lunch is not a sandwich'. There was cutlery, and a glass of chilled white wine, and when Damir investigated further he found his favourite cheese and ham omelette with potatoes fried with onions and garlic. The aroma drew him in and he sat down with his back to the kitchen window to eat it.

It would have been impossibly churlish not to thank Antonia. He could have messaged her or left a note, but instead he went inside, and once he had put his plate in the dishwasher, he pushed open the door to the hall and called her name. After a few moments she appeared at the top of the stairs.

She grinned down at him. "Are you after dessert? There's fruitcake in the larder."

And for some unfathomable reason Damir found

himself saying, "I was going to make coffee. Do you have time for one?"

"I'll make time."

Why the hell had he said that? He'd had no intention at all of talking to her, so now what would he say? He set about boiling the water and brought the fruitcake through to the kitchen. After a few moments Antonia appeared and sat down at the table.

"How's the trough going?" she asked. "It looked pretty water-logged this morning."

"I managed to mop it out, and put in the first layer of concrete. If the weather holds for a few more hours it should dry."

"Vincenzo wants to know if he should bring the mould tomorrow."

"I... I don't know." He spooned the coffee into the smaller jug and poured on the boiling water, stirring while it reheated on the stove.

Behind him Antonia said nothing. Without turning he asked, "Do you think I am stupid to refuse his help?"

"No. But I think perhaps you are confusing building the trough with processing the news about your mother."

Damir continued to stir. Her words made absolutely no sense at all.

"I can see," Antonia continued, "that the fact your mother is alive is something deeply personal that maybe you need to come to terms with on your own, but surely you could accept some help with the trough. Especially when the harvest is just weeks away and it would save so much time."

"I suppose... it would be practical."

"Yes."

Damir poured the coffee into mugs and sat down opposite her. Antonia cut him an enormous slice of cake and everything felt blessedly normal. So normal and comforting that perhaps he could put at least some of these awful thoughts and fears into words. Antonia knew the whole story, so she would completely get why his mother had walked out on him.

"You are so good to me," he said. "I wanted to thank you for my lunch."

"Anything – anything I can do to make this easier."

"You understand then, you can see it too, that my mother did not want to find me."

Antonia's eyes widened, her brows disappearing under the sweep of her hair. Slowly she said, "I have to say that hadn't occurred to me."

"But you do see, now I have said it?" He could not believe this. She had to understand. If she didn't, then she couldn't help him. And if she couldn't, no one could.

"I'm sorry, Damir, you will have to explain. I don't understand why you think that, when she put your name on the missing persons list."

He gripped the edge of the table as he leant forwards. "She probably had to. And she put my birthday wrong so I wouldn't match with anything. She didn't want to know me, that's for sure. She probably deliberately left me in the shelter in the first place. Why else would she not have come back? I have been cursing myself for breaking my promise to my father and not looking for her when all along she didn't even want to be found."

"But I don't think it was like that..."

This was not what he needed, not what he needed from Antonia at all. A terrifying anger coursed through him and he stood, sweeping cake, plate, and coffee mug onto the floor. "And what do you know about it? What the hell do you know?"

He didn't wait for her reply. He grabbed the keys to the people-carrier from their hook by the door and fled.

Although he felt like death the next morning, Damir managed to put on his best smile to wave off the guests at the catamaran. He stood for a long time as it manoeuvred itself clear of the harbour, fingering the cigarette packet in his pocket, then went to look for Antonia in the market. He watched for a while as she moved from stall to stall, picking up produce to inspect, laughing and talking as though she had shopped here all her life. Her dark hair shone as the sunlight nudged its way through the fracturing clouds. Perhaps the Jugo had blown its course for the moment, and it had taken Damir's anger with it.

He had behaved appallingly yesterday and he needed to apologise.

He took the basket from Antonia without a word and she smiled and thanked him, so he followed her progress a couple of steps behind. She selected two shiny pomegranates, paid, and nestled them next to the tomatoes.

"Now, some goat cheese to go with them, and I'm done."

"Time for a coffee?" he asked her.

"Of course. No problem."

When they arrived at his favourite coffee shop overlooking the harbour he chose a table in a corner well away from the owner with his flapping ears and ordered her a *bijela kava* for Antonia, with an espresso for himself and a plate of *kroštule* to share.

She raised her eyebrows at the pastries. "Ah well, you did miss breakfast."

"They are for both of us. And I am sorry. Yet again I am sorry. For missing breakfast, for being so rude to you yesterday afternoon, and for leaving you to cope with everything last night."

"Look, you've had a massive shock so I'm prepared to cut you a hell of a lot of slack. But I still don't really understand why you think the way you do about your mother. I mean, it is possible, but there are other possibilities too."

"Like what?" There was no other option he could see.

"I don't really want to second guess, Damir, but I do know that hundreds of Bosniaks were expelled from West Mostar. Just... rounded up by the soldiers. If that had happened to her, she couldn't have come back for you, or even sent a message. Ages ago I did wonder if she could be alive as some people managed to get to the east of the city, but Declan said it was unlikely because most ended up in concentration camps. So I have no doubt she would not have left you deliberately."

"Even if that is so... why did she not look for me? And why change my date of birth on the missing persons' register?"

Antonia sipped her coffee. "The first, I cannot begin to answer, but I have been thinking about your birthday. You said... you had no birth certificate. Perhaps it was Tetka who got it wrong?"

Damir opened his mouth to argue, but what she said was not impossible. After all, Sanja had told him Tetka had never had anything to do with him before he arrived on Korčula. He shook his head.

"Just when I thought I was beginning to understand who I really am, I can't even be sure about when I was born."

Antonia covered his hand with hers in that oh-so-familiar gesture. "Who you are does not depend on dates or on other people. Who you are is inside you. The person you are right now. Believe it, Damir. Believe in yourself."

"You always think so well of people..."

"I think well of you because I know you. You and you alone have made me feel as though Korčula is my second home. When I thought I was screwing up just about everything and had zero confidence, you took a chance on me and helped me to understand who I really am. Not just someone's girlfriend, not even just a mother, but really, really me."

He looked at her, astounded. "You are just saying that." But he knew from her impassioned speech that it was true. "I'm sorry, I'm sorry," he continued. "But if I have done even half of that…"

"Half and more. You made me feel confident in my cooking and in my language, and in so many other small ways. You've always made me feel that my opinion – and my happiness – mattered. You even said so when Lynn was coming to stay, and that meant so much. And don't forget all you did for the girls."

"I'd say it was nothing, but clearly it was not."

"There's an awful lot of good in you Damir. And I know you'll see it for yourself when you start to feel better."

They sat in silence for a while, their fingers intertwined, sipping coffee and picking up *kroštule* with their free hands. Yes, he remembered all the things Antonia had spoken about, and how he had done them without much thought. Did that make them more valuable, or less? Clearly what was important was that they had meant so much to her. But all the same, the list of people who believed in him was growing: Antonia, Josip, Vesna... and Petar always had. Tetka too. These people knew him; his estranged mother did not. So even if he was right and Antonia wrong, it did not make him worthless.

The thought warmed him, and suddenly he felt quite brave.

"The only way to find out the truth is to meet my mother," he told Antonia.

"Through Declan, or through the Red Cross?"

"Neither. I will ask him again for her address and go myself."

Antonia squeezed his hand. "Do you think that is wise?"

"Wise?"

"Whatever happened, your mother must by now think

you are dead. Just imagine the shock if you turned up on her doorstep. You're probably still in shock yourself. And don't argue – you know you are. Do not imagine for one minute it will not be the same for her. She will need time to adjust too." Antonia ran her finger around the rim of her coffee cup. "And we don't know what she went through in the war. She could be... emotionally damaged."

Antonia's words stopped him in his tracks. He had not even thought about this from his mother's point of view. A fragment of memory burst through the fog in his brain, a fragment he now realised he had been fighting for the last two days: the warmth of her arms around him, her tears in his hair. Kemal was dead, but he was alive, and he had felt as though she would never let him go.

"You are right. I will ask Declan to see her. He will know what best to do."

Chapter Thirty-One

It was the strangest of feelings, meeting his mother by proxy, but both Antonia and Declan had reassured Damir it was the right thing to do. Declan had asked a select few of his colleagues how best to approach her without going through official channels, which they had agreed would take too long. Antonia was worried about Declan putting his job at risk by breaking so many rules, but as they video called him in the kitchen one evening, he shrugged and said he was getting fed up with all the red tape anyway.

After double-checking Damir's mother's address, Declan sent a letter saying he had news of her son. The wait for her reply felt endless as Damir drove guests to and from Vincenzo's, gradually completed the trough using the wooden brace Vincenzo had lent him, and Facetimed Mia to go through her latest drawings. In reality, it was only a couple of days before Declan received a call and arranged to go to Mostar.

He urged Damir to send his mother some sort of message, but he did not know what to say, and none of Antonia or Vesna's suggestions seemed right. So Declan asked if instead he could send a photograph he could show her. Even that was not easy; Damir wanted to email him the corporate one Josip had had taken for their new website, but Antonia was adamant his mother would want to see her son, not some anonymous businessman. So she made Damir sit on the olive press, wearing his usual polo shirt and jeans, with a wriggling Marco on his lap, and snapped away with her phone, admonishing him to smile.

The whole exercise made Damir think about how his mother might look today. The memories of her were coming back stronger, and he found himself gazing at her wedding photograph again and again. But now she would be in her late fifties and very much changed. Her raven hair would be at the very least flecked with grey, and her face lined. Even if she wanted to see him, which part of him still doubted, they would most likely not even recognise each other, and that left him feeling emptier still.

The day before Declan's visit to Mostar, as Damir walked through the olive grove to help Antonia with breakfast, he realised the fruit was beginning to turn from green to reddish brown in large numbers. If he left it much longer before harvesting the olives would be damaged too easily when they were picked; as soon as the last guests left the next day they would have to begin. At least it would be a distraction.

While Damir took the people-carrier to the catamaran on Saturday morning, Antonia raced around the market. He couldn't understand why she had bought so much food, but she said if the harvest was going to take them a few days she didn't want to be going back and forth to town, and Damir supposed she was right. Vincenzo and Petar had offered to help so of course they would need to be fed as well.

Antonia drove home and dropped Damir at the press house to change into his old clothes. On the other side of the mountains, Declan would be heading towards Mostar. Damir had a sudden urge to call him and tell him to stop, but they were well beyond that point now. What happened in Mostar this morning was going to shape the rest of his life. Whether his mother rejected him, or whether she agreed to see him… If she was the mother he remembered, or had been so badly damaged by the war… He sat on his bed to stroke Marco, who was curled next to his pillow, the smooth warmth of his fur giving him comfort. But he could almost hear Tetka's voice telling him he did not have time for this. Already Vincenzo's truck had rumbled past and the olives were calling.

Even though it would take a few days to complete the harvest, Damir had decided to pick the whole crop first, then select olives for curing or to press. It was not ideal, and he was worried the fruit picked first might begin to spoil. If they had more help it could be done so much quicker, but Damir had given nothing to his neighbours this year so could not expect to receive. He put his hand on the old olive press as he passed; he had no idea if it would actually work, but it was a risk worth taking. And a very small one, compared to the risk Declan was taking on his behalf in Mostar.

The crates were stacked in the courtyard so he made his way through the trees, checking the olives again. He would need to show Antonia what to do, and that would take time, but in everything else she had been a quick learner and Damir knew she would not let him down. As he rounded the corner of Vila Maslina he was aware of voices but was still stunned by the sight before him.

Not just Vincenzo and Petar, but Lorena, Sanja, Ivica and his sons, together with several other villagers. Damir stopped and clutched the corner of the wall. He had expected nothing, but here they were. There was a moment of silence, then Ivica told him to stop gawping like a halfwit and tell them where to start.

Now he understood why Antonia had bought so much food, but it was Sanja who would be cooking the lunchtime feast.

"I am too old for clambering around trees," she told him, "and Ivica has brought octopus and bream, so you will not go hungry." Luckily there was wine enough in the larder.

It was late in the morning when Damir's phone started to ring. He was in the higher branches of a tree near the house while Antonia picked the olives she could reach from the ground. He pulled his mobile from his shirt pocket and, seeing Declan's name on the screen, threw it down to her. For a moment she looked puzzled, but Damir nodded and she answered it, walking into a patch of sunlight a few yards away so he could not hear her voice.

Damir rolled an olive between his fingers, smooth and slightly soft, focusing his attention on the fruit. Yes, the picking had had to start that day, and with all these helpers, by tomorrow it would be finished. It was incredible that almost a year had passed since Tetka's death. He pictured her at the last harvest, bustling around, organising their helpers, then disappearing to the kitchen to cook an enormous meal to thank them. He still expected to hear her call, issuing instructions that nobody needed but to which everyone had listened with respect.

Antonia was beneath the tree, gesticulating with his phone. "Speak to him?"

Damir shook his head. Now the moment had come, it was just too frightening.

"He'd like to drive on here now and tell you face to face."

"Is it bad news?"

"Far from it. She seems like a lovely lady."

"And what does that mean?"

"If you won't talk to him then you must wait to find out."

Declan arrived in the early evening, just as their helpers were going home. He had left his car on the port at Orebić, so Damir met him from the ferry, as Antonia insisted she needed a shower. Damir hadn't even had time to change out of his picking clothes, so Declan would have to accept him as he was. Of course, when he thought about it, Damir realised the man had never done anything else.

To his great surprise, Declan gave him a hug. "She's a good woman, Damir, a really good woman."

He nodded, then turned and walked towards the people-carrier. On the drive back to Lumbarda they talked about the olive harvest.

They sat at the kitchen table, drinking wine, the hands of the clock next to the door sweeping slowly around. Damir had given himself a ten-minute countdown, while Declan and Antonia made small talk, but after six he felt ready to plunge in.

"OK, tell me about her."

Declan put his glass on the table. "What do you want to know first?"

Damir shook his head. "I don't know." It was a lie, but it seemed wrong to blurt out that the only important things were why his mother hadn't looked for him, and whether she wanted to see him now.

So Declan told Damir that although his mother had kept his father's name she had married again, to an optician called Harun, but they had no children of their own. They lived in his family home in East Mostar, just south of the Stari Most. Declan asked if Damir remembered the famous bridge, but he shook his head. Of course he had seen pictures, but hadn't paid them much attention. Then Declan asked him what he did remember of Mostar, but Damir shrugged, thinking how unimportant these details were, so Declan carried on telling him about his mother.

He looked at Damir, head on one side. "She has your cheekbones and eyes. Or rather, you have hers. There is no doubt about that. She is small, and her face is quite thin, so they stand out even more. Her hair is cut short in a fashionable way, but she told me she is a hairdresser, so that figures. But most of her work is voluntary; she helps people whose sight was damaged in the war to look their best. It was how she met Harun."

"So that is why you say she is a good woman."

"In part. For the rest, you gain an impression when you talk to someone. And when you see them stripped raw by what you tell them, there is no place to hide."

"How did she react when you told her Damir was alive?" Antonia asked.

"Understandably she was very nervous when I arrived. I am sure she thought it would be bad news. After all, barely anyone is found now, although mass graves are still being discovered. Afterwards Harun told me she had not eaten for two days, and he had been cursing my name for ever sending the letter. I have to say, at that point I was cursing myself too.

"When I told her you were alive, of course she cried. But after a few minutes she raised her head and asked for proof. As much as anything because it was not official. So I showed her the photograph you sent and she knew you immediately. She took my phone, and looked at it from every angle, almost as though you were hidden inside, then gave it to Harun, saying 'my son' over and over again."

There were tears streaming down Antonia's cheeks, and Declan took her hand. They both looked at Damir, but he felt outside himself, as though he was gazing down at the three of them at the scrubbed pine kitchen table. He knew he should be feeling something – anything – but when he looked inside, all he could find was the same old question beating away at his brain.

"So why did she not look for me?"

"The answer is that she did."

"But not here. Not in the most obvious place."

Declan sighed. "This is where my skills are woefully inadequate, so much so that when I was driving here I was beginning to wish I had left it to the authorities. I'm warning you Damir, this is a biggy. You, and only you, can choose who to believe, and you won't even begin to know the answer straight away."

"Then you had better tell me."

"Narcisa said she wrote to your *tetka* after the war, but she replied to say she had no information."

"And does she still have the letter?"

"She said it was not a nice letter, so she burnt it."

"Very convenient."

"Perhaps. But I wish you had seen her face when I said you were living on Korčula and your aunt had brought you up. Even in all my years on the front line working with refugees, I have rarely seen such anguish. And it was then she told me about the letter. I did not have to ask."

"When did she write it?" Antonia asked. "Could it have been before Damir arrived here?"

"No. It was after the war. Nothing is normal in a warzone, you have to understand that. And experiences are not normal, either. She suffered greatly at the hands of the soldiers who took her; more so I think because she told them she was married to a Croatian. It seems they held her for days before finally dumping her near the front line outside the city, where other refugees found her and took her across to the east with them."

Antonia was saying something about how awful it was, but it was hard for Damir to hear her through the ringing in his ears. She was lying. His mother must be lying. But why? Perhaps her experiences in the war had unhinged her, and he told Declan as much.

He nodded. "It's possible. She suffered such trauma, everything could have become blurred. But do not think she did not try to find you. As soon as it was possible, she ventured back across the city to your old apartment. She even attempted to live there, in case you tried to find her, but it was very difficult. There was too much hatred in people's hearts in the years following the war; so many had died in terrible circumstances. But she stuck it out for quite a while. It was only when she married Harun that she left for good.

"None of the neighbours would even speak to her, although she tried again and again to ask them what had happened to you. One day she returned to find 'better dead than a Bosniak child' scrawled across her door. That in itself tells you a lot about the degree of loathing. At the time there were rumours circulating that some children had been sold for adoption overseas, and rather than believe you were dead, that was what she always hoped for you. A life away from danger and hatred."

"That's what I have had here."

"Perhaps it was what Tetka wanted for you too," said Antonia, as Declan entwined his fingers more closely with hers. "Perhaps she wanted that more than anything, which was why she lied to your mother. If Narcisa's story is true, that is," she added.

Silence fell in the kitchen. A silence that bounced around the walls in search of Tetka's memory, which Damir found strange considering how close she had felt to him all day. Only a year before she had been sitting in the chair in front of the range, and all had been well with his world. He could hardly recognise the boy who'd been at the table, pretending to listen to her while sexting Vesna – or some other woman he'd had on the go.

Maybe Tetka had not always been right. After all, he had become a man who cried, yet he was able to deal with his emotions all the better for it. And he knew he wasn't the finished article she had been so proud of; he, and everyone else, were only works in progress, trying to better their lives as they went from day to day. But, although judging by the measures he'd been brought up to believe in he should have been weaker, he really was beginning to feel stronger inside.

It was Declan who spoke. "Your mother let me take a photograph of her. Do you want to see it?"

He shook his head. He remembered the shock of finding her wedding picture all too well, and this time he needed to be prepared. "Later. Can you send it to me?"

"She also gave me something for you. She found it when she returned to the apartment. The place had been looted, stripped almost bare, but I don't expect this was worth anything – although to her it was a part of you." He reached into his rucksack, with some difficulty given his reluctance to let go of Antonia's hand, and produced a red fabric mouse with an impossibly long tail.

Damir held out his hand. "It was Dusa's. She would play with it for hours, patting it to all corners. I'd hold it up by its tail and she would jump and spin to catch it." And he could see it in his mind's eye, as clearly as if he was a child back in Mostar.

"What happened to Dusa?" Damir asked the question out loud.

"Now that's something you'll have to ask your mother."

"Yes, I will. It will be a place to start." He tucked the mouse into his pocket and stood, placing his chair under the table. "Now, if you will excuse me..."

Damir did not leave by the kitchen door, but stood for a long while gazing at Vincenzo's picture of Tetka, the only mother he had known from the age of six. That was more than twenty-five years. He'd only had to look at her to feel safe. And if that safety had been built on a lie... well, it had also been built on love. He reached up to touch her cheek and the tears started to roll uncontrollably down his own, so, head down, he made for the front door.

The night was chill and the moon hung above the olives in an elegant crescent. Damir made his way between the trees, touching each one that he passed, following the twists and turns in their bark with his fingers. Beneath them was a scattering of leaves, some knocked off by the pickers, but others fallen yellow; the ones the new leaves had replaced. Could you replace a mother? Tetka may have made him who he was, but his mother's blood flowed through his veins. It was the part of him that had been missing for so long. And in that moment, he knew it was what he needed to be complete.

Damir hunched his shoulders further into his fleece and

upped his pace, passing the old olive press with barely a glance. He opened the door to the press house and turned on the light, calling, "Marco, I have a present for you."

Chapter Thirty-Two

Declan's hand felt warm through her glove as he led Antonia down a narrow street.

"Right. Close your eyes."

She did as she was told and his grip tightened as he led her around a corner and the sound of surging water drowned out the traffic they had left behind.

Declan stopped. "OK. You can open them."

In front of Antonia an impossibly fragile-looking bridge raised a single eyebrow arch over a tumble of glassy river, its pale grey stone almost lost in the December sky.

"Wow. Just wow."

"Probably the most photographed landmark in Bosnia from probably the best angle. I so wanted you to see the Stari Most from here. Nothing beats it."

She looked around at the industrial-sized bins and steam belching from the vent of what she took to be a restaurant, filling the air with spices.

"How on earth did you find this place?"

"I had a wander around when I brought Damir to meet his mother for the first time. Not that I had terribly long."

The meeting had not been a success. Antonia had been in England at the time and Declan had borne the brunt of Damir's guilt afterwards. While his mother, Narcisa, had welcomed him with open arms, they were not arms Damir had felt ready to run into and it had put him on the defensive. Their conversation had been stilted at best, all the questions he had longed to ask dried up inside him, and they had sat like strangers, on either side of the coffee table, Narcisa attempting to fill the silence.

Afterwards, he and Declan had walked the streets, Damir berating himself for his lack of affection towards his mother and how he could never now put it right. The most Declan had been able to do was persuade Damir to buy a postcard and write a note to apologise, which he'd delivered after Damir had begun the long, lonely drive back to Korčula.

But if Declan had laid the foundation, it was Antonia who had helped Damir build the bridge, block after painstaking block. She'd returned to Korčula a few days later, full of excitement at the news of Honey and Sara's engagement, only to find Damir as low as she had ever seen him.

So she'd made carbonara – the quickest hot meal she could think of – and told him to open some wine. The kitchen had been warm from the heat of the range and they had talked well into the second bottle.

It had helped that her visit home had made her understand how much her relationship with Honey had changed. For the first time she'd seen her daughter as an independent woman, and although perhaps she leaned on Sara a little too much, her fiancée certainly didn't pander to her every whim. The bonds of motherhood were no less strong, and Antonia had enjoyed spending time with her daughter more than ever now that she wasn't worrying about the ironing, or whether the bathroom was perfectly clean.

So she had been able to tell Damir with some conviction that parental relationships took many forms, and changed over time. She knew from Declan that Narcisa completely understood Damir's reaction, saying she herself had perhaps expected too much, a fairy-tale reunion after the miracle of finding each other, when every harsh reality of her life so far should have told her that wouldn't be the case.

The second meeting had been better. Beforehand, Antonia had reminded Damir how hard he found it to talk about his feelings to strangers, and at the moment that was exactly what his mother was. So she had helped him to compose an email explaining this, and asking if when they next met, Narcisa would perhaps be so kind as to tell him about herself and not expect too much from him.

Her reply had been immediate and Damir had travelled to Mostar the next day. He had listened to her tales of her life with her husband Harun since the war, and Damir had found himself asking a few questions and beginning to like this shyly smiling woman, who was doing her level best to make him comfortable. He relaxed so much that when she mentioned his father, rather than let the awkward silence take over, he had told her Sanja's tale about Ivan and the donkey and they had laughed together for the first time.

It had prompted him to ask about his pet cat, Dusa, and he learnt that just after the war started, when people were fleeing the city, their neighbour had taken her to a cousin in the country. Narcisa had been worried about feeding herself and her child, let alone a pet, although she told Damir how guilty she'd felt when he had cried inconsolably. Damir confided in Antonia that he'd thought about sharing the flashback about the old woman taking the last cabbage, but had decided against it.

They'd discussed this for a long time. Damir knew that to move on he needed to talk to his mother about the war, needed to flesh out and affirm his memories, but the words had stuck in his throat. There seemed to be no way Antonia could guide him past this, and he'd retreated into the work he was doing on the new hotel, spending hours on what was hardly even a building site, as Antonia battled to design Vila Maslina's web pages and had several futile attempts at making soap from the last pressings of their olive oil.

It took Antonia a while to realise Damir's problem was whether or not Narcisa had really written to Tetka, but there was no way of proving it one way or the other. What Sanja had told Declan about Tetka being upset and becoming unusually protective of Damir after the end of the war gave some credence to Narcisa's story, but it was far from conclusive. Antonia and Damir talked around and around it, night after night. At first he said it didn't matter, because even if the letter had come and Tetka had destroyed it, she would have done so from love. That was all very well, but did Damir really believe Narcisa had tried to look for him in the first place? He would find it very hard to trust her if he did not.

When Damir could not bring himself to have the conversation with Narcisa, Antonia wondered whether he was frightened of not believing her. If she suspected Honey had lied to her, what would she do? But it was not the same; she and Honey had a lifetime of love and trust to fall back on. Damir and his mother only had distant memories.

Next time, they arranged to meet for lunch at a small hotel in the Hutovo Blato national park, and Damir asked Antonia to come with him. Somehow, having her and Harun there made conversation easier, and when Damir went outside for a cigarette it was Narcisa who raised the subject of the letter and how she felt it was coming between them. Mother to mother, seeing the pain in Narcisa's eyes, Antonia took the risk of breaching Damir's trust and told her how initially he had felt she had not wanted to find him, and had even left him deliberately.

When Damir returned, Harun offered to show Antonia one of the fishing lakes the area was famous for. An hour later, they'd found Narcisa and Damir sitting side by side on a bench amongst the trees which surrounded the hotel, eyes red, not from the biting wind but from their tears. In that moment Antonia had known Damir had let his mother slip behind his carefully crafted front, and so he would begin to heal.

Declan brought her back to the riverbank and the here

and now. "Come on, there's some bite to that wind. How about we find a coffee?"

Antonia nodded and they retraced their steps before crossing the bridge. At the apex they stopped, gazing at the mountains that seemed to hold the city in their arms, and closer to, the graceful minarets of the mosques rising into the clear grey sky.

"I don't think I expected it to be this beautiful," Antonia sighed.

"Beautiful, but scarred. Old, yet new. And, if I dare say it, east and west."

"Finding a way to live together again."

"Let's hope so."

Antonia would have loved for him to put his arm around her, but in the last month or so they had not progressed beyond holding hands. Tempted as she was to make the first move, she had promised herself she would give him time, but the better she came to know him, the harder it was. The way her heart had flipped when she had seen his face that morning told her, given his reticence, she was falling faster and further than she should.

The coffee shop was in an old stone building, advertising its wares with colourful messages chalked on its folded-back wooden doors. Inside, low sofas and chairs festooned with tasselled cushions and throws were clustered around small tables, and behind the counter rows of copper-plated *dzezva* glowed under the lights. Haunting music, which sounded as though it came from a cross between a sitar and a mandolin played in the background, and when Antonia chose a sofa next to the window, Declan sat down next to her.

Unusually, they remained silent until the owner brought their coffee, the *dzezva* on a beaten metal tray with two fine-china tumblers, two glasses of water, and a plate of what Declan told her were *rahat lokum,* the Bosnian version of Turkish Delight. Before even pouring the coffee, Declan turned to her.

"Can we talk about us?"

"Us?"

"Yes. There kind of is an us, isn't there? But I'd like it to be more."

Antonia ran her finger around the rim of her water glass. "So would I. But I was beginning to wonder if perhaps you were having doubts about me."

"God no, not about you. Never about you. I think I knew almost at once you were the woman for me. I mean, those cheese melts you dished up with my first beer, that incredible moussaka, those tuna steaks… I could go on." His eyes were twinkling and Antonia laughed. "But all the time I was wondering how the hell we would ever make it work with very full-time jobs and six hours of hard driving, not to mention a ferry, between us.

"But when you said about us both being givers, and doing something for myself, I really started to think about it. Could it be possible? I've been backwards and forwards in my mind for weeks and the only conclusion I've come to is we won't know unless we try. So what do you say? I mean, obviously a long-distance relationship at first, but if it works out then I have some savings… I've been wanting to take time out to do an MA for a while now, and I could do it anywhere with remote learning..." He tailed off, looking at her.

This was big, really big. He was offering commitment, but Antonia didn't hesitate. "I say let's give it a go. I reckon it's so much better to be with the right person some of the time than the wrong person all of the time. If we both want it enough then we'll make it work."

Declan took both her hands in his. "Oh, you have such confidence. Can I snuggle up a bit closer so some of it rubs off on me?"

"As close as you like." Antonia laughed, not only because this lovely man wanted her, but because he was right, she did have confidence. Compared to where she'd been a year ago, that was a miracle in itself.

Antonia knelt on her suitcase and finally managed to snap it shut. She'd over-bought Christmas presents yet again, but she and Declan had found a wonderful winter market in Mostar, and wrapped in the glow of their decision – not to mention a significant caffeine high – they had gone slightly mad. Never once had it entered her head how she'd get it all back to England, nor he to Ireland where he was spending the festive season with his sister.

Luckily, she could leave most of her clothes here. It didn't feel strange at all that this attic room had become as much her home as her cottage. Honey, Sara, and her parents may be in England, but here she was surrounded by friends. And

Declan, who had already visited for a weekend. Half-lost in the memory, she gazed out of the window over the olive trees, their leaves sparser than they had been in the summer months, towards the cove. Today the water was calm, barely ruffled by the Jugo's icy partner, the Bura, which was sweeping in from the north. It would be a good day to travel.

Damir had installed a wood-burning stove in the old stone trough in his living room, but this morning no smoke issued from the metal chimney that rose above the old press house. After the harvest the press itself had refused point blank to work, but instead of throwing a strop, Damir had simply sent the olives to the co-operative and proclaimed he was going to repurpose it into a water feature. She presumed he'd told the architect, Mia, because now something very similar had appeared in her design for the new hotel, which was to be named Vila Nada after Tetka.

As if on cue, she heard the kitchen door slam and Damir's footsteps pound up the steps, two at a time. Reaching the landing he called to her, asking if he could come up.

"Of course."

The racing steps continued and he appeared in front of her, a shirt on a hanger in each hand.

"Which one, do you think, for Josip's party?" One was white, buttoned-down formal and the other open-necked with zig-zagged blue and cream stripes.

"Will Mia be there?" she asked, grinning at him.

"And that makes a difference?" The shirts cartwheeled as he waved his arms.

"The zig-zags are far more striking."

"Too striking?"

"Damir, if anyone can carry it off, you can. If not, I suggest you take it back to that very expensive designer shop you bought it from and try something else."

"I thought, with the charcoal suit…"

"You'll look a million dollars."

He grinned at her. "One day."

Antonia rolled her eyes.

"How long before we have to leave?" she asked him.

"About forty minutes. Then even if the drive to Dubrovnik is slow you will be at the airport in plenty of time."

"Right. I'll make the coffee while you finish packing."

Taking one last look around the room, she followed his retreating footsteps downstairs, checking all the windows were securely fastened for one last time. Vila Maslina would be standing empty for almost a week, because after Josip Beros's party, Damir was heading for Mostar to spend Christmas with his mother. This had surprised Antonia, knowing they were Muslim, but December 25th was a holiday in Mostar and Narcisa's birthday was the next day, so there would be many reasons to celebrate.

Antonia set the larger green *dzezva* on the range to heat the water then wandered back into the hall to gaze at Tetka's picture. What would she think of everything that had happened since she died? Impossible to tell, but Antonia knew in her heart of hearts she would be pleased Damir was building a new life without her, a very different life, but one that had every chance of making him truly happy.

Returning to the kitchen, she spooned the grounds from the canister into the small navy jug. You needed both *dzezva* to make coffee. One would not do. They weren't a pair – far from it – but they went together and that was that. She laughed to herself. Which one was she? Chipped as it was, Damir would probably lay claim to the exuberant green, but she certainly didn't feel blue anymore. She shrugged. It really didn't matter. After all, as he had told her right from the start, what mattered in Croatia was the perfect cup of coffee. And a good friend to share it with.

Acknowledgments

There is always a fascination for readers where ideas for books come from and sometimes it is hard for a writer to pinpoint, but with *The Olive Grove* I know exactly the moment I decided it was a story that had to be written. I was sitting in the dining room of one of the many small cruise boats that ply the Dalmatian coast, while our Bosnian guide told the group about the Yugoslav wars in the 1990s. And he didn't just tell us the history – he told us his own astounding story about growing up in Mostar during the conflict too.

The guide's name is Darko Barisic, and without him I could not have written this book. But let me stress it is not his story. For a start, he was a little older during the war, and although his mother disappeared and he was cared for by neighbours in the shelter, thankfully she did come back. But he has been generous in talking about his wartime memories – including being injured by Serbian soldiers while his mother was trying to protect Bosniak neighbours, and the joy of receiving certain food parcels – on countless chats over Zoom, as well as filling me in on the finer details of life in modern Croatia. If I have made any mistakes in that respect, they are mine alone.

The sad truth is that almost no searches for people missing after the war result in happy endings. It is incredibly hard to pin down the stats of how many people went missing, but just after the war the UN reported 30,000. But with around 12,000 still unaccounted for, 7,000 of those in Bosnia, and some sources saying 80% have been traced, the figures simply don't add up. Either way it is too many. And the end of uncertainty for most people comes through DNA linking and the discovery of another mass grave.

Children react to being in a warzone in different ways and reading Lynne Jones's *Then They Started Shooting: Growing up in Wartime Bosnia,* a research study she carried out over many years, was invaluable. And harrowing. As was watching the 1993 BBC documentary *Unfinished Business – War in Mostar*. It is the film Antonia watches in the book, and if you would like to find out more about that dreadful time then I recommend it to you.

I knew, when I had just the germ of an idea in my mind, that I wanted this book to be commissioned before I would write it. It needed the right publisher. I am so grateful to Charlotte Ledger at One More Chapter for believing in it too, and to Lydia Mason, Jennie Rothwell, and the whole editorial team for improving it so much with their ideas, encouragement and enthusiasm throughout the editing process.

The book was written between August 2020 and March

2021, so much of it during Covid lockdowns, not at my own desk, but at a good friend's kitchen table. Many people have had tragedies to deal with in the last year, but it became real for us when our dear friend Gordon died from cancer in October and my husband and I decided to form a support bubble with his wife Cynth, so she would not be locked down alone. This book is dedicated to both of them too.

Although writing is a solitary career, none of us work in isolation, and as ever a big thank you goes to my word-count buddy Kitty Wilson, who chivvies me along on a daily basis. As I write, I cannot wait to see her and our other close writing pal Cass Grafton just as soon as we are able to meet.

Thanks also go to Susanna Bavin for her tireless encouragement; Rosanna Ley, for the marvellous writing retreat in Spain just before Covid last year during which I learnt so much, and for the support of my fellow retreaters on Zoom over the months since. Also, my Apricot Plots buddies, and the members of the RNA's Cariad Chapter. Meeting you all regularly online has most surely kept me sane.

Last but not least, as ever the biggest thank you is to my husband, Jim. Ever patient, ever supportive – I could do none of this without you.

If you would like to find out more about my books and be the first to know about special offers and exclusive deals, please:

- Sign up for my newsletter here: *https://mailchi.mp/99543ad90bea/sign-up*